NO WAY OUT

A NOVEL

JOEL GOLDMAN

Contents

For my nieces and nephews,
Jessica, Ariel, Michael, Josh, Elise, and Jacob.
Make sure your parents buy you a copy.

Chapter One

Eldon Fowler's Ruger Redhawk .44 Magnum revolver was missing. He was certain it had been lifted on the last day of the gun show, some asshole rewriting the Second Amendment to include a right to steal arms. Didn't matter. It was gone, and there was nothing he could do about it now except curse getting too old to protect what was his from some punk.

That, and file an insurance claim, which meant making a police report and turning over records to the cops that the government had no right to force him to keep in the first place as far as he was concerned, which was why he didn't have the papers. Better to let the Redhawk go than have to deal with those bastards.

He'd set up three U-shaped tables under a banner he'd paid good money for that read ELDON FOWLER'S GUNS at the Expocentre in Topeka, Kansas, laying out a hundred and six semiautomatic assault rifles and fifty-two handguns for the Labor Day weekend show. For three days, he'd sat on a high bar stool with a swivel seat to keep an eye on everything, climbing down to talk only if a customer showed real interest, with the off-duty cops providing security to back him up, and still, he'd been robbed.

The Redhawk had been in the middle of a spread of new and used handguns, including Glocks, Smith & Wessons, Berettas, and Sig Sauers; another professionally made sign advertising them as the best in personal protection. It was a beefy gun that thrived on hot magnum loads, a gun he just had to have the instant he saw it in a pawnshop in Oklahoma two years ago. He was a shooter, not a hunter, and sometimes all he wanted was to feel the power of a gun in his hand. No gun did that for him like the Redhawk. And now it was gone.

More than six thousand people had come to the show. There were more lookers than buyers, one run-down man poor-mouthing him earlier in the day.

"C'mon Eldon, give me a break," the man said, reading his name on the banner, acting like they knew each other and crying about hard times when Eldon wouldn't sell him the Redhawk for less than Eldon had paid for it. Eldon had priced it too high to sell even in good times, just wanting to show it off.

"No, sir," Eldon told him, grinding his tobacco chew, spitting in a cup. "Your troubles are not my troubles. I've got plenty of my own."

"You act like you don't even want to sell it," the man said.

Eldon shook his head. Pathetic, that's what the man was. "I'd rather pack up my whole inventory than give a single goddamn piece away. You can't afford it, don't buy it."

Another customer had called to Eldon from the next table over, and Eldon left the man behind. He didn't notice the Redhawk was missing until he began packing his inventory that night after the show had ended. He couldn't prove the man had stolen the Redhawk, but no one would ever convince him that he hadn't.

He was in the empty parking lot at the Expocentre, the last dealer to leave, the back end of his four-by-eight trailer open, assault rifles, each in a soft case, packed in canvas bags, his name stitched on the bags and the bags suspended on hooks lining the trailer walls. The handguns were on trays, the trays fitted inside two footlockers. He'd sorted through them three times, checking the guns against his inventory sheet, confirming again and again that the Redhawk was gone, slamming the trailer door closed, turning when he heard the low rumble of an approaching gray Dodge Ram pickup truck.

The driver slowed, giving him a nod, a ball cap pulled low, hiding his face. Eldon didn't recognize the man or his truck, and that was what bothered him. Neither belonged in the parking lot this long after the show had ended.

The men who sold guns at these shows traveled a circuit, knew one another, what beer they liked, what they drove, and which marriage they were on. There were regular customers, too. People who followed them from show to show like a woman he once knew that followed Elvis Presley when he was on tour. After twenty years, Eldon knew the regulars. The man in the truck wasn't one of them. Neither was the man who tried to buy the Redhawk on the cheap.

It was enough, in an uncertain world, to make Eldon uneasy, especially after what had happened last month in Nebraska and Iowa. Thieves had followed two dealers home from shows and robbed them of their guns, the thieves quick and professional enough that the dealers never had a chance to draw their weapons, one that tried getting a bullet in the leg for his trouble.

The security in the hall had done him little good. He was down the Redhawk. But outside, there was no protection for the dealers, many of them, like him, transporting enough weaponry to start a small war. No one complained because everyone was armed and certain he could take care of himself and because his brothers in arms were always close at hand. Tonight Eldon was alone and had his doubts.

He was seventy and felt eighty, jolts of pain coming and going in his chest, cutting off his breath and leaving a sour taste in his throat he couldn't cough up or wash down. He was due to see his doctor in the morning, a woman half his age who'd tell him to quit smoking, lose weight, and bend over while she stuck her finger up his ass and warned him he'd keep getting up to pee every hour during the night unless he cut back on his caffeine.

Eldon breathed easier as he watched the driver of the Dodge pickup follow Expocentre Drive onto Topeka Boulevard, heading south, the opposite direction he was going, his route taking him north to Highway 24, east on 24 to the county roads and back roads leading to his house at Lake Perry. It was a forty-five minute drive with steady traffic in the city that thinned out the closer he got to the lake, especially this late.

The show had ended at six, and it was close to nine. He'd hung around telling lies with his buddies, drinking beer in the parking lot, taking his time packing up. He checked the trailer hitch, making certain it was secure, and climbed in his truck, a Ford F-150, thinking about the stolen Redhawk, the dealers who got hit in Nebraska and Iowa, and the man in the Dodge Ram. He pulled out onto Expocentre Drive and stopped, squinting as he scanned the traffic on Topeka Boulevard for any sign of the Dodge but not seeing it.

He called his wife on his cell phone, relieved when she answered on the first ring.

"I'm just leaving the Expocentre," he said.

"How was the show?"

"A lot of people but not many with money to spend."

"Did you do all right?"

"Fair, except for somebody lifted the Redhawk."

She paused, drawing a deep breath, knowing his fondness for that gun. "Oh, honey, I'm sorry." She paused again. "You must be so tired."

She worried about him; saying he must be so tired was code for she hoped he wasn't having more chest pains. He'd made the mistake of telling her about the pain, and she hadn't let loose until he called the doctor and made an appointment.

Their house sat by itself at the end of a mile-long winding gravel road, midway down a slope, secluded and sheltered by a tall stand of trees, overlooking the lake. He wanted to ask her if she'd seen anyone around the house but didn't, afraid she'd panic. She knew about the robberies in Nebraska and Iowa and had begged him to give up the shows until the thieves were caught. *And do what?* he asked her. She didn't argue, knowing there was no point in it. He'd do what he wanted to do, just like he'd always done. It was enough to hear her voice, quiet and steady like it had been for almost fifty years, the one sound that always calmed him.

"I'm okay. See you when I get there."

"Buckle up, dear."

"Sure," he said. His wife knew that he hadn't used a seat belt since the state passed a law making it mandatory.

He was carrying a Glock 22 .40-caliber semiautomatic pistol and had a 12-gauge Browning Maxus Stalker semiautomatic shotgun mounted on the rack behind his head, both of them loaded. It would be enough firepower if it came to that, but paled in comparison to his assault rifles, making him wish he'd brought ammunition for one of them. He laid the Glock on the seat next to him and put the F-150 in drive as a light rain began to fall.

Chapter Two

Ask someone from New York or California to describe Kansas in one word and they'll say it's flat. West of Salina, they'd be right, but northeast of Topeka, they couldn't be more wrong. It's hill country, a rolling timbered landscape; some parts are like those around Lake Perry thick with woods, a refuge for white-tailed deer, bobcats, and red foxes.

Eldon favored the deer, putting out feeders to attract them, admiring the doe's graceful, shy, quiet personality and the power of the big antlered buck, imagining a bit of his wife and him in the animals, happy to give them a safe haven when the archery and muzzleloader hunting season started in three weeks and the regular firearm season came in December.

He thought about the deer, his wife, and the home they'd built thirty years ago on that hillside in the woods, how their safe haven could have become a trap if the man in the Dodge Ram had gone north instead of south and followed him there to steal his guns. The narrow road dropping toward his house was the only way in and out, easy enough to cut off. The nearest neighbor was too far away to hear or see anything. The boat he kept docked was in for repairs, the lake as big as an ocean without it.

Each month, he shot hundreds, sometimes thousands of rounds of ammunition, practicing his marksmanship, putting his guns through their paces, noting each weapon's idiosyncrasies from trigger pull to recoil, adjusting his aim and grip to compensate. But he'd never shot a man or an animal, never served in combat, never been under fire. Lessons learned in a self-defense class years ago were a faint memory. He wasn't a paranoid survivalist who longed for battle. He was a man who loved his wife and his guns in that order and who wanted the government to leave him the hell alone. That's all he was. If the man in the Dodge Ram came for him, he didn't know if he could pass the test.

He turned on the radio, hoping a honky-tonk country tune would put him in a better mind, but switched it off when the hard-driving drums and guitar put him more on edge. The rain had picked up, a steady rattle that blurred his vision and wore on his nerves.

Highway 24 was a four-lane divided stretch, and he stayed in the right-hand lane holding at sixty, glancing at the F-150's oversized side mirrors to keep a watchful eye on traffic behind him. There wasn't much, and what there was had no trouble passing him. A convoy of semi tractor-trailer rigs roared and rumbled by, throwing sheets of water and road grit at him. He fought the wheel when a blast of wind threw the F-150 toward the rigs, his trailer shimmying behind him.

The semis well ahead, he looked in his side mirrors again, sighting a pair of headlights a quarter mile behind him and closing. They were too high and wide for a sedan, matching the dimensions of a pickup. He waited for a car going west to pass, hoping its headlights would illuminate the vehicle, but the median was too wide and the distance too great.

His exit, a left turn across the westbound lanes of the highway, was coming up in less than a mile. He wanted to change lanes to make the turn, but the other vehicle had gotten too close. He could make out its shape as it began to pull even. It was a pickup, the trailer's taillights reflecting red off the Dodge Ram logo on the center of the grill. He grabbed the Glock, holding it in his lap as his chest tightened like someone was cinching a leather strap around him, his breath stuck in his throat.

Was it the man from the parking lot? How had he found him? What did he want? Would he roll his window down and shoot him through the glass or aim at his tires and watch as he lost control and ran into a ditch? Could he shoot him first? He felt like one of his deer, caught in the crosshairs, only he couldn't outrun his pursuer, not pulling a trailer. He was certain of one thing. He wouldn't let a thief decide his fate any more than he'd let some bureaucrat tell him to buckle his seat belt.

He laid the Glock on the seat, lowered his window, and reached behind him, yanking the shotgun from the rack, leveling the barrel on the window frame and releasing the safety, his finger on the trigger.

The nose of the Dodge eased past. It was blue, not gray, a man behind the wheel, a woman in the passenger seat holding a baby, screaming at the driver, waving at Eldon like she was trying to swat a fly, the man leaning over looking at him, his eyes wide, flooring the Dodge, the truck bucking as it blew by him.

Stunned at what he'd almost done, Eldon stomped on his brakes, the F-150 swerving and spinning on the slick, wet pavement and the trailer whipping side to side behind him like a water-skier jumping the wake. The shotgun slid back inside the truck, the butt dropping on the cab floor between his feet, the barrel aiming under his chin. He grabbed the barrel, pulling the shotgun up and away from him with his right hand, his left on the wheel, fighting the swerve.

He let go of the barrel, trying to get both hands on the steering wheel, his fingers getting caught inside the trigger guard instead, clamping down. The shotgun fired two rapid deafening rounds, blowing a hole in the passenger door, filling the cab with smoke as the truck came to a stop straddling both eastbound lanes. Deaf and blind, he collapsed against the wheel, his chest heaving as the truck's horn wailed.

The smoke cleared, and he sat up, having enough presence of mind to get moving before a semi doing eighty miles an hour rear-ended him into the next county. He reached his exit, easing the F-150 onto the county road, stopping on the shoulder to check the trailer hitch and his load.

The rain felt good, cooling him down, his breathing labored, the pain in the left side of his chest radiating into his shoulder, neck and down his left arm. The hitch was wobbly, but he thought it would hold until he got home, the canvas bags tossed around the inside of the trailer, piled on top of the footlockers. He climbed back into the cab and returned the shotgun to its place on the rack, rubbing his chest with the palm of his hand.

He knew he was in trouble, figured he was having a heart attack. The nearest hospital was in Topeka, a distance he didn't think he could make, and, if he could, he didn't trust a stranger to look after his guns. He'd die or he wouldn't, but if he was going to die, he'd do it at home in his wife's arms, not with some nurse telling him to fill out a bunch of forms before he saw the doctor. He put the truck in gear, eating up the county road as fast as the F-150 would take him.

The turnoff onto the gravel road leading to his house was at the top of a rise. He made the turn, his breath ragged. The cool chill from the rain had given way to a sickly sweat and queasy stomach. Combined with the pulsing pain in his chest, it was all he could do to hang on to the wheel. Even had he felt well, it would have been too dark for him to notice the pickup truck backed into the woods on the opposite side of the county road. The three men in the pickup waited until Eldon took off down the gravel road, the driver following him, lights off, relying on Eldon's taillights to show him the way.

Eldon knew the road, knew each dip, curve, and turn as it wound through the woods, lower and lower toward his house. He'd come home drunk a time or two, navigating the passage without so much as a scratch on the paint, knowing better than to brag about it to his wife, even if she forgave more than most women would. But the paint was taking a beating as he sped past tree limbs and brush, getting too close. The truck careened from one side of the narrow road to the other until he rounded a bend, catching a two-hundred-fifty-pound, eight-point buck jumping across the road in mid-flight.

The collision threw Eldon backward, his head bouncing off the gun rack, his body rebounding against the air bag as it exploded out of the steering wheel. The deer catapulted over the hood and through the windshield, head first, its antlers piercing the air bag, impaling Eldon and pinning him against the seat. The F-150 skidded sideways to a stop, blocking the road. The trailer broke free from the hitch and rolled onto its side, the doors flying open, guns spilling out.

Eldon felt the buck writhing, trying to free itself, its antler digging deeper in his chest, surprised that he could feel anything at all. With his right hand, he groped across the seat, finding the Glock, wrapping his fingers around the grip, wondering if he could raise his hand and pull the trigger and, if he could, whether he should shoot the buck or himself, both of them needing to be put out of their misery.

He heard an engine, blinked when high beams invaded the cab, heard doors open and slam closed, one man saying "Holy shit," another adding "Motherfucker, motherfucker, motherfucker." He turned his head toward them and saw that the engine belonged to a gray Dodge Ram pickup. One of the men was wearing a ball cap pulled low on his face. Another man opened the driver's door on the F-150, looking at Eldon, then at the deer, raising a handgun. It was the Redhawk. The man stepped back, firing once, a bullet to the deer's brain. Eldon nodded and closed his eyes for the last time.

Chapter Three

Lucy Trent wanted a short end of ribs with pit beans, crispy fries, and cold beer. I wanted the same thing, the only difference being that I wanted it while sitting in my easy chair in front of my television. It was Sunday in October, a day intended for artery-busting barbeque and football.

We were at LC's, a dive on Blue Parkway, a road that ran through Kansas City's east side. The name was a misnomer; the closest parks were the ballparks where the Chiefs and Royals played, a few miles away off of I-70. LC's sat next to Parkway Auto Brokers. LC ringed his place with wrought-iron security bars, Parkway preferring chain link and razor wire. They knew their neighborhood.

LC was behind the counter, ribbons of heat rolling over him from the open smoker as he checked slabs, briskets, and chickens, wiping sweat from his dark brown forehead. The fifty-inch television hanging from one corner of the ceiling was on the fritz, all snow and no football.

"Quit moping," Lucy said. "You'll be home in time for the late-afternoon game and the night game."

"Yeah, but I'm missing the first game."

"Who's playing?"

"Who cares? What matters is that I'm not watching."

"Poor Jack Davis. He lives a life of unrelenting cruelty."

"Are you making fun of me?"

"If you have to ask, it's not nearly as much fun."

"Order up," LC said.

Lucy brought our food to the table carrying a tray in one hand

and a brown bag, grease staining the paper, in the other.

"Simon's dinner," she said, setting the bag on an empty chair.

Lucy was an ex-cop, ex-con, and private investigator for Alexander Investigations. Her boyfriend and my best friend, Simon Alexander, was the owner. Simon specialized in cyber crime. Lucy worked the human side, investing her heart in her clients. I was her part-time gun. A convicted felon, she couldn't possess a firearm, but I could even though I had a movement disorder that made me shake and had forced me to retire after twenty-five years with the FBI. Who said justice was blind?

"Simon gets barbeque *and* he gets to watch the game?" I asked.

"Yes," Lucy said, patting me on the head. "And you got barbeque and a trip to the Municipal Farm to visit Jimmy Martin. Aren't you the lucky man?"

"Luckier than Jimmy. Did you really think he'd tell us where he buried his kids?"

"Evan and Cara are missing. No one says they're dead."

"Evan is six and Cara is eight years old, and they've been missing for three weeks as of yesterday. How many of those kids come home?"

"Not many. I know. But that doesn't mean he killed them."

"Let's see," I said, ticking the facts off one by one. "Jimmy and his wife are in the middle of the divorce from hell. She threw him out and had to get an order of protection against him. He can't see Evan and Cara unless it's with a court-appointed social worker. The kids disappeared the same day he was arrested for stealing copper wire and tubing from a construction site."

"I know. I know," Lucy said. "We've been over this. His lawyer asked the judge to release him on his own recognizance since he wasn't a flight risk because he wanted to be with his kids."

"And?"

Lucy leaned back in her chair, arms crossed, reciting as if she was being coerced. "And, his wife was in the courtroom and whispered to the prosecutor to ask Jimmy where the kids were, and Jimmy refused to answer, so the judge said no bail and sent him to the Municipal Farm because the county jail was full. He didn't even take the Fifth. Just acted like he didn't hear the question."

"That's the great thing about the privilege against self-incrimination. You can't exercise it without everyone thinking you're a criminal. So, either he killed his kids so his wife couldn't have them, or he's torturing her by making her think he knows where they are even though he doesn't. I don't know why you were so hot to talk to him. If he won't tell his wife or the judge what he knows about the kids, assuming he knows anything at all, he sure as hell isn't going to tell us."

"I get that, Jack. But it can't hurt to try. Their mother hasn't given up hope. That's why Peggy hired us. So, I'm not giving up either." Lucy slowly stirred the pool of ketchup on her plate with a cold french fry. "It's just so hard to believe he'd let her suffer like that, make her wonder what happened."

"Never underestimate an angry man's capacity for cruelty. There was a case in Alabama where a father killed his four children, threw them off a bridge, to torture his wife."

"Which is worse? Mourning their deaths or never knowing if you can?"

I took a deep breath, thinking about my dead children. "I've done both and wouldn't wish the choice on anybody."

"I know," she said, taking my hand, "and that's why I asked you to go with me to see Jimmy Martin. You don't really miss watching that football game, do you?"

I smiled and shook my head. "Not for a minute. Eat your lunch before it gets cold."

Chapter Four

Two women and a man were sitting at a corner table near the television. They had more on their plates than ribs. The man was facing us, the women giving us their backs; the other eight tables were empty. They gave off a vibe of bad news getting worse. I couldn't help picking up on it, blaming too many years spent finding trouble before it started.

Their postures were stiff, their voices rising and falling, the buzz from the television muffling what they were saying. One thing was clear: They weren't having a party.

The man's totem head was square. His eyes were heavy-lidded, the left one lazy. His neck was short and squat, his shoulders rolled with fat. I put him at forty, maybe less. He drummed meaty fingers on the Formica tabletop, his lazy eye drifting my way, catching me watching them, his glare telling me to butt out.

The woman sitting on the end of the table pointed her finger at him. He grabbed her hand, squeezing until the woman sitting next to the wall pulled them apart, the man gritting his teeth, folding his beefy arms over his chest, the first woman slumping, elbows on the table, her face in her hands.

The woman who'd separated them came out of her chair like a charmed snake, the man flattening his hands on the table, staring up at her, his mouth a dumb scar. Purse on her shoulder, she turned and sauntered past our table, crossing the black-and-white checkerboard linoleum floor, chewing her lower lip and glancing at me before disappearing down the narrow hall between the open kitchen and windows blanketed with wrought-iron bars, heading,

I guessed, for the bathroom. She was young, early twenties, slender with a ropy muscular build, sporting a lip ring and auburn hair streaked with bright red and cut close to a face midway between pretty and incredible.

"I think she likes you, Jack," Lucy teased.

"My lucky day."

"What do you make of them?"

"From the looks of things, I'd say they aren't having a good day, especially those two," I said, aiming a rib at the man and woman still at the table.

The man leaned toward the woman, whispering, hunching his shoulders, his arms wide, making a plea, the woman crossing her arms, shaking her head. The man pressed, chopping the air with an open palm. He wasn't asking; he was telling, his my-way-or-thehighway message plain enough. The woman pulled back, turning away from him and toward us, her eyes widening, her mouth locked in a tight grimace.

"Why'd they have to pick LC's to have a fight?" Lucy asked. "The guy with the lazy eye makes me nervous. Angry, unhappy people do crazy stuff, and I've got a bad feeling about them. Why did you have to leave your gun at home?" she asked.

"You know why. I couldn't take my gun into the Municipal Farm, and I don't like leaving it in the car. Besides, you see the sign on LC's door, the one with the gun inside a red circle and a line drawn through it?"

"You think they look like the kind of people who care about a sign on the door?"

Voices rose from the corner table, drowning out the static from the TV. The woman turned toward the man, reached across the table, and slapped him.

"I won't have it, Frank. I'd rather lose everything!"

She knocked her chair over as she got up, the man she called Frank matching her move, grabbing her wrist. She gave him the back of her other hand this time, her ring cutting a bloody groove across his cheek.

He let her go, wiped his cheek on his sleeve, and reached inside his coat, pulling a gun. The woman skittered backward, her hands raised. Frank fired once and she crumpled to the floor, faceup and dead, laugh lines and crow's feet soft and slack, her gray eyes open, locked and puzzled.

Lucy and I froze in our seats. There was nowhere to hide. Frank gazed down at the woman and then pointed his gun at us, his hand wobbling, waiting for something to happen.

"Goddamn it, Frank! What in the hell is wrong with you?"

It was the woman who'd left the table before the shooting started, her voice behind us. I stole a look over my shoulder. She was standing next to LC behind the four-foot-high counter, a drywall pillar obscuring her head and shoulders.

"It wasn't my fault, Roni," Frank said, his voice quivering. "She started yelling at me—then she slapped me. Slapped me twice and cut me too."

"You could have walked away or slapped her back. Why'd you have to shoot Marie? And where in the world did you get a gun?"

He shook his massive head, blinking at the body lying at his feet as if it had fallen out of the sky. "I didn't mean to. It just happened, that's all."

"Is she dead?"

He nudged Marie with his shoe. "I expect so. I shot her pretty good right in the chest."

"Well, that's just great, Frank. Really, it is. Just great."

The big man heaved and rolled his shoulders. "I'm sorry, Roni. I guess we better get out of here."

"And go where? Look around the room, Frank. There are three other witnesses besides me. How far do you think you'll get?"

"A lot farther than if we stick around. Now let's get out of here!"

She stepped away from the pillar into the open, raising a gun at him in a two-fisted grip, her voice strong and steady. "Don't make me shoot you."

"Aw, hell, Roni. You're not gonna shoot me. You never shot anybody in your life."

"Every girl dreams about her first time, Frank. I just never figured it would be you."

Frank leveled his gun at her, no wobble in his grip, his lazy eye closed in a squint. Lucy and I were trapped in their cross fire.

"I don't want to shoot you," he said. "But I'll do it if I have to. And them, too," he added, tilting his head at us. "And the colored guy."

"That's a lot of killing to have on your conscience, Frank."

He swelled up, stuck his chest out, stretching his gun hand toward her. "I can carry the freight."

"Now, Frank," she said. "I'm a much better shot than you. I work at it, and I've never seen you at the range, not one time. With that lazy eye of yours, you're just as likely to shoot yourself as anyone else. Only reason you hit Marie was she was standing on top of you."

"Don't push me, Roni," he said, his voice low and hard. "That's what Marie did, and you see what it bought her."

"She couldn't protect herself. I can. Do you have the nerve to pull the trigger a second time when you know I'll shoot back?"

Frank was sweating, his neck red, his face purpling, the gun now bobbing in his hand as he fought to breathe. "I come this far! Don't think I won't do it!"

"All right then," she said, bending her knees slightly, lining him up in her sight. "You better not miss because I got you dead to rights."

They stood like that for a few seconds, Lucy and I flipping back and forth between them until Frank relaxed, lowered his gun, and turned sideways and Lucy and I started breathing again. Roni straightened, easing her stance, when Frank jerked his gun hand up and fired, missing her. She ducked and pulled the trigger, hitting him in the thigh. He dropped his gun, clutched his leg, and twisted to the floor.

"You shot me!"

She ran over to him and picked up his gun, sticking both weapons in her belt.

"The moon is pink," she said.

"I can't believe you fucking shot me!"

"The moon is pink," she said, pressing her hands over his wound.

"The moon is pink! What the hell is that supposed to mean?"

"It means you weren't listening to a word I said, you dumb son of a bitch. I told you I would shoot you. I might as well have been telling you the moon was pink for all the good it did."

"I heard you. I just didn't believe you."

"Same difference," she said.

She looked at me, her brows raised, her mouth open, asking for help without saying it.

"I'll call 911," I said.

She nodded. "Appreciate it if you would."

Lucy knelt next to Marie, checked for a pulse, and shook her head at me. She traded places with Roni alongside Frank, pressing her hands against his wound, stemming the blood flow to a trickle. Frank turned pale and laid his head on the floor.

Roni stood, wiped her bloody hands on her denims, and walked to my table as I closed my phone and stood.

"Help is on the way," I said. "I'm Jack Davis. Who are you?"

"Veronica Chase. Everyone calls me Roni." She reached for a cameo hanging from a gold necklace, rubbing the charm between two fingers, and looked at Marie and Frank, then at the blood on her hands and jeans, her face turning green. "Oh Lord, I think I'm gonna be sick."

And she was.

Chapter Five

Roni was too weak to protest when I pulled the guns from her belt and helped her to another table. LC swabbed the floor where she had thrown up, handing me a damp dishrag to wipe the blood off her hands. He gave her a Seven Up to calm her stomach and gave me a carryout bag for the guns. His was a Bersa Thunder 380, and hers was a Beretta 8000 9-millimeter, both guns ideal for concealed carry and personal protection.

Her eyes were glassy, her movement slow, shock dulling her senses, staving off the whirlwind of emotions that sweep through people in the aftermath of violence. The coolness with which she'd confronted Frank was a good sign that she would be able to handle the replays that would haunt her sleep in an endless loop. Her color improved from green to pale as she watched Lucy tend to Frank. His eyes were closed, and his breathing was shallow.

"Is he going to die?" she asked.

"Eventually," Lucy said, "but not today."

Roni nodded, saying "Bless the day," and took a sip from her Seven Up, the fog lifting as she focused on me.

The internal pressure that erupts into my shakes and spasms burst loose, fibrillating my torso as my neck arched and stiffened, aiming my chin at the ceiling. I grunted like I'd been kicked in the gut, letting out a long breath when the spasm passed.

"What's the matter with you?" Roni asked.

"I've got a movement disorder."

She nodded, lips pursed, swirling her drink. "Ever wonder why you?"

"Why not me?"

She wiped her mouth and nodded. "I don't know you well enough to say. You do that all the time?"

"Just enough to keep life interesting, especially when I get caught in the middle of a shoot-out. Who are they?" I asked, pointing at the floor.

"Frank and Marie Crenshaw."

"Frank and Marie always get along that well?"

"Actually, they were real good together until the last year or so."

"What happened?"

"The same thing that's happened to a lot of people since the economy went south. Seems like everyone has either lost their job or their business or they go to sleep every night scared to death of getting out of bed in the morning because it might be their turn. I don't think Frank has slept in a month."

"What's your relationship to them?"

She took a sip of her Seven Up, leaned back in her chair, and closed her eyes for a moment, opening them when she answered.

"We have a history."

"What kind of history? Are you related to them?"

She sat up, studying me, her eyes narrow and cautious. "They've got a scrap business off of Independence Avenue in Sheffield. I keep their books."

"So, you work for them."

"Not like that. I've got my own business. Chase Bookkeeping. They're one of my clients."

"You don't look the bookkeeper type."

She smiled. "It's really my mom's business, but she had a stroke last year. I'd just gotten my accounting degree at Park University so I kind of took over. First thing I learned: when you're the boss, no one can tell you what you're supposed to look like."

She fished in her purse for a business card and handed it to me.

"You also don't look like the type who carries a gun and knows how to use it."

"That was my Grandma Lilly's rule. She said the women in our family had to know how to take care of ourselves."

"Why?" I asked.

She gave me another smile, this one with her mouth closed. "You might say we've got a history too."

"Grandma Lilly ever shoot anyone?"

"Not in a long time, but she says it's never too late. She's sixty-five and still goes to the shooting range."

"I can't wait to meet her. Where's she live?"

"With me and my mother in Pendleton Heights."

"Where's that?"

She squinted, giving me a microscopic look as if I was from a foreign country. "It's a neighborhood in the northeast part of town. West of Sheffield."

I'd lived in Kansas City long enough to know the east side from the west, the Country Club Plaza from the mega malls and strip centers in Johnson County, and where the state line divided Missouri and Kansas. I knew that Northeast KC was bounded by The Paseo on the west, Interstate 435 on the east, Gladstone Boulevard to the north, and Truman Road to the south; that Independence Avenue ran east and west from downtown to the Interstate, bisecting Northeast into northern and southern hemispheres.

Though I didn't know the names of its neighborhoods, I knew that Northeast had a history of mansions on Gladstone Boulevard, hookers on Independence Avenue, and gangs south of the Avenue. And I knew one other thing. It was where Peggy and Jimmy Martin and their two kids lived, a coincidence that shrunk my Sunday afternoon world to claustrophobic dimensions.

"It's Sunday. What are you doing working?" I asked her.

"We had some things to go over. It was the only time we could meet."

"What kind of things?"

She folded her arms across her chest. "What are you? A cop?"

"Retired. FBI."

"If you're retired, why are you asking me all these questions?"

"Old habits die hard. Frank killed Marie, and you shot Frank.

Anybody would want to know why."

"Like I said, I keep Frank's books. His scrap business is underwater, too deep to keep the doors open.

He's known for a while, but he couldn't bring himself to tell Marie. He asked me to do it. Frank said she loves LC's Bar-B-Q. He thought it would go down better if we did it here."

She finished her Seven Up and turned in her chair to take another look at Frank. His color had gone from sheet white to gray, his breathing from shallow to feathery.

"You sure he's not going to die?" she asked Lucy.

Lucy didn't answer, craning her head, searching out the windows for an ambulance.

"The police will be here in a minute," I said. "They'll read you your rights. Bottom line, you don't have to say a word until you've talked to a lawyer."

"You saw what happened. Frank was going to kill the rest of us. He took a shot at me so I shot him back. It's all pretty simple."

I shook my head. "The police will ask you a lot of questions about who you are and what you were doing here, where you've been and where you were going. They'll run all three of you through the computer to check for prior convictions and outstanding arrest warrants. They'll want to see the permit for your gun if you have one, and they'll want to know where you got it if you don't. They'll search your purse and Marie's and Frank's wallet and the car you were driving. They'll want to know everything the three of you talked about since you got up this morning. And down the road, Frank's lawyer will tell him that keeping him off death row may depend on how many people he can offer up in return for his life. So, trust me. Simple is the last thing this is going to be."

A shiver ran through her, remnants of adrenaline or newborn fear. I couldn't tell which it was, but the cloud that came over her eyes as she took another look at Frank said it was more likely fear. She hugged herself, her face rounding back into a normal hue.

"If you used to be an FBI agent, how come you're trying to help me?"

I could have told her, but this wasn't the time or place for my history. She smiled, the expression lighting her face and brightening her eyes, making her young again.

"I know why," she said. "It's because I saved your life. You and your wife."

"She's not my wife."

She glanced at my left hand. "No ring. Girlfriend?"

"Friend."

Three patrol cars skidded to a stop in the parking lot, a pair of ambulances trailing them, the restaurant filling with people in uniforms, ending our conversation. A paramedic took Lucy's place with Frank. I handed one of the cops the bag with the guns and gave them a quick and dirty rundown, telling them who everyone was. They put each of us at separate tables, two of them keeping an eye on us while the other two secured the perimeter of the parking lot with yellow crime-scene tape.

Quincy Carter arrived in time to hold the door for the paramedics wheeling in gurneys for Frank and Marie. Carter was a homicide detective, tall and broad-shouldered; his black head shaved and glistening from the rain. He was a solid cop who knew the book well enough not to go by it all the time. One thing he didn't like was people meddling in his cases, especially people that didn't go by any book at all. People like Lucy and me.

Chapter Six

I had lived by the book most of my life, in the FBI and in my marriage, and had been kicked out of both. The FBI let me go because of my movement disorder. My ex-wife, Joy, let me go because we had caused each other too much pain to stay together. She'd had the insight to understand that at a time when I was still making excuses.

The FBI didn't look back, but Joy and I did. After we divorced, we found a slender thread to keep us connected. Our dogs, cockapoos named Roxy and Ruby, needed playmates and a place to stay if one of us was out of town. Taking care of them gave us time and space to reflect on our past without walking barefoot on the broken glass left by the deaths of our son Kevin and daughter Wendy, Joy's alcoholism, and my inability to come to grips with any of that.

When she was diagnosed with breast cancer a little over a year ago, I asked her to move in with me. She said yes, and we learned to take care of each other all over again. Her disease and my disorder became bridges instead of roadblocks.

Chemo, radiation, and surgery had subdued but not defeated her cancer. The disease had metastasized to her lungs. She was sober and alive. Neither condition, she reminded me, were guaranteed more than one a day at a time. Her oncologist was more precise. She'd die sober sometime in the next one to two years, later if she were lucky, sooner if she wasn't.

There was no getting used to her dying, no clever phrases to buck each other up. We climbed up and down the seven stages of grief, landing in a different place each day. So we fell back on the only one that we could make work, taking it one day at a time. We threw out the calendar our insurance agent sent us as a Christmas gift and did as much as we could as often as we could, lucky that Joy had more good days than bad.

My movement disorder was manageable as long as I said no to Lucy and Simon more often than I said yes. Joy understood how hard it was for me to tell them no, holding me up when I stumbled.

We skirted whether we'd fallen in love again, uncertain what that meant at this point in our lives, at ease living in the same house, our children's ghosts forever hovering in the near distance. It was an odd, ill-defined, and still-evolving relationship that worked because we didn't expect more from it. Ours was a hard-earned wisdom born from losses we thought we couldn't survive but did. We understood that second chances were precious and rare, even more when they came with a premature expiration date.

Through it all, I had learned to leave the book behind, the list of expectations, requirements, and metrics that forced square people into round holes. It helped that I wasn't accountable to anyone and that no one was filing quarterly reports assessing my fitness and performance and that the government sent me a disability check every month that was enough to make my mortgage payment, buy twenty-dollar Dockers at Costco, drive a six-year old Camry, and let the phone ring without answering it. I was fifty-three and aboveground. Life was good.

The one thing I couldn't let go of, and didn't try to, was the debt I owed to my kids. We'd lost Kevin to a child predator when he was eight and Wendy to a drug overdose when she was twenty-five. Grief and guilt, I'd learned, simmer forever. They can eat you alive or boot you in the ass, reminding you not to let it happen to someone else's kid. So, I signed on to help Lucy find Evan and Cara Martin, and I prepped Roni Chase for what lay ahead for her, and I lied to Quincy Carter when he asked me if he was going to have to put up with me again.

"I'm just an accidental witness. That's it," I told him.

"For today, maybe," Carter said. "But I know you. It's tomorrow I'm talking about. Tell me what went down here."

He'd already talked to Roni, Lucy, and LC. I talked, and he nodded, asking occasional questions.

"Matches what the others told me," Carter said when I finished.

A uniformed cop approached and waited for Carter to notice him.

"We've got nothing on the female shooter," the cop said when Carter finally nodded at him and cupped his elbow, turning both their backs to me. I stood, stretched, and eavesdropped.

"What about the other two?" Carter asked.

"Frank Crenshaw, age forty-one. Did six months for stealing a car when he was nineteen, clean ever since, but he's a convicted felon. Can't legally possess a gun. The victim is his wife, Marie, age thirty-nine. We've got nothing on her."

"Any history of domestic violence complaints?"

"No, sir. If they were having problems, she didn't call 911."

"What were they talking about?" I asked.

Carter pivoted and cocked his head at me. "Who?"

"Frank, Marie, and Roni."

He raised his eyebrows. "Why do you care?"

"Lucy and I were having a nice lunch. Then they started shouting and shooting at one another. Ruined our meal. I'd like to know why."

Carter shook his head. "Un-uh. No way, no sir. Not today. You told me you were just an accidental witness. That's it. You've got no dogs in this fight, and I'm not going to give you one. You and Lucy get your butts downtown and write out your statements, then go home."

"What about Roni's gun? Did she have a permit?"

Carter sucked in a breath, glared at me, and turned away.

"C'mon, Carter. That's not classified information. Don't make me work for it."

He stopped, took another deep breath, and did a slow half spin.

"Do me a favor," he said. "Don't work for any of it."

"You've got three eyewitnesses that say it was self-defense. The media will make her an overnight sensation. The prosecutor isn't going to charge her. The chief will probably give her a medal. So throw me a bone."

He held up his index finger. "One bone. She had a permit."

"What about Frank?"

He wagged his finger at me. "Are you blind and deaf? One bone. Go downtown and then go home."

Another detective, a young guy with short, mousse-spiked hair and teeth bleached iridescent white, cut through the crowd, holding up his phone and pointing to the e-mail on his tiny screen.

"We got a match on the serial number on Frank Crenshaw's gun," he said to Carter. "It was one of the guns stolen last month from that dealer who lived at Lake Perry."

Carter closed his eyes and shook his head. "Yardley," he said to the detective, "go away so I don't shoot you."

"What'd I do?" Yardley asked.

I stood and clapped Yardley on the shoulder. "You threw me a bone, son. And that's Carter's job, not yours, and he still owes me another one."

I left them and found Lucy outside. The rain had eased to a thin mist. We watched as Roni was ushered into the backseat of a squad car. She gave me a thumb's-up, the gesture more important to me than her optimism because it meant that she wasn't handcuffed.

"You know anything about a gun dealer up at Lake Perry who was robbed last month?" I asked Lucy.

She thought for a minute, scrunching her brow, the brown curly hair that billowed out from her face hanging damp against her cheeks, topping off a lean and lanky frame. She was another testament to second chances, having served a sentence for felony theft after pocketing loose diamonds she found at a murder scene. She lost her sheriff's deputy badge, but built a new life when she got out.

"Yeah, don't you read the papers?"

"Sports and comics. What happened?"

"The guy was driving home from a gun show in Topeka. There was something weird about the way it happened, out in the woods or something like that. He hit a deer and had a heart attack. I don't remember the details. Why?"

"Frank shot Marie with one of the handguns."

"No kidding! What's Frank do for a living?"

"Roni says he's in the scrap business."

"Much scrap value in stolen guns?"

"Depends on whether you want to melt them down or sell them," I said.

"What's Roni's connection?"

"She kept his books."

"You think she's out of the woods on this?"

"Not so much. Guess where they live?"

She looked at me, blinking the mist from her eyes. "Don't make me beg."

"Northeast."

She hugged herself. "Small worlds are too crowded. I hate them."

Chapter Seven

I don't drive much. Thirty minutes one-way is as far and as long as I go if I can help it. More than that and my head gets fuzzy, which means the shakes can't be far behind, especially on the return trip. Jackknifing with spasms while in the driver's seat is not something I'm anxious to do. So I take the bus, which teaches you patience and the importance of a warm coat during the winter and a daily shower during the summer.

Joy and I live in a midtown neighborhood called Brookside where the trees tower over the rooftops and the houses are modest and close, like the people who live in them. Lucy inherited it from her father and sold it to me when she moved in with Simon. The house is a couple of blocks from Sixty-third and Brookside Boulevard, an intersection where I can catch a bus headed in any direction.

Monday was a bus day. I got off near Thirty-eighth and Broadway and walked to Simon's office, which was on the second floor of a two-story, block-long building. The first floor was anchored on the north by a bar called Blues on Broadway, the rest of the block filled with a dry cleaner, tattoo parlor, health food emporium, and used bookstore. Wilson Bluestone, aka Blues, owned the bar and the building.

Simon's office was on the south end of the second floor, five hundred square feet filled with his computers and flat screens, and Lucy's file cabinets. He was digital, handling his cases electronically, and she was analog, preferring hard copy.

A sometime lawyer named Lou Mason had the office on the

north end. He was as likely to be tending bar at Blues on Broadway as standing before the bar in court, depending on the status of his license and his latest run-in with judges that didn't admire his hit-and-run style.

The middle space was for lease. The last tenant had been Decision Making Consultants, run by Kate Scranton. Kate was a psychologist and jury consultant who could read lies in the involuntary facial movements none of us can suppress. We met while Joy and I were still married, Joy accusing me of having an affair with her. Though I wasn't yet sleeping with Kate, I gave her my heart and left Joy with my pain. After the divorce, I saw my future with Kate until her ex-husband moved to San Diego, taking their troubled teenaged son, Brian, with him. Kate couldn't bear being separated from her son and followed them to California. She asked me to come with her, telling me there was nothing to keep me in Kansas City.

That's when Joy's cancer was diagnosed and I realized that Kate was wrong. When I asked Joy to move in with me until she was better, I asked Kate to understand. Kate tried, but couldn't. I postponed my trip to San Diego. Kate returned my phone calls with e-mails and answered my e-mails with silence.

One door opened as another closed. At first I thought Kate and Joy had done the opening and closing. Then I realized that those doors swung both ways, that the choices had been as much mine as theirs, and that I was where I needed to be, with Joy, whether her time was long or short. Still, I lingered outside Kate's door for an instant, jiggling the knob, images of her flashing in my mind. It was unlocked, but I didn't go in.

Simon was at his desk, which is to say that he was in heaven, three twenty-one-inch monitors arrayed before him, his hands flying across his keyboard, windows flashing on the screens, his head nodding to an internal rhythm. He was a computer genius, catching bad guys in a net of ones and zeros.

"You're late," he said, not breaking eye contact with his screens.

"I can't be late. I'm a consultant. We have no hours, and you and I don't have an appointment."

"A consultant is someone who travels, and you don't travel."

"I took the bus. That qualifies. And, I have miles to go before I sleep."

"What about promises, Robert Frost?" he asked, spinning around in his chair to face me. "You have any of those to keep? Like the one you made to me that you'd watch Lucy's back. She told me what happened at LC's. For Christ's sake, Jack, how could you have left your gun at home? She could have been killed!"

"Slow down, Simon. I couldn't take my gun into the Municipal Farm. I don't like leaving it in the car, and, besides, LC had a sign on his door that said no guns. That's the law."

"How about today? Are you carrying?"

I was, my Glock 23 holstered on hip, beneath my jacket. Carrying it was more a way of staying connected to what I used to be than it was a necessity. My work for Simon and Lucy rarely required that I be armed, and, notwithstanding yesterday's barbeque shoot-out, Kansas City wasn't a war zone.

He jumped out of his chair and snatched a page from his printer. "I looked up Missouri's concealed-carry law, and guess what, it's not a crime to take a gun into a public place that posts one of those signs as long as it's not a church or a school. If LC had found out you were carrying, he could have asked you to leave and you could have been fined if you refused, but it wouldn't have been a crime if you had done your job and protected Lucy."

Simon was five-five on a tall day and pudgy enough that he needed more time in the gym and less at his desk. He was bald on top, thin on the sides, with a light complexion that flushed full red whenever he got angry, like now.

"There was no way to know what was going to happen."

He slapped his palms together. "Exactly my point. That's why you don't leave your gun at home in your underwear drawer. I'd rather pay your fine than pay for Lucy's funeral."

When I was with the FBI, my friends were the agents I worked with and depended on. The job didn't leave time for another life.

When my movement disorder forced me out of the Bureau, those friendships faded, not because they weren't real or strong, but because they were born out of shared lives we didn't share anymore. It didn't help that some of my brethren believed I should have taken the fall for corruption in the Violent Crimes squad I led. With the exception of one of my agents named Ammara Iverson, there were no mutual promises made in good faith to stay in touch only to be broken without malice. There was only a double yellow line between then and now.

Not long after I left the Bureau, Simon asked me to help him with a case he believed in but couldn't prove. He needed someone who knew how to interrogate witnesses and put together a case that depended on the human elements of motive, means, and opportunity that eluded computer analysis. He'd read the newspaper coverage of my last case with the FBI and asked me if the rumors about my involvement in the corruption were true. I told him no, and he didn't ask again.

I put the case together for him, and that led to as much work as I could manage and a friendship that grew beyond our work after I introduced him to Lucy. She was my surrogate daughter, which made him my surrogate something or other. Together with Joy, I had more family than I'd had in a long time, and family members are entitled to yell when they are afraid for one another.

"Okay," I said, my hands up in surrender. "Next time, I'll shoot the people who catch us in a cross fire. I'm sure they won't panic when they see me reach for my gun and shoot me before I can get it out of my holster. And, if they do notice what I'm doing, I'll just ask them to wait a minute so you won't get mad at me for not killing them first."

He flipped the paper onto his desk, shaking his head, unable to hide his grin. "Fine, fine, fine. Make fun of me, but remember this. Nebbishes like me don't get women like Lucy. I mean never. She's smart. She's pretty. She's funny. And she's got the longest legs I've ever seen up close. And, you know what is the most amazing thing of all? She loves me! Me! And I love her. Sometimes I can't tell whether the gods are smiling on me or laughing because they're going to pull the rug out from under me."

"The gods are smiling, so enjoy what you've got and don't worry so much. Life is too unpredictable. I can't shoot everybody."

"Which makes you a lousy consultant. Lucy says Jimmy Martin stiffed you on the kids."

"That he did."

"Where's that leave you?"

I shrugged. "Same place as the FBI and the cops. No place. Some of the neighbors are sticking up fliers with the kids' pictures all over Northeast, and they've organized search parties."

"Where are they looking?"

"Kessler Park, the bluffs, and the river, anyplace you could bury two little kids without being noticed."

"Any chance they aren't dead?"

"Not much. There's been no ransom demand. The FBI has checked out the rest of Jimmy's family to make certain he didn't stash the kids with one of them, and they've run down his known acquaintances and come up empty. If Evan and Cara are still alive, someone has to be taking care of them, and there aren't any likely candidates."

"What else can you do?"

I shook my head. "Keep looking, go back to the friends and family, and hope somebody remembers something or lets something slip. It's not much of a plan, but it is what it is."

"So what can I do?"

"A couple of things. A gun dealer that lived at Lake Perry died on his way home from a gun show in Topeka last month. Hit a deer and had a heart attack. Somebody stole his inventory before his body was found. See what you can dig up on it."

"Because someone is going to pay me or because you're asking me?"

"Because you're a humanitarian. And, because one of the stolen handguns was used in the shooting at LC's."

"Lucy told me, the guy who killed his wife. Why do you care?"

"Roni Chase, the woman who shot him, may be in over her head."

"Is she going to pay me?"

"I was thinking it would work the other way. You pay her."

"That would make me a moron, not a humanitarian."

"Actually, it would make you her employer. You've been looking for someone who can help you analyze financial records. She's got an accounting degree and runs a bookkeeping company. You remember the Jensen case from last year, the one where the bookkeeper embezzled a couple hundred grand from that construction company?"

"Yeah."

"Give me a set of the records, let her take a look at them, see if she can put it together. You already know what's there. If she can find it, maybe you can use her. Plus, she's a good shot and takes her gun into restaurants."

He shrugged and pursed his lips. "I've got a better idea." He pulled up a file on his middle screen, tapped a few keys, copied it to a CD, and handed it to me. "These are the financials on a new case I've got for an electrical supply company. I redacted the company name. Tell her if she finds what I think is buried in those numbers, she can be a consultant making the middle money just like you."

"What are you looking for?"

He smiled. "Like I'm going to tell you."

"Why not tell me?"

"Because I know that look on your face. This Roni reminds you of your daughter, Wendy, or someone else who reminds you of Wendy, so if I tell you, you'll tell her because you think if you save enough stray cats and dogs you'll pay a debt you don't owe and couldn't pay if you did."

I slipped the CD into my side jacket pocket, not arguing because he was right.

"Thanks."

"Jack, do both of you a favor and just give her the disc. Let her save herself."

Chapter Eight

I changed buses at the Transit Plaza on Tenth and Main, picking up the Number 24, which runs the full length of Independence Avenue. Two-person bench seats separated by an aisle lined each side of the bus. I slid across a bench, sitting next to the window, watching a wide-hipped Vietnamese woman, stoop-shouldered from carrying stuffed shopping bags and the clutch of two small children, settle onto the bench behind me, gathering her possessions.

Three Hispanic teenage boys, jeans sagging off their hips, strut-walked down the aisle, the number fourteen, four dots, the letters *NF*, and a sombrero speared with a machete dripping in blood, inked on their hands and necks, tattoos of the Mexican drug cartel Nuestra Familia. The cartel was affiliated with gangs by the same name that originated in California prisons in the 1960s, spreading through the southwest, eventually making their way to Kansas City, recruiting kids whose idea of the good life was a street corner they could call their own, dealing dope, and standing strong against the cops and the competition.

The one in the lead, a skinny kid weighed down by gold chains bouncing against his chest, bumped into a slight, older white man wearing a loose-fitting barn jacket, knocking him onto my bench. The kid snickered, his friends joining in the laughter. One of them slapped him on the back, calling out "Yo! Eberto," as they each claimed a bench. The man righted himself, smoothing his thin gray hair.

"Time was," he said, "I would've kicked all three of their asses."

"Time was, I would have helped you."

He chuckled. "Wouldn't have needed the help."

"Wouldn't have mattered."

He looked me up and down. I'm six-foot and more muscle than fat, though the fat is catching up to the muscle. I gave him the hard stare I'd learned to use with the FBI, trying to convince both of us.

He didn't blink. He had a smoker's aged face, his skin yellowed and drawn, cheeks sunken. His dark eyes were deep set and clouded. He let out a long breath and coughed, a wet raspy hack, and grinned.

"First liar doesn't stand a chance, does he?"

I grinned back. "Nope."

"Punks like that are the same all over. Some turn out okay, others don't last long enough to find out."

We left it at that, both content to watch the streets pass by. There are two cities named Kansas City, one in Missouri and one in Kansas, their borders rubbing along a shared state line, staring at each other across the confluence of two rivers bearing the names of each state. Both grew outward from the rivers, their older cores encircled by ever-expanding rings of new development with predictable patterns marked by the common modifier predominantly—as in Black, Hispanic, or White; rich, middle class, or poor. There are five counties, two in Kansas and three in Missouri, with suburbs and towns that melt and meld into Census Bureau calculations, each carving out an individual identity while still a part of something as ambiguous as Greater Kansas City.

Though Kansas City is more than the sum of its parts, some of its parts bear little resemblance to one another. Whether by design or happenstance, you can drive from Northeast to the southern limits of the Kansas side suburbs, where new rooftops stretch to the horizon and there is little color in the cul-desacs, and conclude that you haven't just left town, you've entered a parallel universe.

More than a hundred years ago, Northeast KC became the city's first suburb, led by wealthy lumbermen who built its mansions, followed by Italians, some of whom never left, and Jews who did, moving steadily south and west, and working-class people of all stripes. In recent years, it had become the new home for immigrants and refugees from Somalia, Sudan, Burundi, Mauritania, Ivory Coast, Cuba, Myanmar, and Vietnam.

Bright lines are hard to come by, but Independence Avenue comes close, defining and dividing the Northeast. Everything is available on the Avenue, from sex to groceries, from salvation to cemetery plots; everything, including Frank Crenshaw's scrap and Roni Chase's bookkeeping. It's where life happens.

North of Independence Avenue, people fight to put their homes on the national register of historic places, to put their kids through school, and to gain a foothold in a strange new land. South of the Avenue, they fight to survive poverty, gangs, and despair.

The Vietnamese woman with her two children, the older man, the three teenagers, and I got off at the intersection of Independence Avenue and Brooklyn. It was late morning, the sun was playing tag with the clouds, and a crisp breeze gave the low fifties a chill. The man buttoned his jacket, pulled a watch cap from one pocket, covered his head, and waited for a break in the traffic. He crossed the Avenue, slow, sure steps taking him north on Brooklyn. The woman shepherded her children a block east before turning south onto Park.

I watched the gangbangers study the man and the woman; their eyes narrowed to predatory slits, whispers and looks passing between them, casting their votes with shrugs and tilted heads. When they took a step toward the curb, aiming toward the old man, I let them see the gun on my hip, closing the distance between us.

Eberto caught my advance, stopped, and stared, his eyes shifting from my face to my gun and back again. He was wearing a ball cap turned backward, both hands in the pockets of his zippered sweatshirt. He ran his tongue across his lips, took off his cap, and swept his hand across his buzzed scalp. He shifted his weight from right to left, his eyes flickering. His boys were behind him. They were young and thought themselves tough, outmatching a middle-aged man, yet they saw something more than my gun that made them hesitate. They saw that I was willing.

I took another step toward them, Eberto backing up, one foot slipping off the curb. The woman was gone, the man nearly out of sight.

"Don't need this shit today," he said.

He turned and shuffled west toward Woodland, the other two trailing him, reclaiming respect with a slow retreat. I waited until they disappeared before collapsing on the metal bench at the bus stop.

Looking up, I saw a flier with Evan and Cara Martin's pictures on it taped to a light pole. The photographs, headshots, had been taken at their elementary school, Evan's cowlick standing at attention, Cara's grin gap-toothed; both smiles were full-faced and easy, their place on the light pole unimagined and unimaginable. Beneath it was another flier with a picture of another child, Timmy Montgomery, his image faded from too many months on the pole, the flier listing the date he was last seen as two years ago. I took a deep breath, hugged myself, and shook so hard the bench rattled against the bolts locking it to the concrete.

Chapter Nine

I was in Simon's office the first time Peggy Martin called. Lucy answered, warm but professional, listening, her jaw easing open, her eyes widening.

"Hang on. I'm going to put you on speaker. I want my partners to hear this," Lucy said, punching a button on the phone, shifting from professional to soothing. "Start over, Mrs. Martin."

"He took my kids," she said, her voice cracking. "You've got to find them."

Lucy grabbed a notepad and pen as Simon and I pulled our chairs closer to the phone.

"Start from the beginning, Mrs. Martin. Take your time."

Her voice caught as she fought back tears. "I'm sorry. It's just that the police say they're doing all they can, but my kids have been gone for two weeks. Why would he do a thing like that? What kind of man kidnaps his own kids, for Christ's sake?"

"I don't know, Mrs. Martin. Where are you?"

"Home. I'm at home. I'm afraid to leave in case the police call. Please, you've got to help me."

"It would be better if we talked in person. Give me your address." Lucy wrote it down and glanced at her watch. "We'll be there in thirty minutes." She ended the call and looked at me. "You in?"

She knew without asking. It was the hardest kind of case, but neither of us could say no. Kids disappear for all kinds of reasons, none of them good. Parents wake up and die each day they're gone, the uncertainty of what may have happened and the unspeakable fear of what did happen a daily acid bath. And no matter how it ends, it never ends. I was living proof that survivors don't heal and ghosts don't rest.

"I'm all in."

Peggy Martin lived in a small house on Wabash between Third and Fourth Streets, a few blocks north and east of my bus stop bench. Her house sat above a two-car garage, wooden steps leading up a flight from the driveway to the front door, white paint cracked and flaking off the wooden siding.

Lucy and I sat at her kitchen table, looking at pictures of Evan and Cara, both fair-skinned with blue eyes and light brown hair, like their mother, listening as she talked about them. Cara was all bones and crooked teeth, a gawky girl who danced, played basketball, loved to draw, and cried herself to sleep when her parents fought.

Evan was her devil child, a spark plug full of mischief and laughter, throwing himself around his mother like a shield when things got hot between his parents. He was the first son in four generations not named Jimmy. Her husband was Jimmy Martin, III, his father was Jimmy Martin, Jr., and the old man who had started it all and dropped dead of a heart attack three years ago while chewing out a cashier he claimed had shortchanged him was Jimmy, Sr. Her husband had wanted Evan to be Jimmy the Fourth, but she'd refused.

Jimmy worked construction, but the recession had knocked the pins out from under builders. With forty hours a week hard to come by, he started going crazy and turning mean from long stretches with nothing at all. Peggy worked part-time at a nursing home, barely making enough to cover the cost of someone to look after the kids. They were three months behind on the mortgage, and she didn't know what they were going to do or where they would go when the bank made good on its threat to foreclose.

Her husband had beat her and accused her of cheating on him, a charge she dismissed with a bitter laugh, but didn't deny, saying who could blame her if she did, being married to him. Her lawyer got a restraining order against Jimmy when she filed for divorce, telling her that the piece of paper was about as much protection as a condom with a hole in it, but short of a shotgun, it was the best the law could do.

She wore no makeup. Her cheeks were sunken, her bloodshot eyes suspended above dark bags, and her unwashed hair hung loose around her thin face. Though disheveled, there was beauty behind her pain, features that in another time had turned heads. She trembled as she spoke, her party days, if there had been any, behind her. She was holding herself together with bubble gum and string.

"Why do you think your husband is the one who took Evan and Cara?" Lucy asked.

"Who else could have done it? He's that hateful!"

"When did you discover that your children were missing?"

She sniffled and wiped her nose with a dish towel.

"It was Saturday morning, almost two weeks ago. They was watching television, and I told them I had to run out to the store. I was only gone a few minutes. When I come back, they was gone. I ran all over the house, hollering, but they didn't answer."

She dissolved in tears, ducking her head, looking up at us. Lucy flinched for an instant, resisting the impulse to comfort her, not ready to sacrifice the objectivity she needed to decide whether to take the case. That decision depended on whether she thought Peggy might have had something to do with her kids' disappearance. She wouldn't be the first parent to kill her kids and beg for help to find who did it.

"Was this the first time you had left them home alone?" Lucy asked when Peggy stopped crying.

"I left them once or twice before. Just for a few minutes. Oh, I know everyone says they was young to be left alone, but Cara, she's real responsible."

Lucy nodded, meaning only that she had heard what Peggy said, but Peggy brightened, interpreting the gesture as one of forgiveness and understanding.

"I'm sure she is. Did you lock the doors before you left?"

"I know I did, not that it would make a difference. Jimmy's got a key, and the kids would have let him in anyway. The police said there was no sign of forced entry."

"What store did you go to?"

"The QuikTrip up on Independence Avenue. We was out of milk."

"What have the police told you about their investigation?"

"Adrienne Nardelli is the detective in charge of the case. She says she talked to the neighbors but no one's seen anything."

"Have you talked to your neighbors? Sometimes they'll tell you more than they'll tell the police."

She started crying again, wiping her face with the towel when she stopped.

"Them people have been so good to me. Ellen Koch, she lives across the street. She's organized the volunteer searchers, and she's talked to everyone and they all say they didn't see nothing or nobody. The police are looking and my neighbors are looking, but nobody's seen my babies. And Jimmy, he went to jail just so he wouldn't have to tell what he did."

"Why did you call me?"

"Ellen give me your number. She said she seen you on the news last spring when you found that little boy after his father kidnapped him." She reached behind her, picking up an envelope from the kitchen counter, handing it to Lucy. "Ellen took up a collection. There's nine hundred eighty-seven dollars in there. It's all I can pay you."

Lucy had made a splash six months ago in a custody case. The father, who had been denied custody because he was a drug addict, had taken the boy to Toronto. Lucy tracked them down, bringing the boy back and leaving the father in a Canadian jail. She picked up the envelope, ran her fingers across it, but didn't look inside.

"Okay, Peggy. We'll give it a shot."

Adrienne Nardelli had accepted our involvement without enthusiasm, reluctantly admitting that she was nowhere on the case, adding that Quincy Carter had told her she would be sorry and warning us that we'd better make a liar out of him. We had made no more progress in a week than she had in two. Evan and Cara Martin had vanished, and their father was the only suspect.

Chapter Ten

Roni Chase's office was behind me, one of four tenants in what used to be a Denny's restaurant, the logo still visible in white letters painted on the asphalt parking lot. The owner of the building had gutted and subdivided it into Chase Bookkeeping, Payday Loans Today, New Life Chiropractic, and Andy's Bail Bonds, each with its own entrance.

I hauled myself off the bench, leaving Peggy Martin's ball up for grabs, certain that Lucy would catch it for now, and grabbed the one with Roni Chase's name on it. I stopped in the parking lot, watching Roni through the plate-glass storefront window of her office. She was sitting at her desk, holding a pen in her right hand, twirling it from one finger to the next and talking to someone whose back was to me. He was wearing blue jeans and a denim jacket, leaning over the desk, hands planted, his head bobbing. I couldn't see his face, but hers was set hard and tight. She pushed back from the desk when I stepped through the door, folding her arms across her chest and cocking her head toward me, signaling that they had company.

"You take walk-ins?" I asked, letting the door close, blocking the exit.

Her guest straightened and turned, arms loose at his sides, cool dark eyes taking my measure. He had close-cropped dyed blond hair, a natural brown chinstrap beard, and a pierced eyebrow. The T-shirt under his open jacket was stretched tight across his body. He was ripped, flexing his hands, balling them into fists, shaking them loose and ready. I put him at five-ten, one-eighty, mid twenties, willing and probably able.

Roni dipped her chin, the corners of her mouth curling into a reluctant smile. "Sure, why not. I'll catch up to you later, Brett."

He gave her a narrow look, jamming his hands into his coat pockets. "You remember what I told you," he said to her.

"Yeah, like I haven't heard it a million times before."

"I mean it, Roni. I'm not buying your funeral dress yet. You keep this shit up, I'll let the county bury you in a pine box in your goddamn underwear."

She got up, came around to the front side of the desk, hands on her hips. "And let all the money you've been saving for my dress go to waste? I don't think so."

"Girl, you are out of your mind."

I stepped aside, holding the door open for him. He hesitated as the wind blew in, fluttering papers on Roni's desk, and gave both of us a last look, shaking his head, pointing at her, talking to me.

"I shit you not, dude. She is absolutely fucking out of her mind."

He climbed into a Ford Fusion parked in front of Roni's office, backed up, spun the wheel hard, and fishtailed toward the street, wheels spinning on loose gravel.

I looked around her office: maple desk and credenza, low-backed swivel chair, flat-screen computer monitor, printer on a stand, twin file cabinets, a fern in one corner, a ficus in another, and paintings of seascapes and meadows on the walls. Her mother's office, not hers.

"Brett who?" I asked.

"Staley."

"Let me guess. You and Brett have a history."

She laughed, easy and relieved. "A lot of history. His family and mine."

"He your boyfriend?"

"Depends on the day."

"Is he a client too?"

She cocked her head, hesitating before taking a breath. "No, but I do work for his father, Nick. He has a little grocery on St. John. Brett works for him but not for much longer."

"Another victim of the recession?"

"Yeah. When times were good, Nick bought a couple of rental properties, figured real estate was a safe investment for his retirement and the mortgage broker made him a sweet deal. That was when the banks would finance anyone with a pulse and a ten-dollar balance in their bank account. Then, when the economy soured, he used the rent money to keep the grocery going instead of paying the mortgages, and now he's going to lose his store and the rental properties."

"You think he'll take it better than Frank did?"

"You can't tell how anyone will take something like that. He's an ex-Marine who still thinks he's a drill sergeant and Brett's one of his grunts."

"Let me guess. Nothing Brett does is good enough for his old man. The harder he tries, the worse it gets. So he puts on the tough guy act to convince you and him that he's a man."

Her eyes popped, and her chin dropped. "How could you possibly know that?"

"My old man was a Marine. Rode my ass until one day I took a swing at him."

"You hit your father?"

"In the mouth. Knocked him to his knees. I was eighteen and angry."

"What happened?"

I let out a sigh. "He got a fat lip and I broke a knuckle, but I got his attention. He started cutting me some slack, and things smoothed out after that. I found out years later that he bragged to his buddies how his kid had tagged him. He was proud of me for not taking any more crap from him, even if he couldn't tell me to my face."

She shook her head. "I don't know. I'm pretty sure if Brett hit his dad, his dad would be bragging to his buddies about how he broke every bone in Brett's body."

"Hey, I'm not recommending it. I'm just saying how it was for me. That stuff about your funeral dress. That about what happened at LC's?"

She went back to her desk chair, motioning me to a pair of black leather chairs in front of the desk.

They were the nicest furnishings in the office, Roni's mother understanding that the customer came first. I sat opposite her. She ran one hand through her hair, took a deep breath, and let it out slowly, nodding her head.

"Yeah. Brett's a romantic."

"Romantic isn't the word I'd use to describe him."

She laughed. "I know, but he's all hard muscle and soft heart. I think he was more scared than mad."

"The woman I was with, her boyfriend got on me the same way Brett got on you."

She sat up. "Got on you? Why? What did you do?"

"Left my gun at home."

"That's what I don't get. Why do men always assume they have to save us?"

"That's the way people think about the ones they love."

"Oh, c'mon. It's more than that. It's the *you're the weaker sex so watch me flex my pecs* bullshit mentality guys are born with. You saw the way Brett looked at you when you showed up."

I nodded. "He lifted his leg a little bit."

"Like you didn't. Jeez, men are so pathetic. You should have seen yourself. You had a look on your face, eyes all bunched up, mouth tight like you were about to spit and couldn't wait for Brett to start something."

She was right. That's what I'd done with the gangbangers from the bus, and I'd done it again with Brett. The first time, I knew it. The second time, I was oblivious, on autopilot.

"You don't even know me," she added. "And you were ready to throw down with someone half your age and twice as tough because you thought you had to save me. What is up with that?"

I shrugged. "We've all got a history."

"Yeah, and who's going to save us from that?"

Chapter Eleven

History comes with options. We can ignore it and repeat it. We can learn from it or revise it, changing winners into losers. It gives us opportunities and excuses, lifting us up or weighing us down. Though our history is as embedded in our DNA as the genes that make us tall, dark, and handsome or short, fat, and good company, it doesn't have to be our destiny. The hard part is being able to tell the difference between being chosen and choosing.

Simon and Roni had told me the same thing: Let her save herself. But here I was anyway, unsure if she needed saving or, if she did, what she needed saving from. Whether I had come to her office because I was gallant or guilty, I was there, and she'd told her boyfriend to leave and asked me to stay.

"Maybe we'll save each other," I said.

She smiled. "It's like I said yesterday. I saved your life, and now you owe me."

"And I pay my debts in full. So, how're you doing?"

Her face darkened, and her shoulders sagged. "I don't know. I didn't sleep so good last night. I kept seeing Marie lying there on the floor. She was always nice to me. And that stupid asshole Frank tried to trick me so he could kill me too. And he'd only known me my whole life! He was at my Communion, and he was going to kill me and you and your friend and LC. And for what? Because Marie pushed his buttons one too many times?"

She stared at me, her eyes filling, hands gripping the edge of the desk, demanding answers that wouldn't tell her what she needed to know.

"If you want it to make sense, you won't get past it because it never will."

She sniffled, wiping her eyes and nose. "The other thing that gets me, the thing I keep seeing over and over is me shooting Frank." She shook her head, eyebrows raised. "I didn't hesitate. I just pulled the trigger. The really crazy part is that when I see it in my head, I'm watching me do it, like I'm having an out-of-body experience. And, I'm not sorry I shot him. I'm just amazed I did. Is that wrong? What does that make me?"

There are no rules for how to cope with shooting someone. Circumstances matter, whether it was premeditated aggression, self-defense, or the heat of the moment, but each person has to navigate through the shock, sorrow, and amazement that follow. Though the law will impose its judgment, Roni was the type for whom the personal verdict would matter most.

"No, it wasn't wrong. It makes you someone who can be counted on. It makes you a survivor."

"Maybe, but I like it better when the bad guy just gets voted off the island."

"Kind of takes the TV out of reality TV."

"Yeah, and now the TV stations won't leave us alone. Same for the newspaper reporters. Grandma Lilly unplugged our phone and threatened to shoot the next one who came to the door."

"Good for Grandma Lilly. All that will pass. The media is a movable beast. They'll find someone else soon enough, and you'll be forgotten."

"Not soon enough to suit me. You can have my fifteen minutes of fame."

"What have the police said about whether you'll be charged?"

"Detective Carter said it's up to the prosecuting attorney, but he didn't think that I had anything to worry about on the shooting."

I knew Carter well enough to know that he chose his words carefully. If he'd said she had nothing to worry about on the shooting, he didn't mean she had nothing to worry about. Frank Crenshaw shot his wife with a stolen gun during a meeting with

Roni, who returned the favor and shot him. Carter was leaving his options open, waiting to see where his investigation would take him.

"You should talk to a lawyer."

"What for? Detective Carter said it was self-defense."

"All the same. I can give you some names, make an introduction, if you change your mind. What do you hear about Crenshaw? How's he doing?"

"He's at Truman Medical Center. I went to see him last night, but a policeman was guarding his room and the nurse at the nurse's station wouldn't even let me go down the hall. I asked her how Frank was doing, and she said she couldn't tell me anything because of privacy laws. On my way out, I ran into another nurse who knows my mom. She told me that she heard that the bullet didn't hit bones or nerves. He lost a lot of blood, but it looks like he's gonna be okay."

"The cop is there to make sure Crenshaw doesn't check out against medical advice before they can lock him up and to make sure you don't shoot him again."

She gave me a sour smile. "Very funny."

"Don't be bitter. The state is very particular about these things. You had your crack at killing Frank. Now the state wants its chance."

"Yeah, that's wild, isn't it? Save a life to take a life."

"Everybody has a job to do."

She pointed to a stack of papers on her desk. "Tell me about it."

"I'd rather you tell me about it. What were you doing for Frank Crenshaw besides keeping his books?"

"Trying to figure out a way to keep him afloat, but business had dropped too far off and, in this economy, it wasn't going to come back soon enough. He's like a lot of my clients. They aren't perfect people, but they've worked hard all their lives and now they look around and it's all gone because an economy they can't begin to understand collapsed on their heads. Some of them, I don't know how they're going to survive."

"How did Marie react when you told her how bad it was?"

"She was mad, not about the business so much as she was mad at Frank for not telling her sooner how bad it was."

"You think she knew he had a gun?" I asked.

"I'd be surprised if she did. Frank wasn't into guns."

"I had a good look at Crenshaw. He seemed unhappy, but he didn't strike me as homicidal. What were the three of you talking about before you got up from the table to go to the bathroom?"

"Marie kept asking me what else they could do to hold on to the business, and I told her there was nothing they could do, that Frank had tried everything."

"What do you think set him off?

She shook her head. "He'd been under a lot of pressure since the first of the year, but it had gotten worse in the last couple of months. I had trouble getting him to focus, and he blew up at me a few times on the phone. Hung up on me twice. Even so, I never figured him to go nuts like that."

"Had he talked about what he was going to do to earn a living?"

"Nothing more specific than look for a job even though there aren't any jobs."

"I guess Frank was really up against it," I said.

"I suppose so."

"That can make a man do things he never imagined."

"He did. He killed his wife and tried to kill me."

Chapter Twelve

"What else do you hear from the police?"

"Detective Carter was here a couple of hours ago with a search warrant for all of Frank's files. He even took my computer."

"What about your other clients? Aren't their records on there too?"

"That's what I told him. All my stuff is supposed to be confidential."

"What did Carter say?"

"Hire a lawyer and take it up with the judge."

"Are you going to do that?"

"I don't have the time. Frank Crenshaw and Nick Staley are like a lot of my clients. They're small-business people who don't have time to pay all their bills, file their quarterly reports, do their payrolls, and run their businesses. My mom knew that so she did that for a bunch of them, and they all expect me to do the same. So I'm more interested in making sure that gets done on time than going to court. I'll tell my clients that the police are looking at their records and they can hire a lawyer to do something about it if they want to, but none of them will because they can't afford it."

"How are you going to do that without your computer?"

"I back everything up at the end of the day to an online server. I'll pick up another PC and download my stuff. That will put me a day behind, but I'll catch up."

"I heard one of the detectives at the restaurant say that the gun Frank used to shoot Marie was stolen from a gun show last month. Any idea how Frank got a hold of a stolen gun?"

"No. This can be a rough part of town. A lot of people own guns and carry them."

"The detective also said that Frank stole a car when he was a teenager. Did you know that?"

"That was before I was born. What's that got to do with anything?"

"Since he was a convicted felon, he couldn't buy a gun. Who would you talk to around here if you wanted to buy a gun without a background check?"

She crunched her forehead. "And why do you think I would know something like that?"

I shrugged. "You're third generation down here, which means you know a lot of people and a lot of their secrets. You don't have to be a crook to know crooks. You just have to pay attention. And, this being a rough part of town, not everyone who wants a gun can get one on the up-and-up like you and your Grandma Lilly."

She straightened in her chair, her cheeks turning rose. "This may be a rough part of town and my grandmother and mother may have taught me to take care of myself, but that doesn't mean we're either criminals or know criminals because I'm not one and I don't know anyone who is."

"I know a little bit about Northeast, and I'd know where to look."

"Where?"

"I'd start with a drug dealer and move up the chain, asking without pushing because those people don't like to be pushed, but drugs and guns go together like pancakes and syrup."

"So why ask me if you already know who to ask?"

"Because I don't know any drug dealers down here."

She folded her arms across her middle. "But you assume that I do? Why? Because I'm young? Because I have a lip ring and red dye in my hair? Does that make me a freak in your eyes?"

She did remind me of Wendy, the way she didn't back down when I tried to pigeonhole her, throwing my stereotypes in my face.

"A lot of people your age do drugs, and if they don't, they know someone who does and someone else who deals. I'm not attacking you. I'm trying to help you."

"I haven't asked for your help, and I don't need it."

"You will if this doesn't go away. Maybe Frank had something going on the side to try and pay the bills, something he couldn't put on his books or tell you about. While you're in the bathroom, he tells Marie, and she freaks out. That's when she jumped out of her chair and said she'd rather lose it all."

"That's hard for me to believe," Roni said. "Frank played it straight on his taxes. He wouldn't take any chances on an audit, and Marie was the kind of person who if she found a dollar on the ground would spend the rest of the day looking for whoever dropped it and if she couldn't find them, she'd give the dollar to the church."

"Anything in Frank's financial records that doesn't match up to his normal business activity, something he could have been doing to cover his nut?"

She shook her head. "I've been over all of that with Detective Carter. If Frank was trying to launder money through his scrap business or cover up something else, I sure didn't see it. I'm telling you, his business was ready for last rites. There wasn't enough cash to wipe your nose, let alone launder."

"Would you have seen it?"

Roni straightened and squared her shoulders. "I know what I'm doing, if that's what you mean."

She was cooperating with the police, and she wasn't hiring a lawyer. That's what innocent people did. Naïve people did the same thing, as did arrogant crooks that were certain they were too smart to be caught. She may be naïve, but she wasn't arrogant. That left innocent. I tossed Simon's CD on her desk.

"That's what I mean. I'd like you to take a look at the financials on that disc. Let me know if you find anything that doesn't fit."

"Who wants to know?"

"Simon Alexander. He runs a private investigation company

called Alexander Investigations. The woman I was with yesterday, Lucy Trent, she's his partner. I do odd jobs for them. Simon is looking for someone who can decipher dollars. I told him he should give you a shot."

She picked up the disc, turning it over in her hand, her eyes lighting up. "What am I looking for?"

"Simon wouldn't tell me."

"Why not?"

"Because he was afraid I'd tell you to make it easier on you."

"Would you have?"

"Probably."

"To save me?"

"Something like that. Simon told me to let you save yourself."

She smiled and nodded. "Cool. I think I like him better than I like you."

"I don't blame you." I handed her a business card. "My home, cell, and office numbers are on the card. Call me when you figure it out."

Chapter Thirteen

I'm at my best in the morning. I shake less, think more clearly, and get more done. I usually exercise in the afternoon, figuring that the better shape I'm in, the better I can shake off the shakes, though my workouts are a double-edged sword, triggering the tics even as they harden me against them. Evenings are an adventure—sometimes easy; other times a pounding combination of tremors and fog, my head feeling as if an invisible hand is squeezing my brain, trying to wring the last drops out of a soggy sponge.

I've seen a lot of smart doctors, but none of them can tell me what causes tics. That only seems fair because they don't know how to cure it either. The upside is that they assure me it won't kill me and it won't turn into something worse that will, and that counts for a lot.

I've tried the drugs that work for some people. One knocked the bottom out of my blood pressure while the other knocked me for a loop. Neither one worked. The heavier pharmaceutical artillery warns of side effects like Parkinson's syndrome, so the only drug I take is chocolate. Joy insisted I try neurofeedback, biofeedback, meditation, acupuncture, Rolfing, and subtle energy therapy, none of which helped, but it made her feel better and left me straddling life between taking it easy and taking as much as I can take.

That said, most people don't know there's anything wrong with me. I don't shake, rattle, and roll all the time or most of the time. When I'm with the uninitiated and my neck and head rear back for a direct shot at the heavens or I break out into a speech-throttling stutter, I explain that I have a movement disorder and leave it at that unless they ask for details I'm happy to provide. I'd rather people understand than speculate, but I don't want to bore them with the details.

It was midafternoon when I got off the bus in Brookside, the long, jostling ride the last straw in a day that didn't fit my tic-management routine. I grabbed hold of a NO PARKING sign, my knees buckling, my chin locked on my chest, my eyes shut tight as I corkscrewed toward the sidewalk, people skirting me, leaving me blessedly alone. The spasm passed, and I pulled myself up, took a deep breath, and walked home, wobbly at first, finding my legs, my head clear by the time I walked in the door and Roxie and Ruby jumped me.

There is only one thing better than a puppy, and that's two puppies, even when they are no longer puppies. Roxie is white with a faint honey streak down her back you can see only on the day she's groomed. Ruby's coat is amber except for her white socks and chest. She's the dominant sister, though Roxie is smarter, scratching at the door so that we'll open it so that Ruby will go outside and she can steal the toy they were fighting over. They greet me like a liberator every time I come home, a few minutes on the floor with them climbing in and out of my lap, licking my ears, and nipping at my nose the perfect tonic.

"They're glad to see you," Joy said.

I was sitting on the faded oriental rug in the living den, a room whose hybrid name made up for what our house lacked in space, one room serving as two, the dogs flanking me, their front paws on my thighs. They'd met me at the door, sliding across the hardwood floor, attacking my knees until I surrendered.

Joy stood in the doorway to the kitchen, a dish towel over one shoulder. She'd lost her hair to chemo, but it had grown back, a thin, white downy layer. She called it low maintenance, claimed it was every woman's dream. She was sickly thin, her clothes hanging off bony shoulders, and straight-line hips. The difference makers were the way her eyes glowed, the ease of her smile, and the sure way she carried herself, the combination saying that she'd taken her turn in the barrel and was determined to live as well and as long as she could. It was enough for her, and it was enough for me.

"Who can blame them?"

"Don't kid yourself. They do that for everyone that comes in the door except they don't get so excited that they pee when they see you."

"Familiarity breeds continence."

Joy rolled her eyes. "Save it for the revival of Urinetown. How's that girl, Roni Chase?"

When I was at the FBI, I didn't talk with Joy about my cases because our investigations were confidential and because I thought I was protecting her from things that would only make her worry. It wasn't until after our divorce that I realized that the wall I'd built to keep her safe had kept us apart. I may have been slow to learn, but I was educable. I followed her into the kitchen and told her about my day, my visit with Roni, the old man on the bus, and the gang bangers.

"So, is Roni going to be okay?"

I shrugged. "Hard to tell. Depends on what happens. Quincy Carter won't leave it alone. If he can tie Frank Crenshaw to the robbery of the gun dealer, some of that could splash back on Roni since she kept his books."

"I'm not talking about that. I'm talking about the shooting. Is she going to be okay with that?"

That was Joy, more interested in people than problems, a lesson she says she learned the hard way. Fix yourself first and worry about the rest later.

"I think she's strong enough to handle it. She went to the hospital to see Crenshaw, but the cops wouldn't let her near him. She'll probably feel better once she sees him up and around, even if he's wearing a jail jumpsuit."

She nodded, opened the refrigerator, the door hiding her face but not the catch in her throat. "That thing with the boys on the bus. I wish you wouldn't do that."

"I'm sorry. It just happened."

"All the same."

She closed the fridge, crossed her arms, and leaned against the counter, biting her lower lip. I put my hands on her shoulders, and we leaned into each other. I rested my face against her neck as a flurry of tremors bent me at the knees. She gripped my arms, and when the shakes passed, I whispered in her ear.

"Okay."

Chapter Fourteen

Simon called as we were finishing the dinner dishes. I followed the dogs outside, letting them take me for a walk.

"The gun dealer's name was Eldon Fowler," he said. "He was hit for a hundred and six assault rifles and fifty-one or fifty-two handguns, depending on who you talk to."

"Who did you talk to?"

"County sheriff's deputy who was first on the scene and Fowler's wife."

"What about ATF? Wouldn't they be running an investigation like this?"

"They are running it. They just aren't talking about it. The sheriff's deputy said it was one for the books. Fowler hit a deer. They figure he was going fifty miles an hour, which is a hell of a speed for a narrow gravel road in the woods, especially pulling a trailer full of guns at night in the rain."

"Was he drunk?"

"He'd had a couple of beers with his buddies at the gun show, but he tested legal. Anyway, the deer smashes through the window, a big-assed buck, and spears Fowler in the chest with his antlers."

"Christ! That's a helluva way to die."

"Only it didn't kill him. He had a heart attack."

"What happened to the deer?" I asked.

"That's when things get really interesting. Someone put a bullet in the deer's brain."

"Fowler?"

"Don't think so. The bullet they took out of the deer was a .44

Magnum. Fowler's wife said he was carrying a Glock 22 .40-caliber pistol, but the sheriff's crime scene people didn't find it. She said he also kept a Browning shotgun on the rack in his pickup, but they didn't find it either. Thieves must have taken both guns."

"Sounds like the thieves were following him and one of them took pity on the deer."

"That's what the deputy said. I talked to Fowler's wife, and she told me that Fowler had called her when he was leaving the gun show in Topeka. He told her that someone had stolen a Ruger .44 Magnum Redhawk from him during the show. Said it was his favorite gun. The sheriff's deputy found Fowler's inventory sheet for the guns he took to the show. Fowler had checked off what he sold and what he was bringing home. The Redhawk wasn't checked off."

"That's why they don't know whether the thieves stole fifty-one or fifty-two handguns," I said.

"Right. And there's one other thing. Highway Patrol got a call from someone an hour before Fowler's wife found his body. Caller said he and his wife had passed a crazy man in a pickup truck that was pointing a shotgun out the driver's window as they passed him on Highway 24. Fowler's wife said he always took that highway. There was a hole in the passenger door of Fowler's truck. The deputy told me it looked as if someone had fired a shotgun at point-blank range. Doesn't make sense."

"Part of it does. The thieves were on him at the gun show, at least one of them cocky enough to shoplift the Redhawk. Fowler realizes his favorite gun is missing and gets antsy, figuring they may be after the rest of his inventory. He thinks he's being followed when he points the shotgun out the window. The driver who called the Highway Patrol, what was he driving?"

"I didn't ask."

"Well, ask. The thieves may have been driving something similar, and that's what spooked Fowler. And that means Fowler thought he'd seen the thieves and what they were driving."

"I can buy that, but it doesn't explain Fowler's passenger door,"

Simon said.

"Who knows what was going on inside Fowler's pickup? Guy is in a panic, maybe already having a heart attack. He's got the shotgun off the rack. He's pointing it out the window and pulls it back when he sees who's in the other vehicle. A loaded shotgun is harder to handle than a cell phone while you're driving and scared shitless. It's a wonder he didn't blow a hole in himself. What are those guns worth?"

"Retail, the handguns would go for an average of four to five hundred and the assault rifles from eight hundred to a grand, same for the shotgun. Makes the lot worth around a hundred and fifty thousand," Simon said.

"Less if you're fencing them one at a time."

"Maybe more if you're selling them as a lot to a motivated buyer."

"Such as?" I asked.

"Cartels in Mexico. Drugs are a big business down there, and a handful of gangs and cartels are fighting each other and the government over it. They all need guns, and they're getting some of them from the U.S."

"How?"

"They have affiliates in this country. The American gangs steal the guns and smuggle them to Mexico," he explained.

"I saw a kid on the bus today inked up with symbols of Nuestra Familia. Is that one of the cartels?"

"Yeah, along with Gran Familia Mexicana and the Cholos and some others. Is that what you wanted to know, or do you want me to keep digging?"

"I'll settle for that for now. Take the rest of the day off."

Frank Crenshaw was a charter member of the Upright Citizens Brigade. Worked hard, paid his taxes on time, and tried to protect his wife from bad news. I understood how someone like that, who'd played by the rules, could break under the pressure of losing everything, how in a mad moment, he could go crazy and kill his wife. It was the kind of sad crime that was committed countless times all across the world. But, how, I wondered, did a guy like that end up with a stolen gun? That was hard to do.

Chapter Fifteen

The phone rang at nine-thirty. I was dozing through the news. Joy was reading, the dogs asleep at her feet. I picked up the cordless phone.

"Who is it?" Joy asked.

"Caller ID says unknown."

"Let the machine answer. You can always call back if it's someone we need to talk to."

She didn't like calls from unknown callers, especially late-evening ones. The ringing triggered the primeval fear that had never left her since we lost Kevin. There had always been calls in the night when I was an FBI agent. They were part of my job. She hated those as well because they took me away, leaving her alone, uncertain when or if I'd come back.

"It's probably nothing," I said, answering the phone. "Hello."

"Mr. Davis. It's me. Roni Chase."

I was surprised by her formality but realized she hadn't called me by name at LC's or at her office. Her voice was strained and hushed.

"Roni, you can call me Jack. What's up?"

"Frank Crenshaw is dead."

"I'm sorry to hear that. What happened? I thought that nurse told you he was going to be okay."

"He would have been except someone else shot him."

"Who?" I asked.

"It wasn't me, but I don't think Detective Carter believes me."

"What makes you say that?"

"I'm at the hospital, and he won't let me go home."

"Are you under arrest?

"I don't think so. Detective Carter hasn't said that, but he told me I couldn't leave."

"Has he read you your rights?"

"Like I have a right to remain silent? All of that?"

"Yeah. All of that."

"Not yet."

"What happened?"

"I came to visit Frank. I wanted to see for myself that he was okay. It's not that I'm sorry I shot him. He didn't give me a choice. But I am sorry in another way, even if he did kill Marie. Does that make any sense?"

It was the same thing she'd told me earlier in the day. She'd keep asking herself and anyone else who would listen the same questions until it did make sense or she could live with the possibility that it never would.

"It makes perfect sense to me because I've been there."

"You've shot people?"

"A few."

She hesitated. "Any of them die?"

"Some."

"And you're okay with that?" she asked.

"I am. What about Grandma Lilly? She's the one who made sure you knew how to use that gun. What does she have to say on the subject?"

"Her mother, my great-grandmother, was shot to death. Grandma was fifteen. She saw the whole thing and says she never got over it."

"It's not about getting over it. It's about what you do with the experience. Your Grandma didn't want you to end up like her mother. If she hadn't taught you that lesson, you could have ended up like Marie."

"Maybe, or maybe Frank would have just run off and left us all there and I wouldn't have shot him and he wouldn't be dead."

"But that's not what happened. I'm more interested in what happened tonight."

"When I got to Frank's floor, a nurse told me I couldn't see him, so I asked to talk to that nurse I told you about who's a friend of my mother and she said no way and got real pissy and we got into it and the next thing I know we're both screaming at each other, she's calling security, and the cop guarding Frank's room comes running over. When security finally showed up, the cop went back to Frank's room. Next thing I know, he comes running out yelling to call a doctor because Frank's been shot."

I understood why Carter wouldn't let her leave. Intentionally or not, she'd created a disturbance that left Frank Crenshaw unprotected long enough for his killer to finish what she had started.

"Have you told Carter anything? Answered any questions?"

"He asked me what I was doing at the hospital, and I told him I just wanted to see how Frank was doing and then me and the nurse got into it and she called security. That's when he gave me a look like *I don't think so* and put me in an office and told one of the cops to make sure I stayed there. I didn't know what to do, so I called you."

"Okay. Don't answer any more questions. I'll be there as soon as I can."

"I don't get it. I didn't do anything wrong. I just wanted to see Frank."

"No good deed goes unpunished."

I hung up and looked at Joy. She'd put her book in her lap and was staring at me, expectant, biting her tongue.

"How'd she get our number?"

"I gave her a business card today. It's got the office number and my home and cell. I have to go," I said, telling her what had happened.

"No, you don't. She needs a lawyer, not a retired FBI agent."

"She needs someone who knows how to handle something like this."

"You're not the only one who does."

"I'm the only one she knows who does."

"It's late. You're tired. You shook most of the evening until you fell asleep in your chair ten minutes ago. You're in no shape to drive, and what good will you do her if you show up shaking so bad that you can't stand up?"

She was right about the driving and could turn out to be right about the shaking. I was pretty good at scheduling my life to manage my symptoms but lousy at scheduling the lives of other people. Roni hadn't asked me to save her, just help her. I could shake and do that. It was simple multitasking. Like walking and chewing gum.

"I'll call Lucy."

She sighed and stood. "No, you won't. I'll take you."

"Why? You don't even want me to go."

"That doesn't mean I don't know why you have to go, but you're wrong if you think going will make up for Kevin and Wendy."

"I know that. Nothing will. But I can't stop trying."

"I know that too. That's why I'm taking you."

Chapter Sixteen

Truman Medical Center is on Hospital Hill at Twenty-third and Holmes, the location so named because it is a hill and because the hill has been occupied by hospitals since City Hospital was built on it in 1872. In 1908, the city built a new General Hospital on the hill, designating it for whites only, leaving the original for Blacks and Hispanics. By 1914, the General Hospital for Negroes, also known as General Hospital No. 2, though owned by the city, was run by African Americans with a staff of Black doctors and nurses. Years later, the city merged both hospitals to create the medical center named after Harry Truman.

From Hospital Hill, you can see downtown to the north, the World War I Liberty Memorial to the west, the high-end shops and high-rise condos of midtown to the south, and, to the east, the rundown homes hugging the hills in the city's poor, Black neighborhoods. For many of them, the successor to General Hospital No. 2 remains the first and last resort for the beginning and end of life and all the aches, pains, and wounds that lie between.

Truman is a level-one trauma center, maintaining one of the busiest emergency rooms in the city. I'd been there with victims and their families as well as criminals and, sometimes, their families, watching doctors and nurses fight to turn back the clock, winning more than they lost but not often enough to satisfy them.

A volunteer at the front desk told us that Frank Crenshaw was on the fourth floor. When the elevator opened, a uniformed cop met us with a raised hand.

"I'm sorry, folks. No visitors allowed on this floor right now."

I read the name on his badge. "Officer Fremont, tell Detective Carter that Special Agent Jack Davis is here. He'll want to see me."

"ID, sir?"

"He's retired, officer," Joy said. "He forgets sometimes. Just tell Detective Carter, please."

"And who are you, m'am?"

"I'm Special Agent Davis's ex-wife. I don't have a badge, but I earned one being married to him."

Joy slipped her arm through mine, tilted her head at me, and smiled at Fremont. Though she was hard to resist, Fremont smiled back but didn't budge. I did a quick shimmy with my head and neck, hardening Fremont's hesitation.

"Just call him, officer," Joy said. "Better to let Detective Carter decide whether to let Agent Davis in than have to explain later why you made the decision for him, don't you think?"

Fremont's eyes flickered. He'd lost even if he didn't know it. Joy smiled again, and this time he reached for the radio clipped to his shirt.

We waited five minutes for Carter to show, trudging toward us, his tie hung loose around his neck, a mustard stain on his white shirt. The bags under his eyes said he'd started on the day shift and was a long way from home.

"So," he said, letting out a sigh that was all regret, "Roni Chase called you. Why am I not surprised?"

"You should have kept questioning her, not given her the chance."

"I talked to her. Between what she told me and what the other witnesses said, I got the basics nailed down before I put her in that room. I'll get back to her when it's time."

"You left her alone with her cell phone. What did you think she was going to do?"

"If she called anybody, I figured it would be a lawyer."

"She doesn't need a lawyer. She didn't do anything wrong."

"Listen to you. She told you that, and you're convinced."

"Not a bad place to start."

"Get real. You've been off the job so long you forgot that everybody lies."

"You haven't arrested her, so let her go. She lives with her grandmother and her mother who's disabled from a stroke, and she runs her own business. She isn't going anywhere."

"This investigation just got started, and Roni Chase is right in the middle of it. She's not going anywhere until I say so, and I'm not about to let you help her get her story straight before I take another run at her."

"I can have a lawyer down here in less than an hour who will make sure you arrest her or let her go. In the meantime, I already told her not to tell you a damn thing. And, if you arrest her, her lawyer will make sure she tells you even less. Let me see her and I may be able to persuade her to cooperate with you. Your call."

One of the other elevators opened, and Brett Staley stepped out. Officer Fremont gave him the raised-hand greeting.

"No visitors."

"I'm not visiting anyone."

"State your business," Fremont said.

Staley looked around, saw me, squinted, and then opened his eyes wide, remembering me.

"Dude, you get around."

"I do my best."

"Hey," Carter said to me. "Who is this guy?"

"Friend of Roni's."

"What'd she do? Send out invitations?"

Chapter Seventeen

"What's your name, son?" Carter asked.

"Brett Staley."

"What are you doing here?"

"Meeting my girlfriend, Roni. She's visiting Frank Crenshaw."

"So you two have a date, or what?"

"Nah. I was just trying to catch up to her."

"Lemme see some ID."

"Why? What's going on? Where's Roni?"

Staley thrust his chest out and squared his shoulders, not intimidated by Carter and the cops that had formed a ring around him, blocking the elevator door. His mix of bravado and cool made me suspect that this wasn't the first time he'd done this dance.

I stepped in front of Carter, keeping my voice low, facing Staley. "She's fine. The police are trying to sort out something that happened while she was here. You can help her by cooperating with them."

"And who the hell are you?"

He barked the question, not backing down.

"My name is Jack Davis. I was at LC's when Roni shot Frank Crenshaw, and right now I'm the only friend she has here that can do her some good and I'm the only one standing between you and a disorderly conduct beef that will cost you a night in jail, plus bail, a fine, and the price of a lawyer, all of which I'm betting will royally piss off Roni. So save the strut for somebody who cares and show the man your ID."

His eyes darted between Carter and me. His stiff neck eased, and his quick breathing slowed.

"You sure she's okay?"

"I'm sure. So take your wallet out real slow and hand the man your ID. And if you're carrying anything that would make these guys nervous, now is the time for show and tell."

"Shit, dude. I'm not stupid."

He brokered a broad grin, slipped his hand into his back jean pocket, pulled out his wallet, and handed his driver's license to Carter, who glanced at it before giving it to Officer Fremont and motioning Staley to a bench between the elevator doors.

"Have a seat, Brett. We'll get back to you in a few minutes."

"I don't have a record," he said, sliding onto the bench, slouching against the wall, fingers tapping a beat on his knees. "Not even a traffic ticket. You'll see."

"That's real reassuring, son," Carter said. "Your mother must be proud."

Carter looked at Joy and then at me. "You going to introduce us?"

"Sorry. Joy Davis, say hello to Quincy Carter."

She smiled and took the hand he offered. "Jack and I used to be married. Now we're just roommates."

Carter shook his head. "I don't know whether that's a promotion or a demotion, but do me a favor, Joy, and keep Mr. Staley company while your roommate and I have a talk."

She joined Brett, and I followed Carter around the corner, past the nurse's station.

"Okay," he said. "Here's how it is. You can talk to Roni Chase, but I'm going to be standing right next to you. Take it or leave it."

The nurse's station was the hub in a wheel with three spokes, each one a hallway leading to patient rooms. Activity was concentrated at the far end of one hall; cops gathered outside a room, a forensic crew shuffling in and out. An exit sign hung from the ceiling just past the door.

"You put Crenshaw in a room at the end of the hall next to a stairway? Could you have made it any easier for the shooter?"

Carter bristled. "It was the only room available when he came in, and we had no reason to think someone would try to take him out."

"Is that the excuse the cop on the door gave for not staying put?"

Carter waved his hand at me. "Yeah, yeah, yeah. Any excuse is a lousy excuse after the shit flies. Now, like I said, you can talk to Roni but not alone. Deal?"

I ignored his offer again. "Any witnesses see whoever it was went into Frank's room?"

"No. It's after visiting hours. The only nurse at the station was hollering at Roni, who was busy stirring up a shit storm."

"Which let the shooter use the stairs—quick in and out. What about surveillance videos?"

"We're checking them."

"Anybody hear a gunshot?"

"No."

"Are the rooms that soundproof?"

"They're pretty quiet, and all the doors were closed. The patients in the rooms next to Crenshaw and across the hall were post-op and sleeping off anesthetic. They wouldn't have heard a bomb go off. The other patients on his wing were sleeping or watching TV. None of them heard anything."

"Maybe the shooter used a silencer. Or, he could have made it easy and used a pillow."

"No pillow unless he took it with him," Carter said.

"A contract hitter would have used a silencer and would be out of town by now."

"You going to keep pretending you didn't hear what I said about talking to Roni?"

"Let me finish working this through. You put Crenshaw in a room at the end of a hall next to the stairs. You got a cop on the door that screws up the one thing that should be impossible to screw up. You got a shooter who knows what room Crenshaw is in and times the hit for the exact moment Crenshaw is unprotected and anyone else who might see or hear anything is zoned out. Those are a lot of planets to line up."

"And I'm no astronomer, but that's too much for the shooter to count on unless he knew Roni was going to mix it up with the nurse. If he did, odds are Roni knew about the hit."

"You swept her office this morning. You find anything that would give her reason to do something so stupid as that?"

Carter grinned. "Figure out which side you're on and I'll tell you."

"You don't have anything, because if you did, she'd be downtown by now. Which means there are at least three other possibilities. The shooter was checking out the setup, making a dry run, and saw his chance and took it. Or, he could have been planning to take the cop out too and got lucky or the cop was in on it. Which one do you like better?"

"I don't like any of them any better than I like you."

"I don't blame you, but you're stuck with them and me. One last question?"

Carter heaved. "What?"

"You ever work the gang squad?"

"Spent some time."

"Does Nuestra Familia operate here?"

"They've just about got an exclusive on the drug trade in Northeast. It's Cesar Mendez and a couple dozen of his closest friends and relatives, plus a waiting list of wannabes. Why the interest?"

"What about guns?"

"You know a gang that isn't armed to the teeth?"

"Any chance they're branching out from drugs, adding another line of merchandise?"

"Make your point."

"Frank Crenshaw killed his wife with a gun that was traced to the robbery of that gun dealer last month. Maybe Mendez pulled that job. Maybe he's arming his boys or maybe he's filling an order from the folks back home."

"How's someone like Frank Crenshaw hook up with Cesar Mendez?"

"It's the law," I said.

"What law?"

"The law of supply and demand."

Chapter Eighteen

Carter pointed toward the elevators. Joy looked at me as we waited for one of the doors to open, her eyebrows raised in a silent question I answered with a shrug. Her shoulders deflated, and her eyes lost their luster. She tired easily, no matter how much rest she got, always needing more, raising questions we couldn't answer.

How do you live when you know you are dying? Do you ignore what's happening inside you, conceding nothing? Do you conserve your strength, spending it only on the things that matter the most? Do you do the most and best you can and not worry about the rest? Joy's answer was yes to all of that. I didn't know how she did it.

Staley ignored us, earbuds plugged into his phone, listening to music and texting. I leaned toward her, a hand on her shoulder, whispering, "You okay?"

"Sure," she said. "You?"

"Marvelistic."

"We're both lousy liars."

"Long as we know it. Hang in there. This won't take long."

"Take as long as it takes. This is the most comfortable hospital bench I've sat on all day."

"You're too good for words."

"I know," she said, smiling and stroking my face with her palm. "Don't forget you said that because I won't."

Officer Fremont motioned to Carter from the nurse's station, and Carter joined him. Fremont said something I couldn't make out, but Carter's grimace said it wasn't what he wanted to hear.

"Bad news?" I asked when Carter returned.

Carter bent over, tying a shoelace that wasn't untied, pretending he hadn't heard me. The elevator arrived, and we stepped on, the doors closing, the car giving us a jolt before it began its descent. I leaned against the handrail, closing my eyes and clenching as the day rattled my cage.

"Still with the shaking," Carter said.

I took a deep breath as the tremors passed. "Yeah."

"Be better off home in bed."

"Lot of ways to be better off."

Carter nodded, watching the numbers for each floor flash by. "I get what you do. The whole protect-the-weak-and-innocent bit."

My torso pretzled, my chin planted on my shoulder for a three count until the spasm let me go. "Keeps me busy."

"Trouble is, you start out from the wrong place. You want people like Roni to be innocent so bad you quit thinking like a cop. You push things the way you want them to go instead of going where the evidence takes you."

"You're kidding yourself if you think anyone starts in neutral, not even a good cop like you. It's not a level playing field for people like Roni. Somebody has to push back."

"There's a difference between pushing and getting in the way."

"Meaning I'm still a pain in the ass?"

He smiled as the doors opened. "Big time."

"Good to know."

Roni was sequestered in a first-floor conference room in the administration wing of the hospital, a cop on the door, this one not going anywhere. She was sitting at a long oval table, rotating her swivel chair side to side while plugged into her phone and texting, a mirror image of Brett Staley, the two of them leaving an electronic trail for Carter to follow.

Cops believe in causation, not coincidence. If Roni Chase had intentionally caused a disturbance so someone could kill Frank Crenshaw, Brett Staley climbed to the top of the shooter short list when he showed up at the hospital, his timing too good and any alibi he may have too pat. The shooter would have to have been someone Roni trusted, and who would she trust more than the man who was saving up to buy her funeral dress? It made sense if she was guilty.

Carter and I were coming at the case from opposite directions. He suspected she was guilty, and I hoped she was innocent, the truth hidden somewhere between certainty and doubt.

She looked up when we entered the room, taking off her earbuds and sliding her phone into her jean pocket, gathering her jacket around her like a protective shield, her face brightening for an instant when she looked at me, then darkening when she focused on Carter.

"So," she said, "can I go home now?"

"Soon, I hope," I said. "Detective Carter says you and I can talk, but only if he gets to watch and listen."

"Can he do that?"

"Depends on how hard he wants to play this. He can hold you for questioning here or take you downtown. He knows that if he doesn't let you go home in the next five minutes that you're going to call a lawyer and if you don't know who to call that you're going to ask me to call someone, and he knows that whoever I call is going to turn his long day into a shitty night. Either way, he knows he's not going to get diddly-squat out of you tonight. Except for what you've already told him, which is that you had nothing to do with Frank Crenshaw being murdered in his unguarded hospital bed."

Her grin split her face. "So," she said to Carter, "am I under arrest?"

Carter, hands planted on his hips, blasted me. "That's what you call getting her to cooperate?"

"Here's how it is. You want anything else out of her tonight you're going to have to give us the room. I'm not promising anything after that, but I'm sure as hell not going to serve her up to you for a midnight snack."

Carter glared. I stared, and Roni waited, wisely swallowing her grin.

"Motherfucking pain in the ass," Carter said, wagging his finger at me. "That's what you are—a royal, motherfucking pain in my ass."

"I'll take that as a yes," I said, pointing to the slack-jawed uniform cop standing in the door. "I'll have him call you when we're ready."

Officer Fremont knocked on the conference room door. "Detective Carter, the ATF agent is waiting for you upstairs. I told him you were interrogating a witness and I didn't know how long that would take. He said to tell you he wasn't much interested in waiting around. Guy's a fed through and through, thinks his shit don't stink."

"So that was the good news Fremont gave you," I said. "Don't worry about us. We can come back tomorrow if that's more convenient for you."

Carter aimed his finger at me again, his caramel complexion purpling. "You keep pushing and you're gonna push too far."

Chapter Nineteen

Roni clapped her hands. "Dude, that was sweet!"

I sat in a chair across the table from hers. "You have no idea how much trouble you could be in, do you?"

Her mouth and eyes stretched wide. "Me? I told you, I didn't do anything!"

"Listen to me. I'm not your lawyer. I know a fair amount about criminal law because I put a lot of crooks away, but I'm not an expert on criminal procedure or the rules of evidence and I'm lousy at reading juries. So I can't help you shape your testimony so that you slide by on some narrow ledge between innocent and guilty. Nothing you tell me is privileged. I get called before a grand jury or summoned to testify in court, I'll have to tell them everything you tell me."

Her cheeks lost their pink. "What are you doing? Are you trying to scare me?"

"Just shut up and listen. Don't talk until I'm finished. Here are the known facts. Yesterday you shot Frank Crenshaw, and then you came to the hospital to see him and were told you couldn't. You came back tonight, after visiting hours, and raised a ruckus when you were told the same thing you were told the day before. Then you made enough noise that the cop guarding Crenshaw came running, giving the killer a clean shot at him. Quincy Carter is no dummy. It isn't hard for him to connect the dots and tie you and the shooter together like a tag team setting up the hit on Crenshaw. Then your boyfriend shows up, saying he thought it'd be fun to hang out at the hospital."

"He's not my boyfriend."

"Maybe not on your dance card, but that's how Carter sees him."

"I can't help that. Sometimes, he drives me crazy."

"And now Carter is going to turn him inside out to see if he might have finished what you started at LC's. Case like this, the first one to make a deal serves the shortest sentence. Carter won't care which one of you flips, so long as one of you does. So you telling Carter and me that you had nothing to do with anything won't cut it."

She went from pale to red hot in a flash, coming out of her chair, planting her fists on the conference table.

"I shot Frank Crenshaw to save my life and yours, and I haven't kept a meal down or slept since. I don't know who killed him, but it wasn't Brett. He was hanging out with my mom and grandma tonight until he came over here. So, fuck you if you don't believe me!"

"He's not your boyfriend, but he hangs out with your mother and grandmother?"

"Sometimes he is my boyfriend. Just not when we fight."

"Then what was he doing hanging out with you and your family?"

"My grandmother likes to have people for Sunday-night dinner. She invited him."

I liked that she was mad. I liked that she didn't curl up into a ball and cry, and I liked that she didn't tell me to call a lawyer. I didn't like that her family was Brett Staley's alibi because families are the first to lie to protect loved ones, and, if Staley was spending his evening with her mother and grandmother, odds were he'd get the family treatment.

"What time did he leave your house?"

She straightened, throwing one hand at the walls before wrapping her arms around her chest.

"I don't know. We had dinner and sat around talking and watching TV. I said I was going to see Frank, and he tried to talk me out of it because they wouldn't let me see him yesterday. We got into it, nothing serious, just yelling like we do all the time, and he says if I go, he isn't going with me, like I even invited him. So I left him there."

"You want me to call a lawyer?"

She dropped her arms to her side, her initial outburst spent. "How can I need a lawyer when I'm innocent?"

"The system doesn't always get it right."

"But if I get a lawyer, it will look like I've got something to hide, and I don't. Besides, I can't afford a lawyer. It costs a lot of money to take care of my mom. She didn't have health insurance when she had her stroke. She's in a wheelchair, and her speech is pretty garbled."

"I'll find someone who will work with you on the fee."

She came back to her seat, folding her arms on the table. "Why are you doing this for me?"

I smiled. "Like you said, you saved my life."

She reached across the table, taking my hand in hers. "Well, at least I did one thing right." I patted her hand, letting go and easing back in my chair. "What about the lawyer?"

She chewed her lip, focusing on the table, then swiveled in her chair, looking out the windows to the west. The torch at the top of the Liberty Memorial was lit, a ring of fire glowing in the dark. She wheeled around, facing me, hands in her lap, her face cool and calm.

"I'm not guilty of anything, and I'm not going to act like I am. Tell Detective Carter I'll answer his questions."

I nodded. "You know it's not always enough to be innocent. Sometimes it's smarter to be innocent and have a lawyer to make sure you stay that way."

"I've got you. That makes me smart enough."

"Okay, then. Let's run through it a few times. Make sure I know what you know."

She was a solid witness, recalling details as we went through it until she had it nailed down, serious until I gave her a taste of a bad-cop interrogation, leaning on her. She bit the inside of her cheek to keep from giggling, gave up, and dissolved into laughter.

"Hey, I'm not practicing my stand-up routine, here."

She wiped tears from her eyes and sat up straight. "Sorry, I couldn't help it. I promise to be really scared when Detective Carter asks me how I'm going to like being a girlfriend on a chain gang."

"All I said was that you could go away for a long time, maybe the rest of your life."

She started laughing again. "I know. I know. I can't help it. What can I say? You kind of scared me at first, but now you don't. Is that a bad thing?"

My head tilted back, my chin elevating past the perpendicular, my neck telescoping and leaving me hanging until the spasm evaporated and I found Roni's eyes again. They were narrow and sober, her lips pursed as if she had been twisting beside me. I took a deep breath, restoring order for both of us.

"Only if you don't listen to me. That could really get you in trouble."

She nodded. I opened the door and told our sentry that we were ready to talk to Detective Carter. A few minutes later, Officer Fremont appeared at the door. I looked past him at Joy, who was standing alone at the entrance to the administrative suite.

"We're ready," I said.

"Detective Carter said to tell Ms. Chase that she can go home. He'll give her a call tomorrow and set something up."

Roni and I exchanged glances. Her quick smile vanished when she realized the same thing I did.

"What about Brett Staley?" I asked.

"Detective Carter says Ms. Chase shouldn't wait up for him."

"What? No way!" she said. "He didn't do anything wrong, and I'm not leaving without him."

"I'm sorry, miss. He's already gone."

"Gone! Where? With who? Is he under arrest?"

"You'll have to talk with Detective Carter about that, miss."

I grabbed Roni's arm when she bolted for the door, clamping

her to my side.

"Tell Carter I want to talk to him."

"Next time I see him."

"What do you mean next time you see him?"

"Detective Carter packed it in for the night. Said if you wanted to talk to him to call and leave a message. He'll get back to you soon as he can."

Officer Fremont walked us to the lobby and watched as we stood outside the hospital entrance. Roni called Brett's cell phone and left a message when he didn't answer, doubling up by sending him a text. She hugged me, and I made her take a blood oath not to talk to Carter alone.

She nodded, squinting, her brow furrowed, half-listening and looking over my shoulder as if Brett would emerge from the shadows. We were parsing the same puzzle, neither of us certain what had just happened or why, the worry lines around her eyes and mouth telling me the one thing that was certain: Despite her protests, she would let Brett buy her funeral dress, though not for a long, long time. I watched until she got into her Toyota Highlander and drove away.

Joy didn't add much to what we knew. Soon after Carter and I left to talk with Roni, Fremont told her to leave. The last time she saw Brett Staley he was still sitting on the bench next to the fourth-floor elevators. She waited for us in the lobby until she saw Fremont and followed him into the administrative suite.

My movement disorder does more than put me through impromptu and involuntary gymnastic routines. It stresses the rest of my brain, sometimes gumming up the gears and making it impossible to concentrate, other times giving me jelly legs. When that happens, I'm no good to anybody. I closed my eyes on the drive home, my questions bogged down in neural quicksand. Joy held my arm as I stumbled into the house, staggering up the stairs and into bed.

"You'll figure it out tomorrow," she said, turning off the light. " Too late. Whatever's happened has happened."

"It's never too late, Jack Davis. Not for any of us."

Chapter Twenty

Lucy called at seven-thirty Tuesday morning.

"I wake you?"

"Roxy and Ruby beat you by an hour and a half."

"Simon told me you want to hire Roni Chase, give her a shot at one of our cases. Not that I'm surprised, but how'd that go?"

"Hard to tell." I gave her a rundown on my day and night.

"Some people are trouble magnets."

"I don't know. Maybe Roni was just in the wrong place at the wrong time. Twice."

"Not her, moron. You. That's what you get for trying to fix the world one messed-up kid at a time."

"I thought I did okay with you, but keep giving me grief and I may have to rethink that."

"Wait until I tell you who called me yesterday."

"Who?"

"It's a beautiful morning. Go outside and play with the dogs, and I'll pick you up in thirty minutes."

Fall in Kansas City is a season of gentle regret, evoking good times past and trials yet to come as summer surrenders to September and October's fiery leaves drape the city in a fragile rainbow canopy backlit by the sun, low and sharp, nature's high-definition broadcast. November's cold, cleansing rain readies us for December's frozen, pale shroud, the promise of spring faint, distant but certain.

I waited for Lucy in the front yard, the dogs swirling around me, chasing squirrels because that was their job. They were unburdened by the past, oblivious to the future, living in the moment while I straddled all three dimensions.

Lucy was wrong about one thing. I wasn't trying to fix the world one messed-up kid at a time. I was trying to fix me, put the pieces back together that were shattered when Kevin and Wendy died. There was nothing gentle about my regrets, nothing soothing about my dreams. Memories of my children were a saw-toothed reminder of broken promises. If I could help Roni Chase and if I could find Evan and Cara Martin, I might save myself.

My cell phone rang. It was Roni.

"Detective Carter wants to meet me at my house at three o'clock. Can you make it?"

"Sure. Don't start without me."

Lucy pulled up just as I finished talking with Roni.

"Had breakfast?" Lucy asked when I got in her car.

"Coffee."

"Good. We're going to the Classic Cup."

"Because?"

"Because we're having breakfast with Ethan Bonner."

"Jimmy Martin's lawyer?"

"One and the same."

"Who's buying?"

"He is. Jimmy told Bonner we came out to the Farm to see him on Sunday. Bonner called me yesterday afternoon. I thought he was going to chew me out, tell us to stay the hell away from his client. But he didn't. Instead, he asked us to meet him for breakfast."

"How's a blue-collar guy like Jimmy Martin afford a lawyer like Ethan Bonner?"

"Beats me."

The Classic Cup is on the Country Club Plaza, Kansas City's Spanish-inspired signature shopping district, located in midtown. There's enough power at its breakfast tables to light the shops at Christmas.

Bonner was waiting for us, his scuffed shoes propped on an empty chair, glasses halfway down his nose, long hair pushed behind his ears, reading the *New York Times*. He was wearing jeans and a corduroy blazer over a Grateful Dead T-shirt and a three-day growth of beard. He was a solo practitioner, mixing criminal defense with plaintiff's personal injury work; winning more cases than most with strategy and tactics few had the balls to use when someone's life was on the line.

He had the perfect Kansas City pedigree. He grew up in Mission Hills, home to old money and older mansions. He graduated from Pembroke Hill, the city's premier private school, before going to Yale and then Harvard for law school. He worked for the law firm his grandfather had founded and his father ran for an entire week before he quit and opened his own shop, his father saying that his son didn't just march to the beat of a different drummer; he was playing an instrument no one had ever heard before.

Bonner dropped his feet to the floor, shoving the chair away from the table, folded his newspaper in half, and waved us to our seats.

"Jack," he said, extending his hand, "I haven't seen you since the Janice Graham case. You remember her?"

"Sure. She and her husband were in the residential mortgage business. She was charged with stealing Social Security numbers belonging to dead people and selling them to illegal immigrants so they could get fraudulent home loans."

"I thought I was going to lose that one, sure as hell."

"So did I until you blew our star witness out of the stand. Been so long I can't remember her name."

"Kendra Wood. Wasn't hard once I figured out she was in love with Janice's husband. She wanted to get rid of Janice so she could run away with him. Turned out she was the one running the scam and had set Janice up."

"We checked her out six ways to Sunday and didn't come up with that. Janice's husband had no idea Kendra felt that way about him. How did you tumble to it?"

"You looked in the wrong places."

"What's that supposed to mean?"

"You looked at Kendra from the outside, at all the stuff you could see. She worked for Janice and her husband. Always showed up on time. Always got good performance reviews. She was married with kids, went to church on Sunday, and didn't stay out late."

I nodded. "The kind of upright citizen with enough guts to blow the whistle."

"That's who you saw. I saw a woman who betrayed the people she was closest to outside of her own family. We weren't talking about a drug addict that needed a fix or a gangbanger looking to get right with the cops before it was his turn to take the needle. Shit, upright is easy compared to betrayal. Upright takes guts, but betrayal takes loathing and guts. I wanted to know where the loathing came from, so I looked at her from the inside out."

"How'd you do that?"

"I'm like a magician. I never give up my secrets. Kendra Wood was living a fantasy, and no one knew it because she came across so normal she'd bore you to death. Crazy how people can hide shit like that."

"Not as crazy as Jimmy Martin killing his kids." Bonner leaned back in his chair. "Point taken. Except for one thing. He may not have done it."

"May not have done it? I thought defense lawyers stuck with innocent until proven guilty."

"Jimmy Martin is charged with two things: stealing and contempt of court. He stole to support his family, and the judge held him in contempt because he's pissed at his wife. He hasn't been charged with killing his kids."

"Yet," I said. "There's a reason the cops are looking at him so hard."

"You and I both know that doesn't mean they're right."

A server took our orders. Three men in suits, carrying briefcases, filed past our table, one of them telling Bonner he'd see him in court after lunch. Bonner got up, followed the man to his table, wrapped his arm around him, whispered, patted him on the back, and came back to his seat.

"Just settled a case. Now I can pay for breakfast. What if Jimmy Martin didn't kill his kids?"

"Then he should tell his wife where they are," Lucy said.

"If it were that easy, we'd all have to find another line of work. Look, I don't know what happened to his kids. Jimmy won't talk about them. Not one fucking word."

"At least he treats you the same way he treated us," I said.

"I don't mind. Sometimes it's better not to know. Lets me sleep at night. This time, I'm not so sure. Best chance I've got to get Jimmy a deal on the theft charge is find those kids and hope they're still alive when I do."

"Then tell him to talk to us," Lucy said.

"Won't do any good. He won't talk to me about the kids. He's not going to talk to you. But you guys can still help me."

"How?"

"His wife Peggy hired you. Tell her to let you work with me. We want the same thing, to get the kids back, and I need investigators Jimmy can't afford."

"Can he afford you?"

"Nope. Public defender is refusing to take any new cases. Their workload is so heavy they're probably committing malpractice every time they answer the phone. The judge asked me if I'd take the case. Looked like a simple deal—work out a plea on the theft charge—and then this thing with the kids came up. Be a big help if we work together."

"Are you out of your mind?" Lucy asked. "Peggy hates Jimmy. Why should she help him? You're just trying to find out what we've got on Jimmy so you can get him off."

"That's what I'd think if I were sitting where you're sitting," Bonner said. "So, here's my offer. I've hired someone to help me with this case. Anything she comes up with, you can have. The three of you can work together."

"You can't afford to pay investigators. How are you going to pay someone else?" I asked. "She owes me a favor. Here she comes," Bonner said, pointing over my shoulder.

NO WAY OUT

I turned around, stood up, and started to shake.

"Hello, Jack," Kate Scranton said. "How are you?"

Chapter Twenty-one

My body can be like a teenage girl living on the margins where everything is either the best or worst that ever happened. The ordinary ups and downs of daily existence may pass me by, water off a duck's back, or unleash the demons. There's little predictability to what will flip my switch except that, when it happens, it happens without warning or opportunity to steel myself. Mine is an erratic vulnerability that drives me crazy, leaving me weak when I have to be strong and causing me to lose control when I have to be in control.

I might have shaken just as much had I known Kate was going to be at breakfast. Wound tight with anticipation, I still may have spun out like a top when I saw her. But her unexpected appearance was a gut punch that never gave me a chance. We had too much unfinished business, neither knowing what came after hello.

Traces of silver had found their way into her dark hair along with creases above her brow and a softening of her cheeks, concessions to her mid-forties that gave her a settled beauty. Standing two feet away, her head cocked at a slight angle, she carried herself with the same certainty that had first drawn me to her, observing and absorbing everyone and everything, intense blue eyes instinctively probing for secrets hidden in our facial expressions, body language, and the way we didn't say what we really meant. Then and now, that was also one of our problems, the way she made me feel exposed, laying bare things I didn't want to admit or share, no matter how open and obvious they were to her.

"Never better, Kate. Good to see you."

She took half a step closer, palms out to catch me. I gripped the table with one hand, held her off with the other, not wanting to fall into her arms. Lucy quietly angled my chair away from the table, giving me a safe place to land.

I corkscrewed into my chair, ignoring my spasms as if everyone's chin was supposed to be pinned to their shoulder, and pointed her toward the empty seat next to Ethan Bonner. He was sitting upright, eyes pinched with detached clinical concentration, like a scientist watching lab rats, making me wonder if he knew about my disorder and whether he had orchestrated this moment and why he would want to make me shake.

I glanced at Lucy, her red-faced glare at Bonner pinning it on him. I wasn't so certain. Some things are just going to happen no matter what you do. And, I had to admit that I wasn't shaking only because I was taken off guard. Uncomfortable or not, I was glad to see Kate.

"So, down to business," Bonner said, signaling our server. "The omelets are terrific, and the coffee is passable. What's everyone going to have?"

Bonner's effort at forced normalcy worked for me. I didn't have answers to the questions rattling around in my head and wasn't certain I'd trust the ones he would give me.

"Veggie," I told the server. "And toss in some bacon."

I looked at Lucy, her face finding its normal hue even as her eyes widened at me. I nodded, telling her that she was on deck and to let it go. Everyone ordered, and everyone breathed. I led us in idle chitchat about Kate's son and my dogs, her neuromarketing firm, and my gig with Simon and Lucy until our food came, keeping it up while we ate, using the time to restore my equilibrium and get used to being with her again.

I thought back to the Janice Graham case, trying to remember whether she'd been in the courtroom at the defense table, deciding she hadn't, guessing that she'd nonetheless been the unseen source of Bonner's magic, wondering what debt she owed him that she was paying off at breakfast and whether she could pick Jimmy Martin's lock and find out what happened to his kids.

Bonner looked at me and brought the conversation back to his client. "Kate's going from here to the Farm to talk to Jimmy. I'd appreciate it if you'd go with her."

"I assume you mean both of us," Lucy said.

"No," he said, taking a sip of coffee and smiling an apology to Lucy. "I mean Jack."

"Bullshit!" she said, coming halfway out of her chair. "This is my case!"

Bonner was smooth, treating the question of whether we had agreed to work together as settled.

Lucy's reaction to his suggestion was as predictable as mine was to Kate's presence, their argument irrelevant unless we were all partners.

"Three people are too many," he said. "Jimmy will think you're ganging up on him, and he'll clam up even more."

Lucy had interrogated enough witnesses to know that Bonner was right. She glanced at Kate. They had been close before Kate moved to San Diego. They'd kept in touch, Lucy telling me that Kate was doing fine and had stopped asking about me. Kate nodded at her, and Lucy sat back in her chair, arms folded over her chest, narrowing her eyes at me, not surrendering and demanding I do something.

"We can't agree to anything until we talk to our client," I said. "Peggy gives us the okay, we can decide who does what."

"Kate is only here for a couple of days. You take too long and your client will be the big loser."

"What's your schedule?" I asked Kate.

She sighed. "It's up in the air. There are some things happening at home. I may have to go back sooner than I'd like. Maybe tomorrow."

I studied her, looking for a downturn in her mouth, a break in eye contact, or a lift in her lip that would tell me what she was thinking and feeling. She called these involuntary twitches micro facial expressions because they lasted a fraction of a second, too short-lived to be recognized and translated by someone not trained in her dark art. I didn't see any of that. Instead I saw a wistful look in her eyes and a hopeful smile, maybe because that's what I wanted to see.

"Then, I'll tell you what," I said to Bonner. "Kate joins our team for now. She and I go see Jimmy. Whatever we get stays with us until we have a chance to talk with Peggy. If she signs on, we'll share and share alike. If she says no, Kate can stick with us or go home."

Bonner put me back under the microscope. We both knew that Kate didn't need me or anyone else with her when she talked with Jimmy Martin. He wanted something else, something he needed us for, and it wasn't chasing down leads.

"One condition," he said. "After you're done at the farm, Kate interviews Peggy Martin and tells you and me what she thinks. If we don't have a deal, Kate keeps working for me and you guys are on your own."

There it was. Bonner didn't think Kate or anyone else could get anything out of Jimmy Martin, so he didn't care who talked to him. Peggy Martin was a different story. She wore her emotions on both sleeves. Kate would have no trouble reading her. If Peggy wasn't being straight with us, I needed to know. I knew one other thing with equal certainty. Never underestimate Kate Scranton. Bonner had done that, his deal now worth more to me than it was to him.

"You know," Kate said, "this isn't the third grade. We aren't on the playground, and Lucy and I aren't waiting with bated breath to see which team we get to be on. It sounds like Peggy hired Lucy, not you, Jack. And I'm here because Ethan called in a favor, but the favor didn't include being used as a bargaining chip."

She said it with a steel smile, the knife going in deep enough to make her point without injuring any nerves. Bonner looked at me and shrugged, conceding the moment.

"Kate," I said, "are you okay with Bonner's deal?"

"Only if Lucy is okay with it."

"Lucy," I said, "let me go with Kate. This could be our best crack at Jimmy Martin."

"What am I supposed to do? Stay here and order another cup of coffee?"

"You've got the closest relationship with Peggy, and you know that Kate can help us find Evan and Cara. Talk to her and convince her that this is the right thing to do. Besides, we both know Bonner is right. Jimmy will feel like we're ganging up on him if all three of us show up for the interview."

She thought for a minute, turning her glare back to Bonner. "Okay, but it's not Kate I'm worried about."

Bonner took her shot with a smile. "I wouldn't be worried about Kate either if I were you."

Chapter Twenty-two

"Why do they call it the Farm?" Kate asked.

We were eastbound on Blue Parkway in her rented Chevy Malibu approaching LC's Bar-B-Q.

"Turn here," I told her, pointing to a street called Sni-A-Bar that fed onto Blue Parkway, one side of the triangle framing LC's. "Before it was the municipal jail it was a farm, a two thousand–acre hog farm. The city bought it, sold the hogs, and built the jail. It opened in 1972. There are two hundred acres inside the fence. Now the city is talking about shutting it down to save money and moving the inmates to the county jail."

"Ethan told me that Jimmy should be in the county jail but they didn't have room for him."

"That's today. Long term, the city says it'll be cheaper to pay the county to house their inmates than to keep the jail open. The county wants the money and is talking about building a new jail."

"Which is less lousy, the Farm or the county jail?"

"Security isn't as tight on the Farm. There are two dormitories, one for women and one for men. Unless they put you in an isolation cell for protection or discipline, you do your time on an open floor, like an old hospital ward with rows of beds, only the beds are made of steel and the mattresses are thin enough you can use them to floss your teeth."

"No stars from Zagat?"

"Not when the majority of inmates have some kind of mental illness and even more of them have drug and alcohol problems. Plus, most of them are homeless, which means they're happy to have a roof over their heads and that they aren't likely to be violent. The food sucks, but the body odor quotient makes you forget how bad the food smells."

"Can't wait. What was Jimmy like when you and Lucy saw him?"

"Like a guy who spent all day practicing his poker face. Lucy asked the questions, but she didn't get any answers."

"What did he say? What was he like?"

"He didn't say much. Just listened but acted like he didn't hear a word she said. Only time he showed any reaction was when Lucy asked him why he'd make his wife suffer, not telling her what happened to their kids."

"What did he say?"

"Said, 'Ask the bitch.' Kind of smiled when he said it."

"Charming. Did you?"

"Did I what?"

"Ask the bitch?" I laughed.

"Peggy doesn't strike me like that, though you never know what someone's really like until you're married to them. She says he's doing it out of spite. Says he's a mean prick. Says he accused her of cheating on him and smacked her around. She got a restraining order against him a month before he was arrested. He couldn't see the kids except with a court-appointed social worker."

"What do you know about the kids?"

"Evan is six, and Cara is eight. They look like their mother."

"That's it? That's all you know?"

"They're little kids, they're missing, and good things don't happen to little kids when they go missing. That's all I need to know."

"Well, it's not all I need to know."

She followed Sni-A-Bar, turning onto Ozark Road, continuing until we came to the entrance to the Farm. A two-story chain-link fence topped with razor wire and curved inward like a baseball backstop surrounded the complex of one-story buildings.

"Ethan told me he arranged for us to meet Jimmy in the

Women's Recreation Area, wherever that is," Kate said.

We announced our presence to an intercom and a camera at the gate and waited for an unseen hand to push a button, gears groaning as the gate slid open. A guard met us inside the administrative building and searched Kate's shoulder bag. A woman wearing a gray pantsuit, her blond hair, sparkling eyes, and perky smile contrasting with the dreary surroundings, introduced herself as Superintendent Annette Fibuch, confessed her love of corrections, told us that the guards were corrections officers, not guards, and escorted us to the Women's Dormitory, telling us that's where we'd find the Women's Recreation Area.

Lucy and I had met with Jimmy Martin in the visitor's area, talking to him through a phone, separated by a bulletproof glass barrier, a setting that nurtured evasion and invited denial. The Women's Recreation Area could have passed for a community college rec room; it was the one space I'd seen at the Farm where inmates could feel at ease and Kate might learn something from Jimmy.

It was a long, rectangular room, its cinder block walls painted yellow with red trim on three sides, the pattern reversed on the exterior wall, the upper third of which was a bank of windows. Sunlight poured into a carpeted room furnished with a Ping-Pong table, a game table, a chalkboard, and a quartet of soft, black club chairs clustered together in a tight square.

"An officer will bring Jimmy here in a few minutes," Superintendent Fibuch said. "He'll wait outside the room if you need him. Jimmy isn't thrilled with the company he's keeping, but I don't think he'll cause any trouble. Feel free to stop by my office on your way out if you need anything else."

"She seems more like a concierge than a jail superintendent," I said, after she left.

"Ethan says she takes good care of him because he worked with her on getting the inmates decent mental health care. He says a lot of them used to live in state mental health facilities but those days are over, thanks to budget cutbacks. Now, this is their ticket to the help they need."

"That Ethan is something else. One step removed from sainthood."

"Do you have a good reason to dislike him, or are you just oozing resentment because he hired me instead of you?"

"I don't like surprises and setups."

"Meaning?"

"Meaning he should have told Lucy you were involved in this case."

"Why? Because you and I used to be together?"

I felt the heat rise in my neck. "Yeah. That's right."

"So you naturally assumed that he knew about us."

"I assumed you told him if he didn't know already."

"Why would I tell him, and why would you think he would know if I didn't tell him? You and I didn't make the society page, and I didn't put my relationship status on Facebook. Honestly, Jack, no one cares what happened between us."

"I care."

The words tripped out as unexpected and involuntary as the stutter that accompanied them, a guilt-laden tremor rippling through my torso for punctuation. Joy was dying, and I was playing wounded Romeo.

Kate caught her breath, her face coloring as her mouth hardened.

"So you do."

The door opened, the officer, a towering black man, led Jimmy Martin into the room, cupping Jimmy's elbow in his massive hand. He had a good six inches and fifty pounds on Jimmy, his gray uniform and dark skin a sharp contrast to Jimmy's orange jumpsuit and pasty complexion.

Jimmy was nondescript, the way so many people are, his features even and bland. Comb his brown hair back, dress him in a blue suit and he could have been a bank vice president though he looked just as at home wearing the latest in jailhouse fashion. His clothes outlined him, but he filled in the empty spaces when he opened his mouth.

"You be nice to these people, Jimmy," the officer said.

Jimmy shook off the officer's touch, his flat expression in place. "I don't need you to tell me shit, nigger."

The officer cuffed him on the back of the head. "Mind your manners, Jimmy. You don't want these people getting the wrong idea about you. And, don't forget, you and me got a long walk back to the men's dorm. Lot of places along the way a man can slip and fall, especially the sorry shape this place is in." The officer looked at us, smiling. "Don't worry about me and Jimmy. We got an understanding. I'll be right outside if you folks need anything."

Kate waited for the officer to leave before walking toward Jimmy, her hand extended, Jimmy's red, puffy eyes darting from her to me and back to her, his arms at his side, clenching his fists. She waited, her hand outstretched, Jimmy studying it like it was a hot poker before giving in and slowly raising his. Kate took hold, not letting go.

"Jimmy, I'm Kate Scranton. Thank you for agreeing to talk to me. Let's sit down and figure out how I can help you."

Chapter Twenty-three

She set up a miniature video camera mounted on an eight-inch tripod, aiming the lens at Jimmy.

"What's that for?" he asked.

"So I don't have to take notes," Kate answered.

That wasn't the only reason. I knew Kate would study the video later, breaking it down frame by frame, deciphering Jimmy's involuntary expressions, deciding whether to believe him.

We sat in a semicircle around a gray hard-plastic coffee table, Kate and I flanking Jimmy. He fidgeted, trying to find a safe place for his hands, locking them in his armpits. The chairs looked sturdier than they were, each of us sinking into the sagging cushions. Kate leaned back, legs extended, shoulders soft, her hands in her lap. His posture said he was tense, uncertain, while hers was open, reassuring, telling him she wouldn't bite. I followed her lead, my legs crossed at the ankles, hands resting on the arms of my chair.

"Looks like you could use a good night's sleep," she said.

Jimmy licked his lower lip like he was searching for a cigarette and didn't answer.

"I hear the beds are made of cold steel and you can floss your teeth with the mattresses." A closed, hard smile creased his mouth. "It's jail. It ain't the Ritz."

"I don't know how you stand the smell, living with all those people on top of you, especially with that officer putting his hands on you and treating you like a child."

He narrowed his eyes, his back stiffening. "I can do the time."

"I'm sure you can, but why do it if you don't have to?"

He stared at her, taking short breaths before answering. "I told my lawyer and I told your friend there and I'm telling you. I'll do the time. I got nothing to say about my kids."

Kate leaned forward, her hands clamped on her knees. "And I'm not going to ask what happened to your children."

He straightened and dropped his hands onto the armrests. "Then what do you want?"

"You're going to trial on the theft charge. My job is to make sure the jury that decides whether you go free or go to prison is on your side."

He rolled his eyes. "Now how you gonna do that? Who the hell is gonna be on my side?"

Kate smiled. "The economy is in a shambles. Millions of people have lost jobs they are never going to get back, and the money they put away for retirement, they would have been better off burying it in a tin can in their backyard. They're angry and scared, but they don't have the nerve to do more about it than stick their heads out the window and scream that they can't take it anymore. You'd be surprised how many of them wish they had the balls to do what you did to support their family."

He smirked. "They caught me with some copper. Don't mean I stole it."

"When the police arrested you, you were driving a truck loaded with five thousand dollars worth of copper tubing and wire they traced to a construction site. You claim you paid cash for the copper to someone who gave you a phony name and address and, so far, the police can't find him. That's like the drug dealer who claims someone planted crack in a condom and stuck it up his ass. You want to ride that horse to the finish line, that's your choice. But, if you want a fighting chance, you'll work with me."

"So what can you do about it?"

"My job is to figure out which jurors will hurt you and which ones will help you. Ethan Bonner can keep a lot of the bad ones off the jury, maybe not all of them but maybe enough to give you a shot at acquittal or a hung jury."

"My lawyer said the jury was supposed to be fair and impartial."

"The more people want to serve on a jury, the more they think they can do that, but half the time, they don't even know they're prejudiced against short people, fat people, or people who part their hair on the right instead of the left. They decide guilt or innocence without being aware of all the subtle things that go into their decision. You need an edge, and I'm your edge, that is, if you let me."

He nodded, turning to me. "What about him? He works for my wife. What's he doing here?"

"He's my edge. He'll find out what we need to know about the people in the jury pool, all the stuff that isn't on the questionnaire the court makes them fill out." He squinted at me, and I nodded in reply, backing Kate up, wondering where she was going.

"Why would my wife let him help us?"

When he referred to the two of them as *us*, I knew that Kate had him. She sat back, knowing it too. "Now why do you think your future former wife would want to keep you out of jail?"

Jimmy thought for a moment, his eyes widening when he figured out the answer. He shook his head, offering his first real smile. "Alimony."

"Bingo," Kate said.

"I'm not paying her one goddamn cent!"

"If you're making twelve cents an hour scrubbing the penitentiary bathroom floor, you're right. At least if you're out on the street making a decent wage, you'll have something worth fighting over."

He smiled again. His uneven teeth were stained with tobacco and coffee, his grin crooked and dirty. I was wrong to think that a blue suit was all he needed to pass for a banker. Everything you needed to know about Jimmy Martin was right in front of you each time he opened his mouth. He rubbed his hands together.

"Okay, then. Where do we start?"

"It all starts with you, Jimmy," Kate said. "If Ethan is going to sell you to the jury, I need to know everything there is to know about you. When were you born?"

She got him started, and it was hard to get him to stop. He told her about growing up in Northeast, how his father had smacked him and his brother around; how he'd stumbled through high school, barely graduating; enlisting in the Marines, doing two tours in the first Gulf War, getting in enough trouble that they offered him an honorable discharge in return for his promise not to re-enlist; and finally pulled himself together working construction, mostly residential, drywall and carpentry, some electrical and plumbing, whatever needed doing. He bragged about all the women he'd known, marveling how Peggy had somehow worn him down until he gave in and married her.

"And the next thing you knew, you had two kids and the party was over," she said.

The air went out of him. "Yeah."

"And with the recession, work dried up and money got tight, which wasn't your fault, and you and Peggy started fighting and you'd come home at night and she'd say she was going out with her girlfriends, only it wasn't always her girlfriends."

His eyes flickered, his lips trembling even as his jaw tightened. "How'd you know about that?"

Kate reached into her shoulder bag, pulling out a sheaf of papers, setting them on the coffee table. "Ethan showed me what your divorce lawyer filed in response to Peggy's divorce petition, and I read the rest of it between the lines. That had to be tough to take."

He looked away, staring out the windows, coming back to her, his jaw set. "Who gives a shit? Somebody wants her, they can have her. I'm through with the bitch."

Kate reached into her bag again, pulling out a manila folder and setting it on the coffee table. "But she was only half of the problem. Even if you were through with her, you still had the kids."

She opened the folder, not taking her eyes off of him, spreading eight-by-ten color photographs of Evan and Cara out on the table, Evan posing in his Cub Scouts uniform, Cara wearing the one from her basketball team. Jimmy scanned the photos, locking in his flat expression.

She pulled out another folder, laying a color photograph of two dead children, their bodies bloody and sightless, on top of the pictures of Evan and Cara. Jimmy's head spun clockwise like he'd taken a right cross, his jaw slack, his eyebrows arching over full-moon eyes.

He shook his head, bringing his glare back to Kate, not looking at the photographs, grabbing his thighs, fighting to stay in his chair and losing the fight. I beat him to his feet, chest bumping him and pinning his arms to his sides.

"Those aren't my kids' bodies! What the hell are you trying to pull on me?"

"Easy, Jimmy," I said.

"Take your fucking hands off of me!"

The officer opened the door, making me wonder how private our conversation had been. "Like the man told you," the officer said, "go easy, Jimmy."

Jimmy sucked in a deep breath, and I felt the tension drain out of him. I released his arms, and he raised his hands in mock surrender, walked past the officer and out into the hall without saying another word. The officer winked at us before following him.

Chapter Twenty-four

I waited until we were back in Kate's car, the barbed-wire gate screening our view of the Farm.

"What was that about?"

She shook her hair. "What was what about?"

"The con you just tried to run on Jimmy Martin. You convinced him you could fix the jury so he could skate on a felony theft charge even though he's guilty, all so you could try to blindside him into admitting he killed his kids. If there's a code of ethics for jury consultants, I'd say you violated all of them except for the one about sleeping with the judge, but I guess you have to save something for the trial."

She put the key in the ignition but didn't start the engine. "Is that all?"

"No, that's just for openers. This is Jimmy's first felony beef, so he's not going to do enough time for styles to change even if he's convicted, which is going to happen no matter how much fairy dust you sprinkle on the jury. Your Robin Hood defense doesn't stand a chance, especially since Jimmy will have to testify how much he loves his wife and kids, which guarantees he'll be convicted once the prosecutor tells the jury that Peggy is divorcing him and that he won't tell anyone what happened to his kids. No lawyer would hire a jury consultant for this case, especially one as good as you. It's a lost cause, and you're too damned expensive. Jimmy doesn't have two quarters to rub together, but he's got you on his team because Ethan Bonner says you owe him. How does that happen?"

"Is that all?"

"That's enough for now."

"Good," she said, firing the engine. "How do we get to Peggy Martin's house?"

"We aren't going anywhere until I get some answers."

She sighed, pulled out Peggy's divorce petition, found her address on the cover sheet, and entered it in the GPS built into the dash. A moment later, a mechanical female voice instructed her to proceed to the highlighted route, and she put the car in gear.

"Your deal with Ethan was clear. I interview the Martins and tell you and him what I think. That doesn't entitle you to an explanation of my methods."

The warm greeting she'd given me at breakfast had faded, replaced by a cold front, the tipping point coming when I blurted out that I cared about what had happened to us. It wasn't hard to understand why my confession had stirred up a storm. When she asked me to follow her to San Diego, I had answered by saying that I'd asked my ex-wife to move in with me and would she mind being patient while I saw how that worked out. I would have sworn it somehow had made sense to me at the time even though anyone else would have realized it was a one-sentence application for Moron of the Year.

"I'm sorry."

She nodded, keeping her eyes on the road. "Good for you."

"Not about today, about San Diego."

She bit her lip. "I believe you are sorry, Jack, but I'm not sure what it is you're sorry about. Whether it's that Joy got sick and you decided you were the only person on earth who could take care of her or that you chose her over me or that you hurt me or that you realized you made the biggest mistake of your life. But whatever it is, don't tell me you care about what happened to us because people who care don't just walk away even if they think they have a good reason. It's been a long time since I've had to deal with all of that and doing it in the middle of this case isn't my idea of fun. So let's just stick to business."

My head and neck whip lashed against the headrest, my right

shoulder dipping as my left twisted until it was perpendicular to my sternum, the spasm holding me for a five count.

"Fair enough," I said when I could breathe again.

She turned toward me, her eyes wet, her mouth soft. "I hate it when you do that."

"Don't say that. I don't like people feeling sorry for me."

"It's not that. When you shake, it takes the fun out of beating up on you, and I really feel like beating up on you."

"Get in line. So, tell me. Did Jimmy Martin kill his kids?" She gathered herself, squaring her shoulders to the road. "I don't know."

"You don't know? What happened to divining the truth hidden in facial expressions?"

She took another breath, suppressing her irritation. "There's been a lot of new research. Turns out that liars don't avert their eyes on average any more than people telling the truth do."

"What about body language, posture, things like that?"

"Same story."

"So, are you running a scam on Ethan?"

"Are you trying to piss me off?"

I grinned. "You made it clear I already did. I'm just trying to give you another reason so you'll forget why you were mad at me in the first place."

"A simple plan for a simple mind," she said, patting my cheek. "I started with Jimmy's earliest memories growing up, something he'd have no reason to lie about. That gave me a baseline on how he communicates. I'll compare that to the rest of the interview for differences that suggest deception, but since he refused to talk about his kids, there's only so much I can do."

"Like what?"

"I'll have a better feel for him after I study the videotape and break his expressions down frame by frame. But, his body language, his facial expressions, everything about him was defensive whenever I got close to talking about Evan and Cara. He relaxed when I got him to talk about himself, which is no surprise since that's every man's favorite subject. He likes portraying himself as the victim, and, no matter what goes wrong, he'll tell you that mistakes were made but not by him."

"He's not an overachiever, that's for certain."

"His reactions to the photographs were interesting and confusing."

"When you showed him the pictures of Evan and Cara he acted like he'd never met them."

"He tried to, but he couldn't pull it off. His involuntary micro-expressions showed me a lot, but I'm not certain what they mean."

This was Kate, the scientist collecting specimens, putting them under the glass, pulling them apart, and putting them back together again.

"What did you see?"

"When I showed him the pictures of Evan and Cara, the corners of his mouth turned up for a fraction of a second. That was a smile, or the makings of one. He was happy to see them. Then he got angry, not annoyed but furious. His mouth got hard and tight, and his eyebrows crunched down and together, squashing his eyes and wiping out his smile."

"I didn't see any of that."

"That's why we call them micro-expressions. They don't last long enough for the untrained eye to pick up on them."

"He could have been mad at his kids. He pretty much told you they were cramping his style."

"Maybe, but I don't think so, especially after I showed him the picture of the dead children. Coming on top of the pictures of Evan and Cara, his brain instantly assumed his children were the ones in the photograph."

"But he realized they weren't his kids."

"Not before I saw his uncontrolled, involuntary reactions. He was completely surprised and horrified."

"Isn't that what you'd expect?"

"Not if he killed them. The killer would have shown contempt or disgust, maybe shame, unless he's a total psychopath."

"All I saw was how angry he got after you showed him the

pictures of the dead kids. You set him up, and he knew it. That would piss anyone off."

"Yeah, but that anger was different than the first outburst, the hidden one you didn't see. You saw his anger at being tricked. As outraged as he was, the flash of anger I saw when I showed him Evan and Cara's photographs was more intense. He was snarling, like a rabid dog."

"Are you saying you don't think he killed them?"

"I'm saying I don't know why seeing pictures of his children made him happy at first and then made him angrier than when I tried to deceive him into thinking his children were dead. I don't know what that means."

"There's one other thing you're overlooking."

"What's that?"

"When you showed him the picture of the bodies, he said that they weren't his kids. He didn't say that they couldn't be his kids because they weren't dead. That's what I would have said if I were him and I hadn't killed my son and daughter."

My cell phone pinged with a text message. It was from Lucy. I read it and shook.

"What is it?"

"One of the volunteer search teams looking for Evan and Cara found something in Kessler Park."

"What?"

"Remains."

Chapter Twenty-five

Kessler Park stretches along the northern edge of Northeast Kansas City, beginning near the intersection of The Paseo and Independence Avenue on the west and continuing east to the intersection of Gladstone and Belmont, a rambling, undulating green border covering more than four miles. Built beginning in the 1890s as the first of the city's ten thousand acres of parks, many of its hilly and hardscrabble wooded areas remain hard to reach. Drug dealers and prostitutes long ago replaced families out for a Sunday horse and buggy ride, plying their trade in after-dark seclusion, turning indifferent eyes to the stolen cars and dead bodies dumped and buried in the park's shadows.

Cliff Drive snakes through the park past the Kansas City Museum, edging along limestone bluffs overlooking the Missouri River, continuing past North Terrace Lake, the Carl DiCapo Fountain, a disc golf course, and Indian Mound, a Native American gravesite. The city and local neighborhood associations have fought to reclaim the park, closing Cliff Drive to motor traffic on weekends and cracking down on illegal activity. But the park is too big, too rugged, and too thick to be tamed by traffic engineers and irate homeowners.

Lucy's text message had said to meet her at North Terrace Lake, an irregular-shaped pond in the center of a broad, grassy basin set below street level. Cliff Drive, Chestnut Trafficway, and Lexington Avenue bordered the lake on three sides, a widening stand of thick trees and tangled underbrush rising behind the lake across the face of a steep slope. The grass was stunted, stained dull beige, ready for winter, the trees half-stripped of their leaves, those hanging on, dry, brown, and frail.

We parked on Cliff Drive at the end of a line of police cars. Two clusters of people, fifty feet apart, were gathered on the near side of the lake along a bike path. The sun was overhead, the air crisp but not cold enough to force them to huddle together for warmth though they stood hunched shoulder to hunched shoulder, larger rings circling smaller ones, a lone woman at the center of each group.

Standing on the side of the road and looking down at the lake, I recognized Peggy Martin as the solitary woman in the group farther from us. She shuffled her feet, strained to see over the heads blocking her view, and then dropped her chin, eyes on the ground, repeating the routine again and again. Even at a distance, one thing was certain. She wasn't cold, and the people around her weren't there to keep her warm. She was scared, and they were protecting her.

The police had established a perimeter along the outer edge of the distant trees, stretching yellow crime-scene tape trunk to trunk. A uniformed cop held the leash on a search dog, the German shepherd lying at his feet, ears pricked, tail slapping the hard ground with an impatient beat.

The woods were too thick to see what was going on inside the tape, but I knew that a forensics team was spooning away dirt and rock until whatever had been found could be identified as human and a preliminary assessment of gender and approximate age could be made. If the remains were human, they would be excavated with painstaking care, each bone and bone fragment photographed, location and position recorded, the surrounding soil sifted for clothing, bullets, and anything else that would help identify the victim and cause of death. Once the remains were tagged and bagged, the investigation would fan out in widening circles searching for more evidence.

That's when someone would emerge from the trees and talk to the women who were waiting inside their friendship circles, too afraid of answers to ask questions. What did they find? Could it be my son, daughter, sister, brother, father, mother? Who did this?

A television news chopper hovered overhead, rotors thumping. Remote broadcast vans, satellite dishes aimed skyward, jockeyed for position as two cops directed them to a staging area. A reporter, trailed by a cameraman, approached Peggy's circle and was rebuffed. She shrugged, signaling to the cameraman to follow her to the other group, where she found someone anxious to make the six o'clock news.

Kate and I walked down the slope from Cliff Drive toward the bike path, our route taking us past the group that welcomed the reporter. One of the women was holding a copy of the flier I'd seen tacked to the light pole on Independence Avenue near Roni Chase's office. I couldn't see the picture on it, but I could make out Timmy Montgomery's name. Several other women were wearing sweatshirts screen-printed with a logo that read *Have You Seen Me?* and Timmy's image.

The woman in the center of that circle had been waiting two years for the answers to her questions. A crack opened in the wall her friends had built around her. She was staring at the ground, rocking back and forth and hugging her body. Her hair was pulled back, her face pale and flat. A man elbowed his way toward her, hands outstretched, calling her name, "Jeannie!" She twisted away without looking at him. He dropped his hands and melted into the crowd.

"Do you think this will be the day?" Kate asked.

"For what?"

"When God decides to ease her pain."

"You think that's how it works?" I asked.

"I hope so."

"I don't think God is going to choose between these two mothers."

"You think it's just a matter of luck, then?"

"I don't believe in luck, good luck, bad luck, or no luck at all."

"What do you believe in?" Kate asked.

"A world where everyone takes his turn in the barrel."

"Maybe they're both in the same barrel."

"What do you mean?"

"Maybe the disappearances of their children are related. Maybe the same person is responsible."

We stopped, both of us looking back and forth at the two groups and the two women at their center. Adrienne Nardelli, the detective in charge of Peggy Martin's case, hadn't said anything about possible links to other cases when Lucy and I met with her.

We were too focused on Jimmy Martin to have asked, making the mistake of seeing the world through our client's eyes instead of following the evidence wherever it led us.

"Maybe."

Lucy waved to us from the edge of the second group, and we joined her. "How's Peggy?" I asked. "Holding up, but only barely."

"What have you found out?"

She pointed toward two people standing apart from the group. "That's Ellen Koch, Peggy's neighbor, the one who organized the volunteer search teams. The guy is her son, Adam. This area had been searched a couple of times, but Ellen decided to give it another try today. She brought her son and a few other people with her. She and Adam were up in the woods above the lake and stumbled across something that looked like a bone, and Ellen called the police."

"Did you talk to the son?"

Lucy cocked her head, one eyebrow raised.

"Okay, sorry I asked. What did he tell you?"

"Not much. He's a pretty boy, pouts a lot and looks bored. Said he was just walking along and saw something sticking out of the rocks he thought looked like a bone. He told his mother, and she called the cops."

"What's the mother say about her son?" Kate asked.

"She says he graduated high school last year, tried junior college but quit. She says he's looking for a job, but the way she says it, I don't know how hard he's looking. She wants him to join the army, but he isn't interested."

"I'd like to talk to him," Kate said.

"Sure. I'll introduce you."

Ellen and Adam were watching the tree line, Ellen's hands in her coat pockets, her face drawn, crow's feet fanning out from the corners of her eyes, her mouth turned down and sour. Adam was slender and handsome, jet-black hair falling to his eyebrows, smoking a cigarette, fingers of one hand tucked inside his pants, posing like the lead singer in a boy band waiting for the girls to go crazy.

Kate didn't wait for an introduction. "Adam, I'm Kate Scranton. I understand you and your mother found the body. That must have been something."

He nodded and dropped his cigarette to the ground, letting it burn until his mother glared at him, then grinding it under his heel.

"Yeah."

"Tell me about it?"

He squinted at her. "I already told the police."

"Which is a great help for them but not for us."

"And I already told her," he said, tilting his head at Lucy.

"The more people talk about this kind of thing, the more they remember."

He made us wait while he rolled his shoulders and breathed deep, swelling his chest.

"Okay. We were walking up in the woods, about halfway up the hill. There was some rocks, and we seen somethin' stickin' out didn't look right. I pulled on it, and it come out. I could tell right away it was a bone. Looked like a leg bone. So my mom called the cops, and that's about it."

"Had you been in those woods before?"

He looked away. "Nah."

Lucy interrupted, pointing toward the woods. "Here they come."

Chapter Twenty-six

Four paramedics carried a gurney out of the woods, a black body bag strapped to it, the bag flat, holding individually wrapped remains too sparse to give it shape or dimension. They stopped, released a wheeled frame tucked beneath the gurney, rolling it across the uneven terrain, a lone woman trailing them.

I recognized Detective Adrienne Nardelli's stout frame and deliberate walk. She was solid and calm, naturally deadpan, saving any hidden sense of humor for off-duty hours. When Lucy and I met with her about the Martin case, she laid down two simple, non-negotiable terms: be straight with her and she'd tell us what she could; fuck with her and she'd fuck us up. She was Quincy Carter without the charm.

Both waiting groups lurched into motion, blending into a single human wave rising and cresting, rolling toward the gurney, Peggy Martin and Jeannie Montgomery squeezed together in the center of the swell. The gurney's wheels bogged down in a soft spot, the paramedics hoisting it to their waists, setting it down when they met the crowd on the open plain. The lake was a glistening mirrored backdrop, the rumble, whine, and whir of passing traffic an everyday overture. The crowd spread out and parted, paying silent homage as the paramedics passed among them, some gasping, others crossing themselves, still others silent and weeping. The two mothers, side-byside, hands clasped, faced Detective Nardelli.

"We found a body," she said. "It's definitely an adult, probably female. I'm sorry."

Peggy let out a low moan that exploded into a guttural wail, collapsing to her knees. Jeannie hung her head, turned, and walked away, no one touching her, no one coming close. Peggy was dying. She was a ghost.

I knew from hard experience that grief born of a lost child begins as a bottomless well; that those black waters eventually dry into a thick wall separating the before and after. Then one day, if we're lucky, we wake up and find that the wall has eroded and all that's left is a harsh filter through which the rest of our life passes, every moment measured against what might have been and what should have been.

But when there is no end to the beginning, when we cannot clutch our child to our breast a final time, we suffocate in uncertainty, beyond rescue or comfort, and those who try trip over clumsy words and gestures before retreating to a safe distance. So it was, as Jeannie made her way alone and Peggy's friends fell away, all except for Ellen Koch, who helped Peggy to her feet, cupping her elbow as if she were a wayward drunk, guiding her toward a pickup truck parked on Cliff Drive where her son Adam waited behind the wheel, engine running.

"Lousy deal for them," Detective Nardelli said to us. "Stand out here half the day, get all worked up for nothing."

"There's nothing else they can do," I said.

"Doesn't make it any less lousy. You have any good news for me?"

"We took another run at Jimmy Martin this morning, but he's sitting on whatever he knows."

"If he knows anything," Nardelli said.

"Oh, he knows something. That's for certain," Kate said.

Nardelli turned to her with a narrowed gaze. "Do I know you?"

Kate offered her hand. "I'm Kate Scranton."

Nardelli shook her hand, studying her face. "I've heard of you. Jury consultant, right?"

"Among other things."

"So why do you think Jimmy Martin isn't telling us what he knows? Except for the fact that if he killed his kids, he'll get the death penalty and that's not the kind of thing he's likely to confess until he's more afraid of his nightmares than the needle."

Kate summarized her interview and impressions. It was easy to read Nardelli's reaction. She did everything but smirk and spit, turning to me.

"That's how you've been spending your time?"

"I'd listen to her, if I were you. The science is solid, and she's usually right."

"That so?"

"Yeah," Kate said, her eyes firing up. "It is so. And if you'd consider the possibility that I know what I'm talking about, you'd spend some time with Adam Koch, the boy who found the body. He's not telling us everything he knows either."

"And which secret expressions of his told you that?" Nardelli asked.

"They aren't secret. They just happen so quickly you'll miss them unless you're trained to see them. Adam had a gestural slip when I asked him to tell me what happened. He raised his left shoulder for a fraction of a second."

"His left shoulder? For a fraction of a second? My, that does sound incriminating."

Kate smiled, her expression cool and patient. "It's a half shrug. In a full shrug, both shoulders rise, stay up and then drop. Tough questions can make a person feel helpless, especially when they're lying, and people who do a half shrug feel helpless. He did it a couple of times. The last time was when I asked him if he'd been up in those woods before. He said no, but I'm pretty sure he was lying."

"All because of the shrug?"

"Partly. His lips also stretched horizontally. That's a micro-expression of fear, and it's involuntary, just like the half-shrug. These gestures and micro-expressions are universal. They show up in every culture, and they mean the same thing. By themselves they might not mean that much, but when they happen together when he's talking about finding a dead body, it's very likely that he's not telling us everything he knows."

"So you're like a human lie detector, is that it?"

"More like a lie catcher, and I've got a better track record than any lie detector."

"Any judge ever let you testify in court that someone's a liar?" Kate took a deep breath.

"That's not how I work."

Nardelli shook her head. "Course not. Why would you when you can catch people lying by watching how they shrug their shoulders?" She turned to Lucy and me. "I should have listened to Quincy Carter. I'm going back to the woods. You find something a judge will let into evidence, give me a call."

"Hang on a second," I said. "Any chance there's a connection between the Montgomery and Martin cases?"

Nardelli hesitated, staring at me. "Ask your lie catcher. She's the one with all the answers."

Kate waited until Nardelli was out of earshot. "I'm right about Jimmy Martin and Adam Koch."

"That's good enough for me. We'll talk to Adam again," Lucy said.

"Talk to his mother too," Kate said.

"Why?"

"I watched her when she was helping Peggy to the pickup truck. She was flashing unilateral contempt the whole way. The right corner of her lip was tight and raised. That indicates arrogance or a feeling of moral superiority. Maybe she does that all the time, but I'd bet against it. She's helping Peggy even though she doesn't like her."

"Then why bother?" I asked.

"And," Lucy added, "why doesn't she like her?"

"All good questions," Kate said, turning to Lucy. "What about Peggy Martin? Did she agree to let me interview her?"

Lucy nodded. "She didn't like the idea at first since you started out working for her husband, but I convinced her."

"How?"

"I told her that you didn't care who hired you, you'd do the same job, and that if we were going to find her kids, we needed your help."

"That's all it took?" Kate asked.

"That's all."

"Did you tell her that I'd know if she was lying to me?"

Lucy shook her head. "No. I didn't want to put any more pressure on her. Besides, nobody tells the truth, or all of it, all the time or all at once."

"Then we're all on the same page here."

"Chapter and verse," Lucy said.

"So let's go talk to her," Kate said.

I looked at my watch. "Can't. Not till later. I'm supposed to meet Roni Chase at her house pretty soon. Quincy Carter is going to interview her again. I don't want him to have another shot at her alone, and I need some time to prep her. She doesn't live far from here. It won't take long."

"Kate and I can talk to Peggy while you go see Roni."

"I don't have a car."

"Take mine. I'll ride with Kate. You up to driving?"

The day was wearing on me, twitches and shakes coming and going like wind changing directions, but Roni's house was close enough that I could make the drive.

"That's not the point. I need to be there when Kate talks to Peggy."

Lucy raised one eyebrow. "Needing and wanting isn't the same thing, Jack," she lectured. "Roni Chase may be your latest reclamation project, but she isn't mine. Finding those kids is the only thing I care about. And you're the one who told me I had to sit out the Jimmy Martin interview because three people were one too many."

"Don't you hate that?" Kate said, grinning. "You raise them, and then they turn on you."

I stuck my hand out. "Keys."

Chapter Twenty-seven

There was enough to tie the disappearances of Evan and Cara Martin together with the disappearance of Timmy Montgomery to ask whether it was possible. All three kids were of the same age and lived in the same part of town. Although they vanished two years apart, there was reason to look for other connections.

Did the families know one another? Even if they didn't, did they have friends in common? Did their kids go to the same schools? How else might they have crossed paths?

Those questions focused on the possibility that the kids were taken by someone who knew them, but that theory didn't suffer much scrutiny. If Jimmy Martin killed his kids to punish his wife for her real or imagined sins, it was unlikely he'd have had any reason to kidnap and kill Timmy Montgomery two years earlier. The same would no doubt be true of any member of the Montgomery family.

If there was a connection, it was more likely that the kidnapper/killer preyed on small children, indifferent to whether his victims came from happy or unhappy homes, caring only whether he could have them. And that meant he probably lived in Northeast, probably hadn't started with Timmy and wouldn't stop with Evan and Cara. It was an incendiary conclusion that would terrify families from one end of Northeast to the other.

Adrienne Nardelli had ducked my question about a connection, and that was enough to scare me. Regardless of why she had avoided answering me, it was clear she wasn't going to share anything she had, at least not until I had something to offer her in return. Her lack of cooperation made my job harder but not impossible. I left a message for Simon Alexander describing what I needed and left another for the one friend I still had at the FBI, Ammara Iverson, asking for a favor, hoping I hadn't gone to the well once too often.

The bones dug out of the woods above North Terrace Lake would distract Nardelli, not because one victim was more important than the other but because the job demanded that she work the cases at the same time. A housewife had disappeared from her Northeast home a few months ago, her husband refusing to cooperate with the police in their investigation. Without a body or other evidence of a crime, the husband had gone on with his life, raising their kids. Maybe the bones were hers, or maybe they were those of a prostitute who'd gone with a john into the woods for her last trick. Regardless, missing kids and bleached bones would divide and subdivide Nardelli's time and attention.

I was no better off than Nardelli. I'd spent last night at Truman Medical Center worrying and wondering about Roni Chase, her relationship to Frank Crenshaw, and the possibility that her boyfriend Brett Staley had killed Frank, with or without Roni's help.

The murdered and missing don't take a number, waiting their turn, hoping people like Adrienne Nardelli and me can work them into our schedule. No matter how long they have been silenced, they scream for our attention, refusing to take no for an answer, and I never stop hearing their voices. Lucy may have shut out everything except the voices of the Martin kids, but Nardelli and I couldn't. We'd keep doing the same thing: press on. Because that was the only thing we knew how to do.

Chapter Twenty-eight

When I pulled up in front of Roni Chase's house, I double-checked the address, wondering how a bookkeeper afforded a mansion, even one that had to be at least a hundred years old. The three-story asymmetrical design was topped with eyelid dormers on the third floor, set beneath a steeply pitched roof offset by a two-story turret on the northeast corner that was capped by a witch's-hat roof. An ornate wooden rail framed the porch extending across the front of the house.

It wasn't quite as impressive close up. The exterior paint was faded and chipped in places, wood rot evident around the windows, the floorboards of the porch creaking and sagging. The house needed a lot of work.

Roni answered when I rang the bell and led me inside through a set of double doors into a small foyer, through another set of carved wooden doors and into a wide space with a high vaulted ceiling, a white flagged floor, and stained-glass windows on the stairway landing leading to the second floor. I raised my head at the ceiling, rotating my gaze. Yellow watermarks and spidery cracks in the plaster were more evidence that the house would soon turn into a money pit if it hadn't already.

"They call this the receiving area," Roni said.

"Who does? The tour guides?"

She laughed. "The people who put this place on the National Register of Historic Places. It's a Queen Anne–style house. A rich lumberman built it in 1886 for his new wife who was living in Europe, but she died before she ever set foot in it."

"How'd she die?"

"Do you ever stop playing the cop?"

"No."

She shook her head. "It must be weird to live like that, to wonder if every bad thing that happens is a crime."

"I never thought it was weird."

"How do you think of it?"

"Me? I wonder what happens when things go wrong, especially when people think no one is watching. Sometimes it's a crime, and sometimes it's just life."

"That's pretty depressing. I'd rather wonder what happens when things go right, like falling in love."

"Well, Brett Staley will be ready when you do. Can't get more romantic than wanting to buy your funeral dress?"

She gave me a wistful, uncertain smile. "It's his way of saying he wants to spend the rest of our lives together, but I'm not sure. We grew up together. I was five years old the first time he told me he loved me."

"But you're not in love with him?"

"More comfortable than in love."

"Don't settle for comfortable. You can get that with an easy chair or a dog from the pound."

"I know what you mean, but he's all I've got."

"You don't strike me as someone who's afraid she can't do any better than the boy she grew up with. You're smart enough to run your own business, pretty enough to turn heads, and ballsy enough to carry a gun and use it. That's a powerful combination."

She blushed, dipping her chin. "I guess we don't always see ourselves the way others see us."

"And a philosopher to boot. So what went wrong with the wife who never saw the house her husband built for her?"

"The ship she took to America sank. The husband lived in the house for a couple of years, but he was too heartbroken to stay. He set up a charity named after his wife, Rachel, and turned the house into a home for unwed mothers and orphan girls called Rachel's

House for Women."

"How did you end up with it?"

"It's Grandma Lilly's, not mine. She was one of the girls who lived here. Her mother left her some money, and Grandma hung on to it and used it to get an education. She got into selling houses and did well enough to buy this place twenty years ago when the charity went broke. My mom and I lived in a duplex off of Lexington, but we moved in here after she had her stroke so Grandma could help me take care of her."

"This place is big, but it doesn't look big enough for very many unwed mothers and orphans."

"There was a dormitory attached to the back, but Grandma had it torn down."

"You haven't said anything about your grandfather."

"I never knew him. Grandma won't talk about him. She got pregnant with my mom while she was a teenager living here, but she never got married. Whenever I asked her why, she said that she'd give up a lot for a man, but the one thing she wouldn't give up was her name."

"Did you mention that she could have gotten married and kept her last name?" She laughed. "Yes, and when I did she said the moon is pink."

"The moon is pink? Why?"

"It's what she always said if she thought I wasn't listening or didn't understand what she meant, like she just as well have said the moon is pink for all the good it did."

"That's what you told Frank Crenshaw after you shot him."

"Yeah, well, I guess I picked up a few things from my Grandma."

"How about your mother? How did she feel about not knowing anything about her father?"

Roni took a breath. "She said everyone is entitled to their own mysteries and that was Grandma's."

"Did she ever try to solve it?"

"No. She said she didn't want anything to do with a man who wasn't good enough for Grandma. My mom never got married either, except she waited until she was a lot older to have me."

"What about your father? Is he in the picture?"

She shrugged. "Almost the same story as Grandma. Mom says they dated for a week between Christmas and New Year's. He took off before Mom knew she was pregnant. She didn't know how to reach him, so he never knew about me. Mom said it was just as well because he wasn't the kind to stick around."

"You ever try to find him?"

"No. Half of my friends' parents were divorced, so it was no big deal living in a one-parent home. One of my friends was adopted and made a big deal about finding her birth parents. When she did, they didn't want anything to do with her. That's when she realized her real parents were the ones who raised her. I know that there's a piece of me that's missing, but I don't see how a stranger who doesn't know I exist can fill it in. Grandma likes to say you can't fix your past but you can make your future."

"So where does the funeral dress figure into the family tradition."

She chuckled. "You'll be glad to know it starts with a criminal, my great-grandmother Vivian Chase."

"That's okay. Everyone has at least one relative that climbed out of the wrong side of the gene pool."

"She was a robber back in the 1940s, banks, drugstores, anyplace with cash. She left Grandma at Rachel's House when Grandma was eight years old because she knew she couldn't raise her and rob banks too. But, whenever she could, she came to see Grandma, and she always gave some of the money she stole to Miss Moore, the lady who ran the home, to make sure they took good care of Grandma. One night after she dropped off some money, her partner showed up. They got into a gunfight right out on the curb and shot and killed each other. Miss Moore used some of the money to pay for my great-grandma's funeral and for the dress. Grandma named my mother after her. And this," she said, fingering the gold chain and cameo around her neck, "belonged to my great-grandmother."

"That's a nice keepsake."

"She left it to my grandma, who gave it to my mother, and she gave it me. It keeps us connected."

"You must have told that story to Brett Staley a hundred times when you were growing up."

"Didn't have to. His grandfather Bobby Staley drove my great-grandma Vivien to the hospital the night she died and dropped the dress off at the funeral home the next day. He and I grew up hearing the same stories."

"And you ended up with the house."

She did a slow turn, one arm extended, fingers tracing a pattern on the wall. "Sometimes I think we're trapped in this house."

"It's just bricks and mortar. You can always sell it."

She shook her head. "Grandma says it would never sell, not in this economy and not with all the things that need to be fixed that we can't afford to fix."

"Can't you borrow against the house to pay for the repairs and pay the loan back when you sell it?"

"Not now. Grandma borrowed against it to pay my mom's medical bills. There's not much equity left, if any, the way home values have dropped."

"Well, I guess you'll have to ride it out until the economy gets back on track."

She shivered, wrapping her arms across her chest. "I hope we can. Sometimes this place feels like ivy wrapped around my ankles, creeping up my legs, and one day it's going to strangle me if someone doesn't take me away from here."

"I thought you didn't want to be rescued."

She tilted her head to one side and loosened her arms, a sad smile capturing her ambivalence. "I don't, but if that's the only way out, I wouldn't turn it down."

"Why not just leave?"

"And go where? Do what? I've got to take care of my mom, and sooner or later, I'm going to have to take care of my grandma, and they will never leave. I'm stuck, so I've got to find a way to make it work, one way or the other."

The doorbell rang. I looked at my watch. Quincy Carter wasn't due for another fifteen minutes.

Roni left me in the receiving area, returning with an older man, his eyes beaming, grinning like a pauper who'd been invited to see the prince. He was tall, his hair sand and silver, his features fine and handsome. He was missing the top third of his right ear, his only visible defect. Roni made the introduction.

"Terry Walker, say hello to Jack Davis."

Chapter Twenty-nine

"Lilly didn't say anything about other guests," Terry said.

"That's because she didn't invite me," I said, extending my hand.

"I invited Jack," Roni said. "Grandma and Mom are in the morning room. You can go on back."

He brightened again, his smile stretching his face. "Nice to meet you," he said, giving my hand a quick, firm shake, turning to Roni. "I'll find my way."

I waited until Terry Walker had disappeared into the house. "Who's he?"

"An old friend of my grandmother's. They knew each other when they were kids. He moved away. He's in town on some kind of business. They haven't seen each other in years."

"Quincy Carter is on his way here to question you in a murder case, and your grandmother is having a reunion?"

"It's not a reunion, and I didn't tell her about Detective Carter until I got home a few minutes ago. I didn't want her to worry. Besides, it's a big house. Anyway, you might as well meet the rest of my family."

I followed her through the living room with its intricate woodwork and fireplace flanked by matching sculptures of cherubs, into the kitchen where Queen Anne had given way to Frigidaire and Corian counter-tops and into the morning room. White wallpaper with a green leaf pattern gave it an outdoor feel. Sunlight poured in through large double-hung windows on the west side. A mirror hung over a fireplace, the reflection making the room seem larger than it was.

A woman in a wheelchair, her head held in place by cushions on either side of her face, sat in the center of the room. She opened her mouth wide when she saw us, a sound coming out I didn't understand, though Roni did, bending to give her a kiss.

"Hi, Mama. I love you."

Her mother answered. This time her gurgle was easier to decipher. "Love you too."

"I don't blame you," Roni said, both of them giggling.

Terry Walker stood next to Lilly Chase at the windows, one hand on her shoulder, Lilly's gaze fixed on the mid-distance; then she turned toward us, watching Roni and her mother.

Lilly was red-haired with an oval face, her green eyes not dulled by age. She must have been a beautiful woman when she was young, and she was still attractive, her back straight and her carriage square and confident.

Roni's mother stirred in her wheelchair, raising her left hand, tapping the armrest, smiling a crooked smile. Lilly knelt besides her, squeezing her hand as they exchanged looks and murmurs.

"Martha needs to lie down. I'll take her," Lilly said.

"I'll help you," Roni said, following her mother and grandmother.

Terry circled the morning room, admiring the view from the windows, running his hand along the backs of the furniture, taking inventory.

"Good to be home?" He looked at me, eyebrows raised, cocking his head to one side.

"Roni told me," I said, answering his unspoken question. "She said you lived here as a kid but moved away. What's it like after being away so long?"

"It's more strange than good. Nothing's what it was when I left, including Lilly and me."

"What made you decide to come back after all these years?"

He shrugged. "I've spent my whole life on the road, always looking for the next stop and never thinking about where I've been.

Now I'm of an age where there's a hell of a lot less in front of me than behind me. Got me thinking that maybe it was time to circle back, see if any of my old crew was still kicking around. I lived down the street from Lilly. I came to have a look at the old neighborhood and saw her sitting on the porch. Hadn't seen her in fifty years, but I never forgot that red hair of hers. Some things just burn into your memory."

"You planning on staying this time?"

"Not likely. Wasn't enough to keep me here when I was a kid, and I doubt there's enough now. I imagine I'll say my hellos and good-byes and be on my way."

"What about family?"

"Had a brother, but Lilly told me he's dead. Got shot robbing a liquor store thirty years ago, which isn't much of a surprise since he was born bad."

"In the DNA, huh?"

"Hard to say if it's the blood or the time and place."

"Probably some of both. I get the sense that you've been in a few scrapes."

He fingered his clipped ear, smiling. "A time or two. How about you? What's your small-world story?"

"Me? Roni is taking a look at some financial records for me."

We traded smiles, the twinkle in his eyes reminding me again that the first liar didn't stand a chance, but I had no reason to share a murder investigation with Northeast's prodigal son.

"That's so?"

"It is."

The doorbell rang, and I heard footsteps clattering down the stairs. "More company?"

"Not for Lilly. It's for Roni and me, a police detective who's working on the same case I asked Roni to help me on."

"Those financial records."

"Yeah."

"Well then, have at it. I'll show myself out."

Chapter Thirty

Lilly Chase led Roni and Quincy Carter into the morning room. Judging from her stiff posture and stern glare, she wasn't pleased to be entertaining the police. Mindful of the power that beauty and age bestowed, she clasped her hands, commanding the room with a bank robber's brass.

"Detective Carter," she said, "my granddaughter only just now told me you are here to question her. I've told her not to talk to you without an attorney."

"With all due respect, m'am, that's up to her."

"You've no right to harass her. She's done nothing wrong. If she hadn't shot Frank Crenshaw, I'd be wearing black, mourning my granddaughter."

Carter nodded. "I got the word a couple of hours ago from the prosecuting attorney. She's in the clear. He agrees with you and me that it was straight-up self-defense."

"Good," she said, as if checking that off her mental list of deal terms. "That leaves the second shooting, the one that killed Frank. Not that he didn't deserve killing after what he did to Marie, but you can't think Roni had anything to do with that."

"I'm just here to ask her a few questions."

"I know how the police do things. You ask questions, insinuate guilt, and badger people who are innocent into confessing to things they haven't done and wouldn't do. I won't have that. Not in my house."

"We're just going to talk, ma'am. No bright lights or rubber hoses."

She glared at Carter. "Detective, I've spent my life selling houses owned by people who didn't know they were moving to people who didn't know they were buying, so don't try to sell me. I told Roni that she shouldn't say another word to you without having a lawyer here to look after her. But you'd have thought I told her the moon was pink. And, you Jack, for some unknown reason, Roni thinks you're better protection than any lawyer I could hire, though in my experience a man who works for free is rarely as committed as the man whose next meal depends on making the sale."

A spasm squeezed me from the inside out, clenching my eyes, tugging my chin to my chest and pulling it up and past my left shoulder. I managed to keep my mouth shut but couldn't smother the accompanying grunt. When the spasm passed and I opened my eyes, Lilly Chase was staring at me.

"When Roni told me you had a movement disorder I thought you had a bowel problem. Obviously, I was wrong."

"Grandma!"

"It's okay," I said, catching my breath.

"Can't you call it something else?" Lilly asked.

"Mostly, I call it a pain in the ass, but I don't think that solves your problem."

"He shakes sometimes. It's no big deal," Roni said.

Lilly smirked, undeterred. "That's what the seller always says about the water in the basement until it turns out the house is floating on an underground spring. I always tell my sellers to make full disclosure of any defects in their property. Saves a lot of aggravation."

She was pushing, but I didn't blame her. I'd made it a practice to explain my condition, believing that the more people knew, the more at ease they would be.

"It's called tics. It's a lot like Tourette's. It makes me shake, spasm, and stutter."

"Can you control it?"

"Not much."

Lilly crossed her arms over her chest. "Tell me something, Jack.

134

If you were me, would you entrust your granddaughter to a man with the shakes?"

"If it's this man, I would," Carter said. "I know Jack better than I'd like. Most of the time, he's a pain in my butt. Still, if it were me, I'd want him on my side."

"Careful, Detective," Lilly said. "It's very tricky to work both sides of a sale without screwing somebody."

"Lilly," I said. "I told Roni she should get a lawyer. She said she doesn't want one because she hasn't done anything wrong. But you're right that these things can take a turn no one expects. If Roni wants a lawyer, all she has to do is say so. Detective Carter will wait, and I'll go on my way."

Lilly turned toward Roni, one eyebrow raised in an unspoken question.

"No sale, Grandma. I'll be fine."

Lilly stared at her, waiting for Roni to fold. When Roni didn't, she dropped her arms to her side. "Well, let's see what tomorrow brings."

"Thank you, Lilly," I said as she headed toward the kitchen.

"Don't be so quick with gratitude, Jack, because if any harm comes to my granddaughter, you won't be thanking me. Trust me on that."

Chapter Thirty-one

"I'm sorry," Roni said after Lilly left. "She means well."

"There's no question about that," I said. "It's good to have someone like that in your corner."

"Let's get this over with before she comes back and tries to sell me a house," Carter said.

There are all kinds of ways to conduct an interrogation. A lot depends on how much you know going in and your objective. If it's early in the case and you're after information, you take it slow, build trust, ask open-ended questions, and give the witness time to think and reflect.

If the witness is a suspect, you pin them down to their story as soon as possible, investigate, and build the case against them, then come back when you know enough to go after whatever it is they are holding back. And everyone holds something back. That's when craft separates from the manual. Sometimes, I'd hit a suspect right out of the gate with my best shot, catching him off guard. With others, I'd take my time, chipping away at their story until it collapsed. Even though the prosecuting attorney had given Roni a pass for shooting Frank Crenshaw at LC's Bar-B-Q, that didn't mean she wasn't a suspect in his murder at the hospital.

Roni sat on the floral-print sofa, Carter and I taking chairs opposite her. I glanced at Carter, wondering how he would play it. He opened with a hungry smile that made the hairs on the back of my neck stand up.

"Roni, I know we've been over this a couple of times, but I want you to walk me through what happened last night one more time. Yesterday was a long one, and I want to make sure I've got everything right."

She sat straight up on the edge of the sofa, hands in her lap. "Sure, no problem."

He took her through it, five minutes of slow-pitch batting practice, looking at his notes, nodding as she answered each question, adding *that's right* and *yeah, yeah* to her responses. Roni was getting too comfortable, and comfortable people made mistakes. I decided to throw Carter off his rhythm.

"What did you see on the hospital surveillance tapes?"

He looked at me, flashing annoyance, then muzzling it. "The hospital's cameras cover the entrances and lobby. They don't have cameras in the stairwells or on the patient floors."

"So, you didn't see anyone who jumped out at you?"

"Not yet. We're still studying the tapes."

"Any other leads?"

He took the same deep breath he always took when he was trying to decide whether to shoot me. "The investigation is ongoing."

"Then I guess we're done here."

"Yeah, we're done," he said, tucking his notepad inside his suit-coat breast pocket. "By the way, Roni, the gun you shot Crenshaw with, you should be able to pick it up in a couple of days. Just come downtown. There'll be some paperwork, but it won't be too painful. In the meantime, do you have another gun you can carry until then if you feel the need?"

"I do, but that's okay. I never shot anything except a paper target until a couple of days ago. I'm still sorting that out. I don't feel like carrying anything right now."

"I know what you mean. All that time on the range doesn't prepare you for the real thing. What kind of gun is it?"

"It's a Ruger LCP .380."

Carter leaned back in his chair. "Really? That is a sweet little gun, fits right in the handbag. Perfect for a woman. I've been thinking of getting my wife one for her birthday. Mind if I take a look at yours?"

Roni's eyebrows shot up, her mouth opening halfway as she sucked in and swallowed a sharp, shallow breath.

I took my cue. "We'll skip the show and tell. I think we've had enough fun for one day."

Carter stood, leaning toward her, using his height to full advantage to pressure her. "Is there a problem, Roni? Some reason you don't want to show me your gun?"

I came out of my chair, wedging myself between them. "What's going on, Carter?"

"I'm just wondering why Roni about crapped her pants when I asked to see that gun."

Roni retreated, scooting against the back of the sofa, grabbing a pillow and clutching it to her chest. "What's he talking about, Jack? What's going on?"

"Detective Carter is playing you. Do you have a permit for the Ruger?"

"Of course."

"Then he knew about it before he walked in the door. Probably ran your name last night, checking for any other handguns you owned if he hadn't already done that on Sunday. Now he wants you to show it to him, but I don't think that's because he's shopping for his wife's birthday present. He thinks it has something to do with Crenshaw's murder, but he didn't hand you a search warrant for the gun. Why is that, Carter?"

He smiled, his lips bloodless. "Why do you think, Jack?"

It didn't take long to figure out why. I glanced at Roni, who refused to look at me. I shook my head and let out a sigh.

"Because you've already got the gun, you know it was the murder weapon, and you wanted to see her reaction when you asked to see it."

Roni doubled over on the sofa. "Oh my God!"

I shot my hand in front of her face. "Not another word."

"C'mon Roni," Carter said, reaching for her arm. "We'll finish this conversation downtown."

He pulled her off the couch and spun her around, cuffing her hands behind her back.

"What's the charge?" I asked.

"We'll sort that out later, but I'd say she's looking at conspiracy to commit murder at a minimum."

The color drained from Roni's face. Her mouth trembled as she blinked back tears. "Jack, please, I never..."

"No talking, Roni. Don't say a word in the car or when you get downtown. I'll have someone there as quick as I can."

"You! I want you to be there!"

"Sorry," Carter said. "Visiting day isn't until Sunday. I guess you should have hired that lawyer after all."

I followed them outside, standing on the curb as Carter put her in the backseat of his car and drove away. Lilly Chase watched from the front porch, arms folded tight against her chest. I started toward her, but she turned, marched into the house, and slammed the door.

Chapter Thirty-two

I leaned against Lucy's car, bracing one hand on the hood as gut-ripping spasms jacked me to my knees and strangled my breath. On the bright side, the onslaught saved me the trouble of kicking myself in the ass for letting Carter blindside Roni.

I should have known better. He wanted to meet at her house. There had to have been a reason, and I should have been smart enough to figure it out or at least ask the questions that would have tipped me off to the trap he set for her. Worse, I'd let him play me, accepting the pat on the head he gave me in front of Lilly Chase like a schoolboy getting a gold star.

No one touched by violent crime is objective because it's impossible to separate our inner lives from what we do. Pressured to clear cases and win trials, cops settle on a suspect, and prosecutors shape the evidence to prove the cops are right. Needing a big fee to pay for the condo in Aspen, defense lawyers pretend it's all about the state's burden of proof and that their client's guilt doesn't matter. Confusing vengeance with justice and passing it off as closure, victims and their families demand immediate arrests and ironclad convictions.

Memories and nightmares of my dead children haunt my inner life, teasing me with second-chance fantasies that always end badly, waking me in a cold sweat. Helping Roni was my way of doing penance, but I'd let my twin burdens of grief and guilt color my thinking, making me give her too much benefit of the doubt, forgetting that I had to give doubt its due. I'd screwed up because I wanted her to be innocent too badly to consider the possibility that she wasn't.

Her lawyer would fashion an explanation for how her gun became the Crenshaw murder weapon. Odds were it would be some variation of the lost or stolen gun defense offered by way of cross-examination of the state's witnesses, denying the prosecuting attorney the chance to dismember Roni in front of the jury.

When I could stand and breathe, I called Kate.

"I need Ethan Bonner's phone number."

"Why, where are you?"

My vocal cords seized, my answer escaping in short staccato bursts. "Somebody used a gun registered to Roni Chase to kill Frank Crenshaw. Quincy Carter just took her downtown."

"What does she say about the gun?"

"She didn't have to say anything. Carter asked to see the gun, and she came apart. I didn't want her to dig a deeper hole, so I didn't give her a chance to explain. Ethan has to get to her before Quincy Carter gets her in a room."

"Okay, okay, I'll call him. Where are you?"

"In front of Roni's house. Tell me where you are, and I'll meet you."

"The way you sound, not a chance. Give me the address, and if you get behind the wheel of that car, I'll break both your legs above the knee."

I gave her the address, the words fighting their way out of my mouth.

"Good," she said. "Now sit tight until we get there."

"Easy for you to say. You're not the one shaking."

"You are a crazy person. Don't move. Oh shit, I did it again," she said, laughing, and hung up.

I slid into the driver's seat of Lucy's car, my inner schoolboy glad that I'd made her laugh. Ten minutes later, Kate pulled alongside, and Lucy brought me up to date as we traded cars.

"Kate interviewed Peggy Martin and says we've got some problems. I'll let her fill you in."

"What about Ellen Koch and Adam?"

"Nobody answered their door. Adam's pickup truck wasn't there, but that doesn't mean the house was empty. I'm going to go back and wait for someone to show up."

"What about Kate? She'll want to talk to them, probably on video."

"We've got to catch up to them first. Besides, we can't run this case around Kate's schedule."

"You're right."

I got into Kate's rental, a flurry of tremors rippling from my waist to my neck.

"I talked to Ethan. He's probably with Roni by now," she said.

"Thanks. Lucy says you have some problems with Peggy Martin."

"I don't have problems; Peggy does. We'll talk about it tomorrow. You're in no shape. I'm taking you home."

I waved her off. "Not yet. We have to find the Martin kids. The longer it takes, the less chance we find them alive."

"How are you going to do that? At the moment, you can't walk or chew gum."

"I just need some down time, an hour or so. If I go home, Joy will handcuff me to my easy chair."

"Where then?"

"Somewhere quiet where I can watch your interview with Peggy Martin and you can tell me all about her problems."

She gave me a long look and a longer sigh. "You know the brain registers negative comments much more strongly than positive comments. That's why it takes five compliments to make up for one shot below the belt."

"Which means what, exactly?"

"That this is really hard for me, but I know just the place."

"Where?"

"My hotel room." My track record with women made me more of a survivor than an expert. I'd managed to screw up my marriage to Joy and scuttle my relationship with Kate. After digging out from the debris, Joy and I were building something that was fragile and undefined but vital. And now, my ex-girlfriend, who was mad enough at me this morning to spit, was escorting me to her hotel room for some quiet time. Who said God doesn't have a sense of humor? I closed my eyes, pretending that I'd been blindfolded and taken hostage.

"Perfect."

Kate was staying at the Raphael on the Plaza, a Spanish Renaissance Revival–style boutique hotel built in the 1920s as an apartment building. A sign next to the elevators offering a special *Romantic Getaway Package* stopped me in my tracks. I looked at her.

"I don't know about this," I said.

"That's what I say everyday when I wake up. I've got video, and Joy's got handcuffs. Your choice."

My legs buckled, making the choice for me. Kate grabbed my arm, keeping me on my feet as the elevator door opened and we stepped inside. Her suite had a bedroom with a king-size bed and a separate living room. She led me into the bedroom, pulled the spread and blankets back, and pointed at the mattress.

"Lie down," she said.

"You're sure?"

"Positive. I've got work to do. Get in bed, close your eyes, and don't come out for an hour, or I'll call Joy and tell her where you are. And take off your shoes."

Chapter Thirty-three

I woke to raised voices coming from the other side of the bedroom door, several people arguing, though I was too foggy to catch who was mad at whom and why. As my head cleared, I heard Kate say something about a video, to which Lucy answered they couldn't wait. Simon Alexander interrupted her, saying he needed more time, and Ethan Bonner complained that his hands were tied until he could get in front of a judge. Someone's cell phone rang, and they got quiet before I could figure out who was on first.

Propped on an elbow, I blinked at the digital clock on the nightstand. I'd been asleep for three hours, long enough to stifle the gremlins living inside my body. My cell phone was next to the clock, a pulsating red light announcing that someone had left me a message. I picked it up. The ringer was on silent.

It took me a moment to remember that my phone had been in my pants pocket when I fell asleep. I was still wearing my pants, which meant that Kate must have heard the phone ring, taken it out of my pocket, and turned the ringer off. I had been in worse shape than I had thought if she'd been in my pants and I never knew it.

I swung my legs onto the floor, turned on the lamp next to the bed, and opened my phone. There were three voice messages, all of them from Joy, matching the three text messages she'd also sent, each a variation on the same theme. *Where are you?*

I'd learned a few things over the years: sometimes, there's no way to answer a question without lying or committing suicide; there are no secrets; and being innocent won't help if you look guilty. All of these things made my return call to Joy a midnight stroll in a minefield.

"Are you all right?" she asked.

"Yeah. It's been a rugged day, but I'm fine."

"You've been gone so long, and I know how hard that is on you. I got worried when you didn't answer your phone."

"I'm sorry. It's been crazy, but everything is okay."

"What happened?"

"Roni Chase was picked up for questioning in Frank Crenshaw's murder. A gun she owned turned out to be the murder weapon. I'm about to go into a meeting with her lawyer."

"Are you at the jail?"

I knew where this was going, and there was nothing I could do to avoid it except make it worse by forcing her to drag it out of me.

"We're at the Raphael Hotel. I'm with Lucy, Simon, and Roni's lawyer, Ethan Bonner, and his jury consultant."

"Jury consultant?" The pitch in her voice changed from concern for me to concern about me. "Who?"

"Kate Scranton."

No woman wants to hear that her man is at a hotel with another woman he used to sleep with, no matter how many other people are there with him. The other woman part is bad enough, but the hotel part lights a fast-burning fuse.

"Are you in her room?"

"Yes. We're all here."

She hesitated, both of us knowing what was coming next. "Why didn't you answer my calls?"

"I needed some down time so I took a nap."

"In Kate Scranton's hotel room?"

"Yeah. It's okay. It's not like that. I promise."

She sniffed, her brittle voice turning the phone cold in my hand. "Will you be coming home?"

"As soon as I can."

"No hurry. Tell Lucy and Simon I said hello."

That was the end of the conversation and the beginning of a

fight we hadn't had since we were married and Joy was certain I was having an affair with Kate. It wasn't true then, at least not in the physical sense, though I'd later learned that was a distinction without much of a difference.

And it wasn't true now, even if I had to admit that my feelings for Kate were percolating again. I'd promised Joy that I wouldn't put her through that a second time, which reminded me of something else I'd learned. A promise to protect can frighten more than comfort.

"So, you're not dead," Lucy said, opening the door. I stretched, rubbed my face, and finger-combed my hair. "Once again, those reports are greatly exaggerated."

She grimaced. "Okay, Mark Twain; in the other room. Believe it or not, we need you."

Simon was sitting in a chair at one end of a coffee table. Lucy took the chair opposite him. Ethan Bonner leaned back in a desk chair. Kate sat on a two-seater sofa that in other circumstances I would have admitted was a love seat. She was holding a laptop, studying the screen and ignoring me. The coffee table was littered with room service remnants surrounding a covered dish.

"It's a club sandwich on toasted wheat bread, no cheese, light mayo, just the way you like it," Kate said without looking up. "And fresh fruit instead of fries."

"Thanks. You've got a good memory," I said, uncovering the dish, picking it up, and looking around the room for another place to sit even though I already knew the sofa was the only option. I joined her, the cushions collapsing toward the center, drawing us closer together. "What do I owe you?"

"Nothing." She finally looked at me, biting back a smile. "Ethan is paying for it."

"Twelve bucks," Ethan said. "Tax and tip included."

"That's what I get for referring a new client to you?"

"You're lucky I'm not charging you a hundred and twelve bucks."

"That bad?"

He nodded. "Tonight it is. I couldn't get Roni out. They're charging her with conspiracy to commit murder. She's being arraigned in the morning. The judge will probably grant bail, but she doesn't have any money so she may be a guest of the county for a while."

"What do they have on her besides the gun?"

"You mean the murder weapon? If I had a nickel for every time Quincy Carter called it that, I could post Roni's bail. He's hanging his hat on the gun and the disturbance he says she created at the hospital, or as he puts it, the diversion she caused to set up the shooter."

"That won't stand up if she's got an explanation for the gun."

"If she has one, she isn't saying, not even to me. She's covering for someone, and Carter figures to pressure her into giving him up. We'll see if a night in the tank does the job. In the meantime, it would help if you have any idea who she's protecting."

"Best bet would be Brett Staley. He's in love with her, and she thinks she might be in love with him. Maybe she is. Odds are he knew about the gun. He showed up at the hospital right after Crenshaw was killed. Said he was looking for her. Carter questioned him, but let him go before he cut Roni loose."

"Where do you fit into the mix?" Bonner asked me.

"Didn't Roni tell you?"

"I'd rather hear it from you. See how it matches what she told me."

I gave him the rundown, ending with Roni's story about her fight with Brett and how Quincy Carter worked Roni and me, my face reddening as I told that part of the story.

"And that's why I think she's covering for Brett."

"Why would he kill Frank Crenshaw? What's the connection? Did he know Crenshaw? Did Crenshaw owe him money? He'd have to have a reason unless he's a psychopath that roams hospitals looking for someone to shoot," Bonner said.

"I don't know if he's got a connection or, if he does, what it is, but Roni should know."

"She shot Crenshaw the first time. Maybe she meant to kill him and her boyfriend decided to finish the job for her."

"I was there. That was self-defense. He was her client. Why would she want him dead?"

"I'm better at questions than answers," Bonner said. "I keep asking them, hoping someone else will do the rest. Your version fits with Roni's story, except she didn't say anything about an ATF agent. What was he doing at the hospital?"

"There was a gun show in Topeka last month. Thieves followed one of the dealers before he got home and robbed him. They got a small armory of handguns and assault rifles. Frank Crenshaw shot his wife with one of the stolen handguns. If the ATF agent wasn't interested in that, he needs to find another line of work."

"We don't know if Crenshaw's murder was related to the theft of the guns or to something else," Bonner said. "We need to know more about Brett Staley's relationship with Crenshaw. Right now, the only reason he's a suspect is that it looks like Roni is covering for him. Maybe if you go with me in the morning, she'll open up, tell us about the gun. She seems to trust you."

"Not enough," I said. "She didn't tell me about it."

"She'd have had no reason to tell you if she didn't know the gun was missing or that it was used to kill Crenshaw," Bonner said.

"She'd have had less reason to tell me if she did know."

"Her arraignment is at ten. They'll have her at the courthouse by nine so I can talk to her. Can you meet me there?"

"Yeah, but I don't know how much that will help."

"Why not?"

"Roni may not want to be rescued."

Chapter Thirty-four

"Well, no one is going to rescue her before she's arraigned," Bonner said.

Lucy jumped from her chair. "And no one is going to rescue Peggy Martin's kids if we spend all night sitting around here talking about goddamn Roni Chase!"

"Take it easy, Lucy," I said. "We've got to be able to do more than one thing at a time."

She crossed her arms, glaring down at me. "No, we don't, Jack. I can't and I won't. You don't have to help Roni. She can find someone else to do that, and Ethan doesn't have to represent her. The court will appoint a lawyer for her if she can't afford one. She may be in jail, but she's got a roof over her head and isn't scared to death that someone is going to rape and murder her at any second. So, no, I'm not going to do more than one thing at a time until I find those kids, and I need to know that you aren't either."

"I'm on this case to the end, but I've got to help Roni too."

"Jack, you can't save everybody. Sometimes you have to choose."

"Babe, we're doing the best we can," Simon said.

Lucy flung her arm at him. "What is that? You're telling me this is the best we can do? We haven't done shit! Those kids are out there somewhere, and Jack's taking a nap while we ordering fucking room service, for Christ's sake!"

Simon stood, taking her hands in his, his voice low and soothing. "We're doing what we know how to do. We could run out of here screaming into the street, but we'd still have to do the same things. Dig up leads and run them down, talk to witnesses, stir things up until we get a break. If there was a faster way, we'd do it."

They were a mismatched pair, filling each other's gaps. She was a head taller, street savvy and full of fire. He was a round-shouldered numbers guy, a grinder sifting through digits and data looking for a thread to tug on until he unraveled the truth. She took a deep breath, leaned down, resting her forehead on the top of his head.

"They're just babies." He put his arms around her. "And we'll find them."

She turned away and went into the bathroom, coming back a moment later, eyes red but composed. She settled into her chair, rubbing her hands on her thighs.

"So," she said, "what's next?"

"The video," Kate said. She was standing next to a flat-panel television parked on top of a dresser. "This TV has a USB port. I connected my laptop so we can all watch. Let's have a look at Peggy Martin."

Peggy's image filled the thirty-two-inch screen. Her face was drawn and washed out by hours spent waiting in the cold and wind at Kessler Park. We watched in silence as she talked about her children, her marriage, and her husband, Kate not offering any commentary until the video ended.

"First time through was for context," she said. "Now let's take a look at a few key moments. The first is when she talks about her children. See how her mouth turns down, her eyes scrunch up, and her cheeks sag? That's agony."

"What else would you expect?" Lucy asked. "Her husband kidnapped her kids."

"Her kids are missing," Ethan Bonner said. "That's all we know for certain."

Lucy threw him a poisonous look and started to say something, but Kate cut her off.

"The agony is important because it may indicate that she didn't kill her children. If she had, she'd show signs of shame, like she did here."

Kate fast-forwarded to the moment when she asked Peggy if Jimmy's allegations that she'd had an affair were true. Peggy looked down and away, nodding her head, her voice breaking as she muttered her confession.

"Classic expression of shame," Kate said.

"It makes sense that she's ashamed," Bonner said.

"Agreed. It's not unusual for a spouse to be ashamed of cheating, no matter how big a jerk the other spouse is and, having spent an hour with Jimmy today, he is that big of a jerk. The question is whether she has other reasons for being ashamed besides her cheating heart."

"When you asked her who she was fooling around with she wouldn't tell you," Bonner said. "What do you make of that?"

"My best judgment? Revealing her boyfriend's identity would only make things worse. Could be he's someone Jimmy knows, which would make his feelings of betrayal and her shame even worse, maybe unbearable."

"If it was like that, if she was fooling around with Jimmy's best friend or someone else he was close to," Simon said, "it's more likely that he would snap and do something to the kids to punish her."

"Or," Bonner said, "Maybe she's afraid her boyfriend had something to do with her kids' disappearance. That would give her a double dose of shame. She says she left them alone in the house while she went to the store to get some milk. Her boyfriend might have had a key. The kids might even have known him and let him in the house."

Lucy let out a sigh. "It gets worse. Peggy says that when she left the kids that morning that she went to the Quik-Trip on Independence Avenue to buy milk. I talked to the cashier who worked that shift. He remembered her because she's a regular. He says she bought beer, not milk."

Bonner leaned forward in his chair, rubbing his hands together. "I like it. I like it a lot. This has the makings of a fine defense."

Lucy sprang to her feet. "You unholy asshole! That's all you care about! Throwing a load of shit against the wall, hoping enough of it sticks to get your fucking client off!"

Bonner leaned back in his chair. "I'm as worried about those kids as anyone in this room, but I don't have the luxury of being self-righteous and sanctimonious like you do, Lucy. I owe my client the best defense I can give him, and that means I've got to make sure the jury knows that someone besides Jimmy Martin could be guilty."

Hands on hips, she snarled at him. "This morning you were all about how Jimmy has only been charged with theft and contempt, not kidnapping and murdering his kids. So why are you trying so hard all of a sudden to defend him against something he hasn't been charged with? Did he confess? Are you hiding behind the attorney-client privilege and just using us to build a defense when you know he's guilty because, so help me God, if I find out you are, I'll put you in the ground."

Kate was studying Bonner with freeze-frame eyes, a look that could read bar codes a mile away. I needed time alone with her, to ask her what she saw in Bonner's expressions. He ignored her, giving Lucy a tight-lipped smile.

"It's been a while since someone threatened to kill me for doing my job. Bet it happens to you all the time. I bend a lot of rules because I think they're bullshit, but I won't breach my client's confidence because if I do, he's done and I'm done."

"Even if it costs Evan and Cara their lives?" Lucy said.

"Let me put it this way. I won't help Jimmy commit a crime, but I won't turn him in for one he's already committed."

"I couldn't live in your world," Lucy said.

"Okay, okay," I said. "Let's step down to DEFCON Three. Bonner, I know you can't tell us if Jimmy confessed. But if there's a chance that Peggy's boyfriend had something to do with this, we need to take a look at him, and if you know the boyfriend's name, now would be a good time to tell us. At least that way, we could try to rule him in or out."

Bonner pursed his lips, searching for the limits of the attorney-client privilege. "Okay. You don't think I hadn't thought of the boyfriend angle? First thing they teach you in criminal defense school is to give the jury any suspect except the defendant, and Peggy's boyfriend, whoever he is, makes an easy target. I pushed Jimmy to tell me, but all he said was that he'd take care of it himself."

"The guy has pride," Simon said, "even if it's the ugly kind."

"So, he knows or thinks he knows," I said. "If Kate's right about why Peggy is so ashamed, we need to find her boyfriend, and the best place for us to start is with Jimmy's friends, assuming he has any."

"There`was one person he mentioned several times," Bonner said, flipping through a legal pad filled with scrawled notes, looking up from the page. "Guy's name is Nick Staley. That name mean anything to anybody?"

Chapter Thirty-five

Nothing happens in a vacuum. We go through life, content in the belief that our little corner of the world is a gated community, that outside our limited circle of family and friends no one much cares or notices what we do. Politicians and celebrities are criticized for living in a bubble, a closed atmosphere impervious to reality. But the truth is we all live in our own bubbles, ignoring the ripples we create until we bump, trip, or stumble into someone else's world, the bubbles burst, and the ripples well up, becoming shock waves.

"Nick Staley owns a little grocery store on St. John," I said.

"You live in Brookside," Simon said. "Since when do you buy bread on St. John?"

"I don't. Staley has a son named Brett who works at the grocery. He's also in love with Roni Chase."

"Six degrees of separation," Simon said. "Which one was in a movie with Kevin Bacon?"

Lucy scooted to the edge of her chair. "Jack, you can talk to Roni, find out if her boyfriend knows anything, maybe get her to make an introduction to Nick. That way you can come at him without him being on guard. He might open up or at least let something slip."

"So now it's a good thing I'm helping Roni?" She sat back, arms crossed. "If it'll help find those kids."

"It's worth a try," Kate said. "If you show up at his grocery store and ask him if he's sleeping with Peggy and, oh by the way, did he kidnap her kids, he might clam up in spite of your considerable charm."

"Bonner," I asked, "have you talked to Nick Staley?"

He shook his head. "No."

"Why not?" Lucy asked. "You said you'd already thought of the boyfriend angle."

"I left him a couple of messages, but he didn't call back. I tried catching him at the store, but missed him. The kid I talked to must have been his son."

"Mid-twenties, blond, chinstrap beard, pierced eyebrow. Spends a lot of time in the gym and wants you to know it," I said.

"All that and an attitude to match. Asked me for ID, wouldn't tell me when or if Nick would be back or how I could get ahold of him. When I told him I represented Jimmy Martin, he acted like he'd never heard of him, which didn't register with me until now. If his father and Jimmy were buddies, you'd think he'd have been more helpful."

I thought of Roni, how her family's history connected her to the Staley and Crenshaw families. She was third-generation Northeast. It made sense that her roots were entwined with so many others who lived there, loyalty and suspicion of outsiders strengthening the ties. She'd been reluctant to talk about Frank Crenshaw even after he killed Marie and took a shot at her, asking me if I was a cop and questioning why I was trying to help her.

"If Roni won't talk about the gun that was used to kill Frank Crenshaw because she's covering for Brett Staley, there's not much chance she'll help me run a scam on her boyfriend's father. I'd rather Kate and I talk to Nick and leave Roni out of it. Besides, there's another possibility."

"What?" Bonner asked.

"You tell him, Kate."

"Today at the lake, there was another mother, Jeannie Montgomery. She's been looking for her son, Timmy, for two years. He and the Martin kids lived in the same neighborhood. We have to consider the possibility that their disappearances are connected."

Bonner straightened, taking a sharp breath. "You're talking a serial killer that goes after little kids?"

"That's one theory," I said. "I asked Adrienne Nardelli if she had any evidence of that, and she ducked the question. That was reason enough to get it on my radar."

"Great, that makes us worse off than we were," Bonner said. "We go from a boyfriend suspect with real potential to looking for a creep who snatches kid without leaving a trace. How am I supposed to sell that to a jury?"

I looked at Simon. I'd left him a message asking him to dig up what he could on the Montgomery case. "You make any progress?"

"Let's start with the big picture," Simon answered. "According to the Justice Department, in one year they studied, roughly eight hundred thousand kids under the age of eighteen went missing, which worked out to about twenty-one hundred a day or one child every forty seconds. Family members snatched a couple hundred thousand of them and a non-family member but known to the family took another sixty thousand. Classic kidnappings by strangers accounted only for a hundred and fifteen cases."

"The numbers don't add up," Bonner said. "There are over a half million kids left out."

"That's because they're still missing. No one knows what happened to those kids. Even if you extrapolate the statistics to include them, a serial kidnapper killer is way down on the probability scale."

"What about other kids from the area that have gone missing?" I asked. "I'm working on that, but the odds are still against a serial killer."

"Someone once told me," I said, "not to confuse the improbable with the impossible."

"And my statistics professor taught me to trust the numbers especially when you are short on time and resources."

"Tell that to the people who get washed away every spring by the annual hundred-year flood. Bring it down to these two cases. Did you find anything to connect them?"

"The kids went to the same school, and the families belong to the same church."

"Which means they could have come in contact with some of the same people. Anything else?"

"The public record on the Montgomery case is thin, a few stories after Timmy went missing, the usual stuff, appeals to the public for help, follow-up stories that are a rehash. What I need is a look at the files the police put together."

"I don't think Adrienne Nardelli is going to take us into her inner circle, but I've got a call in to Ammara Iverson at the FBI. She might be willing to help."

Bonner stood. "So it looks like we've got a plan. Jack and I will talk to Roni in the morning. Jack will have a go at Nick Staley and, maybe, the feds will throw him a bone. It's getting late, and I'm getting old. I'm going to go home and go to bed."

Lucy grabbed her purse. "You coming?" she said to Simon.

"Where?"

"To see if Peggy Martin's helpful neighbors, Ellen Koch and Adam, are home yet. They can't stay out all night."

"It's almost ten. Can't this wait until tomorrow?" he asked, regretting the words as soon as they left his lips, Lucy slicing and dicing him with a raised eyebrow and a tight, down-turned mouth, not saying a word. "Forget I said that. I'm right behind you."

"Well," Kate said after they left, "I guess it's down to you and me."

I was standing in the middle of the room. She rose from the sofa, closing the distance to half an arm's length, putting herself in easy reach.

"It's down to you. I'm overdue at home."

"Let me drive you."

I shook my head. "Joy left me three voice messages and three texts while I was asleep. I called her back so she knows I'm here, which is bad enough, but having you drop me off is no way to end my day."

"What about tomorrow? If I'm going with you to see Nick Staley, how will you manage that?"

"I thought you had to get back to San Diego."

She smiled. "I moved some things around and bought a few days. I hope I made the right decision." I got lost in her eyes. "I'll take the bus to the courthouse and meet you there."

"Funny, isn't it? There's nothing going on between you and me, but the three of us are acting like there is. I lured you to my hotel room. You're itchy just being here because Joy is jealous, and we're scheming how we're going to be together without her knowing about it. The past has a long half life, and we're living it—again."

"I'll tell Joy everything, and you didn't lure me."

"Then why not let me drive you home and pick you up in the morning?"

I didn't answer, not certain what I really would say to Joy, if anything, knowing that she'd react the same to the truth, a lie, or silence.

She studied me, nodding. "It doesn't matter, does it? I lured you, and I'm not certain why. You hurt me, and I've been angry with you for a long time. I tried to stay with the anger all day, but I couldn't."

"Well, at least the day wasn't a total loss. You got me in your bed."

She smirked, smacking me on the arm. "Smartass! All the good it did me. You didn't even budge when I took your cell phone out of your pocket."

"Better that I didn't."

She dipped her chin, then raised her head, sweeping her hair to one side. "Yeah. I know. It is what it is."

"Joy is a good..."

She interrupted, putting her palm on my chest. "Person. I know, and so are you and so am I. Good people make life harder. You can't hate them forever, and you can't forget why you loved them. You won't have any trouble getting a cab. They're always lined up across the street at the Intercontinental Hotel."

"One question before I go?"

She crossed her arms against her chest. "Of course. I forgot that you're always on the job."

"You had Bonner under the microscope tonight. Is he lying about what he knows?"

She shrugged. "What can I say? He's a lawyer. They all lie."

Chapter Thirty-six

I entered the code on the garage door keypad when a car came to life across the street, pulling into my driveway as the door rose, high-beam headlights blinding me, a replay of the gun dealer robbery. I pulled my gun from its holster, holding it at my side as I backed into the garage.

"Put your gun away, Jack. It's me, Ammara. I'm getting out of the car, so don't shoot me."

The passenger door opened, and she stepped out, her lean frame familiar but not enough to put me at ease since I didn't know who was behind the wheel or why she'd shown up like a thief instead of an old friend.

"Kill the lights."

She motioned to the driver, who cut the engine and the headlights. I blinked, clearing the starbursts from my eyes as the driver's door opened. The driver, burly and broad shouldered, a ball cap pulled down over his brow, stepped out, using the door as a shield. I guessed he was holding his gun out of sight, waiting to see what I would do.

"Jennings," Ammara said, "put your fucking gun away before I tell Jack to shoot you. This isn't a raid. And, Jack, please put your gun away too, before this ATF asshole ruins our friendship."

I slipped my gun into my jacket pocket. Ammara walked toward me, her arms open, embracing me as a round of shakes rocketed from my belt to my chin, buckling my knees. She leaned into me, bracing her body against mine until the shakes passed. I didn't know whether to be pissed or embarrassed so I settled for both, pulling away when I could stand on my own.

"Don't expect me to say I'm glad to see you. Why didn't you call, give me some notice?"

"Wasn't up to me. Jennings and I came by a couple of hours ago. Joy told us you were out and she didn't know when you'd be home. She made it clear she wasn't in the mood for company. The message you left said you were in a hurry for information and, it turned out, Jennings was in a hurry too, so we decided to wait in the car. While we were waiting, he asked me about the stories he'd heard about you, about what happened at the Bureau and with Wendy. I told him the truth, but I didn't think he'd pull something like this."

"Guy's a jerk, lighting me up like that."

"Yeah, but now he's your jerk. He's running the investigation into the stolen guns you asked me about."

Ammara was near my height, all lanky muscle from her college days playing volleyball. I looked over her shoulder as Jennings stepped toward us.

I had asked her for help, giving a thumbnail sketch of the two cases I was working and a quick summary of what I needed, some of which I figured she'd have to get from ATF. When she reached out, odds were that Jennings had reached back with his own wish list. Nobody in law enforcement gives anything away for free, pissing matches over pride and turf too often leaving everyone with nothing to show for it except wet shoes. This was shaping up the same way.

I was still twitching, my left shoulder jerking up and down, alternating with my bobbing chin. Jennings watched me with curious eyes as if I were a magician and he was trying to figure out my sleight of hand. Ammara said he'd heard the lingering rumors at the FBI. People from DC to KC still believed that the shakes were a scam I'd used to duck the indictment I deserved for covering up Wendy's involvement in the drug ring, and that her death was more convenient than tragic. It didn't matter that Ammara had told him the truth. He came at me the way he did to see how

I'd react, testing the rumors against his own eyes before deciding whether to work with me.

"Satisfied?" I asked him.

"Yeah. Sorry about that, but I had to see for myself. Braylon Jennings, ATF," he said, his hand extended. "Can we go inside and talk?"

I ignored his hand. I didn't blame him for testing me, but that didn't mean he wasn't an asshole.

"I don't want to wake my wife." Ammara stared at me with raised eyebrows. "Ex-wife. Forget it. It's complicated, but whatever we've got to talk about, we'll do it right here. You first, Jennings: what do you want from me?"

He tilted his head to one side, weighing the advantages of going first or last, giving in with a sigh. "Ammara says you're interested in the robbery of a gun dealer last month?"

"That's right."

"Why?"

He knew the answer but wanted to hear me say it. I'd passed his first test, and it was time to take another.

"I was having lunch yesterday at LC's Bar-B-Q when a guy named Frank Crenshaw used one of the stolen guns to kill his wife. A woman named Roni Chase was with Crenshaw and shot him but didn't kill him. She went to the hospital last night to see how he was doing, but somebody killed him before she could say hello. The cops say Crenshaw was killed with a handgun registered to her. She's being arraigned in the morning, and I'm helping with her defense."

"You were there when it happened, when Crenshaw shot her?"

"You know I was, so what's the bottom line?"

He nodded. "We're interested in Crenshaw, how he came into possession of that gun."

"I'll bet you are. Too bad someone killed him."

He cocked his head, uncertain whether I was sympathizing with him or yanking his chain.

"What do you know about that, about Crenshaw getting

popped in the hospital?"

I shook my head, stuttering as another round of shakes twisted my vocal cords. "Not much. The cop sitting on Crenshaw's door left his post long enough for the shooter to get it done."

"Roni Chase, what's your relationship with her?"

I took a few breaths, enough to stabilize my voice. "I told you. I met her yesterday at LC's. She's in trouble, and I'm helping her out. What's your interest in her?"

"I'm interested in those stolen guns. She did Crenshaw's books. She was with him when he killed his wife. She shot him and then shows up at the hospital when Crenshaw gets popped. You was me, you'd be interested in her too."

"What else?"

"What do you mean, what else? The stolen guns, that's it."

"Which means we're back to bullshit. You haven't asked me one thing you didn't already know. I assume you were the ATF agent at the hospital last night. Quincy Carter was all over Roni until you showed up. Next thing I know, he's gone, you're gone, Brett Staley's gone, and Roni gets to go home. If you're so interested in her, how does that happen?"

Jennings shot a quick glance at Ammara when I mentioned Brett's name. "You want to help Roni, work with me and maybe I can help her and you."

"Work with you, how?"

"Give me your cell phone."

He added his name and number to my contacts and tossed the phone back to me.

"Anything you get on the stolen guns, I hear about it, including anything you get from Roni Chase. Doesn't matter who it involves or what it is, it comes to me. I call you, you answer. You don't put me on hold, you don't promise to call me back. We tell you to wear a wire, you wear a wire."

He was giving orders, not asking for suggestions, but he didn't own me, at least not yet. Going along was a promise I'd decide later whether to keep.

"Understood. You think Roni knows something about the guns, or do you want to use me and her to get to Brett Staley?"

This time, he held his poker face, making me wish Kate were here to read it for me.

"I'm saying Roni Chase's life can get real complicated. You want to help her, I'm telling you how."

"And what do I get for being your butt boy?"

He looked at Ammara again, nodding.

"Copies of the files on the Martin and Montgomery missing children," she said.

"I need those files, but that won't help Roni."

"Sorry, Jack, it's the best deal I could get. Half a loaf, you know what I mean."

"How does an ATF hump get copies of missing person files?"

"He didn't get them. I did. KCPD asked for our help on both cases. Jennings made the deal with our new SAC, Debra Williams, and I'm stuck with it."

I looked at Jennings. His face was flat, impassive, a brick wall shutting out further negotiations until I had something more to offer than cooperation. He and Adrienne Nardelli were dealing from the same deck. Knowledge was power. They had it, and I needed it.

"When do I get the files?"

"Right now," Ammara said. "They're in the car."

"Who do I deal with? You or asshole?"

She shrugged. "Asshole."

"Hey!" Jennings said. "I'm standing right here."

"Exactly," I said. "Give me the files."

"One last thing," he said. "You tell anyone about this, our deal is off and Roni Chase goes away."

The lights were off when I walked in the house, lurching on uncertain legs, bracing myself against walls, countertops, and furniture. Roxy and Ruby were fast asleep, back-to-back, in their doggie bed on the kitchen floor. I left the files Ammara gave me on the kitchen table, my brain too fogged to make sense of them.

When Joy moved in, she took the bedroom that had been Lucy's. We didn't start sleeping together for a couple of months, and when we did, it was for comfort, sex one of the last things to come back into our relationship and then, only occasionally, given her condition. We were intimate in other ways, though, that held us together, knowing that we were sharing the last months of her life with one another.

Even then, we didn't sleep together every night. It wasn't something we discussed or negotiated. There were times one of us needed the other, and there were times we needed to be alone. We just let it happen as if that part of our life had an identity and will of its own, sometimes going a week or more together or alone as our uneven rhythms dictated, Joy keeping her clothes and toiletries in the other bedroom and bath.

Climbing the stairs, seeing the door to her room closed and mine open, I understood why she wanted it this way. She'd lost too much—our children, our marriage, and the certainty she'd be alive from one day to the next—to trust the future or me enough not to need a place of her own.

Chapter Thirty-seven

I don't get misty-eyed when I walk into a courthouse, kvelling over the nobility of the law. I've learned that justice is more myopic than blind, judges working crossword puzzles at the bench while jurors sleep through trials and lawyers stumble over closing arguments buzzed from a three-martini lunch. I've seen suspects do the perp walk one day and the freedom walk the next, their fate a commodity traded among plea-bargaining prosecutors and defense counsel like baseball cards at an autograph show.

In spite of all that, I was knocked back when I stepped off the bus and saw Roni Chase standing on the steps of the Jackson County Courthouse flanked by Ethan Bonner and Kate Scranton, waving to me, her smile so wide I could count her molars. I looked around. Cars passed back and forth on Twelfth Street in front of the courthouse. People flowed around me on the sidewalk. A pushcart vendor was setting up shop offering bagels, pretzels, and brats. A northbound bus stopped at the intersection of Twelfth and Oak, people getting on and off, the bus pulling away in a sooty cloud of diesel exhaust. Braylon Jennings emerged from the fog, tipping his ball cap at me before turning and walking away, letting me know that he'd made good on his end of our deal and, PS, now he owned me. Roni skipped down the steps, threw her arms around me, and planted a sloppy kiss on my cheek.

"Oh my God, Jack! Can you believe it? They dropped the charges! I didn't even have to go in front of the judge! I don't know how to thank you for getting me such an awesome lawyer!"

Bonner took his time, ambling down the steps, not offering a high five. We exchanged looks, his full of questions, mine saying don't ask me.

"Quincy Carter called me this morning," Bonner said. "Told me they were dropping the charges."

"Any explanation?" I asked.

"None, but Carter said not to get cocky because things could change. My guess is the prosecuting attorney didn't want to get too far ahead of himself. If he moves on Roni before he's ready to go after the shooter, he's got to turn his evidence over to me in discovery. He might be afraid that could hamstring him."

"You don't buy that," Kate said. "Your face is full of doubt. Your eyes are too narrow to see your shoes, and your brow is doing a Cro-Magnon crunch."

He took a breath. "No, I don't buy it. I didn't let them interview Roni, so they haven't even heard her explanation about how the killer could have ended up with her gun. Hell, Roni hasn't told me either. Any other case, the cops would threaten her with spending the rest of her life doing remakes of *Chained Heat* to get her to confess and cooperate. I'm good, but this doesn't make sense. If I didn't know better, I'd say somebody fixed something."

"What do you think?" Kate asked me.

Braylon Jennings was working a simple robbery, but he had enough juice to kick a murder suspect to the curb. That the thieves had made off with a cache of guns didn't change the standard criminal justice calculus. Murder trumps theft every time unless they are tied together. Frank Crenshaw had been murdered while lying in a hospital bed waiting to be charged with killing his wife, and nothing reorders a desperate wounded man's priorities like a death sentence. If Crenshaw had something to offer the cops besides a guilty plea, killing him was the only way to make certain he kept quiet.

Then everything came together. Jennings suspected that Brett was involved with the robbery of the gun dealer, that he'd sold one of the guns to Frank Crenshaw and killed him so that Frank couldn't give Brett up in a deal to avoid a death sentence. And,

NO WAY OUT

when Roni's gun proved to be the murder weapon, Jennings and Carter figured that Roni was covering for Brett.

If they were right, Brett would assume that they cut Roni loose because she made a deal, forcing him to try to shut her up just as he had Crenshaw. Jennings had tossed Roni out like chum for the sharks and told me to look the other way while Brett measured her for her funeral dress. The only thing I could do to make things worse for Roni was to open my mouth. She'd be charged again and be just as vulnerable whether she made bail or sat in a cell waiting for someone to do someone a favor.

"I think we shouldn't look a gift horse in the mouth."

"And I'm not going to," Roni said. "Yeech, look at me. I need a shower and clean clothes. Can somebody give me a ride home?"

Bonner raised his hand. "I'm in the lot across the street."

"Hang on a minute. Roni, we need to talk," I said, taking her by the elbow until we were out of earshot.

"What is it?"

"This isn't over."

Her face clouded. "Of course it is. They dropped the charges."

"For now. Quincy Carter isn't Santa Claus. He can arrest you again."

"Why? I didn't do anything wrong."

"Then tell me what happened to your gun. Did you loan it to someone? How did Crenshaw's killer end up with it?"

She folded her arms across her chest, her lips tight. "It's over, Jack. You don't have to save me anymore."

"Why do you think Frank Crenshaw was killed?"

"I don't know."

"Well, I've got a good idea. The gun Crenshaw used to kill Marie was one of a bunch of guns stolen from a gun dealer. Crenshaw probably didn't know that when he bought the gun, but his killer couldn't take the chance that Crenshaw would give up whoever sold him the gun."

"I don't know anything about the robbery."

"I'm not the one you have to convince."

168

"The police don't think I'm involved or else they wouldn't have let me go. So, who do I have to convince?"

"Frank Crenshaw's killer. If he thinks you made a deal with the cops, he'll come after you."

She took a step back. "You're just trying to scare me."

"That I am. Where's Brett Staley?"

"Brett? What's he got to do with this?"

Her voice jumped an octave, her brows arching and eyes widening. I glanced over my shoulder. Kate had moved to the steps and was watching us. She had a clear angle on Roni's face. I'd wanted to keep our conversation private but welcomed Kate's read.

"An innocent person would have told your lawyer or me or the cops what happened to your gun. A half-smart but guilty person would at least come up with a plausible lie. But you're stonewalling—acting like you didn't even hear the question, which is a piss-poor way of covering up for someone. So tell me, what happened to your gun?"

She looked at the ground, turned away, and then looked at me straight on, teeth clenched.

"I didn't do anything wrong."

"Did you give your gun to Brett?"

Her eyes were on fire. "No."

"Did he steal it?"

Her shoulders sagged for an instant. She took a breath, straightening her spine, holding her head up.

215

"How should I know? I didn't know it was missing until Detective Carter told me someone used it to kill Frank."

"Is that why you freaked when Carter asked you to show him the gun? I thought you were going to crawl inside the sofa pillow and hide."

"Carter scared me, that's all."

"Did Brett know Frank Crenshaw?"

"What difference does that make? If that makes him guilty, they'll have to arrest the whole neighborhood because everybody knows everybody."

"Have you seen him since we were at the hospital Sunday night?"

"No, but he called me yesterday morning to see if I was okay."

"Does he know you were arrested?"

"Grandma Lilly told him. I called him as soon they let me go."

"Did he say anything about your gun?"

"He didn't answer. I left him a message."

"I want you to go home, stay home, and stay away from Brett until this is over."

She raised her hands to her shoulders, ready to push me away. "Look! I'm going home to clean up and see my mom and grandma. Then I'm going to my office to see if I have any clients left who can pay my fees, and if I want to see my boyfriend, I'll see him."

"So now he is your boyfriend? Listen to me, Roni."

"No, you listen to me, Jack. I've known you for two days. I appreciate how you helped me out, but back off. Go find someone else to rescue."

She strode past me, arms at her sides, fists clenched.

I waited until she and Bonner were at the curb. "Hey, Roni!" She stopped, turned, and glared at me. "What now?"

"The moon is pink."

Chapter Thirty-eight

Jennings called my cell before they were out of sight, his way of letting me know I was on a short leash.

"What?"

"What did she tell you?"

"Nothing."

"Don't fuck with me, Jack."

"You're not my type."

I snapped the phone shut. Jennings had made a huge investment in this case—cutting deals with the FBI and KCPD, conscripting me, and risking Roni's life. The question was why he would lay so much on the line for a case that was a blip in the news cycle. Not that gun-dealer robberies and hospital-bed murders weren't cases that had to be solved. They were. It's just that they weren't bet-your-career cases. If Jennings's gamble didn't pay off, his would go south with the case, meaning he'd stay on me or make certain someone else did.

Kate waited until they reached Bonner's car. "So are you going to tell me what that was all about?"

"I pissed her off."

"I had no idea except that you transformed her from bubbly to boiling. What did you say to her?"

"I told her this wasn't over, and she didn't believe me, kept saying she didn't do anything wrong. I asked her what happened to her gun, and she wouldn't tell me. The only straight answer I got was when I asked her if she gave the gun to Brett and she told me flat-out no. When I asked her if he could have taken it, she bobbed and weaved, said how should she know."

"She avoided eye contact and touched her mouth and eyes a lot which are classic deception gestures. There was one time she did look you in the eye. Was that when she told she didn't give the gun to Brett?"

"Yeah. Said it like she meant it."

Kate shrugged. "Could be she's telling the truth."

"Could be? I thought you were the deception expert."

"It's not like on television. One glance and aha, she's lying or she's telling the truth. It's more nuanced than that. I have to have a baseline from talking to her or observing her or watching her on video before I can be more certain. Some people are better liars than others, and some people come across as lying because they're afraid they won't be believed."

"Well, one thing is for certain. She knows more than she's telling me."

"Or she thinks she does and she's afraid she might be right. How strong is her relationship with Brett?"

"She says he's in love with her but she's not so sure how she feels about him. They've been together a long time, since they were kids, really, but she comes across as more resigned than committed."

"What makes you say that?"

"We were talking about their relationship yesterday. She said they were comfortable, and I told her she didn't have to settle for that, but she acted like she did, said that Brett was all she had."

"Sounds like she's put too much in the relationship to let it go even if she'd be better off without him," Kate said.

"Seems likely."

"And now she's making bad decisions because of that, maybe passing up better options without realizing it."

Her voice was loaded with the unmistakable sardonic tone of *can you believe anyone could be so stupid?*, the message clear. She wasn't only talking about Roni and Brett. She was talking about us. I didn't want to go down that road and pretended not to notice.

"She told me to butt out, leave her alone."

"She fired you?"

"Sort of. I don't think you can fire someone you never hired and who works for free."

"Which means you won't leave her alone. That's called stalking."

"I'll get Ethan to defend me. He's good at getting people off, no questions asked."

"I'll give you that. What about the phone call?"

"What call?"

"The call you got right after Roni left."

"It was nothing."

She sighed. "Fine. We both know you're lying.

Your face was twisted like a man possessed the instant you answered your phone. You pulled it back together, but the expression was there long enough for me to see it. If that was nothing, I'd hate to see you when it's something."

"I thought you didn't make snap judgments."

"About Roni Chase? No. But you're another story. I know you."

"Don't thin-slice me." The words came out like razors, the look I gave her just as sharp.

It was an old argument, one that had burdened our relationship from the beginning. Kate couldn't help what she saw, and there were too many times I didn't want to be seen. She had no difficulty keeping her observations to herself when she was working, disclosing them as her professional obligations required. It was different with us, she said, love giving her a license to care and share. We had struggled to find a balance between her need to know and my need to hold back.

"Fair enough."

She bit her lip, turning away, making my stomach churn, the hurt in her voice a reminder that time and distance hadn't healed the raw places that drove us apart or buried the sweet spots that had brought us together. She was trying to help me, and I'd returned the favor by jumping her because I was angry at Jennings and Roni.

"I'm sorry. That was uncalled for. I can't talk about it right now, but I'll tell you when I can."

She gave me a soft half smile, nodding. "It's okay. I forget that you're like one of those Chinese boxes full of hidden compartments."

"And I forget that you can't resist taking them apart and putting them back together again, a perfect combination for driving two people nuts. Looks like we're picking up where we left off."

"I know. And," she said, pausing and taking a deep breath, "while we're at it, how'd it go with Joy last night?"

I shuddered, a mild flurry. "It didn't. She was in her room with the door closed when I got home, and the door was still closed when I left this morning."

Kate raised her eyebrows. "Separate bedrooms?"

"When she needs the space."

"What do you call that?"

"I don't know what to call it. It's not what it was when we were married or when we were first divorced. All I can say is that we're feeling our way."

"Are you in love with her?"

I hesitated, searching for the right words, saying things out loud that I'd struggled to piece together in my mind.

"Crazy, can't wait to see her, rip her clothes off, suck all the air out of the room in love? No. Build a life, laugh and cry, retire and die love? Not that, either. Help each other through the night because we can't do it alone and that's all we've got left and we owe it to one another. If that's being in love, then yeah."

"I'd call that noble and a little bit sad, but I'm not sure I'd call it being in love."

"I'm not saying you're wrong. I'm just saying that's what it is."

"And you're willing to settle for that for the rest of your life?"

I smiled, shaking my head. "It's not my life we're talking about. It's Joy's, and she's dying. The cancer has spread, and there's not much the doctors can do about it except to tell us to think in terms of months, not years."

Kate paled, her hand at her throat. "Oh, my God. I'm so sorry, Jack."

"Like you said before, you don't walk away from someone you

care about even if you have a good reason."

"Well, that's enough to make me feel heartless, rotten, and small."

"Me too. So you get my point."

"Yeah, I get it, but you could have told me, you know, before I made a complete ass of myself." I nodded. "I could have, but I didn't know how to fit it into..."

"Into what?"

"Us."

She thought for a moment, staring at me. "Duty always comes first for you, doesn't it, Jack?" I took a deep breath. "Yeah."

"And what comes next, when you've done your duty?"

"It seems like I never get that far."

"I hope you get the chance to find out. You deserve that. At least your night ended uneventfully."

"Depends on your point of view. Ammara Iverson was waiting for me with copies of the KCPD files on the Martin and Montgomery cases when I got home."

"Another gift horse about which I don't ask any questions and you don't tell any lies?"

"You catch on quick."

"Okay. Where are the files?"

"At home. Lucy is going to pick them up this morning."

"What's in them that we don't already know?"

"I haven't had time to go through them. I'll let Lucy and Simon pick them apart. Let's go grocery shopping."

Chapter Thirty-nine

Staley's Market was near the intersection of St. John and Monroe; a thirty-foot brick and glass storefront shielded by wrought-iron bars, the name spelled out in flickering purple neon stretched across the center panel, flanked by promises of everyday low prices, fresh produce, and cold beer painted in twelve-inch red and yellow script. The aisles were empty, no cashiers ringing up sales, no baggers offering paper or plastic, and no shoppers sorting coupons. A hand-drawn notice was taped on the door, papering over the hours of operation, announcing the market was closed, out of business, impossible to tell which was cause and which was effect. An American flag hung limp from a bracket bolted into the frame.

The lights were off, but there was enough daylight to illuminate narrow aisles of canned goods, cereals, snacks, detergents, lightbulbs, toilet paper, and toothpaste. Refrigerated and frozen cases lined one wall; meat, poultry, and produce the other. Three abandoned check-out lines stood at the front. Powerball tickets offering billion-to-one odds against turning a dollar into fairy dust were looped around spindles next to the registers alongside packages of cigarettes and copies of the *National Enquirer*. I tried the front door, pounding when it wouldn't open.

A man appeared at the back, his head visible over the top of a swinging saloon door, a fluorescent ceiling fixture shedding cool light behind him. He hesitated before easing one side half open, his arm tucked under the apron hanging from his neck. He edged into the store like he was testing thin ice, taking his time getting to the front, his hidden hand gripping something at his waist as he turned the lock and opened the door a crack.

"Looking for Nick Staley."

"That's me, but I'm closed."

He was an older, battered version of his son.

"We saw the sign. You're out of business?"

"You saw the sign. What? You think I'm kidding?"

"Not kidding, just maybe not yet. We don't want to buy anything."

"Neither does anyone else. Not enough, anyway. If you're from the bank, tell them I've got a guy coming to give me a bid on the inventory and fixtures. Tell them they'll get some of what I owe but not all of it. They want to come after me for the rest you tell them they're wasting their time. I'm walking away from here without a pot to piss in. There's nothing they can do to me that hasn't already been done."

I tried pulling the door open, and he raised the hand under his apron, the barrel of a gun outlined against the thin fabric. I stopped, the hard cast in his eyes telling me he was willing. The iron bars testified to the rough neighborhood and hard times, so it was no surprise that he was cautious. The surprise was that he felt threatened by Kate and me.

"You won't need that. We're not from the bank, and we're not armed." I opened my jacket, lifting it above my waist and turning around. "My name is Jack Davis. This is Kate Scranton. We're working with a lawyer named Ethan Bonner. He represents a friend of yours, Jimmy Martin. We'd like to talk to you about him."

He took his time, chewing his lip, making up his mind before motioning to the rear of the store. "We'll talk in the back."

Half-empty shelves confirmed that Staley was going out of business. What merchandise he had wouldn't last a week. I could guess what happened. As his customers got laid off, they stopped buying as much, making it hard for him to stay current with the bank. Roni said he'd diverted rent money from his real estate, but it wasn't enough, forcing the bank to cut off his credit and his suppliers to cut off their shipments and his mortgage lender to foreclose. No customers, no credit, no groceries, no future, a personal pandemic of economic ruin repeated all across the country.

There was a small warehouse on the other side of the saloon door, empty wooden produce crates scattered on the floor, a folding table and chairs butting up against a sloppy pyramid made of overturned cardboard boxes. A calendar hung on one wall advertising a different power tool each month, and a radio sat on a three-drawer file cabinet tuned to an oldies station, the volume low, music mixing with static.

Staley turned the radio off, settled into a chair, and folded his arms across his chest. He had a fighter's face, his forehead layered with scar tissue, his nose crooked and squashed, the look of a man who'd given as good as he got, the split decision written in his washed-out eyes.

"I don't know nothin' about Jimmy's trouble."

"Which trouble?" I asked him.

"What d'ya mean?"

"Jimmy is in a lot of trouble. Which trouble are you talking about?"

"I heard he got busted for stealin' some copper off a construction site. I don't know nothin' about that, and if he's got his tit in the wringer some other way, I don't know nothin' about that neither."

"But you do know Jimmy."

"I know him."

"How?"

He shrugged. "He's from Northeast, I'm from Northeast. Both of us were in the Marines. You live here long enough, you know people. "

"You guys asshole buddies? Get drunk, chase women, play poker?"

He cocked his head, one corner of his mouth turned down and sour. "Shit. I know him, that's all."

"How about his wife, Peggy? You know her?"

He shifted in his chair, uneasy coming back to center. "Seen her around. Same as him."

"You ever see Peggy when Jimmy wasn't around?"

"What are sayin'?"

"She ever come into the store by herself?"

"Now and then. Most everybody in the neighborhood came through here one time or another. Or they did until everything went into the shitter. Now most of the stuff left on my shelves is past the sell-by date. Nobody's got any money. I don't know whose food people are puttin' on their table, but it sure as hell isn't mine."

"Yeah. It's tough all over. Peggy Martin, you get close to her?"

He laughed. "That's what this is about? Jimmy tell you I was bangin' his wife? Even if I was, what's that got to do with him rippin' off that construction site?"

"Were you banging his wife?"

He shook his head, smiling. "Not that I couldn't have if I'd have wanted some of that. Peggy, she gets around. Least that's what Jimmy said; why they split up."

"Jimmy told you why they split up? I thought you and him didn't hang out."

"We might've had a couple of beers now and then. Run into each other at the Jigger, a bar over on Independence Avenue. Lot of the locals get pickled there on Friday nights."

"When was the last time Jimmy and you talked about his wife?"

He pursed his lips, rubbed his chin. "Hell, I don't know for sure; probably a month or so ago. What's this about?"

"Jimmy tell you who he thought his wife was seeing?"

"Said he wasn't for sure but someone was going to pay."

"What do you think he meant by that?"

"Christ, who knows what a man means by anything he says when he's drunk."

"You say that everybody knows everybody around here. You hear any talk about who might have been Peggy's boyfriend?"

He shrugged. "People talk a lot, mostly about stuff they don't know nothin' about."

"We could use a name."

"What's that got to do with Jimmy gettin' busted?"

"No one has seen Jimmy's kids in three weeks. The police think he kidnapped them, maybe even killed them, to punish Peggy. If she has a boyfriend, we want to talk to him, find out if he knows anything about the kids."

He sighed. "I heard about the kids. That's tough, real tough. I wish I could help you. All I can tell you is that Peggy's got a big appetite; you know what I'm sayin'. A woman like that' will do most anything."

"Jimmy's sitting in jail instead being out on bail because he won't answer any questions about his kids. You think he'd hurt them?"

"No way. Man loved his kids. Talked about them all the time. Told me he'd never let Peggy have them and that he was going all out for custody."

I pointed at his belly. "What is that under your apron? A .38?"

He smiled, patting the gun. "Nine-millimeter, man's best friend."

"We scare you that much?"

"These days, mister, getting out of bed in the morning scares me."

Chapter Forty

"That must be a hard way to live," Kate said.

He grunted. "I've had it worse."

She leaned forward. "I can't imagine how."

"I did two tours in the first Gulf War, made sergeant. When I got out, I joined the Guard, figured to pick up a paycheck for one weekend a month and two weeks in the summer. Got sent back to Iraq after 9/11. Spent a year dodgin' IEDs and snipers. Watched a lot of my men get blown apart."

"Is that where you broke your nose?"

He rubbed it with the palm of his hand. "Nah. Did some boxin', local Golden Gloves and when I was in the Marines."

She smiled, knowing that most people can't resist the impulse to reciprocate, the instinctive response building rapport and trust. She made it impossible, using her entire face, eyes lively, cheeks full and raised, mouth wide, framing her perfect gleaming teeth, adding a casual *aren't you something* toss of her hair. His smile came in a flash with a soft blush—primal brain circuits picking up the subtle signal she intended loud and clear.

231

"You risk your life serving your country, come home, build a business, and then lose it because a bunch of greedy Wall Street speculators drive the economy off a cliff. I can see how that would make a fighter like you so angry he couldn't see straight."

He pulled himself up to the table. "You got that right, lady."

"But I don't understand how that would scare a man who's survived two wars so badly he'd go around hiding a gun under his apron." Staley started to rise, his eyes narrow, his jaw tight as she reached across the table and wrapped her hand around his wrist. "Tell us, maybe we can help."

He pulled his wrist free, his voice a low growl. "We're done here."

"Almost," I said, keeping my seat. "What's Brett going to do now that you're closing?" I asked him.

He stiffened. "How do you know Brett?"

"Met him yesterday at Roni Chase's office."

"Roni? What's she got to do with Jimmy's case?"

"Nothing, as far as I know. I'm helping her with something else. Where's your son?"

"What do you want with my boy?"

"Did you know Frank Crenshaw?"

He nodded, dropping into his chair.

"Sure, I knew him."

"What do you know about his murder?"

He glanced from side to side, breathing deeply, touching his hand to his temple and letting it slide across his jaw.

"Brett called and told me about Roni shooting Frank, and then I saw the rest of it on the news about Frank getting killed at the hospital." He clasped his hands, setting them on the table, arms extended. "I been telling Brett since he was old enough to listen that those Chase women are nothing but trouble, starting with the old lady, Lilly. No reason why Roni was gonna turn out any different."

"Did Brett know Frank Crenshaw?"

"Yeah, he knew him."

"They ever have any problems, get into any arguments?"

He sat up. "Hey, what are you saying? You come in here accusing me of screwing Jimmy Martin's wife, and now you're all but saying my boy killed Frank! You got some nerve, mister!"

"Did you know that Brett came to the hospital right after Crenshaw was murdered and that the police questioned him?"

Staley shook his head, dipping his chin. "No. He didn't say

nothing about that."

"When was the last time you saw your son?"

He let out a long breath, looked away, coming back and staring through us. "It's important," Kate said. "Please."

"Sunday night," he said, looking away.

"When?" I asked.

"Late, close to midnight."

"Where?"

He fell back against his chair, dropping his hands in his lap, resigned. "Here. I was finishing up the inventory, what's left of it. The bank wanted it last week, but I figured, what the hell, what are they gonna do if I turn it in late, you know what I'm saying?"

"Was he helping you take inventory, or did he just happen to show up while you were here?"

"I should've been home in bed, but I haven't been sleeping much. Figured might as well get the inventory done. Beats the hell out of lying in bed, listening to my wife snore."

"What was Brett doing here?"

He sat up, reddened again, gripping the edge of the table, spitting his words. "Money. He wanted the cash we use to start the day. Said there was no point in leaving it lying around on account of we were out of business."

Kate reached across the table, covering his hand with hers. "You walked in on him, didn't you? Caught him stealing the money?"

He ducked his head again and then lifted his eyes to meet hers, his face twisted, his voice thick. "Yeah."

"What did you do?" she asked.

"I asked him, 'What's the money for? Why didn't you just ask me for it?' But he wouldn't tell me, just said he needed it, that's all."

"Did you let him have the money?" she asked.

He looked down and away. "No. I smacked him in the mouth and threw him out. Haven't seen or talked to him since."

"Did Brett ever talk about someone named Cesar Mendez?"

Staley spat. "Fucking greaser gangster."

"You know him?"

"He comes in the store."

"Where's Brett live?" I asked.

"Shitty little rental house in Sheffield."

I handed him the notepad I carried. "Write it down and give me a number where I can reach you. I'll call you when I find him. Did he say anything about Roni, about buying her funeral dress?"

"Him and that damn dress! Worst thing that ever happened to my family was Vivian Chase getting herself shot. Ever since that night, the Chases and the Staleys been stuck with one another. Roni tell you about that?"

"She did. Said your father was the one who delivered Vivian's funeral dress to the funeral home."

"My old man," he said, shaking his head again, "he's what they call a real romantic. Loved to tell how he fell for Lilly Chase that night, right on the spot, but she wasn't interested in him or any other man as far as that goes. But Pop kept after her, sending flowers, writin' her poems, waiting for her after school until she took a shot at him one day and he finally got the message."

"He ever get over her?" I asked.

"Pop was the kind of man who fell for pretty girls, especially if they were in trouble, and, if they were in enough trouble, they'd fall for him 'cause he was as loyal as a puppy dog, stick with them through thick and thin. Lilly had plenty of trouble, but she was the kind who handled it on her own, just like her mother. Now my mother was a different story."

"How's that?"

"When Pop fell for her, she said yes, but she spent the rest of her life convincing him he was a fool to have asked her 'cause she was more trouble than Pop bargained for."

"How'd things work out?"

"They're both gone now, so I guess it don't matter talking about it. She was a lot like Peggy Martin in her day. Tore Pop up, her running around on him, but he kept his mouth shut all them years, looked the other way. Not me, boy. First fight I ever got in was over somebody calling my mom names. Now Brett, he's got a lot of his

184

grandpa in him. Been telling me he's in love with Roni since he learned to talk, but she treats him the same way Lilly treated my Pop, only difference is she hasn't taken a shot at him."

"What about your son? Can you think of any reason he would take a shot at Frank Crenshaw?"

"No, sir. That's one thing I can tell you for sure. Brett would never have killed Frank."

"Why not?"

"Because Frank was family. My mom was Elizabeth Crenshaw, Frank's aunt. He was my first cousin and was like a father to Brett when I was overseas. You find Brett, you tell him to come home, tell him I'm sorry. Tell him we'll figure something out."

Chapter Forty-one

Nick Staley let us out, locking the door and retreating to the back of the grocery. He'd lost his business, and now he was scared he'd lost his son, learning the hard lesson that sometimes the only thing that makes you feel better about bad news is worse news and the news about his son was not likely to get better. Brett's relationship with Frank Crenshaw was as likely to be proof of guilt as proof of innocence. Murder in the family was the oldest of crimes.

There were a lot of reasons Brett could have needed money badly enough to steal it from his father, but there was one at the top of my list. He wanted to get out of town, hopefully before he fitted Roni for her funeral dress. Unrequited love is no match for the survival instinct. If Brett thought Roni made a deal with the cops to pin Crenshaw's murder on him, love would turn to rage in a heartbeat.

I called Roni, but she didn't answer, meaning she was probably screening my calls. I left her a message warning her again to stay away from Brett, knowing she'd ignore that too.

I surveyed the block, taking the pulse of a neighborhood on life support. Traffic was light, a handful of cars passing, no one stopping, no foot traffic going in and out of the cleaners, liquor store, or shoe repair shop that occupied the rest of the block, the storefronts on the other side of the street dark.

We were still on the sidewalk when a tricked-out Lexus, with gold-rimmed wheels, windows tinted midnight, slid to the curb behind Kate's rental. A lanky brown-skinned kid stepped out, hands in the pockets of his jacket, the collar turned up. Even with his tattoos covered, I recognized Eberto. He slammed the car door, looked at me like I wasn't there, and tried the grocery's door.

"Read the sign, Eberto," I told him. "They're closed."

He looked at me, this time remembering what happened on the bus, glancing over his shoulder at the Lexus, caught between a locked door and a middle-aged white guy who'd punked him once already, and whoever was behind the wheel, no-man's land for a would-be gangster. He rattled the door a second time, pressing his face against the glass. I followed his eyes. The light in the back was off. I couldn't see Staley but was certain that he was watching from the shadows, the reason he was hiding a gun beneath his apron now clear.

My working theory had been that Brett was in on the robbery of the gun dealer and had given his cousin Frank one of the guns. It was just as likely, maybe more likely, that Brett was the middleman when Crenshaw bought his gun, dealing with someone who knew that business a lot better than Brett, someone who wouldn't hesitate to force Brett to clean up loose ends like his cousin and girlfriend as the price for his life, someone like Cesar Mendez.

Brett had told Roni that Mendez was a regular customer at the grocery. The question was who was buying and who was selling. If Brett was on the run, he might be running from the cops and Mendez, Northeast's small world shrinking fast.

"Like I said, they're closed. There's nobody there. What do you want?"

Eberto went to the Lexus. The driver's window slid down, and Eberto leaned in, talking across the driver to the person in the front passenger seat. Bits of Spanish I didn't understand drifted back to me. The passenger door opened, and out stepped a man, late twenties, tall, broad, and hard, copper skinned, with buzzed head, leather jacket, and a slit-eyed look that straightened Eberto, sending him backpedaling to the grocery, yanking on the door to prove that he wasn't lying about it being locked.

I whispered to Kate, "Get in the car, now."

"You must be joking," she said. "You don't speak Spanish. I do."
"Swell."

"You're welcome." I caught Eberto's eye.

"Aren't you going to introduce me to your boss?" The kid looked like he'd been pimp slapped, his head spinning from me to the other man. I turned toward the man who'd stepped out of the car. "You must be Cesar Mendez."

"Who the fuck're you?" he said.

"Jack Davis."

"Name don't mean shit to me."

"Wouldn't be healthy if it did."

"You a cop?"

"Not anymore."

"What about her?" he asked, pointing at Kate.

"I'm his driver," she said.

The rear doors on the Lexus opened, and two of Mendez's boys got out, flanking him, jackets open, gun butts sticking out of their jeans. Mendez slow walked toward Eberto, the boy's lower lip trembling. Mendez threw his arm over Eberto's shoulder, peppering him with questions in Spanish, Eberto mumbling his answers.

I glanced at Kate, whispering. "Can you hear any of that?"

She kept her eyes on them, her voice soft. "Enough. He asked Eberto how you know his name, and Eberto said something about seeing you on a bus. Does that make any sense?"

"Yeah. You'd be surprised the people you meet on public transportation."

Mendez finished with Eberto, closing the distance between us, rolling his shoulders and shaking his arms loose as he walked, warming up.

"Eberto says you pulled a gun on him. That right?"

"Fuck Eberto. He's a punk. Hassles old men and mothers with small children."

Mendez smiled. "And you run him off. What's that make you, Superman?"

"Makes me nothing I wasn't already."

"You and your driver gonna run me off?"

"Not that we couldn't, but that wouldn't do either of us any good."

He laughed, curious but not afraid. I was on his turf, and he had the numbers and the guns. If it hadn't been for Eberto, he'd have probably ignored us and gone on his way. I was being enough of a smart-ass to pique his interest.

"What good you gonna do me?"

"I don't think either one of us came here to buy groceries. I think we're after the same thing."

"What's that?"

"Not what. Who. Brett Staley."

He shrugged. "Don't know him."

"Sure you do. The two of you did business. Probably a little weed, maybe some blow. Then one day, Brett says, hey, cousin of mine wants to buy a gun, can you hook him up, and you say show me the money. Deal goes down, nothing special, just business. You're selling enough dope it doesn't even register. Then Brett's cousin uses it to kill his wife, and it turns out the gun you sold him was stolen from a gun dealer last month and the ATF is all over that case like stink on shit and your boy, Brett, who you know is such a pussy he'll flip on you the minute the cops say put up your hands, is in the wind. So you've got to find him, make sure that doesn't happen, or you'll end up doing the warden's laundry instead of cruising around in that fine-looking Lexus."

He listened, his face smoldering, turning away without comment when I finished, heading back to the Lexus, his boys following him, one of them opening the car door for him as he gave me a last look.

"I'm headed to Brett's house in Sheffield," I told him. "You can follow me and we'll talk some more, unless you've already been there."

"You know," Kate said after they pulled away, "you sounded like a crazy man."

"I don't care what I sounded like, what did he look like?"

"Well, I don't have a baseline . . ."

"Kate, I don't have time for a baseline lecture. I'll take whatever you've got."

She folded her arms, taking a deep breath and nodding her head. "Okay. You're right. Quick and dirty. I'd say you hit him where he lived. He flashed fear when you talked about the ATF. And he agrees with you that Brett is a pussy. I'd say you're on to something. Not bad for making that story up on the fly."

"I only made part of it up on the fly, but it fits with what we know. And, it explains why Nick Staley is carrying a gun and why he's so worried about Brett. It doesn't explain why Frank Crenshaw wanted a gun so badly he'd get it on the black market. I wonder what scared him."

"He was losing control of his life. His business was falling apart. The gun may have been his way of reasserting control, of feeling strong again," Kate said.

"One dick in his pants wasn't enough?"

"Either that or he was planning on robbing a bank."

"Thank you, Dr. Phil," I said.

"Look, we didn't come here because of Frank Crenshaw or Cesar Mendez. We came here because of Evan and Cara Martin. I'm beginning to think Lucy is right. You keep trying to work both cases and you'll end up going off on tangents without solving either one."

"Then you weren't paying attention when we talked to Nick."

"Are you kidding? He's lost everything. He's scared of whoever might knock on his door, and he's worried about his son."

"How do read his relationship with Jimmy?"

"He's trying to minimize their relationship, but a lot of people do that—pretend they hardly know someone who was their best friend for life until they get arrested. Who wants to claim a crook?"

"I agree. After what happened with his parents, I don't think he was fooling around with Peggy Martin, so we can cross him off our boyfriend list."

"So what's next? Are you really going to drag me to Brett's

house? How much longer can you keep juggling these cases?"

"As long as I have to. Brett's house is a low priority. If he was hiding under the bed, Mendez would have found him."

"What then?"

"I need to borrow your phone."

"What's wrong with yours?"

"Dead battery."

"Tell me the truth. It's easier."

"Okay. No."

She handed me the phone. "I appreciate your honesty. It's so refreshing. And, after you finish your call, do I get to go on a scavenger hunt?"

"Absolutely."

"Where do we start?"

"Peggy Martin's house."

"Why there?"

"Most trouble starts at home."

Chapter Forty-two

Braylon Jennings wanted me on a short leash. That's why he entered his number in my cell phone last night and made an appearance outside the courthouse this morning. Odds were he was also listening in on my calls. If I stopped using my phone, he'd get suspicious, but that was no reason to let him know everything I was thinking. I walked to the corner, keeping my call to Ammara Iverson private.

"I need a favor."

"Jack, don't. I've given you everything I can. You need something else, you'll have to deal with Jennings."

"We both know that Jennings will screw me the first chance he gets. But I can handle him. I just need room to maneuver."

She sighed. "What do you want?"

"Whatever you've got on Cesar Mendez. He runs a gang in Northeast, Nuestra Familia."

"Where's he fit in?"

"They do drugs, which means they do guns."

"So do a lot of people."

"But Mendez is the only one who's looking for Brett Staley."

"Should I ask you how you know that?"

"Probably, next time we have dinner."

"You'll buy. Why is Mendez after Brett?"

"Frank Crenshaw was Brett's cousin. Brett's father owns a grocery in Northeast, and Brett works for him. Mendez was a regular customer; they knew each other. Best bet, Brett hooked Crenshaw up with Mendez, and Mendez sold him the gun he used to kill his wife."

"Which you think Mendez stole from the gun dealer?"

"Bingo. And, when Quincy Carter and Jennings make that connection, they'll be all over Mendez. But, if Brett is too dead to testify against him, Mendez skates."

"That doesn't help Roni Chase unless you can prove Mendez stole her gun too."

"It's a start. Right now, Mendez is at one end of this thing, Roni's gun is at the other, and Brett Staley is in the middle. I've still got a lot of dots to connect."

"Pretty hard not to put Roni's gun in Brett's hand. Makes him a man without much to lose. You made a deal with Jennings. You should take this to him."

"He has enough clout to get the charges against Roni dropped so he can use her as a moving target, hoping that whoever killed Crenshaw will come after her. I'm not telling him anything until I've got this nailed down and I know that she's in the clear."

"Jennings is going to be pissed if he finds out you're holding back about Mendez."

"That assumes Jennings doesn't already know about him. Gangs, drugs, and guns are the ATF trifecta. If I'm right, a lot of this has gone down on Mendez's turf. He has to be on Jennings's short list."

"Then why did he draft you?"

"When I know the answer to that question, I'll start talking to him. Until then, I need your help."

She was silent for a moment. "Okay. I'll do what I can, but watch yourself."

There are a lot of ways to get from dawn to dusk. Most people lean forward or fall back, trading modest risk for nominal gain, hoping to break even when they cash in. Then there are the outliers, the people who hit the gas, turning into a swerve with a wild-eyed grin or who assume the position at birth, ducking whatever life throws at them. I'd spent most of my life in the first group, leaning into punches when I couldn't avoid it. But the shakes changed all that, forcing me to learn how to tap dance on a tightrope, solid ground the only thing that made me uneasy.

"Don't worry. I always do."

Chapter Forty-three

Peggy Martin didn't answer her door or her phone. Her car wasn't on the street or in the garage. There was no mail in her mailbox, and there were no newspapers piled on her driveway. She was out but not gone. Across the street, Ellen Koch watched us from her front window, drawing the curtain when I started toward her house.

"You wanted to talk to her," I said to Kate. "Find out why she showed such contempt for Peggy. Might as well be now."

We rang the bell, and she opened her door a crack, the chain keeping us out.

"May we come in?" Kate asked.

"What for?"

"We'd like to talk with you about Peggy. You've been such a great help to her through all of this."

"I'm worried about her kids. Anyone would be."

"But not everyone would do what you've done. There are people who don't think Peggy is a good mother. They blame her for what happened and use that as an excuse not to help. You're not like that."

Ellen studied us for a moment, removing the chain and opening the door. "It's not those poor kids' fault. They didn't choose their mother."

She led us into the kitchen, warmed her coffee and offered us a cup. "All I've got is decaf."

"Perfect," Kate said. "The caffeine makes me too jumpy."

Kate was in her element, reading Ellen, making a connection, turning it into an invitation. She'd done it with Jimmy Martin and Nick Staley, both times sucker punching them. I made myself part of the scenery, wondering whether she'd do the same to Ellen.

"Me too," Ellen said. "Keeps me up at night."

"My son is almost as old as Adam. He's what keeps me up at night."

Ellen stirred her coffee, eyes on the rising steam. "I know what you mean."

"There's a lot of talk about Peggy, about her being unfaithful. I imagine you must have heard that."

"People talk."

"The police think her husband may have been so mad at her for cheating on him that he did something to their kids to punish her. What do you think?"

She looked up. "Jimmy Martin has a temper on him, that's for sure. And, he's a hateful man. Never said a kind word about anybody that wasn't White, and that's a hard way to be around here with all the Blacks and Mexicans and the other immigrants. Seems like he was mad most of the time, and he and Peggy fought like there was no tomorrow."

"So, you wouldn't be surprised if he did something to his kids."

"Oh, no. I'd be shocked if he laid a hand on them. He has a lot of ugly in him, but every time I saw him with his kids, he was nothing but a good father. One look at them kids and he was a different man."

"Then why do you think he won't help the police find his children?"

"I don't know," she said, looking away. "Maybe he knows they're okay and he doesn't want to let Peggy have them."

Kate reached across the table, covering Ellen's hand with hers. "If you believed Evan and Cara were safe, you wouldn't have raised the money to hire Lucy Trent or organized the volunteer searches, and you wouldn't have been at the lake yesterday."

Ellen raised her head, her eyes moist. "You never know for sure about someone. You try to find the good in them."

"Did you see Jimmy the day the kids disappeared?"

"No. Like I told the police, I didn't see anybody or anything."

"It's possible Jimmy had nothing to do with the kids' disappearance. It's possible that someone else who had access to the house and who the kids knew well enough to let inside may have taken them. Can you think of anyone like that?"

"No," she said, her gaze aimed at the floor. "Nobody I knew of."

"Peggy admitted she was having an affair but wouldn't tell us with whom. We need to talk to her boyfriend. The kids could have let him in, and he could have taken them. Do you know who she was seeing?"

Ellen sagged, shaking her head. Kate squeezed her hand. "I think you do know. I can see it your face.

There's nothing more important than saving Evan and Cara. Please help us."

Ellen withdrew her hand, clutching her arms around her chest.

"It wasn't his fault. He's a good boy, and she's old enough to know better, but she kept after him."

"Who?"

Her chest heaved. "Adam."

"Peggy was having an affair with your son?"

Ellen turned away, crying. "She's nothing but a damn whore! Threw herself at my son. I found out a couple of months ago and made him break it off."

"Did he stop seeing her?"

She shook her head. "He says so, but I don't know."

"Where's Adam?"

"He left a while ago. He didn't say where he was going."

My cell phone rang. It was Lucy. There was a door in the kitchen leading to a small, bricked patio. I waited until I was outside to answer.

"Did you pick up the files?"

"Yes. Simon and I have been going through them all morning."

"Anything?"

"Timmy Montgomery and the Martin kids went to the same school and the same church."

"We knew that. What else?"

"There's a list in the Montgomery file of all the Sunday school teachers at the church and the older kids who helped out in the classroom. One name jumped out; a teenager who was assigned to Timmy's class."

"Who?"

"Adam Koch."

"You and Simon were going to try to catch up to him and his mother last night. Any luck?"

"No. The house was dark. We rang the bell, but no one answered so we waited outside for a couple of hours before Simon made me go home. And, get this. I called the church to find out if Adam worked in either of the Martin kids' classrooms, and he didn't. Turns out that the church gave him the boot a year after Timmy Montgomery disappeared. It seems that a parent complained he'd gotten too friendly with a little girl."

"Did the police question him about the Montgomery boy?"

"Yes, but it was a perfunctory interview, covering the bases. They talked to all the Sunday school teachers and staff, asking them if they'd seen any strangers hanging around the church or the neighborhood, stuff like that. He was never considered a suspect."

"What about the parent's complaint?"

"There's nothing in the file about it."

"Makes sense. The complaint was a year after Timmy's disappearance. No reason for anyone at the church to make a connection and call the police."

"You're right. Only reason I found out was that the church secretary likes to gossip. When I asked her about Adam, she couldn't wait to tell me."

"Did you get the name of the parent who complained?"

"Yeah. I'm going to see her later this afternoon. Where are you?"

"On Ellen Koch's patio. Kate is inside talking with her. She told us that Adam was having an affair with Peggy. He left the house this morning, and she doesn't know where he went. Peggy isn't home either. I'm going to have a look around. If he killed the Montgomery boy, he may have kept souvenirs."

"Timmy's file says he was wearing blue shorts, a *Harry Potter* T-shirt and flip-flops when he was last seen. Any of those would qualify."

Chapter Forty-four

When I came back in the house, Ellen and Kate were still at the kitchen table, Kate holding her hand, their heads bent close together, Ellen apologizing, Kate granting absolution.

"Mrs. Koch," I said, "do you mind if I look around Adam's room?"

She raised her head, red, puffy eyes popping with panic. "Why?"

"The police will want to talk with Adam. It will help if we can tell them we didn't find anything to connect him with Evan and Cara disappearing."

She hesitated, looking at Kate for reassurance. Kate nodded. Ellen surrendered with a weak shrug and quiet consent. "Top of the stairs."

"Thanks. This will only take a minute. Kate will stay with you."

Adam's room looked like any other teenager's, moguls built of dirty clothes, muddy jeans on top on one of them, rose from the center of the floor, his bed unmade, his closet a tangle. I sifted through his clothes and dresser drawers, flipped his mattress and looked under his bed without finding a thing.

The hallway outside his room led to a bathroom, which revealed nothing more incriminating than a brown bathtub ring. The other bedroom was Ellen's. Unlikely as it was to yield anything, I did a quick search, coming up empty. I headed for the stairs until I noticed a pull-down panel in the hallway ceiling. When I opened it, a rickety wooden cross between a stairway and a ladder unfolded to the floor.

The stairs led to the attic, pink insulation stuffed between two-by-fours, plywood laid over floor joists, a bare bulb hanging from the ceiling. I turned on the light, scanning the dim empty space. Straddling the joists, I lifted one of the plywood panels, finding a laptop computer half-buried in insulation.

There was enough juice in the battery to boot it up. I clicked on the Internet browser, not surprised that it wasn't password protected, teenager logic dictating that a good hiding place beat a password every time.

I knew what I'd find even before I opened the hard drive, flashing back to a time too many years ago when Joy, Kevin, Wendy, and I were living in Dallas. A neighbor had offered to give Kevin a ride home from school. When Kevin didn't come home, Joy went to the neighbor's house to look for him. The door was unlocked, a treasure trove of child pornography spread on a table. He killed Kevin and himself as the police and I closed in on him.

Adam's computer was loaded with hundreds of the same kind of images. I pulled up the other plywood panels. Lodged deep in the insulation beneath one of them was a soft package bound with yellowed newspaper. I unwrapped it, confirming what I felt in my bones. It was a child's bloodstained *Harry Potter* T-shirt.

I set the T-shirt next to the laptop and called Adrienne Nardelli, told her where I was and what I'd found.

"I'm on my way. Put my evidence back where you found it and don't touch another thing."

Kate and Ellen had moved to a small sofa in a den cluttered with half-finished knitting projects, a crucifix on the wall above the television. Ellen was leafing through a family album, Kate oohing and aahing at Adam's baby pictures, shielding Ellen a while longer from the storm about to rain down on her. They looked up as I walked in the room.

"Mrs. Koch, the police will be here in a few minutes. Do you have any idea where Adam is?"

She went pale, cradling the photo album to her breast. "Why are the police coming? What did you find?"

"Did Adam know a boy from your church named Timmy

Montgomery who disappeared a couple of years ago?"

She melted into the sofa, the photo album sliding from her limp arms onto the floor, muttering. "Oh, no, oh, no, oh, no."

Kate looked at me, eyebrows raised, her question obvious. I answered it with a quick nod. She turned toward Ellen, gently rubbing her shoulder with one hand, holding Ellen's with the other.

Parents' worst fear is that something horrible will happen to their child. They cannot imagine the flip side of the nightmare, how much worse it would be if their child committed a terrible crime, especially against another child. Ellen's response spoke to the suspicion, guilt, and fear she harbored about her son, worries she had spent years tamping down with denial, unable to face them and her own failings as a mother. Her world, built on thin reeds of self-deception, was collapsing.

I understood now why she had led the neighborhood search efforts for Evan and Cara and raised the money to hire Lucy. Knowing that Adam was sleeping with their mother, suspecting him in Timmy Montgomery's disappearance, she had to find them, if only to hold on to her sanity. Hating Peggy Martin was her last lifeline, giving her someone else to blame for the child she could face only in her darkest moments.

"Adam hid something in the attic that might have belonged to Timmy. What do you know about that?"

She folded forward, rocking slowly back and forth, shaking her head without answering.

"Ellen," Kate said. "Adam is in trouble, and he needs our help. It will be easier for him if Jack finds him before the police do."

She sobbed and shuddered, forcing deep breaths into her lungs until she could speak.

"He was out all night and wouldn't tell me where he'd been and wouldn't tell me where he was going when he left again."

"There's a pair of muddy jeans on top of a clothes pile in his room. Is that what he was wearing last night?"

"He tracked mud all over the house. I cleaned it up this morning, but I told him I wasn't going to wash his clothes."

If Adam had spent the night digging in the dirt I had a good idea what he was doing and where he was doing it.

"Kate, I need the car keys."

"Where are you going?"

"To find Adam. I need you to stay here with Ellen until the police come. I'll be back as soon as I can."

She straightened, ready to argue, but let the moment pass and handed me her keys. "Do you know what you're doing?"

"I get lucky every now and then."

Chapter Forty-five

It was easy and irresistible to convict Adam of Timmy Montgomery's murder. The church connection, the parent's complaint to the church, the child porn, and the bloody T-shirt marked a straight line from delinquency to a death sentence. But resisting the irresistible is what separates good cops from sloppy cops.

I would wait until Timmy and the rest of the evidence that was buried with him was unearthed. I would wait until Adam confessed or didn't, until he pled guilty or not and a jury extracted the truth from the witnesses and exhibits.

If Adam had killed Timmy, the chances that we would find Evan and Cara alive had all but evaporated, a child predator's habits one of life's sad and predictable patterns. His affair with Peggy Martin may have been nothing more than an escalation of his perverse sexual fantasies: screw the mother, then kill the kids. And, if it was, their bodies wouldn't be far from Timmy's.

Adam had lied to Kate about having been in the woods above North Terrace Lake before yesterday. If that's where he'd buried Timmy Montgomery, he couldn't take the chance that crime scene investigators would find the body, and there was no way for him to know whether they'd be back today for another pass. They were careful and thorough, the odds of them finding something they weren't looking for too great for Adam to risk.

It was a problem with a simple solution. Dig up Timmy's remains and find them a new home before the police did it for him, meaning he had to dig in the dark when no one was looking. But there would be proof: fresh dirt where it didn't belong, trampled undergrowth, overturned rocks, the sort of thing a disorganized, immature teenage killer would ignore.

I found Adam's pickup on Cliff Drive in the same spot where he'd waited for his mother and Peggy Martin the day before. He hadn't made any attempt to hide his truck, making it virtually certain that someone would see him going into the woods and coming out with a bag of bones. Either he was an innocent kid going for a hike or he was in full-blown panic, oblivious to risk, and, if the latter was true, there was another possibility. He wasn't planning on moving Timmy's body. He was planning on joining him.

I parked behind his truck and made my way down the bike path, around the lake and to the edge of the woods. Flecks of crime-scene tape clung to a few tree trunks. CSI had finished its work, leaving a trail of flattened grass and rutted gurney tracks leading to the spot where the dead woman had been found buried beneath rocks on a rugged slope midway between the tree line and a ridge above the site.

I stood at the foot of her open, empty grave, doing a slow turn. A lot of people had been in these woods yesterday, poking and prodding the surrounding area, scooping up soil, rustling through deadfall. Separating out CSI's effort at discovery from Adam's effort at recovery was beyond my outdoor forensic skill set, but the extent to which the ground in the immediate vicinity had been disturbed convinced me that if there had been a child's body buried nearby, CSI would have found it.

That didn't mean Adam hadn't buried Timmy here; it just meant that he hadn't buried him *right here*. I began walking back and forth across the face of the slope, working my way up to the top of the ridge until I reached the outer perimeter CSI had established, marked again by fragments of crime-scene tape, the grave a hundred yards or so below me.

The ground on the other side of the ridge fell away into a ravine, a thin creek running along the bottom, cutting through muddy banks. I scrambled down the slope, crouching close to the ground along the creek, finding a trail of muddy footprints.

Adam Koch was younger, stronger, and faster than me, a probable killer who may also be suicidal, operating on little sleep and running on fear, someone who would flee if he could and attack if he couldn't. I was unarmed and had to assume that he wasn't, that whether he had a gun, knife, or sharp-edged shovel, he was more of a threat to me than I was to him.

All of my training and all of my experience in the FBI screamed at me to wait for backup, but I was deaf, though I knew why. I missed the man I used to be too much to listen. Mine was a phantom pain, only instead of reaching for a lost limb I was searching for a missing person last seen with steady hands and a badge, hoping to redeem him by a grand gesture in a moment such as this.

But I had no trouble hearing the voices of Timmy Montgomery and the Martin kids, all the justification I needed for pretending not to know any better. It was enough to make me shake, and I did, a full torso, neck, and head, knee-bending twister, putting me on the ground, my hands grasping the soft earth.

I've heard it said that losing one of your senses sharpens another, acute hearing compensating for failing sight. I was about to find out what happened when you lost all your senses.

The footprints ran along my side of the creek for twenty yards before jumping to the other side, a crossing made with the help of a large rock in the middle of the stream, before disappearing in the underbrush. Adam had left the creek and, unless he'd backtracked, had to have gone up the slope I was facing, a gentler hill than the one behind me. I stood still, listening, letting the woods tell me which way to go, the sharp sound of steel slamming into rock answering my question.

The sound came from the other side of the rise in front of me, the elevation enough to blind me to what was there. Not wanting to reveal myself too soon, I skirted the rise, moving to my right slowly and carefully, stealth more important than speed, stumbling when I stepped into a shallow depression, going down on one knee, my hands planted at my sides. The dirt was fresh, the edges of the hole well defined, the length sufficient for a child's body.

Brushing my pants off, I stood, certain I'd found Timmy's empty grave until I scanned the surrounding area and saw three more just like it scattered amongst the trees, shrubs, and vines. The first grave plus two others would have been enough for Timmy, Evan, and Cara, but I'd found four, raising mind-numbing possibilities, the continuing metallic clang renewing my alarm.

Sidestepping the graves, I climbed through the brush, emerging into a small clearing, Adam's back to me, a short-handled shovel raised over his head. It was the kind you could carry on a camping trip to dig a fire pit and cover ashes, not the kind you'd use to dig graves. The short handle made it easier to wield as a weapon, though he would have to get closer to me than he would like to do real damage.

Shirtless and mud-stained, he speared the ground with the shovel and sank to his knees, hanging his chin, gulping for air, his shoulders heaving. The ground around him was pockmarked with half a dozen shallow graves, all of them empty, jagged edges of rock aimed skyward.

"Adam."

He jumped to his feet, snatched the shovel, and whirled around, cocking it like a baseball bat.

"Put the shovel down, Adam. It's over."

He took a step toward me, sweeping the air with the blade. "Go away! Leave me alone!"

I held my ground. "Can't do that. I found your laptop, and I found Timmy Montgomery's T-shirt. Your mother told us about you and Peggy Martin. The police are at your house by now. It's over."

His eyes billowed. "My mom told you about Peggy?"

"Yeah. She's worried about you. She wants you to come home." I glanced at the empty holes he'd dug. "Where's Timmy's body?"

He bounced on the balls of his feet, a slight bend to his knees, twirling the shovel's blade, panting, nostrils flared.

"You see a body here? If there's no body, there's no crime. You can't prove I done anything!"

"The police won't need Timmy's body. They're going to find your DNA on Timmy's clothes, and that's all they will need."

"Then what do you care about his body?"

"I don't care, but Timmy's mother does. Now put the shovel down and tell me where you buried him."

He narrowed his eyes, his face turning red as he screamed at me. "They'll put me away, maybe even give me the death penalty!"

"You'll go to prison, that's for sure. Whether you die there depends on what happens right now. This is your last chance to help yourself."

He took a deep breath, lowering the shovel. I took two steps toward him when he raised it over his shoulder and swung it at me in a wide arc. I ducked beneath the blade, diving at his feet. His momentum spun him around out of my grasp. Before I could scramble to my feet, he slammed the shovel between my shoulder blades, flattening me on the ground.

My back felt like it was on fire. I couldn't breathe. All I could do was cover my head with my arms and curl my knees to my chest, waiting for the next blow, but none came. I raised my head, made it to my knees, and looked around. I was alone.

Chapter Forty-six

Adam could have run in any direction, but the only one that made sense was back toward his truck and he had enough of a head start to get there before I could catch up to him. He'd left the shovel, his shirt, and a denim jacket lying on the ground. I searched the jacket pockets, finding the keys to his truck. Time was on my side again.

I was wobbly and my back was throbbing, but my limbs were working. Using the shovel as a walking stick, I leaned forward, retracing my route, stumbling through the woods. When I got to the edge of the woods overlooking the open ground and the lake, I saw Adam, his head under the hood of his pickup. He darted back and forth from the cab to the hood, trying to hot-wire the truck, kicking the tires when he couldn't make it happen.

If he saw me, he'd run. Staying inside the tree line, I skirted the lake, staying below his line of sight until I reached Cliff Drive. I'd parked my car behind his truck. That gave me additional cover. I ran, the shovel tucked under my arm, stopping behind my car as he slammed the hood of the truck and jumped into the cab.

The truck's engine rolled over. Adam gave it gas, revving it, making certain it wouldn't fail him. I sprinted toward the truck. He saw me in his side mirror, throwing the truck in gear as I pulled even with the driver's door.

He yanked the wheel hard left as I swung the shovel at the driver's window, glass exploding. The blade caught him on the chin, knocking him sideways on the seat, his foot still on the gas.

I swung the door open, climbing into the cab and shoving

him aside. A minivan swerved around us, rocking and skidding past, the driver laying on the horn and giving me the finger. I hit the brakes, stopping the truck in the middle of Cliff Drive. Adam raised his head and grabbed my arm, letting go when I elbowed him in the throat.

I backed the pickup onto the shoulder, cut the engine, and took a closer look at Adam. He was conscious, glassy-eyed and bleeding. He'd need stitches, but he wasn't going to bleed to death. There were rags on the floor of the truck. I put one in his hand and pressed it against his wound. When his eyes focused, I pulled him from the truck, setting him on the ground, crouching down at eye level.

"Last chance, Adam. What happened to Timmy Montgomery?" His mouth quivered. He spit blood and began to sob.

"It was an accident. I never meant to kill him. Things just got out of hand. He started yelling. I told him to shut up, but he wouldn't. He just kept yelling and I had to make him stop so I put my hands over his face, and the next thing I knew, he wasn't breathing. If only he'd have shut up like I told him, none of this would have happened."

"And that's what you'll tell the police, but I need to know. Where's Timmy's body?"

Bitter laughter replaced his tears. "I am such a fuckup. I can't even remember where I buried him. I thought I knew, but I can't find him. What am I going to do now?"

"The police will find Timmy's body, but the more you help them, the easier it will be for you. You understand how that works?"

He nodded, the enormity of his situation sinking in. "What about my mom? What's she gonna say?"

"I can guess. She'll want you to be a man and do what's right, tell us everything that happened."

"I told you. It was an accident."

"I know. But that's about Timmy. He's dead, and you can't un-ring that bell. Evan and Cara Martin are a different story if they're still alive. Tell me where they are, and you've got a good shot at avoiding the death penalty. Otherwise, you're headed for death row."

His squinted at me, trying to understand what I was saying, shaking his head, recoiling. "I didn't touch those kids."

"C'mon Adam. No one is going to believe that. Not after what you did to Timmy. Not after you were shacking up with their mother. I'm telling you that you've got one chance to grow old. Don't blow it."

He struggled to his feet, sputtering and angry, but I clamped my hands on his shoulders, pushing him back.

"I'm telling the truth. I didn't do it!"

"Why should I believe you?" He took a deep breath, looking away and then back at me.

"I was with Peggy the night before Evan and Cara disappeared. She called me after they went to sleep and begged me to come over. Said she needed some company. My mom had found out about us and made me promise to stay away from her, but I couldn't."

"Why not? The sex was too good?"

"Yeah, but not the way you think. I knew there was something wrong with me before Timmy. I couldn't stay away from the kiddie porn. After what happened with him, I was so scared. I tried to quit the porn and leave the little kids alone, but I couldn't."

"A parent of one of the kids in your Sunday school class complained to the church about you."

He hung his head.

"I know, but I never hurt that little girl. I was trying not to. I really was. You don't know what it's like to want to do something so bad and you know it's a sin to do it, but you can't stop wanting it no matter how hard you try. Then, when Peggy came on to me, well, I thought maybe if I had sex with a grown woman like her, that'd cure me. I wouldn't get off on the kids anymore."

"How'd that work out for you?" His slumped, his chin on his chest, fresh tears falling off his face. "So you went over to Peggy's that night. What happened next?"

"What do you think happened? We did it. I wanted to go

home after, but she wanted me to stay. Said she felt safer having a man around since she'd had to get a restraining order against her husband. So I did. Next morning I woke up, and she wasn't there. I didn't know what to do. I didn't know if the kids were still asleep, but I didn't want them to catch me there. I opened her bedroom door a crack, and that's when I saw him."

"Saw who?"

"Jimmy Martin. Peggy's bedroom is at the top of the stairs. When I opened the door, I could see down to the front door. He was on his way out with Evan and Cara, telling them to hurry up if they wanted to have ice cream for breakfast."

"You're sure it was Jimmy?"

"Oh, yeah. I'm sure."

"How were the kids? Were they glad to be going, or were they upset?"

"They were laughing. Cara even said that their mom would kill them if she knew they were having ice cream for breakfast, and Jimmy said not to worry cause she'd never find out. That's the last thing I heard, and that's the truth."

"Why didn't you tell the police?"

He looked at me, wide-eyed at my stupidity. "Are you kidding me? My mom would have killed me if she knew I was back with Peggy."

"Did you tell Peggy?"

"Yeah. I knew she wouldn't say anything to my mom."

"What did she say when you told her?"

"She said she knew it had to be Jimmy, that no one else would do something like that."

Liars work from a script, the fewer details to remember the better. Ask them what happened, and they'll tell you the bare bones. Ask them again, and they'll repeat it, sometimes verbatim, sticking to their story so they don't screw it up. An honest person isn't afraid of the truth and the more often they tell what happened, the more details they remember, adding information because they want to be helpful and have nothing to hide.

I took Adam through the events again and again. Each time he gave me more information, descriptions of what Jimmy and the kids were wearing, the wine he and Peggy had drank the night before, the music on Peggy's iPod they'd listened to lying in bed after they had sex. He told me about coming down the stairs and peeking out the window cut into the front door, watching until Jimmy drove away in his pickup truck, remembering the first part of the truck's license number, guessing at the rest.

All of it was helpful, some of it easy to check out, none of it conclusive proof that Jimmy had taken his kids, confessed child killers being low on the credibility pyramid. Adam had good reason to tell the truth and better reason to lie, knowing that Jimmy was in jail for refusing to talk and that the police already suspected him. Corroborating his story depended on two things that had yet to happen: Peggy telling the entire truth, and Jimmy telling anything at all.

I called Adrienne Nardelli. She was still at Ellen Koch's house. I told her not to go anywhere, that I was bringing her a present, gift-wrapped, following that with a call to Lucy, telling her to meet me there.

"Okay, let's go," I told him.

"Where?"

"Home."

"Oh, man! My mom is going to totally kill me."

"Trust me, that will be the easy part."

I put Adam in the backseat of Kate's rental, pushing him to the center, belting him in, crisscrossing the shoulder straps over his chest.

"Hey," he said, "what about my truck?"

"Don't worry. You're not going to need it for a long time."

Chapter Forty-seven

"You did good," Adrienne Nardelli said.

We were in Ellen Koch's kitchen, Ellen sitting mute in the living room and Adam bundled in the back of a squad car. I'd spent an hour running it down for Nardelli, letting her work me the way I'd worked Adam, keeping my memory fresh, scraping all the details she could onto her notepad, pausing as successive waves of tremors and spasms ripped through me, petering out in a final soft ripple. Kate was on one side of me, Lucy on the other, each with a hand on my back when I stuttered and shook.

"Thanks."

"But going after him the way you did wasn't the smartest thing you could have done, you do know that?"

"Yeah, I know it."

"Any point in me telling you to butt out of my case and not to pull another fool stunt like that again?"

I didn't answer.

"Figured as much," she said, turning to Kate and Lucy. "Take him home. Make sure he takes the rest of the day off."

"After we talk to Peggy Martin," I said.

"Wrong," Nardelli said, "after *I* talk to Peggy Martin. I've got an officer babysitting her across the street."

"Anyone tell her about Adam?"

"Not yet. She came home half in the bag while you were out chasing him through the woods. I had an officer escort her inside and told him to keep her off the phone and to keep the press and neighbors out of the house, but she was watching from her front window when we cuffed Adam and put him in a squad car. Won't surprise me if the prosecuting attorney charges her with obstruction for not telling us about her husband taking her kids."

"She did tell you," Lucy said, "from day one."

"But," Nardelli countered, "she didn't tell us that her baby boyfriend was the one who saw him do it. What kind of mother holds back something like that?"

Lucy squared off at Nardelli, hands on her hips. "So she's not a perfect mother. So she's not even close. She cheated on her husband, and she drinks too much. But that doesn't mean she doesn't love her kids. And even if Adam is telling the truth, which is the Pikes Peak of ifs, Jimmy isn't talking. So any bad decisions Peggy made hasn't changed this case one damn bit."

"There's something else about Adam's story," I said. "Unless Jimmy confesses, there's no way to prove which one of them is lying. Peggy wasn't there. She only knows what Adam told her. If Adam took the kids, blaming it on Jimmy would be the easiest and smartest thing for him to do."

Nardelli pointed at Kate. "Then let your lie catcher figure it out. Pick the one that twitches the most."

"Maybe," Kate said, "it's neither of them."

"What's that supposed to mean?" Nardelli asked.

"It means that you're trying to pick a winner between two people who have every incentive to lie, as if they are the only possible suspects. That's not an investigation. It's tunnel vision."

"So who's your dark horse in this race?" Kate drew a reluctant breath. "You have to consider Peggy Martin."

"Wait a minute!" Lucy said. "Last night at your hotel when we watched the video you took of Peggy, you said that she showed agony when you asked her about Evan and Cara and shame when you asked her about her affair. You made a big deal about that, about how she would have shown shame when you asked her about the kids if she'd killed them."

"That's right," Kate said. "But like I keep telling Jack, context is everything. I was working off what we knew at the time, which didn't include her relationship with Adam."

"What difference does that make?" Lucy asked.

"It could make all the difference, especially if they're in this together, which would explain why she showed such shame. She accuses Jimmy from the beginning and primes Adam with the story about seeing Jimmy take the kids. She doesn't want Adam telling the police right away because that would mean disclosing their affair. So she keeps that in her back pocket, figuring to use it if the police find out about it. When the affair comes out, Adam's story about Jimmy deflects attention from her and puts the spotlight back on her husband."

"You think Peggy has that kind of a hold on Adam?" I asked.

"He admitted as much when he told you he was having sex with her to cure his pedophilia and that he kept seeing her after his mother told him to end the relationship. Plus, when she called him the night before the kids disappeared and told him to come over, he snuck out of his house. He wanted to go home after they had sex, but she made him stay. He's young, vulnerable, and easily manipulated."

"And," Nardelli added, warming to the possibility, "if she knew about his pedophilia or even had an idea that he'd killed Timmy Montgomery, she knew he'd go along, and if he didn't she could threaten to tell the police about Timmy."

"Given all that, I'd say she could make him jump through almost any hoop," Kate said.

"Why?" Lucy asked. "Why would a mother who loved her kids do that?"

"Nick Staley told me that Peggy is a party girl," I said. "Maybe the kids were cramping her style."

"That's a crock of shit!" Lucy said. "Peggy hired us to find her kids. I've handled enough of these cases to know how they tear parents up, and Peggy is in shreds. I know she isn't going to win Mother of the Year, but you can't fake that kind of pain. No one knows that any better than you, Jack."

My belly shook, my back bowed, and my neck arced toward

the ceiling, Lucy's last shot triggering a flurry of spasms. She turned red, covered her mouth with her hand, and looked away.

Nardelli threw up her hands. "What is it with you people? Don't you want anybody to be found guilty?"

"Sure we do," I said when the spasm died. "As long as they are guilty."

"Look," Kate said to Nardelli, "I admit it's not the most likely explanation based on what we know. But I was right when I told you that Adam knew more than he was telling us and that he was lying when he said he hadn't been in those woods before yesterday. I wasn't there when Jack interviewed him, so I can't say whether he was telling the truth about having seen Jimmy take the kids. But, if I'm right, Jimmy's refusal to cooperate is playing right into Peggy's hands."

"Only now we've got a witness who will testify that Jimmy was the last person seen with Evan and Cara," Nardelli said. "Once he knows that, he may open up, if only to defend himself."

"Depends on who asks the questions and how they are asked. Come at him hard, threaten him, try to scare him, and he'll shut down."

"I've done this once or twice before," Nardelli said. "And you've gotten nothing out of Jimmy," Kate said.

"Same as you."

"Actually, no. I got a lot out of him."

"Like what?" Nardelli asked.

"Like he loves his kids and is scared for them."

"Right," Lucy said. "That's exactly what you told us about Peggy."

"I should just leave you people alone and let you kill each other. Would save me a lot of trouble," Nardelli said, letting out a long breath, studying us, and then pointing at Kate. "Okay, then. You tell Jimmy about Adam."

"Me?" Kate asked.

"Yeah, you and me. Let's go. And call Ethan Bonner. Tell him to meet us there. Anything comes out of Jimmy Martin's mouth, I want to be damn sure a jury gets to hear it one day."

"So much for going home," I said.

"I didn't invite you," Nardelli said.

"The three of us," Kate said, "are a package deal."

"And we talk to Peggy Martin first," I said.

Nardelli shook her head. "I should have listened

to Quincy Carter and arrested all of you."

"For what?" I asked. "For being a pain in my ass."

Chapter Forty-eight

A crowd had gathered in the street between Ellen's and Peggy's houses, word of Adam's arrest racing through the neighborhood and leading the breaking-news updates being broadcast from adjacent driveways. Reporters swarmed toward us as we left the house, cameras and microphones aimed at our faces.

Nardelli declined comment, and we followed suit, a lone woman pushing her way past them, reporters jostling her, holding her back. I recognized Jeannie Montgomery.

"Let her through!" I said, brushing them aside, making room for her.

I took her by the hand, leading her away from the reporters so we could talk without having our conversation lead the six o'clock news. Her hand was cold, the bones slipping side to side, her fingers rolling together. I eased my grip, but she tightened hers. We found a quiet spot on the side of Ellen's house. She searched my face, still holding my hand.

"Is it true?"

"Yes."

"What happened to my boy?"

"Adam told me it was an accident, that he didn't mean to hurt Timmy, that things got out of hand."

"Is that supposed to make me feel better?"

"No. I think it's supposed to make him feel better."

She nodded, my answer matching hers. "Have they found my son's body?"

"Not yet, but they will."

"What will happen to Adam?"

"That's up to the court, but there's a good chance he'll spend the rest of his life in jail or be executed."

"His life for my son's. It won't change a thing. I'd never make that trade."

"No one would."

She let go of my hand. "Thank you."

"I'm sorry for your loss."

"At least I know for sure."

"That's something."

"It's all that's left," she said and walked away.

She was blind to the waiting cameras, deaf to the reporters' shouted questions. The crowd of neighbors shrank from her, and she passed through them untouched as before.

Nardelli tapped me on the shoulder. "Let's go. City doesn't like paying me overtime."

Peggy Martin watched us from her open front door as we climbed the long flight of stairs from her driveway, a uniformed cop peering over her shoulder. She was pacing from side to side in the doorway, clutching her body and biting her lip, her eyes wide, darting from the cop to us to the floor and back to us.

Nardelli was on point, nodding to the officer, who motioned to Peggy, leading her and the rest of us into the house. We gathered in the small living room, circling around Peggy, our reluctant, beer-soaked, scraggly-haired host. In need of a strong cup of coffee and a shower, she tottered, reaching out to Lucy, who guided her to a lumpy sofa. Kate sat next to her, and Nardelli and I stepped back, giving them room, Lucy taking the lead.

"How are you holding up?"

Peggy stared at the floor. "How do you think I'm holding up?"

"I can't imagine. I don't know how you get through the day."

She raised her head. "I can't take much more of this. I swear to God, I can't."

Her speech was clear, no slurring, just a drunk's self-pity, one thing jumping out at me. She hadn't asked whether her kids had been found, and she hadn't asked why Adam had been arrested.

"Kate needs to ask you a few more questions. Are you up to that?"

She looked at Nardelli, stiffening as if sensing a threat. Nardelli's face was flat, making no promises. Peggy shrugged.

"Sure. Why not?"

"Peggy, we're doing everything we can to find Evan and Cara," Kate said. "We may have gotten an important break, and we need your help to figure out if we're on the right track."

She looked at Kate, her face quivering, eyes welling. "It's about Adam, isn't it? About Adam and me."

"Yes."

She buried her face in her hands. "I am so sorry, so, so sorry."

"What are you sorry about?"

She straightened, sniffling, taking a deep breath. "I should have told the police what Adam told me about Jimmy taking the kids, but I was too afraid."

"Of what?"

"I thought Jimmy took the kids just to push my buttons. I thought he'd bring them back in a day or two at the most. I never thought he'd hurt them. But I was scared he'd get custody of them if he found out about Adam and me."

Nardelli interrupted, unable to hide her disbelief. "Your husband was arrested for stealing. The judge won't let him post bail because he won't tell us a damn thing about your kids, and you kept quiet because you were afraid he'd get custody? He'll do two to five years on the theft charge alone. You think he was going take the kids with him?"

She winced, like she'd been slapped. "Jimmy's the kind who gets away with everything. He got this fancy lawyer. I thought he'd get off."

"Peggy," Kate asked, "what if Adam was lying about having seen Jimmy?"

"Lying? Why would he lie?"

"Did Adam talk to you about any problems he was having,

anything he thought you could help him with?"

"Just his mother. She drove him crazy. Why? What are you talking about? Why would Adam lie to me?" And then she understood and started to shake, terrified at what she may have done. "Oh, my God, is that why the police arrested him? Did he take my babies?"

"We don't know," Kate said.

"Then what did he do?"

"He molested and killed Timmy Montgomery."

The color vanished from her face, her eyes rolledback in her head, and she fainted before she could scream.

Chapter Forty-nine

Kate and I waited outside while a paramedic tended to Peggy, Lucy staying by her side. Kate brushed dirt off my jacket.

"You're a mess."

"Old news."

"Very old. You should ride with Lucy to the Farm. And call Joy. She's probably worried about you. I know I am."

Lucy and Adrienne Nardelli came out of Peggy's house, Nardelli twirling one finger in the air, telling us to get the show on the road.

I settled into the front seat of Lucy's car and called Joy, leaving a message when she didn't pick up that I was going back to the Farm with Lucy and didn't know when I'd be home.

"Everything okay with you and Joy?"

"Yeah, why?"

"You grimaced when she didn't answer, and it wasn't a happy grimace."

"Well, she isn't happy that Kate is working on this case."

"Do you blame her?"

"No, but it's not my fault."

"Doesn't matter. If I lost Simon, all I'd think about is how much I want him back, and, if I got him back, I'd never stop worrying that I'd lose him again."

"Trouble is, that gate swings both ways."

"You and Kate?"

"Yeah. We both thought we'd moved on, but neither of us has moved on as far as we'd like to believe."

"Forget it, Jack. I like Kate, but you can't do that to Joy, not after what she's been through and what she's looking at."

"I'm not doing anything to Joy. I'm doing my job, and right now, Kate's part of the job, but that's all she is. The rest will work itself out."

"That's a half-baked commitment to doing the right thing."

"I'm glad you're so certain about what's right for Joy, Kate, and me. Soon as I figure it out, I'll be all over it."

Lucy grasped the wheel with both hands, biting her lip.

"You're right. I'm sorry, and I'm sorry about what I said about you knowing better than anyone what it's like to lose a child. That was really, really stupid."

"Except you were right about that. I do know better."

"Even so, I shouldn't have said it. Look what it did to you."

I waved off her concern. "Comes with the territory. If I stopped talking to everyone who made me shake, I'd have to take a vow of silence. I can handle it if you can."

She put the car in gear and fell in line behind Adrienne Nardelli and Kate. "So, what about Peggy? Do you think she killed her kids?"

"After that performance, no way. But if it turns out that Adam killed them, she'll drown in a bottle before she turns forty."

"Either way, the press will crucify her," Lucy said. "They don't give anybody a break because they don't think anyone can change, turn their life around."

"Like you did."

She smiled. "Yeah, like I did."

"Is that why you get your back up every time someone takes a shot at Peggy? You think she's getting a raw deal?"

"Maybe. I guess. Probably. Look, just because she's poor and her marriage fell apart and her husband stole so they could pay the mortgage doesn't mean she or her kids deserve any of this."

"It's not about who deserves what. It's about what happens when things go wrong and what you do about it. Besides, look at Joy and me."

"What's that supposed to mean?"

"We had it made. We were both college graduates. I had a good job. Joy wanted to stay home with the kids. We had a nice house in a nice neighborhood, and none of that mattered. One day we let a neighbor give Kevin a ride, thinking we could trust him when all we did was deliver our son to the devil, and nothing, I mean nothing, was ever the same again. Wendy lived another twenty years, but the day we lost Kevin was the day she started to die. So zip code and tax brackets don't have a damn thing to do with it, and if we don't find Evan and Cara alive, Peggy Martin won't make it either."

"Is that why you went after Adam on your own?" I thought of Jeannie Montgomery drifting through the crowd. "We don't need any more ghosts."

Ethan Bonner was waiting for us with the jail superintendent, Annette Fibuch, when we arrived at the Farm. She had arranged for us to meet with Jimmy in the Women's Recreation Area, just as before.

"There's too many of us," Kate said. "We'll overwhelm him, and he won't tell us his name, let alone anything else."

"Kate can go in on her own, but I'm not letting Detective Nardelli in there without me," Bonner said.

"I've got a better chance if I talk to him on my own," Kate said.

"That's not happening," Nardelli said. "I don't want you helping him get his story straight."

"Fine," Kate said. "Do it yourself. You've done a great job with him so far."

"Detective, you can watch and listen from our security center," the superintendent said, confirming my suspicion that our meeting with Jimmy had been monitored.

"Tell you what, Detective," Bonner said. "Give Kate first crack at him. We'll watch from the security center. You don't like the way it goes, you can have the second crack."

"You're pretty confident," Nardelli said.

"I like my team."

A corrections officer took Kate to meet with Jimmy, and the superintendent took the rest of us to the security center where three officers were monitoring a dozen screens displaying every part of the Farm.

"Gene, Mike, and Cheryl," the superintendent said to the officers. "Sorry to barge in on you. Do me a favor and pull up the Women's Recreation Area."

We watched the center screen on the top row, a black-and-white monitor feeding us video of Kate and Jimmy. The camera angle was distant and wide, better suited to capturing inmates dealing drugs. Facial expressions were blurred, and the audio was scratchy. Jimmy's wrists and ankles were shackled when an officer led him into the room with Kate.

Bonner turned to the superintendent. "Annette, what's with the restraints? Jimmy's not dangerous."

"He's suspected of kidnapping and killing his children. He's not our typical nonviolent, homeless resident. I'm not leaving him alone with a woman," she said.

Kate said something to the officer we couldn't make out and pointed to the restraints, the officer shaking his head, Kate pressing him, pointing to the two-way radio on his hip. The officer picked up his radio, his voice coming through a speaker on the security console.

"She wants me to take off the restraints," the officer said.

"Absolutely not," the superintendent said.

Kate grabbed the radio from the officer. "Keep him shackled and I'm wasting my time. Leave the officer outside. Leave the door open if that will make you feel better, but take off the restraints or I'm walking."

The superintendent looked at Nardelli and Bonner, both of whom nodded, though I didn't like it, remembering too well that I'd nearly gotten Kate killed a couple of years ago when I let her talk me into taking a chance that made more sense than this one did.

"Kate," I said, "go out in the hall where Jimmy can't hear us."

She disappeared from the monitor, popping up on another one displaying the hallway.

"Okay. I know what you're thinking, Jack, but this is different. I've had time to study Jimmy. His fight is with his wife, not me. I'll be fine."

"You'll be even better if he stays shackled."

"Stop worrying. I know what I'm doing."

"Kate, this is a bad idea."

"Good or bad, it's not your decision. It's mine, and I've made it."

I looked at the superintendent. "You heard her."

"Okay," the superintendent said, letting out a long sigh. "Let me talk to my officer."

We watched while he removed Jimmy's handcuffs and motioned him to sit down so he could remove his ankle shackles. Jimmy smiled at Kate, and when the officer knelt at his feet and freed his legs, he clasped his hands together, raining double-fisted, rapid-fire hammerhead blows on the officer's neck. The officer collapsed, and Jimmy jumped to his feet, kicking him in the face. Kate started to run, but he grabbed her arm, twisting it behind her, pulling a shiv from his waistband, jamming it against her cheek, and, using her as a human shield, pushed her out into the hall.

Chapter Fifty

I bolted for the door, Lucy and Nardelli racing behind me. It was full dark and cold, stadium lights burning the walkway from the administration building to the women's dormitory, the Farm silent. There was no siren sounding an alarm, no flight of corrections officers toward the dorm, no hint of trouble until I yanked on the front entrance to the dorm and nearly wrenched my shoulder fighting a locked door.

"Great," Nardelli said, flipping her cell phone open, telling whoever was listening to send a SWAT team and a hostage negotiator.

She snapped her phone shut and tried the door again as the superintendent and Bonner caught up to us.

"Door's locked," Lucy said.

"Of course it's locked," the superintendent said. "That's called security." She clicked on her radio. "It's Superintendent Fibuch. Open up if you're secure."

An officer swung the door open, and we stepped into a hall that ran the length of the dorm, the Women's Recreation Area near the opposite end. There was an open sleeping area to our right where two dozen women in jail-issued jumpsuits sat on steel cots, an officer keeping them well away from the hall, the women silent, their faces lit, waiting for something to happen, not certain whom to root for. We joined another officer who was standing ten feet farther down the hall past the sleeping area, not taking his eyes off of Jimmy and Kate.

"What's your procedure?" Nardelli asked the superintendent,

her voice quiet enough that Jimmy couldn't hear.

"There are officers at every exit. The building is secure. There's no place for him to go, so we'll wait him out."

"Who's your hostage negotiator?"

"We don't have one. My officers and I are trained in verbal judo, how to defuse tense situations, but none of us qualify for hostage situations."

"I've got a SWAT team and a hostage negotiator on the way," Nardelli said. "They'll be here in less than thirty minutes. What weapons do your officers carry?" she asked.

"Just pepper spray. Our residents are nonviolent."

"Except for Jimmy Martin."

"He doesn't belong here. I was forced to take him because the county jail was full." The superintendent glanced at the gun on Nardelli's hip. "Firearms aren't allowed in here. I'll have one of my officers take your gun back to the administrative building. You can pick it up when this is over."

Nardelli covered the butt of her gun with her hand. "You've got a man holding a shiv against a woman's neck sixty feet from where we are standing. What's the range on your pepper spray?"

The superintendent reddened. "I run this jail, Detective, and guns are not allowed."

"And this is a crime scene, and I'm running it. You don't like it, take it up with the chief of police tomorrow morning," she said, turning to the officer who'd let us in. "What's he doing?"

"Not much. He yelled at us to back off or he'd kill the woman. We're giving him plenty of space. I can't tell for certain, but it looks like her neck's bleeding."

The hallway was lit with ceiling fixtures that gave a dull yellow cast to the brown walls and checkerboard linoleum floor. Jimmy was holding Kate in a shadowy area between two fixtures, making it hard to tell if the officer was right. The poor lighting worked to Jimmy's advantage, disguising his actions, making it more likely he could stab Kate or slit her throat before we knew he'd done it.

"Did Jimmy know we were coming?" I asked the superintendent.

"Ethan called me, and I told him."

"How'd he react?"

"Indifferent. Same as always."

"Has he been in any trouble since he got here? Any reason he'd have to carry a shiv?"

"No. Most of our residents are drug and alcohol abusers, and they're pretty passive. If they have a history of violence or they appear likely to be violent when we do our intake evaluation, we send them somewhere else. They survive in here the same way they do on the streets, by being invisible and not threatening anyone."

"How has Jimmy gotten along with them?"

"He scares them. They give him room, not trouble. I don't know why he'd risk getting caught with a weapon."

"It's obvious, isn't it?" Lucy said. "He wanted it in case he had a chance to escape, either to overpower an officer or take a hostage, both of which he just did."

"Maybe," I said. "But this isn't an easy place to escape from. Even if he gets out of the building, he's still got to get through a lot of officers, electronic gates, and barbed wire. A shiv will only get you so far."

"Why then?" the superintendent asked.

"Self-protection. Somebody in here scared him. I'd appreciate it if you could give me a list of everyone who's visited Jimmy and everyone who's checked in since he arrived."

"Who are you looking for?" Nardelli asked.

"Someone like Jimmy, someone who didn't belong here."

Bonner cupped his hands, shouting down the hall. "Jimmy! It's me, Ethan Bonner. Let Kate go."

"Fuck that, Bonner. They let me go first, then we got something to talk about."

"Jimmy, you know that's not going to happen. Let her go before this gets any worse."

"Only one way it's going to get worse, and that's if they don't let me out of here."

"Okay, okay. Just take it easy. Let me see what I can do."

Nardelli looked at Bonner. "Don't even ask. You made your fee speech, counselor," she said. "Now sit tight and shut up. We'll handle this the rest of the way." She stared down the hall for a moment and then called to Jimmy.

"This is Detective Nardelli. I talked to you right after your children disappeared. I've got someone on the way over here to talk with you, see what we can work out."

"There's nothing to work out. You heard what I want. Make it happen."

"It's not up to me, Jimmy. That's why I've sent for someone you can do business with. Until he gets here, you've got to make sure Kate doesn't get hurt because if she does, there's nothing anybody can do for you. We clear on that?"

"Either I get out of here, or there's nothing I can do for her. We clear on that, Detective?" he said, stepping into the light.

Kate let out a cry as Jimmy let go of her arm and grabbed her hair from behind, yanking her chin up, the shiv now visible at her neck. He retreated into the shadow, pressing his back against the wall and making himself a smaller target, Kate providing cover.

"He's clear, I'm clear, we're all clear!" Kate yelled. "So do us a favor and move back, give us some room. Jimmy and I have things to talk about, and all this attention isn't helping."

Chapter Fifty-one

Nardelli turned to me, her voice low. "Is she serious?"

"Most of the time," I said. "I'd give her a chance."

"She was the one who wanted Jimmy's shackles taken off. That's not much of a track record."

"She's the only psychologist in the room, and we're out of options until your people get here, unless you plan on shooting him."

"Not that I couldn't, but that's what the SWAT team gets paid to do. They don't like it when someone else does it for them."

"In that case, I'd do what she says."

"Okay," she called to Kate. "We're pulling back to the end of the hallway. Help is on the way."

Ten quiet minutes passed, Jimmy hanging onto Kate's hair. They were talking, though we couldn't hear what they were saying. Jimmy was not relaxing his grip, evidence enough that it wasn't going well.

Sirens pierced the silence, announcing the oncoming cavalry, the thumping of a helicopter hovering overhead upping the ante. Boots clattered on the sidewalk outside the door, enough for a small regiment. Nardelli opened the door, and two men entered, one in full SWAT gear carrying an M24 sniper rifle, the other dressed in jeans, a sweatshirt, and a black leather jacket, sporting bloodshot eyes and a two-day growth of beard.

"I'm Quinn," the second man said. "You're Jeremiah Quinn, the negotiator?" Nardellli asked, raised eyebrows saying she didn't think so. "Don't act so disappointed. Henry Kissinger was busy,"

Quinn said. "Who started this party?"

"The guy down the hall with a shiv up against a hostage's neck."

"What's he want?"

"A get-out-jail-free card."

Quinn shrugged. "Why should he be any different than all the others? Let's see what we got."

The sniper took up position, sighting Jimmy just as he released Kate's hair, dropping his arms to his side. She did a slow pivot, facing him, wrapping her fingers around his wrist, easing the shiv out of his hand, talking. Jimmy answered, and both of them nodded. Kate walked away, leaving him alone in the center of the hall.

Nardelli and the sniper rushed past Kate. Nardelli shouted at Jimmy to get down on the floor, and the sniper grabbed him before he could comply, shoving him onto the tile, jamming his knee into Jimmy's back as Nardelli cuffed him.

I ran to Kate, embracing her, both of us trembling. Pulling away, I tilted her chin to one side, pressing my sleeve against a crimson tear along her pale neck. A paramedic materialized, replacing my sleeve with a pressure dressing and cupping Kate's elbow, telling her to step outside.

"I'm okay," she insisted.

"Let's make sure," the paramedic told her.

"You better take this," she said, handing me the shiv.

It was six inches of hard plastic, tapered at one end to a sharp point. Nardelli and the superintendent studied it with me.

"It's the handle for a toilet bowl brush," the superintendent said. "I recognize the color and shape."

I gave the shiv to Nardelli and went outside, finding Kate sitting on a gurney in an ambulance, the paramedic cleansing her wound and covering it with a small bandage while she talked with Quinn.

"Damn fine piece of work," he told her. "Except for the part where you asked to have the guy's shackles taken off. That's classic too-stupid-to-live rookie bullshit. Don't trust anybody, especially someone who's got more to lose than you do. Makes me want to puke every time I see crap like that on TV."

"Sorry you made the trip for nothing," Kate said.

"You kidding? Nobody died. That's a good day. You ever want to do this again the right way, call me," he said, handing her a business card.

He patted her on the cheek and climbed out of the ambulance, nodding at me as I took his place alongside Kate. The superintendent and Nardelli joined us, standing outside the ambulance.

"Is that guy a cop?" I asked Nardelli.

"No. He's freelance."

"A freelance hostage negotiator? How does that happen?"

"Budget cuts," she said. "We had two negotiators. One retired, the other had a nervous breakdown, and now there's a hiring freeze."

"Are you telling me there are enough hostage situations in Kansas City that a guy can make a living as a negotiator?"

"That's not all Quinn does, and he doesn't just do it around here."

"What else is there?"

"He calls himself a conflict specialist. You got a problem with somebody and you aren't too particular how it gets handled, you call a number, leave a message, and hope he shows up."

"Hard times makes for hard choices," I said. "Kate, you feel like talking about what happened?"

A rose blush crept into her cheeks. "It's my fault," she said. "I completely misread Jimmy. I didn't see this coming."

To their credit, the superintendent didn't say I told you so, and Nardelli didn't crack wise about the vagaries of micro facial expressions.

"How did he fool you?"

"He didn't fool me. I fooled me. He knew what I wanted, and he gave it to me: a smile, a friendly, open face. There was no hint of aggression or violence until the instant before he hit the guard. By then, it was too late."

"He knew we were coming, so he must have planned it," Nardelli said.

"I don't think so," I said. "He couldn't have known you would ask to have his restraints taken off. I'd say it was a spur-of-the-moment decision. He saw an opportunity and took it."

"That's how a lot of escape attempts happen," the superintendent said. "Except I don't think he was trying to escape," Kate said. "He knew he had no real chance of getting away. I think he just wanted out of the Farm."

"What makes you say that?" I asked.

"It's what he told me, in so many words, anyway. Once we were out in the hall and you gave us some space, I asked him why he was doing this, and he said, 'Why do you think?' I said it was pretty obvious that he wanted to break out of jail, and he said, 'Yeah, right, like how far am I going to get armed with a toilet bowl brush.' "

"Are you saying he beat up a guard and took you hostage and risked getting shot just so he could get a transfer?" Nardelli asked.

"Yes. When the SWAT team came through the door, his body went limp like he'd put down a heavy weight, and then he let me go."

"But you stayed to talk to him. What was that about?" I asked.

"I was waiting to tell him what Adam had said about seeing him take the kids from Peggy's house until I could watch his reaction. That's when I told him."

"Did he deny Adam's story?"

"No. It was weird. He smiled, almost like he was glad."

"What did he say?"

"Just one thing. He said, 'Please find my kids.' He's not acting like a man who killed his kids."

"He's playing you," Lucy said. "Just like he did with the restraints. Why would he ask you to find Evan and Cara when we know he took them? He knows where there are, and he knows what happened to them."

"And, first chance he got, he beat up an officer and stuck you with a shiv," Nardelli said.

"But he gave up," Kate said.

"When he was about to get shot," Lucy said. "Give me a break."

The superintendent's cell phone rang. She held her hand up, asking us to wait, listening and thanking the caller.

"I had my assistant check the records on visitors and new admissions. It will take longer to get you the names of his visitors, but I can tell you that we've had seventeen since Jimmy got here, ten women and seven men, all but one of them regulars, repeat offenders who show up here three or four times a year."

"Who's the new kid on the block?" I asked.

"A kid named Ricky Suarez. He came in yesterday, ten days for drunk and disorderly, his first time on the Farm."

Chapter Fifty-two

"You think there's a connection between Jimmy Martin and Ricky Suarez?" Nardelli asked.

"If Kate is right, somebody spooked him," I said.

"How does a blue-collar construction worker like Jimmy get involved with a probable gangbanger?" Kate asked.

"It's not so much the gangbanger as it is the gang," I said.

Nardelli explained. "There are two Hispanic gangs in town. The Cholos work the southwest side of town along Southwest Boulevard, and Nuestra Familia operates in Northeast."

"Which is where Jimmy lives," I said. "Cesar Mendez runs Nuestra. Suarez probably belongs to him."

"Most likely scenario," Nardelli said, "Jimmy bought drugs from Mendez and stiffed him. Mendez finds out that Jimmy is at the Farm and sends Ricky to deliver a message, maybe even kill him."

"A message, maybe, but kill him, I doubt it. This isn't the state penitentiary where a guy can walk into the shower and come out on a slab and no one knows anything about it. And, with all the open spaces, Ricky couldn't touch him without half a dozen correction officers coming down on him."

"So Mendez sacrifices Ricky. He's got a dozen more just like him," Nardelli said.

"The price is too high on a hit like that. Mendez can't take the chance that Ricky would make a deal and trade his life for Mendez's life."

"What then?"

"I don't know. Let's ask Ricky," I said.

I stepped down from the ambulance, my knees giving out as my feet hit the ground. I descended slowly, like I was melting, eyes clenched and my head floating in brain fog until my knees and hands touched the ground. My body was playing out the fundamental law of physics that for every action there is an equal and opposite reaction. I'd pushed far enough and hard enough that it pushed back, calling an all stop.

"Or not," Lucy said.

They talked about me as if I weren't there, Nardelli asking questions, Lucy and Kate explaining, Nardelli saying "Hell of a thing" and "He's no use to anybody like this," Kate volunteering to take me home, and Lucy saying she didn't think so. There was nothing I could do, no point in trying to get up until the moment passed, no reason for Lucy and Kate to help me until I could stand on my own.

"Okay," I said when I could open my eyes and my head began to clear. Lucy hooked her arm under mine, and I made it to my feet. "Welcome back."

"Good to be back. Let's go see Suarez," I said, the words fighting to get out of my mouth, one syllable crashing into the next.

"That train has left the station, and Nardelli and the superintendent are the only ones on it," Lucy said. "I'm taking you home."

My legs were still equal parts jelly and jam, and the rest of me was doing a slow-motion version of twist and shout. The only thing missing was a robotic voice assuring me that resistance was futile.

Joy met us at the front door, Lucy handing me off with a sad smile like I was a favorite uncle who'd had too much to drink at the family reunion. Roxy and Ruby swarmed around me, jumping and scratching my legs, indifferent to my condition as if to say *Don't make your problems our problems*. I couldn't and wouldn't, sliding to the floor and gathering them in my lap.

"Thanks for leaving me a message," Joy said, when the dogs lost interest, having smelled my breath, nipped at my nose, and allowed me to scratch their bellies.

She sat on the floor across from me, her head tilted to one side, her sweater hanging off her shoulders, billowing. Though she ate with gusto, she had struggled to put enough weight back on, and no matter what size she wore, it always looked too big.

"I'm sorry about yesterday. I knew you would be worried, and I should have called."

"It's okay."

"And I'm sorry about Kate. I don't know what to tell you. She just showed up."

She let out a long sigh. "You never knew my mother. She died of breast cancer when I was a teenager. I remember sitting around the dinner table with her and my father and my brothers. Once she knew she was terminal, she talked about what would happen to my father after she was gone. She knew he'd be no good by himself, that he wouldn't be able to take it being alone. She'd look at him across the table, pointing at him with her fork, and tell him it was fine with her if he could find someone who would take him."

"What did he say?"

"He'd laugh and say thanks a lot, but since he'd fooled her into marrying him there wasn't much chance he'd get that lucky again."

"Your father was a wise man."

"Yes, and my mother had more wisdom. She was right about him. And I'm right about you."

"How's that?"

"You're like my father. You're no good alone. So it's okay with me. Whether it's Kate or someone else."

I didn't know what to say, so I didn't say anything. I just hugged her until I felt her tears on my neck. She pulled away, wiping her nose.

"So, tell me what's happening on your cases."

She was letting me know that she wasn't hiding or walking away, that our home was my refuge and she was, in the truest sense of that tired cliché, there for me, making me feel at once grateful and shabby.

"I solved one case today, but it wasn't one I was working on."

She boosted me off the floor, spotting me as we climbed the stairs. I told her about my day, leaving nothing out while we undressed, showered, and fell into bed.

"The boy from the gang who was at the Farm," she said, "you think he works for this Cesar Mendez?"

"I'd bet on it."

"And you think Mendez is also looking for Brett Staley?"

"You're two for two."

"And you said that Jimmy Martin and Nick Staley are friends and that you think Brett Staley helped Frank Crenshaw buy the gun he used to kill his wife."

I rolled over on my side, propped on my elbow. "Don't stop now. You're on a roll."

She gave me a smile, the first real one I'd seen in days, and stroked my face with her palm. "Then they're all connected, Frank Crenshaw, the Staleys, Jimmy Martin, and Mendez. The question is how? Figure that out, and you'll be home in time for dinner tomorrow night."

She kissed me on the cheek and turned off the light. I lay on my back, staring at the ceiling, my eyes adjusting to the dark, the final spasms of the long day bouncing me from the inside out, my brain clear enough to know that her last question was the right question, but too muddled to hazard an answer. I reached for her hand, squeezing it beneath the covers.

"How was your day?"

"Go to sleep. We can talk about it tomorrow."

"I don't deserve you."

"You never did, but that's okay. Even a blind squirrel gets lucky and finds an acorn now and then."

"A blind squirrel? Really?"

"I read it somewhere. No shut up and go to sleep."

Chapter Fifty-three

Braylon Jennings was sitting in my kitchen when I wandered in the next morning, drinking my coffee, reading my newspaper. Joy was eying him with crossed arms, the dogs flanking her, tails down, casting their votes with soft growls. I was wearing the T-shirt and boxer shorts I'd slept in, scratching my crotch, tasting my morning breath.

"You look like hell," Jennings said.

If he'd been a dog, he'd have peed on the floor, staking his claim to my territory, and if I'd been a dog, I'd have bit him in the ass.

"Get out."

He folded the newspaper, sipped his coffee, and leaned back in his chair. "Your ex-wife invited me in. She's got better manners than you do."

"He said it couldn't wait, Jack. I'm sorry."

I picked up Jennings's coffee cup, poured it out in the sink, and pointed to the front of the house. "Get out. You want to talk to me, make an appointment."

"You got a short memory, Jack. Must be all that shaking. Tell you what, I'll wait in my car while you get dressed."

I followed him to the door. He glanced at his watch. "Hurry it up," he said. "I've got a full day."

There were two ways I could deal with Jennings: wait for him to tell me how high to jump, or push back, figuring he needed me enough to take a certain amount of flack until he got what he wanted. If I made it too easy for him, he'd use me till he used me up, and if I busted his chops too hard, he'd make good on his promise to throw Roni Chase back in the soup. It was that prospect that made me shave, dress, strap my gun on my hip, and sneak out the back door, climb over our fence, cut through our neighbor's backyard, and get on a bus at Sixty-third and Brookside, Joy's question from the night before rattling around in my head.

Frank Crenshaw and Nick Staley were first cousins. Jimmy Martin and Nick grew up together and were army buddies. Frank was in the scrap business, Nick sold bread and milk, and Jimmy worked construction. Their relationships were typical, friends and family, lifetimes spent in the daily struggle, grateful for the good times and sorry for the bad times, wondering whether they'd be missed or remembered when it was all over. Brett Staley tied his father and cousin to Cesar Mendez, but that left Jimmy Martin as the odd man out, his connection to Mendez the missing piece of the puzzle.

I would make good on my side of the deal with Jennings and give him what I had about the stolen guns, which was more guesswork than fact, but I wasn't going to do that until I was satisfied that Roni was in the clear. If Frank Crenshaw, the Staleys, and Jimmy Martin were into something with Cesar Mendez, the blowback could easily drown her.

She kept the books for Crenshaw and Nick Staley, and she dated Brett. Those connections would deafen the feds to her denials that she had no idea what they were doing. And she was already working without a net, offering no explanation for how her gun had been used to kill Crenshaw and refusing to talk to me. The only way I could protect her from Jennings and whatever else was happening was to figure out where she fit in.

I got off the bus on Broadway at Thirty-eighth, taking the stairs two at a time to Simon's office. I hadn't spoken to him since Lucy gave him the files on the Martin and Montgomery cases. I needed to work the puzzle with him. I breezed through the door, stopping short when I saw Jennings sitting in my chair, Lucy and Simon standing behind Simon's desk, glaring, Kate along another wall, taking X-rays of Jennings.

He pointed his finger at me. "You got more balls than sense. I give you that. And don't tell me to get out. I let you get away with that crap in front of your ex-wife, but I'm not taking any more shit off of you unless you want Roni Chase auditioning for penitentiary girlfriend of the week."

"How'd you know I'd be here?"

"You didn't come out the front door, so I figured you went out the back. I knew you weren't going to walk all day, which meant you'd take the bus, just like you did going downtown yesterday. I turned the corner onto Brookside when you were paying your fare. When I saw which bus you were on, I guessed you were coming here, and if you weren't, I knew these good people would know how to reach you and that they would understand the importance of cooperating with federal law enforcement."

"You aren't that fast, and you aren't that smart."

"I'm here, aren't I?"

"Did you get the text message I sent you this morning?" Simon asked.

"No," I said, looking at the screen on my phone, Simon's message telling me to come to his office first thing. "I was on the bus and didn't hear my phone."

Simon, his jaw clenched, pointed at Jennings. "That's how he got here. He's monitoring your phone. He strolled in here, flashed his ATF badge, and made himself at home. You care to tell us what he's doing here and why this is the first we know about him?"

Simon was angry with both of us. He didn't like Jennings barging in his office and telling him what to do, and he liked even less that I had left him out of the loop. That was Simon's problem, but I decided to make it Jennings's problem.

He had made me take a blood oath to keep our arrangement private. Yet, here he was putting it on the table in front of the people he wanted me to keep in the dark. His tactics of squeezing me, using Roni as bait, and grandstanding in my kitchen and Simon's office were high-pressure moves, but they put as much pressure on him as on me, each escalation increasing the risks to him that the whole thing would come apart. That's what happens when a case becomes too personal. The question was why he had crossed that line.

"You tell them, Jennings."

He rose from the chair, standing behind it, putting distance between us, stalling, his lack of a ready answer more evidence that he was improvising, making it up as he went along.

"A gun dealer was robbed about a month ago. The thieves got away with sixty-three pieces. A man named Frank Crenshaw used one of those guns to kill his wife. Roni Chase shot Crenshaw but didn't kill him. Someone else finished him off with a gun registered to Roni."

He paused, took a deep breath, and looked at Simon and Lucy.

"We have reason to believe that Jack has been obstructing justice by interfering with ATF's investigation of the robbery. Jack agreed to cooperate with ATF's investigation in return for a favorable recommendation to the U.S. attorney, only he seems to have forgotten what it means to cooperate. I told him I'd keep our deal quiet, but he's forced my hand."

Lucy and Simon rolled their eyes. Kate cocked her head to one side, staring at Jennings. None of them said a word. Lucy broke the silence.

"Why bring it here?" she asked Jennings. "Why involve us?"

"Call it professional courtesy," Jennings said. "No need for any of you to get painted with the same brush if you can persuade Jack to hold up his end of the deal."

"Meaning," Lucy said, "you want us to tell Jack we'll cut him off unless he's a good boy, and, if we don't, you'll gin up a special load of crap for us like the one you just dumped on him."

"Like I said, call it professional courtesy."

"So," Simon said, "what about it, Jack? Are you going to tell the nice man what he wants to know or are you going to let him rain on us?"

"You guys have umbrellas?" I asked.

"Yep," Lucy said.

"And hip waders if we need them," Simon added.

"Keep them handy because right now, I'd say there's a fifty-fifty chance of a shit storm."

"Don't push me," Jennings said.

"Wouldn't think of it. I'll give you what I have, but I want something in return."

Jennings took a step toward me. "You're in no position to negotiate."

"That's where you're wrong. Your obstruction-ofjustice fantasy won't sell. I'm betting that you're one bad break away from taking a long fall and I'm the only guy who can pull you back or push you off the ledge. So, what's it going to be?"

The veins in his neck were popping, and the furies were gathering in my belly, both of us fighting to maintain control. He blinked first, letting out a breath and taking a step back.

"One shot. That's all you get."

Chapter Fifty-four

My head snapped, but the rest of me held steady. "Let's talk about Cesar Mendez."

He nodded, his eyes narrow and wary. "Nuestra Familia."

"They've got the concession on drugs in Northeast Kansas City and, unless you've been drunk on the job, you know that and you know that guns are a growth industry for Mexican gangs."

"None of which is news," he said. "Drug cartels are turning parts of Mexico into feudal states. They need guns, and they're getting a lot of them from this country. They've got affiliates in all our major cities. Mendez has ties to NF in Mexico."

"Which means he's your number-one suspect in the gun robbery."

"And I wasn't drunk on the job."

"Then you must have been totally in the bag when you came up with that crazy-assed story about me obstructing your investigation. So let's talk about Brett Staley."

"You talk. You're the man with all the answers."

"Brett's father, Nick Staley, told me that Mendez was a regular at his grocery, that Brett bought drugs from him. Brett had to know that Mendez was the man to see if you wanted to buy a gun without all the paperwork. Frank Crenshaw was Brett's cousin. He wanted a gun, but he had a record, which meant that he couldn't fill out the paperwork, so Brett hooked him up with Mendez. When Crenshaw killed his wife, Mendez got worried that he would cut a deal with the prosecutor, so he gave Brett a choice. Pop his cousin or get popped. Brett asked Mendez for a gun, but Mendez wasn't that stupid, so Brett stole the only gun he knew about, which happened to be Roni's gun. How am I doing so far?"

"You've got my interest."

"Here's where it gets real interesting. Brett shows up at the hospital right after Crenshaw is killed. He says he's there to meet with Roni, which Roni corroborates. Quincy Carter takes a natural interest in that coincidence, but he loses interest when you show up. Everybody goes home, and Brett drops off the radar. Now I'm just a disabled FBI agent who shakes when he should shoot, but even I can put that together."

Lucy said to Jennings, "Me too. Brett Staley was your informant. You couldn't let him be questioned in Crenshaw's murder without exposing him and losing the chance to take Mendez down."

"Head of the class, Luce," I said. "It's an old problem with no good way out. Your informant commits a crime. Arrest him, and your case falls apart. Cover for him, and your ass belongs to him as long as he lives; he needs money, dope, a woman, or a new address, you can't turn him down. It's worse than having a kid that stays in school forever or a wife that thinks shopping is an Olympic sport."

Jennings's nostrils flared, and Lucy pricked him with another needle.

"That's no way to go through life."

"No, it isn't. Spend your career going after the bad guys, and some punk tries to take it all away from you. But, if the punk goes away, so does the problem."

"Enter Mendez," Kate said. "That's why he was looking for Brett." Jennings swiveled toward Kate, giving her a hard look.

"Sorry, that's one of those things I probably should have mentioned," I said to him. "Kate and I stopped by Staley's grocery yesterday, but it was closed. Mendez dropped by too, and he was looking for Brett. What did you do? Let Mendez know that Brett was working both sides of the street so he'd clean up your mess?"

"You're full of shit," Jennings said.

"You don't believe that," Kate said. "Your pupils are dilating, and the muscles around your mouth are turned down and are doing rapid-fire twitches. You're frightened. The truth does that to people with something to hide."

"And, that's not the scariest part," I said. "Turns out you and Mendez can't find Brett, so you use Roni to draw him out. Get the charges against her dropped, so that he'll think she made a deal to testify against him."

"Assuming she's guilty of anything, which is doubtful," Lucy said.

"And," I said to Jennings, "if Brett was willing to kill his cousin, you figure he won't hesitate to take out his girlfriend, especially after he stole her gun, used it to commit murder, threw it away, and left it where the cops could find it so they'd go after her. Not a bad plan, especially since he figures that he can blackmail his godfather, the ATF agent, into a free pass if the cops get too close to him."

"Except," Lucy said, "Brett didn't count on his godfather going rogue on him. So Jennings makes sure that Mendez keeps an eye on Roni until Brett comes after her, and, when he does, Mendez puts him away. If Roni goes down too, that's a bonus because she's the last of the loose ends. Jennings loses this round to Mendez, but at least no one is going to make him turn in his badge. Besides, going after gangs is nothing but a game of Whac-A-Mole. Put Mendez away today, and there'll be another one just like him running the street corners tomorrow."

"Okay, Miss Da Vinci Code, I get all that," Simon said. "But where do you fit in, Jack?"

"I'm Jennings's insurance policy, another set of eyes and ears looking for Brett Staley. If I find him and tell Jennings, it greases the skids for Mendez."

Jennings fought his control, jittering like me on a good day. "Are you through?"

"Yeah, except for one question. Why did Mendez put one of his boys in the city jail to go after Jimmy Martin?"

Jennings eyebrows jumped, and his jaw dropped. "Who the hell is Jimmy Martin?"

"You don't know?"

"I've got no fucking clue. Who is he?"

"A friend of Nick Staley's. They grew up together and served in Iraq together."

"Why is he at the Farm?"

"Theft of construction materials."

"Since when is that a municipal offense?"

"It isn't. The county didn't have room for him, so they sent him there. He has two kids that are missing, and the judge held him in contempt without bail when he wouldn't cooperate in the investigation of their disappearance, which makes him a kidnapping suspect and, if the worst happens, a murderer."

"How does that get him crosswise with Mendez?"

"I was hoping you'd know the answer to that question. A Mexican kid named Ricky Suarez got ten days at the Farm for drunk and disorderly. He started his sentence two days ago. Yesterday, Jimmy carved the handle of a toilet bowl brush into a shiv and tried to escape. I think he was running from Suarez."

"I talked to Ethan Bonner this morning," Kate said. "He said that Jimmy has been transferred to the county jail. Adrienne Nardelli briefed Ethan after she questioned Suarez. The kid isn't in the gang."

"So that's a dead end," Jennings said. "This guy Martin, he must have been trying to escape because he doesn't want to stand trial for killing his kids."

"Nardelli isn't so certain. She says Mendez could have sent Suarez after Jimmy Martin as an initiation into the gang. Kill someone and you're a member for life. The jail superintendent said that Jimmy and Suarez got into it the day Suarez got to the Farm, but the guards pulled them apart before it got physical."

"That shit happens every day in every jail in the country. It's how the pecking order works. Bottom line," Jennings said, "you don't know anything that ties Martin to Mendez."

"I know you're in a world of hurt if we don't find Brett Staley before he kills Roni Chase."

"You think you can make that work, have at it. But I'm going to be on your ass every step of the way."

Chapter Fifty-five

"Why do people insist they're innocent when it's so obvious they aren't?" Lucy asked after Jennings left. "Jimmy Martin begs Kate to find his kids when we know he was the last one seen with them. And this bozo Jennings says we're wrong about him when he's done everything but draw targets on Roni and Jack. I don't get it. Do they think we are that stupid?"

"Maybe they are innocent," Kate said.

"You've got to be kidding."

"Hear me out. Jimmy Martin and Agent Jennings share one thing in common. They're both afraid of something."

"Great, because I'm afraid of spiders and growing old with flabby triceps, but that doesn't mean I've got anything in common with those two."

"Lucy," I said, "chill. I think I know what Kate's getting at, at least as far as Jennings is concerned. He started something dangerous he thought he could control, and now he's lost the reins. It's a case of go big or go home, only he can't go home."

"That's right," Kate said. "Not to beat the gambling metaphor to death, but Jennings is playing high-stakes poker with Mendez. He went all in, thinking he had a nut hand with Brett Staley, but turns out all he had was a bad beat."

We stared at her, mouths open, waiting for a translation.

"Listen," she said, "there's no better place to study facial expressions than at a Texas Hold'em poker tournament. A nut hand is the best hand at any particular moment, and a bad beat is a hand that looked like a winner but was a loser."

"What's that make Jimmy Martin?" Simon asked.

"A man who bet his kids on a long shot," Kate said.

"I don't buy that," Lucy said, "unless the long shot was getting away with murder. Don't over-science this case. Go back to the beginning. The Martins are lousy spouses and worse parents. I've got no quarrel with that. But Jimmy took the kids. We know that. He swore he'd never let Peggy have them. We know that. He won't lift a finger to find them. We know that. So, what else do we need to know?"

"For starters," I said, "we need to know if Adam Koch is telling the truth about Jimmy taking the kids or whether he's trying to avoid two more murder charges. We need to know if Jimmy is just a down-on-his-luck blue-collar guy who's pissed off at his wife or if he's a psychopath who would murder his kids to keep her from getting custody. Plus, we need to know why Jimmy tried to escape. Let's start with Adam Koch. Simon, did you find anything else in the police files?"

"Nothing that proves whether Adam is telling the truth. The kid is a pedophile and a confessed child murderer who had easy access to the Martin kids, and, most importantly, the story he tells incriminates him as much as it incriminates Jimmy because it puts him in Peggy's house with the kids when they disappeared. If he's lying about Jimmy, that makes him the last person to have seen those kids alive."

"Anything else?"

"KCPD posts crime statistics on their website broken down by offense and location. There aren't any other cases of missing kids in Northeast in the last five years. Predators like Adam tend to stick to their own neighborhoods. The Montgomery and Martin kids were snatched two years apart. That fits with a pattern where the predator holds off as long as he can until he can't resist the urge any longer. Adam knew he was screwed up. He tried to quit the kiddie porn, but he couldn't, no matter how many times he slept with Peggy. His urges may have overwhelmed him, the opportunity presented itself, and here we are."

"Make up your mind," Lucy snapped. "Was it Adam or Jimmy?"

"Sorry, Luce. I'm not ready to pick a winner."

Simon's ambivalence took the air out of the room, all of us sharing his uncertainty. It wasn't only that we wanted to be right, we had to be right if there was any chance we'd find Evan and Cara Martin alive. They'd been gone almost a month without so much as a false sighting, no one sure they'd seen the kids at a mall in Montana, no one swearing they'd seen them at Disney World, SeaWorld, or anywhere in the world. Either they were in a locked room or buried in a shallow grave, and the longer it took to find out which, the more likely it was that we'd find nothing but bleached bones and heartache.

Time was running out for them and for me. Jennings had made his case too personal, letting his future depend on getting it right. I had done the same thing, betting my past against my future—what I should have done to save my children, Kevin and Wendy, against what I'd yet to do to rescue Evan and Cara and protect Roni. No matter how many times I told myself that it wasn't my fault, that bad things happen to good people and worse things to innocent children, I couldn't stop trying to patch my soul. It shamed me to compare my old pain to Peggy Martin's certain anguish, to admit that her loss would compound mine, but there it was, the threat to Roni's life weighing just as heavily. I'd crossed my own line and couldn't see back to the other side.

"What do we do now?" Kate asked.

"Start over with the time line, beginning with when Adam says he saw Jimmy leaving the house with Evan and Cara," I said.

"That was around eight-thirty in the morning," Lucy said. "According to the arrest report, the police picked him up at twelve-thirty that afternoon, which is not a lot of time to kill his kids, bury them where they can't be found, and steal a truckload of copper."

"But it is enough time to leave the kids somewhere, figuring he'd pick them up after the job was done. So, that's what we're looking for. Lucy, go see Peggy, ask her if she knows where he might have left them."

"We've asked her a hundred times," Lucy said.

"Ask her again and talk to Ellen Koch. Get everything you can about Adam, his relationship with Peggy, and what happened the morning the kids went missing. And take a run at Adam if he'll talk to you," I said.

"I'm on it. Where are you headed?"

"Kate and I will take another shot at Nick Staley and Jimmy Martin, and I've got to figure out some way to protect Roni even if she won't talk to me."

"You can't protect her unless you're on her twenty-four seven," Lucy said. "And we don't have that luxury. You're going to have to choose."

"I can't do that. I've got to keep the balls in the air as long as I can."

Kate picked up her purse. "I've got to make a call. I'll meet you downstairs," she said, closing the office door behind her.

Simon opened a desk drawer and handed me a cell phone. "It's clean and prepaid for a thousand minutes. Turn off your cell phone. That way Jennings can't monitor your calls and texts and he can't use cell towers to ping your phone and keep track of your movements."

I slipped the phone in my pocket. "Nice touch. I'll call you if I need you."

"What am I supposed to do while you and Lucy are running around saving the world?"

"Do what you always do," I said. "Something brilliant."

Chapter Fifty-six

I found Kate pacing the sidewalk, phone glued to her ear. When she saw me, she turned and walked the other way, leaving me to wait next to her rental.

"Everything okay?" I asked when we got into the car.

"Sure, fine. Where to?"

"I mean your phone call. It must have been important. You left in the middle of a pretty intense conversation."

She swept her hair back with one hand, turning the key in the ignition with the other. "Sorry. Couldn't be helped."

"You always do that, you know, sweep your hair back whenever you're uncomfortable. I know it's not one of those gone-in-a-flash micro facial expressions that prove Oswald shot Kennedy and Ruby shot Oswald and the cop who shot Ruby was really a mob guy working as an undercover double agent for the CIA and Castro. But you always do it and it means you're uncomfortable, and like you always tell me, lying makes people uncomfortable."

"Unless they're very good liars."

"The good ones don't sweep their hair back. So, are you going to tell me the truth or tell me that everything is okay?"

She pursed her lips. "I hope everything will be okay. How's that?"

"Fair enough. Anything I can do to help?"

"No more than you're doing, especially calling me on the hair-sweeping part. Now, where to?"

"While you were on your call, I tried Roni's cell phone again, but she's still not answering. Let's swing by her office first. If she's not there, we'll try Nick at the grocery, then Roni's house."

Roni's office was unlocked, the lights on and nobody home. There was no sign of a struggle, no drops of blood, no desk drawers and client files scattered across the floor. The cup of coffee on her desk was still warm, a bite missing from the bagel sitting on a napkin next to the cup. Her computer was open to her Google homepage, her calendar blank, her e-mails a junk buffet, an icon visible at the bottom of the page showing that she had opened another window.

I clicked on the icon, her homepage trading places with an Excel spreadsheet laying out the dismal figures for Staley's Market. Roni had either left in such a hurry that she'd left the door unlocked and forgotten to close out of her client's confidential files or she thought she'd be right back. She wouldn't be happy if she walked in and caught me thumbing through her files, but, at this point, I cared more about keeping her alive than keeping her happy.

I studied the numbers for Staley's Market. It was dead in the water, its debt dwarfing its assets, its expenses guzzling a vanishing income stream. Nick hadn't taken a salary for three months, and he'd cut the fifteen hundred a month he'd been paying Brett to half that. Staley's file included financial statements for a company called Forgotten Homes LLC, which I guessed owned his soon-to-be-foreclosed-on rental properties. He'd used the rental income to keep the grocery afloat, but it wasn't enough and now he was losing both, the last rents paid three months ago, expenses continuing to accrue.

Scrolling through her client list, I pulled up Frank Crenshaw's records, his numbers worse than Nick Staley's. Kate was watching over my shoulder.

"Check to see if she did any work for Jimmy Martin."

She did, preparing a joint tax return for Jimmy and Peggy for last year. Their income was half of what it had been the year before, the downturn in construction taking a toll.

Roni was a witness to the economic meltdown in her corner of the world, delivering terminal financial diagnoses to people with whom she'd grown up. The numbers were one-dimensional, incapable of capturing how it must have felt for Frank Crenshaw to tell his wife they were broke, for Nick Staley to shove his son below the poverty line, and for Jimmy Martin to sweat about how he'd keep a roof over his kids' heads.

"All of them, Crenshaw, Staley, and Martin were going down at the same time," Kate said.

"I wonder if they were going down together."

Frank Crenshaw had let Roni break the news to Marie Crenshaw at LC's Bar-B-Q and then leave them alone to talk it over while she went to the bathroom, Frank saying something to Marie that bought him a slap across the face, a blow he answered with a gunshot. I'd asked Roni if she thought Frank was doing something illegal to earn money he needed to keep his scrap business afloat. She'd said Frank was too honest to try and that Marie was too honest to let him, but I knew that honesty was no match for desperation.

If Frank or the others had made that leap, they would need a legitimate business to launder the money or they'd have to bury it in their backyards. I searched her client list, looking for another business or partnership owned by all or some of them, finding none, realizing that there was another reason to doubt that scenario. If they had had any extra cash, Crenshaw and Staley would have used it to keep their businesses alive, and Martin would have used it to pay his mortgage instead of stealing copper tubing from a construction site.

I quizzed the tenants on either side of Roni's office. One of them said she'd been there earlier in the morning, but he hadn't seen her leave and hadn't seen anyone going into her office. We'd been there long enough that she should have been back if she had planned to be gone a short time. I called her again.

"She hasn't answered any of your calls. What makes you think she's going to answer now?" Kate asked as we headed for Staley's Market.

"Wayne Gretzky."

"Hockey? You're a hockey fan? You never told me."

"Never watched a game from beginning to end, but I've liked Gretzky ever since I heard him say that you miss a hundred percent of the shots you don't take."

I braced myself, one hand on the dash, as I shimmied and grunted, collapsing against the car seat.

"Left turn onto Lexington," I said, as if nothing had happened.

"You don't quit, do you?"

"Try not to."

"It's heroic, but only to a point. You can't keep it up, and sooner or later you really will shake when you should shoot and you won't be able to shake that off."

"Thanks for the vote of confidence."

"Notice that I left my hair alone. I'm telling you the truth, and you know it. You can't spend the rest of your life asking for do-overs for Kevin and Wendy. First there was Lucy, fresh out of jail. You got her a job and a boyfriend and ended up with her house. Not a bad deal in the redemption sweepstakes, but you should have quit while you were ahead because Roni Chase is up to her eyeballs in who knows what and Evan and Cara Martin may, God forbid, be past redemption."

It was as if she had read my mind the moment before she left to make her phone call.

"So what would you have me do? Walk away? Hope Adrienne Nardelli and Quincy Carter and Braylon Jennings handle it?"

"It's their job."

"And they don't have the time or resources to do it. Nardelli and Carter have too many other cases, and Jennings is too busy trying to save his ass."

"That doesn't mean it always has to be you. Next time say no. Go fishing. Take up golf, photography, or painting. Or write a book. That's what everyone does when they can't think of anything else to do."

"I'd rather shake."

"I know. That's what scares me."

The things in life you can't consign to memory's dustbin fall into three categories: first, last, and best. Stick the modifier in front of most any noun, and you'll see what I mean—friend, dog, job, child, lover, and sex. Kate scored on three out of six of these forget-me-nots.

"Why are you here?" I asked her.

"You don't drive much, remember?"

"That's not what I mean. Why did you take this case?"

"I told you. I owed Ethan Bonner."

"Why?" We stopped for a traffic light. She looked at me, deciding what to say, until the light changed and the driver behind us honked at her to get moving. She jumped on the gas, the car jerking into the intersection.

"Six months ago, Alan got into some trouble."

Alan was Kate's ex-husband, a skinny, humorless, short, hairless, chinless man who crawled under my skin and never left because Kate found something in him that she fell in love with that I couldn't see, didn't have, and wished I did even though she and I weren't together.

"Alan who wouldn't say shit if he had a mouthful?"

"No. Alan who is the father of my son, Brian."

"What did he do?"

She sighed. "Went crazy the way middle-aged men do when they think their belly is growing and their dick is shrinking. A woman he met at a speed-dating event accused him of putting something in her wine so he could have sex with her when she was passed out. I called Ethan, and he dropped everything, flew to San Diego, and got it cleared up before it made the paper."

"How?"

"He was able to prove that she passed out because of a reaction between the wine and a couple of different medications she was taking and that she'd made up the rest."

"They didn't have sex?"

"Before she passed out, not after."

"Why'd she make the accusation?"

"She got mad when Alan didn't ask her out again."

"Boy, Brian didn't deserve that."

"Neither did Alan."

I smiled at her. "You're good to the ones you love."

She smiled back. "And now you know why I'm here."

Chapter Fifty-seven

Traffic was blocked off at both ends of the block, police barriers and uniformed cops keeping us from getting close to Staley's Market, a small crowd forming along the line of sawhorses. I got out, gripping the open car door, and scanned the street. A squad car, an unmarked Crown Vic, and two ambulances were parked in front of the market, a body lying in the open doorway too distant to make out race or gender.

"Oh, my God," Kate said. "Who do you think it is?"

"No way to know from here. Could be someone was trying to rob the store and ran into Nick Staley and his nine-millimeter."

"Why rob a store that's out of business?"

"Yeah, I know."

"You don't think it could be . . ." She stopped, unable to complete the sentence.

"Roni?"

Kate nodded, echoing the fear that was turning me inside out. Everywhere I went in this case, I got there too late.

I signaled to one of the cops on the line. When he turned, I recognized him from the hospital.

"Fremont!"

He hesitated a moment, matching my face to his memory, meeting us at the center of the intersection. "Agent Davis. What are you doing here?

"We were on our way to see a man named Nick Staley. That's his grocery. What's going on?"

"Double homicide."

260

"Any ID?"

"None yet, one older and one younger, that's all I know. I just got here."

"Who's got the scene?"

"Detective Carter."

"I may be able to identify at least one of the victims."

"I'll call him, see where he wants you," he said.

"He's probably pretty busy. Don't worry," I said, patting him on the shoulder, "I'll tell Carter you weren't here yet."

It was all I could do not to run down the block, visions of Wendy lying on a New York City street, face against the curb, telling me she knew I would come for her as I scooped her into my arms, hugging her, watching her die. Fearing my nightmare's renewal, I held myself in check. I'd get there soon enough.

Crime scenes are organized chaos, everyone doing their jobs, no one paying much attention to anyone else, assuming that whoever is there belongs there. No one stopped us, asked us who we were or what we were doing until I reached the body in the doorway, taking a deep breath, bending over, hands on my knees when I saw Eberto lying in a pool of blood.

"Eberto Garza," Carter said.

I hadn't seen Carter; I was too relieved that the dead body wasn't Roni, imagining the sorrow of Eberto's mother that it wasn't someone else.

"I didn't know."

"Know what?"

"His last name, Garza."

"But you knew him. How's that?"

I ignored his question, relief giving way to anxiety. "Who's the other victim?"

"Nick Staley. Owned the grocery. Now what are you doing in the middle of my crime scene, and how do you know this no-account gangbanger?"

I stepped around Carter, over Eberto's body and into the grocery. Nick Staley's body was propped up on the floor, his back against a crimson stained wall, his chest a bloody mess, his legs folded beneath him.

"They shoot each other?"

"Doubtful."

I looked at Eberto's body, his feet inside the door, the rest of him lying outside on the sidewalk. He was on his stomach, his head turned to the side, arms extended over his head as if he had been shot while in flight, an entry wound visible in the middle of his back.

"The bullet could have severed Eberto's spinal cord, struck his heart or another major artery, or all of the above. Staley was an ex-Marine who'd seen combat. He knew how to shoot to kill. Eberto could have surprised him, fired first and ran. Staley could have lived long enough to return fire, taking him down."

Carter said. "The kid wasn't armed. The only gun we found was a nine registered to Nick Staley. Preliminary indications are that it had been fired recently, but there are no powder burns on Staley's hands. Ballistics will tell us for certain if Staley's gun was the murder weapon, but that seems likely."

"The way that Eberto is laid out, it looks like he was shot in the back, probably while he was trying to get out of the store."

"Coroner says Staley was killed during the night, an hour either side of midnight. Eberto was shot later, probably around dawn."

"You think the shooter spent the night in the store and killed Eberto on his way out this morning?"

"The timing works, but why stick around after killing Staley?"

I thought of his son, imagined him on the run, coming back to the store for more money or to get even with his father for smacking him and for a lifetime of other slights. It was easy to picture them arguing, Nick reverting to form, belittling Brett, his son pulling a gun, Nick laughing, daring him to shoot, both of them astounded when he did. Brett could have been drunk, high, or both and passed out until Eberto woke him.

"Maybe he had no place else to go."

"What killer wouldn't have a better place to go than the murder scene?"

"Brett Staley," I said, telling him that Nick had caught his son trying to rob the store and laying out my scenario.

Carter listened, interrupting with the right questions. "That's as good a take as any. What were you talking to Nick Staley about in the first place?"

"You know the missing-kids case Adrienne Nardelli is handling, the Martin kids?"

"Yeah. She told me how you broke the case on that other missing kid, Timmy Montgomery. Makes me almost want to take back all the things I've said about you. How did you get from there to Staley's Market?"

"Peggy Martin was cheating on Jimmy. She filed for divorce, got a restraining order against him so he couldn't see his kids except with court supervision. The kids disappeared, and Jimmy refused to answer any questions about what happened to them. Peggy thinks he took the kids to punish her, but she wouldn't give us the name of her boyfriend. I was trying to find out who he was."

"You figured if she was cheating on Jimmy with his best friend, that would make him even angrier."

"Right. And Jimmy told his lawyer the two of them were buddies. Nick acted like he hardly knew the guy, but I think Jimmy was telling the truth."

"Only it turns out the wife was banging the neighbor kid, so it was a wasted trip."

"Not entirely."

I told him about seeing Eberto on the bus on Monday and outside the grocery yesterday along with Cesar Mendez. "And you don't think Mendez stopped by the grocery to pick up a carton of milk?"

"I think he was looking for Brett Staley."

I explained Brett's relationship with Frank Crenshaw and Mendez, and my theory that Brett had acted as the middleman on Crenshaw's purchase of a gun from Mendez and that Mendez had forced Brett to kill Crenshaw so that Crenshaw's lawyer wouldn't offer Mendez in a trade for his client's life.

"I worked gangs for a while. Mendez is smart enough not to get blood on his hands and cold enough to make sure someone else does. But I don't think he'd take any chances on a white boy like Brett Staley. He'd get someone he trusts to pop him."

"Someone like Eberto."

We watched as paramedics rolled Eberto into a body bag, zipped it closed, and carted him away.

"You tell all that to Braylon Jennings?"

"Yeah."

"What'd he say?"

"He's real sensitive on the subject of Brett Staley. I think Staley was his CI."

"Which puts Jennings's balls on the chopping block if his CI has graduated to murder."

"Jennings used his ATF clout to get the charges against Roni Chase dropped so he could use her as bait to draw Brett out, make it easy on Mendez."

"Son of a bitch," Carter said, biting off the words.

"No fun to get played, huh?"

"You talking about what I did with Roni and her gun? Tell me you would have done it different. You've forgotten what it means to be a cop. So has Jennings. Where's Brett Staley now?"

"In the wind."

"And Roni Chase, is she riding the breeze with him?"

"I don't think so. Brett's been off the grid since you cut him loose at the hospital Monday night. I stopped by her office this morning. She'd been there, but had stepped out, left it wide open with a warm cup of coffee on the table."

"Maybe Brett called her, said come and get me. Love will make you forget about your cup of coffee."

"Yeah, but I don't think she's in love with him. Besides, her mother had a stroke a while back, and she's taking care of her. I don't see her running off with Brett or anyone else."

"Maybe he didn't give her a choice."

"You don't know Roni. She makes her own choices."

"And you don't know Cesar Mendez. If he's behind all this, I guarantee you he doesn't give a shit what Roni Chase wants, or Brett Staley for that matter. All he cares about is making sure nothing lands on his doorstep."

"Where can I find Mendez?"

"You can't find him anywhere. Go home before he makes you a hood ornament."

Chapter Fifty-eight

I called Ammara Iverson when we got back into Kate's Chevy, using the clean cell phone Simon had given me.

"Sorry," she said, "I haven't had time to get back to you. Believe it or not, there are other crimes that require my attention."

"None as much trouble as mine."

"Amen."

"Then give me what I need and I won't darken your door again."

"Until the next time," she said.

"With any luck. What do you have on Cesar Mendez?"

"He has strong ties to Nuestra Familia in Mexico."

"How strong?"

"Blood strong. His family is the Familia. They sent him here to run things. They trust him to sell their drugs and send them their money. Word is he's also been sending them guns, all he can get."

"How does he get the guns to Mexico?"

"Each shipment is passed from one collection point to the next until it gets to the border. The farther south the shipment gets, the more guns there are. It's like a dirty snowball rolling downhill. It keeps getting bigger. Once the guns reach the border, they're taken across in smaller lots."

"Where does Kansas City fit into the distribution network?" I asked. "Not surprisingly, it's the halfway point on the north-to-south route."

"Which means Mendez is stockpiling guns. Probably has them spread out so if we find one cache, he doesn't take too big of a hit."

"And that's what happens from time to time. Nothing big,

maybe a dozen pieces recovered in a raid on a drug house. Things like that."

"What's the organizational chart look like? Nuestra must have somebody in the States to make sure the trains run on time."

"We assume they do, but nobody knows who that is. Immigration keeps close tabs on all the known gang members in Mexico who are high enough up in the food chain to handle something like that, and they stay pretty close to home," she explained.

"Would they contract it out to someone not in the Familia?"

"Would you?"

"Depends on how much they trusted him. What else?"

"As gang leaders go, Mendez is not a nice man. When he came to Kansas City, the first thing he did was ice-pick his predecessor to death in front of his girlfriend before he raped and strangled her. One of his lieutenants got busted on an undercover drug buy and told us the story. Before we could put him in witness protection he backed out and refused to testify."

"What happened?"

"Mendez sent him a message. He snatched the guy's mother, cut off her ring finger, sent it to him, and promised to send the rest of her one piece at a time."

"End of story?"

"Beginning. The guy lasted twelve hours when he got back on the street. We found his body and his mother's tied one on top of another, both of them naked."

"Where can I find him?" I asked.

"You have to be kidding."

"I don't shake and kid at the same time. Where does he hang out?"

"You're crazy. I'm not going to tell you."

"I'll find out one way or the other."

"Well, it won't be from me. I won't have that on my conscience."

Kate drove two blocks after I finished talking to Ammara, biting her lower lip, glancing at me, giving up.

"You can't go after Mendez."

"Look, I'm not delusional, and I'm not suicidal. I'm not going to take him on one-on-one or walk into his house and shoot everyone in sight, pat myself on the back, declare victory, and go home."

"Then what are you going to do?"

"The more I know, the more options I have. Knowing where he lives, where he goes, and who goes with him is all part of that."

"Then why didn't you tell that to Ammara? She might have told you what you wanted to know."

I looked at Kate, smiling. "She wouldn't have believed me." Kate studied me, taking snapshots. "I don't blame her." I called Simon to avoid telling Kate another lie. "I want you to find Cesar Mendez."

"Of course you do. How about I send him a friend request on Facebook?"

"And if that doesn't work, do something creative, like check property and utility records. The guy has to live somewhere."

"Gang leaders aren't like the rest of us taxpayers. They don't own, rent, buy, sell, or trade. They have people who do that for them."

"Then find one of them and follow the trail but find him."

"Which is more important, finding Mendez or doing something brilliant? Because I'm getting close on the brilliant thing. I can drop it if you want me to. Your call."

Simon didn't like being left behind at the office, even though he knew that was where he did his best work. When pressed, he admitted that Lucy and I had the edge in the field, but that didn't satisfy his desire to be on the front lines until I reminded him that his best weapon was sarcasm and sarcasm never stopped a bullet or a bad guy.

"Give me a taste of brilliant, and I'll let you know."

"We wanted the police files on the missing-kid cases so we could look for similarities and evaluate whether those crimes were part of a serial killer's pattern. We didn't find a pattern, but that doesn't mean we were wrong to look for it. The brain appreciates patterns. It's how we organize, process, and understand our experiences."

Simon's other favorite weapon was the long explanation. "I remember. Get to the point."

"So just because there wasn't a pattern of child kidnappings didn't mean there wasn't some other pattern at work here."

"And you found one."

He couldn't disguise his pleasure. "Indeed I did, robberies of gun dealers. I searched for other reports of gun dealers being held up especially after leaving gun shows. That's when they're the most vulnerable. They've got their inventories in the trunk of their cars or the back of their trucks. They're usually alone and tired after a couple of days at a show, especially these victims, who were all seventy years old or older, guys that can't wait to get home, put their feet up, have a beer, and recite the Second Amendment until they fall asleep."

"Simon, I'm getting old."

"Okay, okay. Here it is. Five gun dealers have been robbed in the last three months after coming home from gun shows. Eldon Fowler was one of them."

"Wasn't he the guy who lived at Lake Perry and died when he hit a deer?"

"Right. He was the fourth one. Numbers one, two, and three occurred in Lincoln Nebraska; Ames, Iowa; and Edwardsville, Illinois. The last victim, a guy named Joe Rosenthal, lives in Kansas City. The thieves followed the victims from the gun shows all the way into their garages and grabbed their guns. Fowler didn't make it that far."

"Any of the other victims hurt?"

"The guy in Iowa went for his gun. One of the thieves shot him in the leg, but he's okay. They tied Rosenthal up and left him in the garage. His wife didn't find him until she took the trash out the next day."

"Every one of those towns is within half a day's drive of Kansas City."

"If KC was the hub, the others would be spokes in the wheel," Simon added.

"Any arrests?"

"All open investigations. Each robbery made the local press, and the papers quote the same ATF agent who says all the usual bullshit that they're making progress."

"Braylon Jennings?"

"His Eminence."

"How many guns total?" I asked.

"More than five hundred split roughly sixty/forty between semiautomatic handguns and assault rifles. Ballpark retail value is close to seven hundred fifty thousand dollars."

"Eldon Fowler's wife told you that he called her from the gun show, said someone stole his Ruger Redhawk. Has that gun surfaced?"

"Not yet. The only gun that's been traced to the thefts is the one Frank Crenshaw used to kill his wife."

"Anything else on the driver that passed Eldon Fowler on the highway, the one who called the Highway Patrol and said a crazy man was aiming a shotgun at them? Did you find out what he was driving?"

"I did. It was a Dodge Ram pickup truck. That's not all. Fowler was driving a Ford F-150. CSI found paint scraped against a tree at the accident scene, but it wasn't from the Ford. It was from a Dodge Ram."

"That's why Fowler had his shotgun in the window. He must have seen the thieves earlier that night, and they must have been driving a Dodge Ram. Find out if any of the people we're looking at own one."

"Make up your mind. You want me to do that or look for Cesar Mendez?"

"I want you to do both."

Chapter Fifty-nine

I'd been to a lot of gun shows; long lines of tables stretched wall-to-wall, offering everything from replicas of 1842 U.S. black powder percussion muskets to World War II Japanese bayonets, to the latest in easily concealed personal protection handguns and assault rifles, plus ammunition for all occasions. I'd seen Scientologists recruit people who had just snapped up a complete collection of John Wayne western DVDs, an army surplus camouflage wardrobe, and a six-month supply of dried survival meals. And I'd watched fathers instruct sons on the finer points of gun safety, duck blinds, and birdcalls.

The gun dealers were mostly white, mostly older, and mostly scared that the government was going to knock on their doors in the middle of the night and take their guns, none of them worried for a minute that thieves would strip them of their weapons in their garages. But there it was, proof that we're often so afraid of one thing that is so terrible and unlikely to imagine that we dismiss the real likelihood of everyday evil, certain that it will always be the other guy who gets hit over the head.

Five robberies in three months in five different states was not a casual undertaking. It required planning, personnel, and precision by a team of trained people dedicated to the mission, disciplined, and trustworthy. They had to spend enough time at each gun show to identify their target without attracting attention, probably even following the victim home on a dry run one night, doing it for real the next. Cesar Mendez had the people and the balls to make sure they did their job.

Storage of the guns was another problem. It required either a number of secure locations or one extremely secure location that was above suspicion and beyond detection. A gang that dealt in drugs first and guns second operated on street corners and in crack houses. Mendez needed someplace else to store the guns, a place that he could control but that couldn't be traced to him. That meant he'd have to rely on someone outside the gang who could front for him.

Brett Staley fit that description. Mendez could have used him as a straw tenant at a storage facility. I sent Simon a text message adding that to his research list.

As much as anything else, Mendez's operation required patience because Nuestra Familia was unlikely to pay him before they took delivery of the guns. In the meantime, he had bills to pay and people to feed like any other businessman.

That the Kansas City robbery was the most recent of the five was also significant. Having collected guns from the surrounding states, Mendez may have added the local job to round out his inventory without the risk of going on the road where a burnt-out taillight or an overzealous, bigoted cop suspicious of a car full of Mexicans might get them pulled over.

There were a couple of things that bothered me. The first was why Mendez would have sold one of these guns to Frank Crenshaw. That was like a mob guy skimming the casino take, small change that could get a local gang leader ice-picked, family or no Familia. But arrogance and brutality breed a conviction of invulnerability, and Mendez may have considered it his right to cherry-pick a stash of weapons he could dole out as he pleased. He wouldn't be the first family member to disappoint.

The second was whether the guns were still in Kansas City or had been shipped south. The way Braylon Jennings was handling this case made me suspect that the guns were still here even though more than a month had passed since the last robbery. That would be one more reason for him to take the chances he'd taken. If the guns had been shipped south, he would have been forced to follow them and worry about a renegade Brett Staley later. Otherwise, his superiors would ask him too many questions he didn't want to answer.

But why, I wondered, would Mendez hold on to the guns this long, unless he planned more robberies to add inventory to a future shipment. Each day brought an added risk of getting caught. It made more sense to ship the guns out immediately after the Kansas City robbery and let the pending investigations die a natural death before starting over. If the guns were still here, it meant one thing: Something had gone wrong.

Crooks, like honest people, screw up, miscalculate, and outsmart themselves. And, when they are members of a multinational gang, the same thing happens to them as happens to the guy running the regional operation of a big corporation. The home office sends someone to straighten things out. That can make the local guy a lonely man in need of a friend, and I was the friendliest guy I knew.

"We're here," Kate said.

I'd been lost in my thoughts, unaware that she'd pulled up in front of Roni's house.

"Sorry, I wasn't paying attention."

"You were on another planet."

"I was trying to piece this whole thing together."

"Which thing? The Cesar Mendez thing or the Evan and Cara Martin thing?"

"Mendez and the guns."

She pocketed the car key and turned toward me. "Tell me about it while it's still fresh in your mind. Maybe I can help."

Kate made me break it down, asking methodical probing questions, forcing me to admit that my scenario made sense because it accounted for most of what I knew and some of what I believed, but that didn't mean I was right.

"A theory of everything is hard to prove," she said when I'd finished. "You want an explanation that picks up every loose thread in a way that makes sense. Nothing in life is that simple or elegant."

"So are you saying I'm completely wrong?"

"Not at all. I'm saying that your theory makes sense, but there are too many things you don't know to be certain, and when you find them out, it may be that you're more wrong than right. But, your theory is valuable because it provides a framework for figuring those things out. It tells you what questions to ask."

"And who to ask."

"Including Cesar Mendez?"

"Might as well start at the top."

"There's no way I can talk you out of doing that, is there?"

"Not unless you can tell me another way to find out what I need to know."

She shook her head. "That's one part of your theory I can't argue with."

Chapter Sixty

Kate stayed in the car when I got out.

"You coming with me?"

"Go ahead. I'll be there as soon as I make a call."

It was the second private call she had to make today. She wouldn't tell me what the first call was about and I didn't think she'd tell me about this one either, but I leaned in the open car door and asked anyway.

"Is everything okay at home, I mean with Brian and Alan and your father?"

She smiled. "Never better. I'll only be a minute."

Kate prided herself on maintaining a cool exterior, but the flicker in her eyes and the slight tremor at the corners of her mouth betrayed her. I'd waived my right to pry, reserving only my right to be concerned, knowing that, whatever it was, she wouldn't tell me until she was ready, if she would tell me at all. I'd learned the hard way that pressing would raise her wall, not lower it.

Making my way up the walk, I imagined the night Vivian Chase shot it out with her partner. I flashed forward to this week, seeing her granddaughter Martha sitting motionless in her wheelchair in the morning room, and her great-granddaughter Roni taking aim at Frank Crenshaw at LC's Bar-B-Q, Terry Walker's words echoing in my head, *It's as much about blood as it is about time and place*, the front door opening behind me, bringing me back to the moment.

"I saw you coming," Roni said.

She was standing in the doorway, wearing black jeans and a body-hugging black turtleneck. I was so glad to see her that I grabbed her by the shoulders before I realized what I was doing—squeezing her harder than I intended, making her wince—but that's what I do when I find someone I was afraid I had lost.

"Where the hell have you been?"

"What do you mean, where have I been?" she asked, pulling my hands off of her, her tone sharp, her mouth screwed tight. "I've been living my life. I go to work, and I come home."

"You had me scared."

"Of what? I don't know what your problem is. I told you, it's over."

"I stopped by your office this morning. You weren't there."

"So," she said, arms crossed, one hip aimed at me, "you naturally assumed the world had ended."

"You left the door unlocked. It looked like you'd left in a hurry."

"I did. My mom fell when Grandma was giving her a bath this morning, and I had to come home and help get her up. Grandma can't do it by herself. I guess I forgot to lock up."

"Is she okay?"

"Yeah, the world is safe for another day. Okay?"

I ignored her sarcasm. "Where's Brett?"

She backed up a step, her face coloring. "Why can't you leave him alone?"

"His father was murdered last night."

Her hand flew to her mouth, her other arm clenching her middle like she'd been gut-punched. "Oh, my God!"

"He was shot to death in his store sometime around midnight. A Mexican kid named Eberto Garza was also shot to death in the store early this morning, around dawn. Odds are whoever shot Nick stayed in the store and killed Eberto. So, like I told you before, this thing is a long way from over. Now where's Brett?"

She staggered to a white wicker bench on the porch, falling onto it, bent over, covering her face with her hands, crying. I gave her a minute, then sat beside her.

"The police think he's killed three people, and I think he may come after you next."

She sat up, wiping away tears with the back of her hand, rocking back and forth. "He wouldn't do that. He'd never do that. He's not that kind of person."

"A week ago you were probably right. But things he never thought would happen did happen. It spun out of control, and now he's in way over his head."

"What things?"

I told her about Crenshaw's gun, about Cesar Mendez and about Brett trying to rob his father's store. She stopped crying, her face hardening, defiant.

"You're wrong. He couldn't have done any of those things," she said, not convincing me that Brett was innocent but confirming for the first time how much she really loved him.

"Where is he?"

I heard Kate's car door slam before she could answer. I looked at her, her head cocked to one side, asking me a silent question— what should she do. She knew what I was going to tell Roni, had seen her reaction, and was waiting for me to signal whether to join us or give us room. I waved her toward us when Lilly Chase appeared on the porch. Terry Walker was right behind her.

Roni turned toward Lilly, crying again. Lilly hugged her without knowing why, giving me a look that said she blamed me for whatever had happened, shepherding Roni inside. Kate followed them.

"What happened?" Terry asked.

He'd neither lent a hand nor offered sympathy. He was flinty-eyed and calm in the way of men who'd seen enough sorrow not to be moved by it, knowing that others were better suited to the task of giving comfort. He was, like me, more interested in the how and why, more focused on cause and consequence than passion.

"Somebody killed Nick Staley, shot him to death inside his grocery store."

"That's it? That's all you know?"

I had shared with Roni my answers to those questions but saw no reason to bring Terry into the loop until I knew more about him and whether his questions were born of natural curiosity or whether there was a more useful purpose to his inquiry. He'd said that he had come back to Kansas City to see who was left from the old days, that he'd seen Lilly on the porch and remembered her red hair. That was enough to get him into Lilly Chase's house but not into my business.

"All I know for certain."

"And you know better than to flap your lips to somebody you hardly know. Don't blame you, but you can't blame me for asking."

"I don't. Roni is in pretty bad shape, but I'll let her tell you about it when she settles down."

"She won't know anything. If I'm going to find out what happened, I'll have to get you to tell me."

"Why do you think I know so much about it?"

He snorted. "Let's cut the crap. Lilly told me about Roni shooting that fella at the barbeque joint and the rest of it, how somebody finished him off at the hospital. And Roni told me how you've taken such an almighty interest in her welfare, which she says was kind of sweet at first but is really chapping her ass right about now. So, I figure if anybody knows what's what, it's you."

"Chapping her ass? She said that? Doesn't sound like something she'd say."

"My translation. She also says you've got something wrong with you that makes you shake. Is that so?"

The tics arrived on cue, a quick flurry ricocheting from my sternum to my chin and back again. "It's not a big deal."

"Maybe not when you and I are just passing the time, but I'll wager it's tough in a crunch. How'd Roni say you put it, that you shake when you should shoot? Now that's a rough way to be when a bad man is coming after you. All of a sudden you're jumpin' and jukin' and the next thing you know, you're down and out. No wonder the FBI let you go. Can't count on a man that can't count on himself. Too bad, I say, but all we get is the chance to play the game, not make the rules."

Chapter Sixty-one

He said it as if my fate were as certain as tomorrow's sunrise. I didn't want to tell him he was right, that I often woke up in the middle of the night, sweating and trembling, certain that one day his prediction and my nightmare will come true. I was used to shaking in front of other people, letting it pass as if it were nothing more than a sneeze or cough, but this time was different. When the next flurry struck, whipping my head up and back, Terry's quick, satisfied smile and measured eyes made me feel exposed and weak.

One of the curious things about my disorder was that talking about it, especially with someone I didn't know well, could trigger the symptoms. I changed subjects, hoping to regain control.

"Why are you so interested in the details?"

"I'm no different than anybody else. An airplane falls out of the sky or a pitcher throws a no-hitter, good or bad, we all want to know how in the world something like that happened."

"That's what newspapers and cable TV are for."

"Man, you are a tough nut. I'm just an old man looking for a little excitement in my old neighborhood, and you're acting like I need a top-secret clearance to find out how a man died."

"You need a better reason than that."

He pursed his lips, nodding, looking past me, down the street and back, taking a breath and letting it out with his slow confession.

"My family lived down the street in that house," he said, pointing to another down-at-the-heel mansion two doors away. "It was a boardinghouse. The Staley family lived there too."

"When did you leave?"

"Fifty years ago, the night of the Electric Park fire."

"What's Electric Park?"

"It was an amusement park at Forty-sixth and Troost, all kinds of rides, games, and pretty girls. I was there when it caught fire."

He got a faraway look in his eyes, the memory coming back to him, nodding as the images came into focus.

"Man oh man, you should have seen it! That fire was a beast, chewing up the park. Hell, the whole place wasn't more than a bunch of kindling glued together. You ever been in a blaze like that?"

"Can't say that I have."

"Well, trust me brother, you don't want to be. Even the air was on fire, and the noise it made, I swear it was the devil's own voice hollering *Look out 'cause I'm coming for you.* And the people running wild trying to get away wasn't nothing but a mob the cops couldn't control any more than the firemen could the fire."

"What did you do?"

He smiled again, this time softly, shaking his head.

"That devil voice, it was calling me, telling me it was time to chase the darkness, and I couldn't do nothing except answer. But, I'll tell you what, it taught me one of life's most important lessons. One man's trouble is another man's chance if you've got the steel to take it."

"I've got a feeling you're not talking about picking up quarters someone left lying on the ground."

"No sir. I was just a dumb kid couldn't see farther than the end of my dick. Hated my parents because my old man beat my brother and me, and my mother didn't give a shit so long as he didn't hit us with any of her whiskey bottles. They was so beat down all they could do was beat someone weaker and smaller. I swore to Christ I wouldn't end up like them. I was seventeen, and there were only two things I ever thought about: getting laid and getting out."

"And the fire gave you a chance to get out."

"You're damn right it did. The smoke was so thick, I couldn't see where I was going, and it didn't help that no one else could either. I stumbled into the park office. The clerks had taken off, and the day's receipts were just sitting there waiting to be burnt to ash, three thousand six hundred seventy eight dollars, a lot of money in those days and more than I'd ever seen or thought I ever would see. There was a satchel on the floor, and I stuffed it full of cash and took off. Had my stake and never looked back."

"Where'd you go?"

He laughed. "Not as far as I thought I'd go but as far as the money took me. Got to Matamoros, a little border town in Mexico, before I blew it on a gal with big brown eyes and bigger tits who swore she loved me long enough to get me drunk and in bed. Next morning, she and the money were gone, and I was hungover and broke. So I walked back across the border into Brownsville, Texas, lied about my age, and enlisted in the army. Got sent to Korea and bought a ticket home with a bullet in my leg."

"You came back to Kansas City fifty years later to see Lilly Chase. You ever go back to Matamoros to see that pretty girl?"

He laughed. "A time or two. Never did catch up to her though."

"That's some story."

"Best part is that it's true, enough of it anyway."

He slapped me on the back, went inside, leaving me alone on the porch, realizing I still didn't know where to find Brett Staley.

Chapter Sixty-two

They were gathered in the morning room, Roni on the sofa, hands folded in her lap, quiet but composed. Lilly stood next to the fireplace, turning her attention from Roni to Martha Chase, who was in her wheelchair, parked in front of the windows, both absent and present, her view limited to the squirrels chasing one another in the backyard. Terry Walker stood near Lilly, arms at his side, shifting his weight from one foot to the other, looking for a place to land. Kate sat in a chair across from the sofa, watching and listening, dissecting and cataloguing. No one looked my way when I entered the room.

"See to your mother," Lilly said to Roni. "She needs to lie down."

Roni rose from the couch, her head bowed, biting her lip. I followed Roni as she wheeled her mother from the room, down a hallway and to an elevator. She pushed the call button, and the elevator door opened.

"Sorry," she said, backing the wheelchair into the elevator. "No room."

I took the stairs, meeting them when the elevator reached the second floor. Roni didn't speak as she pushed her mother past me and into a bedroom, closing the door and leaving me in the hall.

"We have to talk," I said when she came out. She tried to walk past me, but I blocked her path. "You can be as angry as you like, but you have to talk to me."

"Why?"

"Because Brett is in a lot of trouble."

"And you're the only one who can help him, right?"

"No, but I'm the only one willing to help him. You can help him, but you won't."

"There's nothing I can do," she said, bulling past me.

"Yes, you can. Tell me about your gun, the one used to kill Frank Crenshaw. What happened to it?"

She took a deep breath. "I don't know. I kept in my dresser drawer, with my underwear, like everyone else does. Grandma Lilly picked me up at the police station on Sunday after I shot Frank. When I came home, I took a shower, and when I opened my dresser drawer, it was gone."

"Who knew that's where you kept the gun?" She folded her arms across her chest. "Just Grandma and Brett."

"Then why are you protecting Brett, especially now?"

"Because he didn't kill Frank or his father. He couldn't. He wouldn't. And neither would my grandmother. I don't know who took my gun or why, but it wasn't Brett."

"Why didn't you tell the police?"

"You don't believe me. Why would they? Now for the last time, leave me and my family alone."

The hall where she'd left me ran the width of the house, intersecting at one end with another that extended from the front of the house to the rear. I took a quick walk through both corridors. What had once been a home to dozens of young women and girls had been remodeled into a series of suites, each with a sitting room, walk-in closets big enough for me to live in, and spacious bedrooms. Lilly's was on the back of the house with a view of trees, their remaining leaves a collage of red, yellow, and orange. Roni's was next to her mother's, joined by connected bathrooms.

I made a quick search of her bedroom, finding nothing of significance. She was neat, but not obsessive. She had three books on her nightstand, one a mystery, one about running your own business, and one about understanding strokes. There were no guns, holsters, or ammunition and no love letters from Brett, though there was a framed picture of them, arm in arm, sporting smiles big enough to swallow one another.

Standing at the entrance to her bathroom, I had a clear view of Martha lying in bed on her back. It was a hospital-style bed with a mattress that adjusted up and down and side rails to keep her from falling out. Walking softly so as not to disturb her, I crossed both bathrooms and into her room, watching her chest rise and fall in a gentle rhythm, wondering what life was like for her.

My mother had Alzheimer's, and once, while visiting her in the nursing home, I remarked to a nurse how awful it was for her. She rarely spoke, spending most of her waking hours staring into space, oblivious to everyone and everything around her. The nurse surprised me when she asked me how I knew it was awful for her, making me realize that I was viewing my mother's illness through my eyes, not really knowing what she was experiencing. Perhaps, said the nurse, she was content the way she was because she didn't remember the way she used to be. Since there was no way to know what my mother knew or didn't know, what she felt or didn't feel, why, the nurse asked, should I assume it was awful for her when that would only make it worse for me?

I thought about Roni's mother, trying not to see her through my eyes. She turned her head, opening her eyes, staring at me or through me, I couldn't tell which. I wanted to ask her what she saw, but she closed her eyes again before I had a chance.

When I returned to the morning room, Roni was standing at the windows, her arms crossed. Terry, his hands in his pockets, was making a slow circle around the room, studying the floor. Lilly stood in another corner, talking on her cell phone with someone about funeral arrangements. Kate was still in her chair, entering all of them into her mental database. I caught her attention and signaled to her that it was time to go. Terry Walker was the only one who noticed us leave, raising his head, his eyes creased, his face grim.

"What did you find upstairs?" Kate asked when we got outside.

"How'd you know I was searching?"

"Like I haven't seen you work. You never pass up an opportunity to snoop. And, Roni was in a real snit when she came back downstairs."

"I didn't find anything. She knew I wouldn't. That's why she left me up there."

"If she doesn't have anything to hide, why doesn't she just tell you that?" Kate asked.

"She didn't have anything to hide in her bedroom. As for anything else, I can't get her to talk to me."

"That's because she doesn't want to lie to you. Some people are so uncomfortable with deception they go out of their way to avoid lying. That doesn't mean they don't have something to hide. They may be willing to do the wrong thing even if they have a hard time covering it up. Instead of lying, they use hostility to discourage too many questions."

"Knowing that doesn't make me any smarter. She keeps a picture of Brett and her on her dresser. It's one of those *we're so much in love we can't stand it* pictures."

"I thought you said she couldn't make up her mind about him."

"Her mind was sure made up when that picture was taken. And, when I told her about Nick being killed and that Brett was at the top of the suspect list, she wouldn't have any of it. She's still defending him. Says he couldn't have done it. What did you pick up from the people in that room?"

"When Lilly told Roni to take care of her mother, Roni bristled. Lilly runs the show, and Roni may have had all of that she can take. I watched her with her mother. She loves her and resents her, which is par for the course when the child becomes the parent."

"And Lilly?"

"She's a very strong woman who is short on patience and can't stand weakness. You remember how Ellen Koch showed contempt for Peggy Martin? That's the way Lilly looked at Roni."

"What about Terry Walker? How did Lilly look at him?"

"That was a puzzle. She hasn't seen him in fifty years, but one minute she's mad as hell at him and the next she's all gaga and dewy-eyed."

"Any idea how he feels about her?"

"He's pretty distant. I'm not sure he has much feeling about anybody."

Chapter Sixty-three

"I hope Lucy is having a better day than we are," Kate said.

"I don't know. It will be hard for her to top two dead bodies and one fractured family."

"Don't say that. You could be describing the Martins."

She was right, but the Martin family wasn't the only one to which that description applied. Frank and Marie Crenshaw were dead, their children orphaned, and, depending on what happened to Brett Staley, the description could fit his family as well. It was as if someone had singled out these three families for destruction.

In a world where chaos and randomness held more sway than five-year plans, such misfortune could be nothing more than a commentary on harsh reality. But these families were too closely connected for their pain and suffering to be dismissed as a run of bad luck. The Crenshaws and Staleys were joined by blood and marriage, while Nick Staley and Jimmy Martin had grown up together, gone to war together, and come home together.

"Not just the Martins, all of them, the Martins, the Staleys, and the Crenshaws," I said, running down the list of missing, dead, and damaged. "There must be something else that ties them together, something that would explain all of that."

"Why? Remember what I said about looking for a theory of everything. It's like when there's a cluster of brain cancer cases in one small community and right away people start claiming they're all victims of a corporate conspiracy to pollute the water supply, only it turns out that the cluster is just one series of random events among billions of random events. We live in a world governed by physical laws we can't control or change, and bad things just happen."

"And that world is populated by people with free will who screw up, go nuts, and make a hell of lot of those bad things possible. These three families had one other thing in common. They were all on the ropes financially," I said.

"What difference does that make? Almost one in ten people in this country are out of work, and we're in the worst recession since the Great Depression."

"It could make all the difference depending on what they decided to do about it."

"Okay," Kate said. "Start with Jimmy Martin. He stole five thousand dollars worth of copper tubing, but it was worthless to him unless could sell it to someone. Frank Crenshaw was in the scrap business. He could have parceled the copper out with other scrap and split the money with Jimmy. It may not have been enough money to keep them both above water, but it was a start."

"Which could explain why Frank wanted a gun. Selling stolen property may have made him nervous.

And, just before he shot Marie, he told her something that really set her off. That could have been it."

"But that leaves out Nick Staley. Where does he fit in?"

"Hey, aren't you the one who said I should quit looking for a theory of everything?"

"No. I'm the one who told you never to remind me of what I just said. I could be wrong. Maybe we need to look at it another way."

I thought for a minute, charting the permutations in my head, a light going on. "Maybe Nick Staley isn't the one who doesn't fit in. He and Frank Crenshaw are both dead, which could make Jimmy Martin the odd man out because he's still alive."

Kate grinned. "A theory of everything after all."

"Almost everything. What about Evan and Cara Martin? No matter what Frank, Nick, and Jimmy were into, I don't see how that puts Jimmy's kids in the mix."

"It doesn't have to," Kate said. "Think of the two cases like circles that touch at a single point but don't overlap. One circle is Staley, Crenshaw, and Martin, and the other circle is Evan and Cara. Jimmy Martin is the point of contact between the two circles, but that doesn't mean one has anything to do with the other. Don't forget that there are lots of other circles, including one with Adam Koch's name on it, and his circle definitely overlaps Evan and Cara's."

"I'll give you that. Adam is a lot easier to sell on the kidnapping than Jimmy Martin."

"Which means I'm right and the order of the universe is restored," she said.

"And I'm hungry. It's after one o'clock. I need a burger, and I know where I'm going to get one."

"Where? I only ask because I'm driving. I can circle the block while you eat if you prefer," she said, giving me a gentle poke in my ribs, her eyes bright and filled with mischief.

She was at her most irresistible when she was alive like this, at turns funny, indignant, insistent, and brilliant, enriching her beauty, masking her fears and insecurities, making me forget about mine and the flaws in our relationship. It was a moment filled with promise and pain and one that I had to let pass.

"Westport Flea Market. Best burger in town. I'll call Lucy and Simon and tell them to meet us there."

It took twenty minutes to get to Westport, a midtown collection of bars and restaurants, some more downscale than others. The Flea Market was the only one that counted a serial killer as one of its vendors back when it was just a flea market. Bob Berdella, who kidnapped, tortured, and killed at least six men in the mid-eighties, sold trinkets at the flea market. He died in prison of a heart attack, the Flea Market switched from trinkets to burgers, and the world became a better place.

The restorative power of the Flea Market's cheeseburgers, fries, and rings may never be documented in a double-blind, peer-reviewed study published in the *New England Journal of Medicine*, but that's only because the editors do not understand that holistic nutrition means eating the whole thing. While stuffing our faces, we traded notes.

"Ellen Koch is a mess," Lucy said. "She alternates between blaming herself for what Adam did and insisting that she had no way of knowing there was anything wrong with him and that, if there was, it was all her ex-husband's fault."

"Besides playing dodgeball with her, did you learn anything we didn't already know?" I asked.

"Nope. I had a hard time getting her to focus. I pushed her as hard as I could about the morning the kids disappeared. She finally admitted that she suspected Adam had spent that night at Peggy's. She said she woke up during the night and couldn't get back to sleep. She checked on Adam to make sure he was home. He was gone, but his truck was in the driveway. It wasn't hard for her to figure out where he was."

"Did she see him come home?"

"She says she didn't. Says she tried to wait up for him but fell asleep and didn't see him come in."

"What about Peggy? Did you talk to her?"

"I tried. She hasn't stopped drinking since she found out about Adam, and she's not a clear-thinking drunk. She won't be any help until she sobers up and dries out. While I was at her house, the doorbell rang. It was a couple of the neighbors that had contributed to the fund Ellen started to raise money to hire me. They wanted Peggy to give them their money back."

"What did you do?" I asked.

"I told them that Peggy was broke and that I'd be happy to write them and anyone else who felt the same way a check, but that I'd keep looking for Evan and Cara because it wasn't the kids' fault that their parents were so screwed up. One of them started to cry and said she was sorry and the other one got mad and called me a bitch, but neither one of them took me up on my offer."

"Did you take another run at Jimmy Martin?"

"Not yet. Thought I'd try him this afternoon. How'd you guys make out?"

I explained about Nick Staley and Eberto Garza and how much flak I was getting from Roni Chase. Kate summarized her impressions of Lilly and Roni and Terry Walker. Simon repeated what he'd told me about the robberies of the gun dealers, adding that he'd had no luck getting a line on Cesar Mendez.

"Short of standing on a corner in his neighborhood with twenty-dollar bills sticking out of your pockets and a sign around your neck saying you'd like to buy drugs, I'm out of ideas," he said.

"At this point, it all comes back to Jimmy Martin," I said. "He's the only one left who knows what went down."

"And he's not talking," Lucy said.

"Then I'll have to give him a reason."

"You have one in mind?" Lucy asked. "Because it better be a good one. Finding his kids hasn't done the trick."

"Best one left. Talking to me may be the only way he can stay alive."

Chapter Sixty-four

The Municipal Farm felt like a summer camp gone to seed compared to the Jackson County Jail with its two-person cells, barred slits cut high in the cell wall masquerading as windows, armed guards, and body cavity searches. I left my driver's license and gun with a sheriff's deputy, pocketing my claim check, and followed another deputy to a room where Jimmy was waiting. The room was not much bigger than a closet, with a wall-to-wall table and glass panel subdividing it and a phone we could use to talk to one another, someone else listening and watching, sight unseen.

He was shackled, hands and legs, his face bruised, his nose bent, probably broken, the down payment he'd made for attempted escape and assault with a deadly weapon. Twice before when I'd seen him at the Farm, he had carried himself with a swagger, relishing his defiance of the system, certain he could do the time and thumb his nose at his wife, the court, and anyone else who tried to tell him what to do. That was gone, the chains and the beating he'd taken bowing his stiff neck, leaving him tense, looking over his shoulder even though we were alone. He sank onto his chair, cradling the phone on his shoulder, anxious and jittery.

Adrienne Nardelli had questioned him and gotten nothing. Kate had tried manipulating him, then trusting him, and had a bandage on her neck to show for her trouble. It was my turn.

"You don't look so good," I told him.

"Bad night."

"Escape and assault aren't exactly good career moves."

"Like mine was going anywhere."

"Well, if it makes you feel better, Frank Crenshaw and Nick Staley were in the same boat, career-wise, that is."

He flicked his eyes at me, then down at the table. "I wouldn't know nothing about that."

" 'Course you wouldn't. How do you see this whole thing working out for you now?"

"What's it to you?"

I shook my head. "Nothing. I won't lose any sleep over you. I'm just wondering how you see your options now that you've tacked two big-time felonies onto your theft charge. Your lawyer might have been able to get you a decent deal on the theft, maybe even probation, but now you're looking at a serious stretch. And the whole thing with your kids, you not helping with finding them, the judge is going to screw you down tighter than tight."

"I did what I did. Can't do nothing about it."

"True, but doing the time is the least of your problems."

"What are you saying?"

"I'm saying your biggest problem is living long enough to do the time. Nick Staley is dead."

He squirmed in his chair, his color up and his eyes wide, then narrow and wary.

"Too bad."

"You interested in how it happened?"

"Make a difference?"

"Not to Nick, maybe to you because he didn't die peacefully surrounded by family and friends. He was shot to death in the middle of the night at his store."

He sucked in a quick breath, pushing it out, fighting to stay calm. "Dead is dead. Got nothing to do with me."

"Actually, I think it does. See, I've been piecing this together, trying to figure out what was going on between you and Nick and Frank Crenshaw."

"Nothing's going on. I knew them, that's all."

"A lot better than you let on. That's the way it is in Northeast. Everybody knows everybody, at least that's true for the families that have lived there a long time and you're third generation."

He jolted forward in his chair, the phone falling into his lap, fumbling with shackled wrists to pick it up.

"What if I did, so what?"

"So you lied about your relationships with them or at least you tried to make it sound like you hardly knew them, and there has to be a reason for a man to lie about a simple thing like that. Only reason I can think of is that the three of you were into something you wanted to keep private, something illegal, like stealing copper so that Frank could sell it for scrap."

"I got nothing to say about that. You're not my lawyer."

"The three of you didn't have two quarters to rub together. Frank and Nick were going out of business, and you were out of work. Stealing was one way to get by, and construction materials made sense because Frank could move the stuff for you. But what was in it for Nick? Why cut him in on it when he's not taking any risk or bringing anything to the table? So I think maybe it's just the two of you, you and Frank. Then someone killed Frank and Nick, which leaves you the last man standing, only you're at the Farm, where it's not as hard to kill a man as you might think. A Mexican kid named Ricky Suarez lands there on a drunk and disorderly, you get into it with him before he has a chance to say hello, and the next day you try to escape. There's no way to paint that picture that makes you anything but a marked man."

"I got antsy, that's all. Saw a chance and took it," he said.

"You told Kate Scranton that you knew you couldn't escape and that you just wanted off the Farm. Only county lockup isn't my idea of an upgrade. Lot more bad guys in here, guys who'd put a shank in your back as a favor or just because they're bored. Man has to be pretty damned scared to take a chance like that, and after what's happened to Crenshaw and Staley, I'd say you had good reason."

He looked around again, licked his lips, and edged closer to the glass, his voice a whisper.

"I thought they'd put me in solitary."

"Where you'd be safe."

"Safer, anyway."

"From who? Ricky Suarez, the Mexican kid?"

"I don't know."

"Bullshit. How could you not know?"

"Listen, I'm telling you," he said, his shoulders hunched. "I don't know. I just did my part and kept my mouth shut. I learned how to follow orders in the Army."

"What was your part?"

"Steal the copper. Frank said he could move it, no problem; just mix it in with a bunch of different loads of scrap. We'd done it a couple of other times, small loads, just to see if we could make it work, pick up a few bucks, and it went okay, so Frank, he says it's time to go big. I got a buddy working a job east of downtown. He tells me there's no weekend security on account of the general contractor is going broke and laid them off. Saturday comes, and I drive right onto the site, load my truck, and I'm gone. Not twenty minutes later, some eager-beaver shit-head nigger with a badge pulls me over because I've got an expired tag. Can you believe the shit that happens to me, man?"

"Doesn't seem right."

"You're damned straight it isn't right!" he said, catching himself, pulling back and shutting down, realizing I was pimping him.

"What happened between you and Ricky Suarez?"

"Nothing."

"How did Frank Crenshaw get his gun?"

He stared past me if I weren't there.

"Who was giving the orders?"

He turned his head and coughed, looking at the ceiling.

"You left your house with Evan and Cara at eight-thirty in the morning, and you were busted four hours later. I don't think that was enough time to kill them, bury them, and load your truck with stolen copper. You figured you'd do the job and go get them. Tell me where you left them. It may not be too late."

He folded his arms across his chest, turned his head away, not saying a word. I let the silence work on him, watched him start to squirm, realizing at last there was another possibility.

"Look at you, Jimmy. You haven't had it easy. Guy like you gets hit a lot growing up by an old man whose old man hit him a lot, I'd bet my last nickel that you'd do the same to your kids. That's the way it works. We become the people we hate. And you're full of hate and mad at everyone. I get that. But the people I talked to say you loved your kids; that you lived for them. That may be the one and only good thing about you. A man like that wouldn't hurt his kids and wouldn't just dump them while he pulls a job. No, a man like that would leave his kids with someone he trusted to take care of them. Who was it, Jimmy? Who did you give your kids to?"

"Do I look that stupid?"

"You tell me. A gun dealer named Eldon Fowler was robbed up at Lake Perry last month. The thieves were chasing him down a gravel road in the woods when he hit a deer. Fowler died of a heart attack, but that's enough to make a case for felony murder since he died while a crime was in progress. The crime-scene investigators found paint on the trunk of a tree that came from a Dodge Ram. If Nick Staley, Frank Crenshaw, or you own a Dodge Ram, it won't be hard to tie you to his death. Be better if you tell me now than if you make the prosecuting attorney put it together."

His eyes burned, full and wet, as he spat on the floor. "You go to hell."

Chapter Sixty-five

Kate told me that it takes five compliments to compensate for one insult, a commonsense rate of exchange that resonated as fair. Healing is slow, uncertain, and hard.

As I walked out of the jail, I wondered how many bad traits a lone good one could balance out, whether there was a cosmic calculator programmed with an algorithm to weigh and rank each of us, spitting out the results in this life or the next, if there was one. I wasn't religious, didn't belong to a church or a tribe, and didn't pray or meditate, kneel or genuflect. Though I believed that there were all kinds of reckonings, that reaping and sowing were inevitable and necessary, I couldn't do the math on Jimmy Martin, a man whose anger, hate, crimes, and fear threatened to consume his singular love of his children.

That didn't mean he hadn't killed his kids. People twist love in a lot of different ways, sometimes making it an excuse for murder. But the time line made it more likely that he had entrusted Evan and Cara to someone else. And that didn't mean they were still alive. Joy and I had done the same thing with our son, Kevin.

Jimmy had admitted to stealing the copper, partnering with Frank Crenshaw to fence the goods, and staging an escape to protect him from an unknown but real threat. More important was his Nuremberg defense that he was just taking orders and that he didn't know who was giving them, the latter claim believable but only to a point.

No one would confuse Jimmy with being the sharpest tool in the toolbox. His life had been a series of fuckups. He was the kind of man who could be trusted with doing one thing at a time and not much else. Steal the copper. Whoever was giving the orders forgot to tell him to check his vehicle tag first, exactly the kind of thing that Jimmy would never think to do, blaming everyone but himself when that's what got him caught.

Three other things stood out from my interrogation. The first was his reaction to Nick Staley's murder, the news giving him a kick in the head but not knocking him out, as if Staley's death had been a matter of when and not if.

The second was his pain, not because of the beating he'd taken but because of his kids. It was raw and real and, I realized, the source of his fear. Ever the good soldier, he knew how to take orders and bullets. But it was different with his kids. He knew they were in danger and that the only way he could help them was to keep his mouth shut.

Frank Crenshaw and Nick Staley had been killed to keep them quiet or because they had pissed off the wrong people. Had Jimmy not been arrested, he'd probably be dead by now as well. While it wasn't impossible to kill someone in jail, it was complicated and messy, leaving whomever ordered the hit to trust the least trustworthy.

The easiest way to control Jimmy while he was in jail was to give him a good reason not to cooperate. There was no better leverage than his kids. Whoever had Evan and Cara would need to prove to Jimmy that they were alive and well or he'd have no reason to cooperate. Yet he was afraid for his life, knowing that his death would eliminate any reason to keep Evan and Cara alive, making solitary confinement the safest place for him and for his kids.

I ran through it again and again, each time coming to the same conclusion. Whoever had Evan and Cara wasn't trying to kill Jimmy and, therefore, hadn't killed Frank Crenshaw and Nick Staley. Someone else was collecting dead bodies, someone who had a stake in the theft ring. Which meant that Jimmy was into something else heavy enough that his kids' lives hung in the balance.

The third thing was Jimmy's reaction when I told him about

the Dodge Ram. He was cornered but didn't know what to do except fight.

The county jail was at Thirteenth and Cherry on the east side of downtown. Lucy and Kate had insisted on driving me, but I'd refused and had taken the bus. It was a small-scale declaration of independence, one I made to have time to think things through on my own and to remind myself that there was still such a thing as my own time, my own way, my own life.

The week was piling up on me, and my body was vibrating like a tuning fork. It was late afternoon, the sun surrendering to grimy clouds that matched the fog creeping into my brain. The October air had quickened, turning cold, smelling of rain. I cinched up my jacket collar and began moving, wrestling with the possible permutations, hoping I couldn't walk and shake at the same time.

I started with Frank Crenshaw and Jimmy's construction materials recycling operation. Crenshaw didn't strike me as management. From his lazy eye to the failure of his business to the short-tempered murder of his wife, he wasn't a guy who would know how to put together a stolen-goods ring to pay the bills.

Nick Staley was a better choice. He knew the importance of diversifying, buying rental properties, and he was willing to rob Peter to pay Paul, diverting rental income to his grocery. Most of all, having been an Army sergeant, he was a man used to giving orders. Using Jimmy to steal construction materials and Crenshaw to fence them had to have been his idea. That's what he brought to the table in return for his cut, that and his son, who had to know what was going on and was likely doing his bit for the cause.

Like any plan that looked good on paper, it was undone by human foibles and overlooked details. With Jimmy, it was an expired tag. For Frank, it was the pressure of crossing a line he never imagined crossing and a wife who rejected his midlife career change.

And for all of them, it was Frank's gun that pulled loose the final fatal thread, unraveling Braylon Jennings's investigation of Cesar Mendez. Brett Staley was Jennings's confidential informant, making him the nexus between his father's operation and Mendez. If Mendez found it necessary to have Frank Crenshaw killed to protect his gun trafficking, he'd likely have felt the same about Crenshaw's partners, forcing Brett to act as his proxy.

I liked that mosaic until I tried to fit in the piece with Eberto Garza's name on it. If Brett Staley had killed his father, why would he wait in the store all night only to kill Eberto? It made more sense that Brett hadn't killed his father, that instead the killer was waiting for him to close the circle. Perhaps Mendez had sent Eberto to check on things at the grocery, and in the dark, the killer, exhausted and stressed from killing one man and waiting for another, had shot Eberto by mistake.

It was a way to make the piece about Eberto Garza fit, but it felt like I was squaring a round edge. That was a lot of killing to hide the origin of a single gun. It was like shooting your dick off because you had an itch in your crotch.

There was another problem. Jimmy had to have taken his orders from someone. If it was Nick, he had no reason to lie about it since Nick was dead. Conclusion: Nick was taking orders from someone higher up in the chain of command, and Jimmy didn't know whom that was.

Isolating Jimmy from that information was insurance against him giving it up, but that wouldn't stop him from trying to figure it out. If Ricky Suarez frightened him enough to stage an escape, he must have suspected that Cesar Mendez was on top of the totem pole.

I was migrating north and west, aiming for the Transit Plaza at Tenth & Main with no more of a plan than to take the Number 24 out Independence Avenue, get off, and keep walking until I found Cesar Mendez or he found me. As plans went, it was a lousy one, but it was the best I could do.

I reached Main and turned north, passing a parking garage, feeling more than seeing someone behind me, his footsteps matching mine, keeping a distance I guessed at ten feet for half a block. I stopped at the traffic light at Twelfth and Main, not turning to see what he would do. There were three other people on my corner and more crossing toward me, plus traffic moving in all four directions, making a daylight attack unlikely.

"I hear you're looking for Cesar Mendez," a voice said from behind me.

I turned around. It was the hostage negotiator, Jeremiah Quinn.

Chapter Sixty-six

The thing that most struck me about Quinn when I met him at the Municipal Farm was his nonchalance, his water-off-a-duck's-back reaction to a man holding a woman hostage, a homemade knife at her throat. I'd known guys like him on the bomb squad, guys who looked at a bundle of wires wrapped around a package of explosives and shrapnel the way the people who do the *New York Times* crossword puzzle in ink look at the Sunday edition, an interesting problem to be solved but not one they hadn't seen before.

They lived for the competition, the higher the stakes the better. And like a center fielder that drifts back, loping to the warning track, glove extended at the last second, making a snow-cone catch and bouncing off the wall with a smile before trotting to the dugout, they made it look easy.

I wasn't one of those guys. I sweated a case from start to finish, second-guessing, starting over, feeling a piece of me die if it went bad, thanking a god I wasn't certain I believed in when it went right. In the years since I began shaking I sometimes wondered if going all in all the time hadn't taken a toll on my brain, stressing a neural connection until it short-circuited. The doctors told me no, but what did they know? They couldn't even come up with a better name for my movement disorder than "tics."

The light changed, people sliding past us, scattered wind whipping raindrops splattering at our feet. I flashed on images of Quinn talking to Kate in the ambulance, handing her a card, and of Kate walking out of Simon's office saying she had to make a call and staying in the car when we got to Roni Chase's house to make another.

"Kate Scranton called you," I said.

"She's persistent."

"What did she tell you?"

"That you're proud, stubborn, and resistant to reason."

"That's it?"

"And she said you need a minder."

"What did you tell her?"

"I told her I don't babysit."

"What do you do?"

"I help people make peace or make war."

"I thought you were a hostage negotiator," I said.

"That's the peace part. Not every conflict can be resolved. People need help with the fight too."

"How do you do that?"

He shrugged. "Make sure they know what they're fighting for and why and that they understand what they have to do to win. If they can't do it or aren't willing to do it, then it's time to make peace."

"And if they are willing to do it?"

"I show them how."

"Ever do it for them?"

"If they can't and if they pay me enough."

"What if they can't pay you?"

"Maybe. If I care enough about who wins."

"Is Kate paying you?"

"We'll see."

He was shorter than me and younger by at least ten years. He also carried less weight, but more of it was wiry muscle. His leather jacket hung loose, a slight bulge on his right hip I took for a holstered gun. He was willing, that much was for certain, and he was for hire, my gut telling me it didn't matter for which side as long as the money made it into his account. Not my type.

"I'll pass," I said, turning my back and stepping off the curb.

"I found Mendez. He wants to talk to you."

The light turned red again. I came back to the sidewalk. "Why would he talk to you, and why does he want to talk to me?" Quinn smiled. "Two questions, same answer. He realized it's in his best interests."

I didn't like Quinn, and I liked it less that Kate had gone behind my back telling him enough to get Mendez's attention, information that could give Mendez more of an edge than he already had.

"How do I know you didn't tell Mendez too much and that we aren't walking into a trap?"

"This isn't my first dance. Besides, I'm guessing you were about to go hunting him. What were you going to do? Set a trap and use yourself as bait?"

The really annoying thing about guys like Quinn was that they were too often right and they knew it. "How'd you find Mendez?"

"I've done some work with gang task forces. I knew who to ask and where to look."

"What did you do? Invite him to meet you at Star-bucks so you could buy him a latte?"

He shook his head, letting out a long breath. "Kate was right. She said you'd make this difficult, so I'm going to make it easy. I've been following you since you left the jail. You're shaking and wobbling, just like Kate told me you would. She said that you wouldn't listen, that you'd turn me down, and that when you did I should tell you that the moon is pink, whatever the hell that means."

I chuckled. "She said that?"

"She did. And she said to tell you that if you try to do this on your own and get yourself killed, Joy will never forgive you, and she won't either."

"And how are you going to keep me from getting killed?"

He reached into his coat pocket and pulled out an orange. "With this."

"A piece of fruit?"

He opened his coat, showing me the butt of his gun. "In case the orange doesn't do the trick."

Chapter Sixty-seven

Quinn drove a stripped-down black SUV wrapped in dark tinted windows, stick shift and rubber mats, no sound system for talk radio, top forty, or hard rock, the cup holders stuffed with gum wrappers, loose change, and wadded scraps of scribbled paper. There was a canvas bag on the front passenger seat that smelled like old sweat but rattled like it was packed with steel when I moved it to the back.

"More oranges?" I asked him.

"Odds and ends," he said, settling behind the wheel and tossing me the orange. "Whose orange is that?"

"Yours, I guess."

"Don't guess."

"Okay. It's yours."

"Based on what?"

"You gave it to me."

"Whose name is on it?"

I rotated the orange, finding the familiar stamp. "Sunkist."

"My name Sunkist?"

He was making a point that began to dawn on me. "No, and neither is mine."

"Exactly. So you've got the orange. That gives you a possessor's rights. Maybe that's enough for you to keep it, maybe not. But I want the orange. I tell you it's mine, that I bought and paid for it and I want it back. Naturally you say bullshit because you've got the orange and I don't have a receipt for it and my name isn't Sunkist. Now make peace."

I laughed. "When my kids were little, I'd tell them to work it out or I'd take the orange and neither one of them would get it. They'd both be mad at me, and I'd end up with an orange I didn't want."

"And," Quinn said, "if you were Solomon, you'd tell them to cut it in half."

"But you wouldn't."

"Nope. They'd still be mad. The real is question is, why do you want the orange?"

I shrugged. "I'm hungry. I want to eat it."

"And I want to use the peel to bake a cake."

"You don't look the type."

"I'm not. I prefer moon pies. But if I was, we can both get what we want. You can have the fruit, and I can have the peel. We can make peace because knowing why we want what we want lets us expand the pie and meet both of our needs."

"That's swell, Dr. Feel Good, but suppose I don't give a shit about you or your cake and I want the whole thing because I don't share well with others."

He smiled. "That's when we find out how hungry you are and how badly I want to bake that pie."

"What are you, an ex-cop, a lawyer, a shrink, or just a guy who sells fruit?"

"My father is a psychiatrist and my mother is a psychologist, which means every time I farted when I was growing up, I got analyzed. I broke their hearts when I applied to the police academy instead of Harvard. I spent six years on patrol, another ten as a detective, went to law school at night, passed the bar but never practiced. Couldn't see selling slices of my life measured in tenths of an hour. Stayed a cop and ended up a hostage negotiator until I quit the force and opened up my own fruit stand."

"Why'd you quit?"

"They gave me a choice. Quit or get fired."

"Why?"

"When the fruit is rotten, someone has to take the fall. It was my turn, which was only fair because it was my fault. Two people died. One of them was a hostage, and one of them was a cop."

"But they still use you as a freelancer?"

"The department ran out of negotiators, which made it easy for them to forgive even if they didn't forget. Kate told me what she knows and thinks she knows about your case. I need you to tell me the rest."

I started to talk, but my vocal cords froze, my chin bobbing, my torso following suit, the words finally coming in a stutter.

"It's not a short story. Be better if we stopped somewhere for a few minutes."

"No problem. Mendez won't start without us."

"Are we on a schedule?"

"Anytime after dark. I'll send him a text message when we're ready."

"You must be good if you've got him sitting by the phone waiting for you to call."

"I let him pick the place as long as I got to pick the time. Turf is a big issue for him. It's one of the ways he defines himself. I'm not into real estate, but going in unprepared can get you killed. This way he'll feel like he's in control and we'll be ready."

A powerful spasm jerked me forward, bending me at the waist, twisting me clockwise. I grunted and braced myself, one hand flattened on the dash, the other on the passenger door, taking a deep breath when it passed, looking at Quinn, wondering if he was having second thoughts. He didn't blink, smile, or frown, his eyes doing all the work, boring in, deciding how, not whether. I was another problem to be solved, more water off a duck's back.

"You have some place in mind we can go?"

"Yeah. You look like you could use some religion."

He parked behind a small, two-story church in Northeast, the first floor ringed in limestone, the second in dark red brick. There were no lights on and no other cars in the one-row parking lot. I followed him out of the car to the back door where there was a keypad lock. He punched in a code and opened the door, turning on lights as we walked down a narrow hall.

"Let me guess," I said, "you're a preacher in your spare time."

"No chance. The only thing worse than the pay is the hours. This church has a small congregation. The building is only open on Sunday and Tuesday. I did some work for them a while back."

"And they let you use the church for client meetings?"

"No, but I was with the pastor one time when he punched in the code for the back door."

We came to the end of the hall, and he opened another door, turning on a single ceiling fixture, casting faint light and long shadows on the bare-bones sanctuary with its hard-backed wooden pews, scuffed and scarred. Stained-glass windows lined the walls, one of them broken out and covered over with plywood. There was a shallow stage with a portable lectern and two leather chairs immediately to our right.

"Take a seat," he said, pointing to the chairs, "and preach to me."

My chair was soft, the room quiet and peaceful. It wasn't a cure for tics, but it was soothing, my body and brain easing as I gave Quinn the gospel, breaking it down into the books of Chase, Martin, Crenshaw, and Staley.

"I think you're right about Jimmy Martin," Quinn said. "He's caught in the crossfire between two sides. Someone is using his kids to keep him quiet, and the other is trying to kill him. If he talks, his kids die. If he dies, his kids die. If that's the world you're living in, solitary confinement looks pretty damn good. Nobody goes to that much trouble for a truckload of copper."

"But they would for three quarters of a million dollars in guns." He nodded, opened his phone, sent Cesar Mendez a text, and looked at me. "One hour."

Chapter Sixty-eight

Quinn drove east on Independence Avenue, slowing down as we approached Roni Chase's office. Night had fallen, and it was dark and deserted, the adjacent storefronts shut down for the day.

"Turn in here. That's Roni's office," I said. "Circle the building. I'll check the door."

"Why?"

"I want to be certain she's not lying on the floor with a bullet in the back of her head."

The door was locked. I peered in the windows, but there was nothing to see, just chairs, her desk, papers stacked in neat piles from one side to the other, her computer monitor turned off, no dead bodies in sight, a light on in the back. Quinn pulled up, leaning out his window.

"The back door is a piece of cake. You want to have a look around?"

"We have time?"

He looked at his watch. "We've got fifty-five minutes. If we can't toss her office in ten, we should hang it up."

Quinn drove, I walked, and he had the door open by the time I caught up to him, his canvas bag open at his feet. He pulled out two halogen penlights, handed one to me, zippered the bag, and put it back in the SUV.

"What are we looking for?" he asked.

"Missing pieces."

"Oh, missing pieces. That's helpful."

I turned off the light in the back of Roni's office, crossed to the front, lowered and closed the blinds on the storefront glass and turned on my penlight.

"If Roni is protecting Brett Staley, she probably knows where he is. We're looking for anything that can tell us where he's hiding."

"You think she's part of this?"

"No. I think Brett is and she's helping him."

"Then that makes her part of this."

"Not in the way you mean it. Whoever killed Nick Staley stuck around in the grocery for a reason. The only reason that fits is that the killer was waiting for Brett. Which means Brett didn't kill his father or Frank Crenshaw. I think Roni is protecting Brett in the truest sense. She's trying to keep him alive."

Quinn's cell phone beeped. He read the screen. "Text message from Mendez. He moved up the meeting time. He says if we're not there in ten minutes we can forget it."

"How far away are we?"

"Ten minutes."

"I'd say Mendez just put your orange peel in his pocket." I took a quick glance at Roni's desk, sweeping everything into a wastebasket and tucking it under my arm. "Let's roll."

Quinn barreled onto Independence Avenue, fishtailing and slaloming through eastbound traffic.

393

"Independence Avenue becomes Winner Road about four miles east of here just before we hit what's left of the old steel mill," he said.

"I've driven past it. There's a building a couple of blocks long that's nothing but a bunch of broken-out windows and aluminum siding."

"That's the billet yard where they stored steel rods and bars. Access is off a side street called Ewing. Winner bridges the steel yard like an overpass. Ewing runs parallel and one-way east down a steep hill. The gate to the yard is at the bottom of the hill underneath Winner."

"We're meeting him at the billet yard?"

"No. There are two layers of ten-foot chain-link fence topped with razor wire to keep people out. The yard is abandoned. No need for on-site security with that fence. We're meeting Mendez at the bottom of the hill beneath the overpass."

"Is that the only way in?"

"There's a road that runs north and south along the yard called Winchester. There's nothing else down there, except a couple of old machine shops and a few broken-down abandoned houses."

"Perfect for Mendez. The overhead traffic muffles any noise. He can put people at the top of the hill on Ewing and down along Winchester in case anyone gets close. This time of night, we should be the only people within a mile. No one will hear or see us. We should have gotten there earlier."

"And done what? Set up an ambush? We're there to talk to the man, not take him down."

"He made sure of that, moving up the timetable."

"This was never about gaining a tactical advantage. There're only two of us, and I don't know how many of them. This is about going in and getting what information we can without giving him a reason to kill us. You want to take a pass, now is the time to tell me."

I shook my head. "This is my deal. Not yours. Drop me off. I'll call you when it's time to pick me up."

He laughed. "I've met Kate Scranton one time, but that was enough to know I don't want her coming after me the rest of my life."

Two minutes later, we stopped at the top of the hill. A burly figure stood five feet back of the curb, camouflaged by darkness, one arm at his side, his hand tucked behind him, no doubt holding a gun. He motioned us down the hill with his other hand.

Quinn let the SUV coast down the hill, headlights picking up the sign above the gate, SHEFFIELD INDUSTRIAL STATION, GATE NO. 2. Another solitary figure stood in front of the gate, hands in his jacket pocket. Rectangular pillars supporting the overpass broke the hill into four segments. The man at the bottom of the hill waved at us, gesturing that we were to pull over into the center, the pillars funneling us toward him. When we were halfway down the hill, he raised his hand, telling us to stop.

High-beam headlights flashed behind us, filling the cab of the SUV. I looked over my shoulder, squinting at three cars that had been parked at the top of the hill beneath the overpass, invisible to us until now. The cars crept closer, the center car holding course, the other two flanking us. Only then did a Lexus sedan emerge from Winchester, passing the man at the gate, blocking us in, its high-beams adding to the blinding glare.

The driver got out of each car on our flanks, opening Quinn's door and mine, motioning us to get out. No one had spoken a word, but there was no doubt who was in charge and what we were supposed to do. They closed our doors, turned us toward the SUV, and made us spread, patting us down and taking our guns and holding them up to the Lexus.

The lights on the Lexus went off, the other cars doing the same. I blinked in the sudden darkness, aware that the passenger door on the Lexus had opened and someone was getting out, my eyes too dilated to capture any other details. I felt a hand on my back shove me toward the Lexus.

There were seven of them, the guy at the top of the hill, the one at the gate, the drivers of the three cars, and the two in the Lexus. They were half my age, faster, and stronger, no doubt armed and anxious to prove themselves in a fight even if it wasn't a fair one.

I looked to my left, expecting to see Quinn, but he wasn't there. Doors on the car next to Quinn opened and closed, the engine racing as it sped away, Quinn staring at me from the rear passenger seat, a gun pressed against his cheek. The numbers had changed, five against one for me and two against one for Quinn. I didn't like either of our odds.

Cesar Mendez stepped toward me as one of the other men handed him the keys to the SUV.

"You wanted to talk," he said. "Let's talk."

Chapter Sixty-nine

"Where'd they take Quinn?"

"That's Quinn's problem, not yours. Luis will take care of him. He's a very safe driver."

Mendez leaned against the front of the Lexus, his hands clasped below his belt, a casual pose, like a sleepy-eyed snake, letting me know that he held my life in his hands and didn't much care whether I lived or died. Guys like him that held back always blew hotter when they finally cut loose. It wasn't much different than what happened to me when I tried to contain the shakes except when I blew, I didn't ice-pick, rape, or strangle anyone. I just fell apart.

"It's your problem if you want any information from me."

"Amigo, you're the one who asked for this meeting."

"And you said yes because you need me."

He spat. "I don't need you, and if I did, I'd take what I need and believe me, you wouldn't turn me down."

We'd skipped hello and gone straight to the pissing match. Two things were likely to happen if I didn't change the conversation. The first was that I'd run out of piss. I was unarmed, alone, and holding a hand that was more bluff than high hole cards. The second was that I would come undone, shake, spasm, and crumble, getting nothing more for my trouble than a kick in the head. The first-round tremors, the little ones, were flickering through me like internal static electricity not yet rippling along the surface. I put my hands in my pockets, pressing down to anchor myself, my right hand bumping into the orange.

"You hungry?" I asked Mendez.

"What? Are you crazy, man? Asking me am I hungry."

I pulled the orange out of my pocket, tossing it to him. "Just asking. You see, that orange is the solution to the problem you and I've got."

He grabbed the orange with one hand, slamming it onto the hood of Quinn's SUV, drew a knife, stabbed the orange, and dragged it across the hood, the blade gouging the paint, leaving the orange to wobble and ooze.

"You are the one with the problem, dragging my butt out here to play games."

The flat thud of the orange being crushed against the hood together with the steel-on-steel screech of the knife scraping against the paint dropped the flag for the gremlins waiting to race through my body. I yelped like I was the one who'd been stabbed, my knees giving way, my upper body banging against the front grill of the SUV as I slid down against it, squatting on the ground, grasping the bumper to keep from falling over.

Mendez stepped back. "What the fuck is wrong with you?"

I laughed, gasping. "That was Quinn's orange, and he's going to be really pissed off that you killed it."

Two of his men grabbed me under my arms, hoisting me to my feet, letting go before my legs were ready to stand on their own, grabbing me again when I started to melt. Mendez stepped into me, clamping his hand around my throat, lifting my chin, starring down at me.

"I got no time to play games with you." I wrapped my hands around his wrist. "It's not a game. I shake. I can't help it."

He tipped his head at the two men holding me up, all three letting me go at once, backing away as I squatted, folding over, my forehead touching the ground, my hands out in front of me like I should have been facing east.

"We're out of here," Mendez said.

I pushed myself up, grabbed the SUV's bumper, then the grill, then the hood, leaning against the car, trying to catch my breath.

Mendez was watching me from behind the Lexus's open door.

"Hang on. I know about the guns."

"What guns?" Mendez asked.

"The stolen guns you're supposed to be smuggling to Nuestra Familia in Mexico."

He came back slowly, reluctant to get too close, as if he might catch whatever I had—the one time ignorance of my disorder had worked to my advantage. He drew a gun, his outstretched arm bringing the barrel a foot from my face.

"I give you one chance to tell me what you got to tell me, or I make sure you don't shake no more."

I took deep breaths, trying to smooth out the tremors, holding one hand up, buying time, stuttering.

"Nuestra Familia sent you here. They need guns. You send them what they need."

Mendez came closer, screwing the barrel of his gun under my chin. "You made a big mistake getting into my business."

"You made a bigger mistake trusting Brett Staley. Now you can't find him, but I can."

He cocked his head to one side, easing back on the gun.

"Tell me where he is and you get to go home."

I took another deep breath, my vocal cords relaxing, my legs holding steady, letting me stand straight. "First, we talk."

"About what?"

"The guns."

He waved his gun at me. "This is the only gun you need to know about."

"Believe me, it's got my full attention, but if anything happens to Quinn or me, you're going to have the cops, the FBI, and the ATF climbing up your ass and coming out of your ears. Work with me and you may get some breathing room, make things right with the folks back home."

His eyes opened wide, his brow popping up. "You're full of shit."

"I don't think so. Five gun dealers have been robbed in the last three months. You were supposed to ship those guns to Mexico, but something went wrong and the guns are still in Kansas City, which can't make Nuestra too happy. Whatever went wrong, Brett Staley is part of it. That's why you've been trying to run him down, and that's what got Eberto Garza killed. In the meantime, ATF is all over you."

"What do you want?"

"Brett Staley."

"Why?"

"I'm trying to protect a friend of mine, a woman. I can't do that as long as Staley is on the street."

"How do I know you aren't working with ATF?"

"One of their agents, Braylon Jennings, tried leaning on me, but I don't belong to anyone. He knows more about you than I do, and once Brett is taken care of, I never heard of you."

"You saying you'd forget about the guns as long as your friend is okay?"

"I'm saying the woman is my problem, the guns are your problem, and Brett Staley is the solution to both our problems."

He thought for a moment. "You got questions, ask me. Then you tell me where to find Brett Staley."

"You do know him?"

He nodded.

"From his father's grocery?"

Another nod.

"You sell him dope?"

He shrugged. "I know he gets high."

"Did he ask you to hook up his cousin, Frank Crenshaw, with a gun?" Mendez shook his head. "Did Crenshaw come to you for the gun?" He shook his head again.

I didn't see any of the tics or twitches that Kate relied on as signs of deception. He was looking at me straight on, not ducking. His answers were all gestures except for one spoken reply that didn't answer the question directly, making it hard to assess his honesty and even harder for me to testify against him.

"Did you sell or give the gun to Crenshaw?"

Mendez smiled, his lips closed. "No."

"Then where did Crenshaw get the gun?"

"He stole it. Now where do I find Brett Staley?"

At first, I thought it was another non-answer, and then I realized he was telling me the truth, the whole truth. I ignored his question.

"Of course. You didn't want to send your people to gun shows, especially in places where they'd stand out. That would've made it too easy for ATF to put you in the mix. Better to contract it out with guys who'd blend in, look like every other redneck with a confederate flag. But I'm guessing they didn't deliver. That's what this is all about, isn't it? You don't have the guns. What happened? Did they want more money or get a better offer?"

"Brett Staley, where is he?"

"I don't know."

Mendez raised his gun an inch from my eye, preparing to squeeze the trigger. "Wrong answer."

Chapter Seventy

Headlights appeared at the top of the hill, a car rolling our way, one of Mendez's men trotting toward it, looking back at him.

"It's Luis—he's here."

The car followed an arc, stopping when it was perpendicular to the driver's side of Quinn's SUV, engine off, high-beams washing over us. Luis stepped out, clinging to the frame of the open door.

"Kill the lights," Mendez said.

Luis ignored him, stumbling toward us, cradling his left arm with his right, his head down.

Mendez lowered his gun, turning toward him, shouting. "What's the matter? Are you deaf? I said kill the fucking lights!"

Luis didn't answer, falling to his knees, then flattening out on the ground. Mendez and the two men who'd been holding me up rushed to his side, the driver of the Lexus hesitating, holding back, his gun aimed at me. The rear door on the driver's side of Luis's car opened. It was Quinn. The driver of the Lexus followed my eyes and saw him, ignoring me, yelling, and taking aim.

I hit the driver in the throat with my elbow, folding him in half, hitting him again, this time on the back of his neck, dropping him to the pavement, a kick to the head putting him out. I grabbed his gun as Quinn drew down on Mendez and the others.

"On the ground, on your face and spread out," I said.

Quinn retrieved his canvas bag from the SUV, sifting through the contents for plastic handcuffs, binding each of them and emptying their pockets. He scooped up their guns, cell phones, and car keys, throwing them over the chain-link fence protecting the abandoned steel mill while I gathered our guns.

"What about the other two?" I asked Quinn, "the guy who was in the car with you and the one at the top of the hill."

"They're resting uncomfortably."

I handed him the orange with the knife still embedded in it. "Mendez didn't want this after all."

Lying on the pavement, Mendez shouted at us. "You're dead men, both of you!"

Quinn walked over to him, pulled his hair, raising his head, and crammed the orange in his mouth. "Not today, amigo."

"So all that win-win, expand-the-pie bullshit," I asked Quinn as we left Mendez behind, "is that just bullshit?"

"The basic principles apply across the board, but the board is a big place. Works great with two neighbors fighting over whose dog barks louder, but not so well with gun-running drug dealers used to getting their way the hard way. Mendez didn't give it a chance, so we had to use a zero-sum strategy he understands. I hope you got what you came for."

"All that and more. Mendez didn't steal the guns. That was Frank Crenshaw, Nick Staley, and Jimmy Martin. Brett Staley had to have been part of it. They were supposed to sell the guns to Mendez, but something went wrong, the deal didn't go through."

"Maybe they got greedy and wanted more money," Quinn said.

"That, or maybe they found another customer and decided to let the market set the price. Nuestra Familia isn't the only cartel buying guns north of the border."

"So Mendez or his competition upped the ante, killing Crenshaw and Nick Staley and going after Jimmy Martin."

"Probably to convince them to sell at the right price. And, right about now, I'd say that the best offer Brett Staley is going to get is his life for those guns."

"That will be the last deal he makes," Quinn said. "No way do they leave him alive after taking out the others. And that means Jimmy Martin is doing time on borrowed time. But why kill

Eberto Garza?"

"Eberto Garza was an accident, a victim of friendly fire if it was Mendez or mistaken identity if it was someone else."

"Who?"

"I don't know. All I do know is that Brett Staley is the key now. He's on the run, and I'm not the only one chasing him."

Quinn nodded. "Where do you want me to drop you?"

"Had enough?"

"I told Kate Scranton I'd get you to a meeting with Mendez and bring you back in one piece. It wasn't pretty, but I did my thing."

"I envy you."

"Why?"

"You know when to quit."

"In my business, that's the name of the game."

"You ever look back, wonder if you should have stuck around or ask yourself if there was something else you could have done?"

Quinn shook his head. "That's the difference between you and me. You're a crusader, and I'm a mercenary. You have to feel that way, or you don't have a reason to get out of bed in the morning. But that's a luxury I can't afford."

"Understood. You can drop me at Roni Chase's house."

"What are you going to do if she stiff-arms you again?"

"Offer her an orange."

Quinn's cell phone rang when we pulled up to Roni's house. He answered and handed me the phone.

"Are you okay?" Kate asked.

"Never better."

"I tried calling you on the phone Simon gave you, but you didn't answer."

I checked the phone. "Dead battery."

"Lucy has been trying to reach you too."

"Tell her I'm fine, and tell her I'm getting close."

"You should call Joy. She's worried."

"You talked to her?"

Kate hesitated. "She called Lucy when she couldn't reach you. Lucy told her about Quinn. She called to thank me for making sure you didn't go after Mendez alone."

"Call her back, tell her I'm okay, that Quinn's taking good care of me, and that I'll be home late."

"It would be better if you called her."

"I don't want to lie to her," I said and hung up.

I shook Quinn's hand, thanked him, and got out of the SUV, watching from the curb as he drove away. He jolted to a stop halfway down the block, brake lights flashing, backing up to where he'd left me, his window down.

"One man's trash," he said, handing me the wastebasket I'd taken from Roni's office.

"I hope is another man's treasure."

I turned on my cell phone. Joy had left me a text message asking if I was okay. I answered, telling her that I loved her. The superintendent at the Farm had also sent me a text message with the names of people who had visited Jimmy Martin, one name raising more questions than it answered.

The front porch light was on. I did a quick sort through the contents of the wastebasket, most of which was mail addressed to Roni and her clients. A collection agency was threatening to file suit against her grandmother, who guaranteed payment of her mother's medical bills. The county sent her a notice of a tax lien that had been filed against the house. There were complaints and demands for a host of other creditors for amounts long since past due.

The mail was no different for her clients, most of them up against the same wall. There was one piece of mail different from all the others. It was a monthly statement showing an account that had been paid on time and in full by a client who couldn't, reminding me again not to confuse the improbable with the impossible.

I rang the doorbell and waited, grabbing the heavy brass knocker on the front door and pounding it against the hard oak when no one answered. Lillian Chase opened it long moments later.

"Where's Roni?"

"Out. She didn't say where."

"I need to borrow your car."

Chapter Seventy-one

She was wearing a warm-up suit, no makeup, looking weary and worried, the lines creasing her drawn face hard won and honest. Her green eyes were cloudy, her red hair brushed out, gray at the roots. It was the first time I'd seen her look her age.

"If you don't have a car, how did you get here?"

"A friend dropped me off. I don't have a lot of time."

"What is that?" she asked, pointing to the wastebasket.

"Roni's mail."

"What are you doing with it?"

"I need to talk to her."

"You're carrying a gun. Why?"

I looked down, forgetting that I was holding the wastebasket under my arm so that my jacket was pulled back, exposing the holster on my hip. I switched the wastebasket to my other hand, holding it at my side.

"It's been that kind of night."

"Is it a good idea for a man with your condition to carry a gun?"

409

I took a deep breath, considering and rejecting the possibility of pulling the gun on her.

"It's a very good idea."

"I see. Then you'll have to tell me what this is all about before I'll let you go running off after my granddaughter with your gun and my car."

I followed her through the receiving area and the living room and into the kitchen. Terry Walker was sitting at the rectangular kitchen table, a pair of glasses slid halfway down his nose, a mug of coffee in one hand, a pen in the other, studying a crossword puzzle laid out in front of him. Lilly ran her hand across Terry's back, pausing to caress his neck. Terry didn't look up from his puzzle. She took a seat at the far end of the table, motioning me to the chair opposite her.

"I'd rather you just give me the keys."

"Sit. Talk and then we'll see," she said.

"There isn't time."

She folded her hands on the table. "I won't let you treat me like you've treated my granddaughter. If you want my help, you'll tell me what this is all about."

I was out of options, so I set the wastebasket on the floor and sat down.

"Nick Staley, Frank Crenshaw, and Jimmy Martin were broke or going broke so they decided to get into the stolen-goods business to make ends meet. Jimmy stole construction materials, and Frank resold them as scrap. Nick ran the show, and Brett helped out."

Terry glanced up at me and returned to his crossword.

"Is that all?" Lilly asked.

"No. That's the least of it. There's a drug cartel in Mexico called Nuestra Familia. Cesar Mendez runs a gang in Northeast by the same name. It's basically a subsidiary of the Mexican cartel. Their main business is drugs, and they've got a lot of competition with other cartels in Mexico. Lately, the competition has gotten pretty rough. The cartels are practically at war with each other and the Mexican government. They need guns, and Mendez is part of a network to smuggle guns to Mexico."

Terry put his pen down. Lilly clutched her robe around her throat.

"Go on," she said. "Finish it."

"Mendez shopped at Nick's grocery. He got to know Brett, probably sold him drugs and probably talked about how he was in the market for guns. Brett must have told his father, who figured out a way to cash in. He and Brett and Frank Crenshaw and Jimmy Martin robbed five gun dealers in the last three months. They had a deal to sell the guns to Mendez, only the deal fell through and now Nick and Frank are dead and so is a kid named Eberto Garza. Jimmy Martin is in jail too scared to talk, and Brett is on the run."

"I've known these people all my life," Lilly said. "That's not who they are."

"It may not be who they were, but it's who they've become," I said. "They were going broke, losing everything they ever worked for or hoped for. I guess they didn't see another way out. So they took a chance, and things got out of control."

She sighed. "I still don't believe it, but I suppose it's possible. What went wrong?"

"They backed out on the deal with Mendez. Could be they wanted more money or they found another buyer. Either way, they made the wrong people mad."

"What does my granddaughter have to do with any of this? Why are you looking for her?"

"I think she knows where Brett is hiding. I think she's trying to protect him. It will be better if I find her before the police do."

"And you know where she is?"

"I've got a good idea. Nick Staley had a couple of rental properties."

"In Forgotten Homes," Lilly said. "I handled the sales. He put them in a company I think he called Forgotten Homes LLC."

"Where is Forgotten Homes?"

"A Northeast neighborhood roughly bounded by Prospect Avenue on the east, Paseo Boulevard on the west, Fifteenth Street on the south, and Ninth Street on the north. All pretty rundown but a few worth rehabbing and renting if you can get decent tenants. I tried to talk Nick out of buying them, but the prices were right and he saw the houses as a way of paying for his retirement."

"The houses are in foreclosure, but the bank hasn't taken them over yet. I think Brett is hiding in one of them."

"I'll get you the addresses," Lilly said, getting up from the table.

"Terry, come with me."

Terry shoved away from the table and followed her. A moment later, Lilly came back in the kitchen, Terry right behind her carrying a gun at his side. I came out of my chair, reaching for my gun, knowing I was too late.

"Relax, Jack," Terry said. "It's Lilly's gun. She wants me to go with you."

"I don't doubt your desire to help Roni," Lilly said, "but I can't leave my granddaughter's safety in the hands of a man who shakes. I'm sure you understand."

Chapter Seventy-two

The houses were next door to one another on Eleventh Street east of Brooklyn, narrow, deep, and close, brick resting on exposed limestone foundations. They shared a driveway, one smaller, on the corner and sitting in the shadow of the other, its second-story windows shuttered with plywood. The lots across the street were vacant, the houses that once filled them long since decayed, destroyed, and bulldozed. A lone streetlight cast dim light on the pavement, the rest of the block dipped in pitch.

There were no cars parked in front of Nick Staley's houses. The records I'd seen on Roni's computer showed that they were vacant. The greater surprise would have been if the lights had been on and the driveway full.

I told Terry, "Circle the block. If they're here, they probably parked and walked."

He made two circles, the second one covering a two-block radius. We passed apartment buildings, a church, an elementary school, and houses alternating with vacant lots like jack-o'-lantern teeth. Dozens of cars were parked on the street, in driveways and parking lots.

We found a Ford Fusion in an alley behind an apartment building that looked like the one I'd seen Brett driving when he left Roni's office on Monday, a Staley's Market bag on the floor of the backseat enough confirmation for me. A Toyota Highlander was parked on the street a block away, the license tag a close match to my memory of the one on Roni's car.

I told Terry to park on Brooklyn. He rolled to a stop fifty feet from the intersection with Eleventh beneath a heavily branched elm tree that hid us while providing a decent view of both houses. He settled back in his seat, drawing his gun from his belt and resting it against his thigh.

I pointed at the gun. "You know how to use that?"

He racked the slide, confirmed there was a round in the chamber, put the safety in the on position, and returned it to his lap, the muzzle pointed at the gas pedal.

"Learned in the Army. It's like riding a bike."

"Range practice is a lot different than hitting a moving target in the dark, especially when the target is someone that's shooting back at you."

"Don't doubt that for a minute. Must be even harder if you're shaking."

"Everybody shakes when the shooting starts."

"Some more than others, I imagine. You been in a shooting fight since you got the shakes?"

"No. I've been shot at, but haven't had to shoot back."

"You scared what'll happen if you do?" Terry asked.

"Never been a time when I wasn't before or since."

"If that's supposed to make me feel better, it don't."

I nodded. "Me neither."

We had a better view of the house on the corner, the one with the boarded-up second-story windows. Ten minutes in, the front door opened. A man slipped out, trotting to the house next door and letting himself in. I couldn't see his face, but his size and shape matched Brett Staley.

"Let's go," Terry said.

"Not yet. Let's wait and see if he's coming or going."

A minute later, the man left the second house, carrying two large duffel bags, straining under the weight.

"What do you figure is in the bags?" Terry asked.

"Something heavy, the way he's carrying them."

"Guns?"

"Seems likely."

"Why move them from one house to the other? Reminds me of being in the Army and having to move a sand pile."

"We'll have to ask him."

A woman opened the door to the corner house, letting the man in, enough light behind them for me to recognize Roni Chase and Brett Staley. We watched as they repeated their routine three more times.

All I could think was that God sometimes gives us second chances. When I met Lucy, I thought she was my second chance to make up for not having saved my daughter, Wendy. Things turned out well for Lucy, but it wasn't enough for me, my debt growing faster than I could repay the principal, a leg-breaker's interest rate keeping me forever in the red. I knew now that saving Roni wouldn't bail me out either, that no one could, that I was the only one who could forgive my debt.

"You still think that girl is just looking out for her boyfriend?" Terry asked.

"To tell you the truth, she reminds me of someone else who got sucked into something she never would have done on her own because she thought she was in love with a guy that was no good."

"How'd that turn out?"

My body trembled, my head twisting as far as it would go. "They both died. The girl was my daughter." Terry had the decency not to tell me how sorry he was, keeping the focus on Roni.

"You think that's what happened to Roni, that her boyfriend sucked her in?"

"We'll see." We waited another five minutes. Neither Roni nor Brett left the corner house.

"Now?" Terry asked.

"Now. Careful and quiet."

We crossed the street, surveying the front of the house from the curb. A light glowed from behind a shade. "Must be a back door," Terry said. "How about if I go around and come in that way?"

"I don't think so. I know what I'm doing, and you don't. I'd rather have you right behind me than not know where you are or what you're doing."

"I'd rather sneak up on them. No reason to make it a fair fight. You start shooting, and I'll start ducking," he said and took off before I could stop him.

Chapter Seventy-three

There was a small porch on the front of the house, a V-shaped portico above the door the only protection from the elements. The windows on either side were far enough from the porch that I could hide between one of them and the door after I knocked, giving me some protection if my greeting was answered with gunfire.

Holding my gun against my leg, I rapped on the door and moved to the side, rapping again when no one answered. A window shade moved an inch, but I had the angle, concealed in the dark. I knocked a third time.

"Who's there?" Roni asked without opening the door.

"It's me, Jack."

She kept her voice low, hissing, "Go away!"

"Too late for that, Roni. Open up. It's either me or Quincy Carter."

She didn't say anything for a moment, opening the door enough to step outside, arms crossed over her chest.

"What do you want, Jack? Why can't you leave me alone?"

Two gunshots echoed from the back of the house, Roni muffling a scream with one hand over her mouth.

"That's why!"

She ran into the house. I tried to grab her, but she slipped out of my grasp, stumbling, slamming the door at me. I caught the door with my shoulder, bulling past it and into the house. There was a stairway in front of me and a room to my right, no furniture, just a dozen or more duffel bags stacked like sand bags against the far wall. I glanced up the stairs. The second floor was dark, muted scuffling sounds coming from somewhere above me, quick and soft enough to be squirrels in the attic roused by the gunfire.

A center hall split the house in half, leading to the back. There was another room to my left, the one with the light on. It was empty, a swinging door on one wall closed, not moving as it would have been if Roni had just passed through it. I took two tentative steps, stopping and listening, not hearing anything until Terry's voice broke the silence.

"Come on and join us, Jack. Things are getting mighty cozy back here. Roni and I are having a regular reunion, but Brett isn't having quite as good a time."

I let out a sigh and a shiver, holstered my gun, and covered the last steps to the rear of the house, stopping at the entrance to the kitchen. Brett Staley was lying on the floor, facedown, blood trickling from beneath his body, pooling in a depression on the warped linoleum floor.

Terry Walker was standing a few feet away, his back to the rear door, one arm locked around Roni's middle, her eyes wide and wet, the muzzle of his gun pressed against her throat. I started to kneel so I could check Brett's pulse.

"Don't bother," Terry said. "He's dead or will be in a minute."

Brett's arms were extended from his body, both hands empty. I looked around the room, not seeing a gun on the floor, table, or counter.

"He wasn't armed. You didn't have to shoot him."

"Not how I saw it. Roll him over."

I turned Brett onto his back. There was a Ruger .44 Magnum Redhawk sticking out of his waistband.

"Now don't get stupid. I need you to pick up Brett's gun and yours, one at a time, by the butt, lay them on the floor and kick them over to me. Two fingers or I'll shoot you where you stand."

I did what he said. "What's it like," I asked him, "to come home and kill the children of people you grew up with?"

"Don't waste your time, Jack. I left these people behind fifty years ago and never looked back. Nothing but a job brought me back, and nothing but bad luck got them killed."

All I could do was keep him talking, hoping he would drop his guard and give me an opening. Roni was trembling, glancing back and forth from Brett's body to me.

"You work for Nuestra Familia or one of the other cartels?" I asked.

"I don't work for nobody but me," he said.

"And you just happen to handle shipments of guns to Mexico. How'd you find out about this one?"

"Old friend of mine from Matamoros. Him and me done a lot of business over the years, and he's close to one of the cartels. He called me last week, said there was a load of guns supposed to go to Nuestra Familia, but Cesar Mendez couldn't close the deal because the seller was trying to hold him up for a last-minute premium."

"Law of supply and demand."

"My friend said there was a play to be made. If I could get the guns he could move them. He said Mendez was dealing with a boy named Brett Staley. I figured he had to be related to the Staleys I grew up with and that would give me an in. I'd pay what needed to be paid, say hello to my old friends, and be on my way."

"Then why kill Frank Crenshaw and Nick Staley?"

"Didn't want to. Tried not to. I tracked Brett down at the grocery last Saturday, told him I wanted to make him a fair offer. He brought Frank and Nick in on it, and they laid the whole scheme out trying to impress me, real proud, telling me that Jimmy was part of it, like that'd make me want to pay more. I made my offer, and Brett said he would get back to me, that he had to talk to someone else."

"Mendez?"

"Had to be. I figured Brett was going to ask him if he would beat my offer. So I said, 'Okay but don't take too long.'"

"And the next day, Frank killed his wife, and Roni shot Frank."

"Which turned a simple business proposition into a cluster fuck. I should have known better than to bother with those boys. They were losers, just like everybody else in Northeast always was and will be."

"Frank was looking at the death penalty. The only chance he had was to trade his life for you and Cesar Mendez."

"Not a deal I could let him make, not with those guns sitting out there somewhere ripe for the taking."

"How'd you convince Roni to give you her gun?"

"I didn't!" Roni said, struggling against Terry's grip. He jerked his arm up, clamping it around her neck, her face reddening.

"She's not lying."

"Then how'd you get it?"

"I was visiting Lilly when Roni called to tell her about shooting Frank. Lilly asked if I'd stay in case Martha needed anything while she went to get Roni. I like to carry a gun in my line of work, but I didn't have one because I had to fly here on short notice, so after Lilly left, I went looking to see if there was any more guns in the house. I found the one Roni kept in her dresser drawer. When she and Lilly came back, I went to the hospital to see if I could get close to Frank."

"You were lucky that Roni and the nurse got into a fight and the cop guarding Frank left his post."

"I've had my share of luck, good and bad. I was checking out the setup on Frank's floor when she got off the elevator. I ducked into an empty room when I saw her. The next thing I knew, she got into it with the nurse and that cop came running. I knew it was going to be my only chance, so I took it."

"And you threw the gun in a Dumpster on your way out. That was sloppy. Your Mexican friends wouldn't be impressed."

He bristled, the first reaction I'd gotten. It wasn't much, but it was something. He didn't like being made fun of.

"It was smart. If the cops found the gun, they'd check the registration and go looking for Roni, not me, and that's what happened."

"You got rid of Frank, but you still couldn't close the deal even though you told the cartel that you had the right connections to make it happen. They must think you don't know your ass from third base. What happened? Was Brett screening your calls?"

His face flushed, and his eyes narrowed.

"The little shit showed me no respect. I went to see Nick yesterday, told him his boy better meet me at the store last night. Nick was there, but Brett wasn't. He pulled his gun, tried to scare me off, but I don't scare. We fought, and his gun went off. I waited all night for Brett to show up, but that damn Mexican kid came snooping around and that took care of that."

"It must have been hard to explain to the cartel that you'd fucked up again."

Terry jammed the gun deeper into Roni's neck. "Why do you keep yanking my chain when I'm the one who had faith in you even if Lilly didn't? I saw that I could sit back and let you lead me to the guns. So who's the fuckup here? You or me?"

"How many people are you willing to kill for those guns?" He tilted his head toward me, then at Roni, counting. "Two more ought to about do it."

"You'd kill your own granddaughter so some ass-hole drug dealer in Mexico can use them to kill another asshole drug dealer?"

Chapter Seventy-four

Roni lost what little color she had in her face, squirming in his grip to look at him. Terry eased the gun away from her neck, squinting at me.

He said, "That's a load of crap."

"I don't think so. There was a reason you came looking for Lilly Chase before you went looking for the guns. Had to have been something more than her red hair that made you want to see her that bad, and she must have been glad to see you because you've been at her house so much I was beginning to think you'd moved in. I saw the way she touched you tonight, running her hand across your shoulders. I'd say she was thinking about asking you."

"That shit don't mean nothing!"

"Here's the clincher. Lilly got pregnant while she was a teenager living at Rachel's House. I did the math. You told me you disappeared the night of the Electric Park fire, fifty years ago. Lilly's daughter, Martha, is fifty years old. She was pregnant when you ran away. She had your baby and never got married because she never got over you. And now you're going to murder your granddaughter, the only child of your only child."

Blood rushed from his neck into his face, turning him red, then purple with rage, his mouth twisting into a snarl as he flung Roni to the floor, raising his gun at me and aiming straight for my heart.

"You son of a bitch!"

The bullet should have struck me before I even heard the sound of shots being fired. In that instant, my body exploded in spasms, my knees buckled, and I wondered why there was no pain, but I knew the pain would come if I lived long enough to feel it.

It wasn't until I saw Terry fall backward and collapse like a rag doll that I realized he'd missed me. As I corkscrewed to the floor, Roni scrambled to her feet, holding the Redhawk over Terry, the muzzle flashing and smoking as she pulled the trigger again and again.

She dropped the Redhawk and fell to her knees, crawling to Brett, turning him over and cradling his head in her lap. I managed to stand, steadying myself with one hand on the kitchen counter, taking deep breaths, drunk-walking the few steps to Terry's body and picking up his gun and mine and the Redhawk, leaning against the refrigerator for support.

She looked up at me. "What now?"

"You surrender."

She nodded. "It was self-defense. Just like before with Frank. I saved your life again."

"And I'm grateful, but the first shot was probably enough."

"Not after what he did to my grandma, leaving her pregnant like that. But everything will be okay now, won't it?"

"Not for a long time. You're in a tight spot."

"But I didn't know anything about the guns."

"Then what were you doing here?"

She glanced around the room, blinking, her hands fluttering, her mind spinning.

"Brett called me. He said to meet him here. He was going away and wanted me to go with him. When I got here, he told me about the guns. He said he needed my help to get rid of them."

"Why was he shuttling them from one house to the other?"

She brightened, her confidence returning. "The bank had a buyer interested in the other house. They were coming to look at it in the morning. He had to get the guns out of there."

"That's the trouble with making it up as you go along," I told her. "It's tough to make all the lies hang together. If that's all he was doing, there was no reason to ask you to help and no reason to get rid of the guns. All he had to do was move them from one house to the other."

"No," she said, raising her hands in protest. "You don't understand. He wanted out, and he wanted me to go with him. That's what he said."

"And you were going to run away with him and leave your mom and grandma without even saying good-bye. Is that it?"

She folded her arms over her chest, bending at the waist. "Yes. When he said he was leaving, I realized how much I loved him."

"Roni, the moon isn't pink. I hear what you're saying, but we both know you're lying. You remember what you kept telling me the last few days?"

"What?"

"You kept telling me that it's over. Well, you're finally right. It's over."

She sat up. "I don't understand what you mean."

"Sure you do. Frank and Nick were lousy businessmen, and Jimmy could barely hold a job. They let you pay their bills because they couldn't even do that on their own. You told them they were finished if they didn't find another way to make money. The stolen goods operation was your idea. You sold them on it and told them what to do."

"No! That's crazy."

"Looking back, you're right. But nobody wanted out of Northeast more than you did. You said so yourself, even your house was strangling you. Getting Jimmy to steal construction materials that Frank could fence was easy, but there wasn't enough money in it to get you out."

She eased Brett's head out of her lap, scooting away, and started to stand. I pointed the Redhawk at her.

"I like you better sitting down."

She slid back to the floor.

"Then one day, Brett told you that Cesar Mendez was looking to buy guns, and that was too good an opportunity to pass up, especially if you could build up an inventory so big that you could squeeze Mendez, maybe even threaten to sell the guns to another cartel."

She ducked her head, avoiding me. "It wasn't me. It was Brett."

"I'm sure you let him think it was his idea. That way you could use him as the front man and Mendez wouldn't know anything about you."

She looked at him, reaching out, caressing his head. "He wanted to impress his father. Show him he really was a man."

"And Nick, Frank, and Jimmy went along because they needed the money."

"They were wiped out. The banks wouldn't loan Frank and Nick another dime, and Jimmy couldn't find work. It was a simple plan. It should have worked." She started to cry, the tears coming fast, easy, and honest, but they were for her, not for him.

"I didn't want any of this to happen," she said. "I just wanted to get the money. Grandma still owed more than a quarter of a million dollars for my mom's medical bills. She'd leveraged the house and everything else she owned. If we didn't come up with the money, we'd end up like the others."

"What happened to the money you got for the construction materials Frank Crenshaw moved?"

"I hid it at the house."

"Why didn't you split it up with the others? Everyone was broke. Didn't they need the money?"

"Yeah, but I needed to keep them in the game more than they needed a few bucks. We were going to get top dollar for the guns, enough to get us all back on our feet. It would have worked, too, except Frank shot Marie."

"You must have thought you were the luckiest girl in the world when Terry murdered Frank because there was no way you could have convinced him to keep quiet."

"It wasn't supposed to happen like that. Everything just got out of hand."

She and Adam Koch were reading from the same hymnal.

"Actually, things started to come unglued when Jimmy Martin picked his kids up to take them for ice cream.

You just didn't know it." She winced, like she'd been slapped. "I don't know what you're talking about."

"Jimmy took his kids out for breakfast the day they disappeared. He was supposed to be stealing copper for you, but he couldn't pass up the chance to be with his kids. I'll bet you called him to see if the job was done and he told you he'd get to it later. That's the way Jimmy did things. When he told you he had his kids, you told him to drop them off with you and pick them up when the job was done. Then, when he got busted, you realized you had a big problem if Jimmy talked, so you went to see him and told him that if he said a word, he'd never see his kids again."

"No!"

I opened my cell phone and read the text message from Superintendent Fibuch. "Then why did you go see Jimmy at the Farm the day he was arrested and once a week after that?"

"I would never hurt those kids, never! I was going to give them back as soon as I got the money for the guns. I swear I was!"

"But Mendez wouldn't pay your price, and you decided to hold out, make him sweat."

"I couldn't believe it! He wouldn't pay, and Terry wouldn't either."

"People like Terry Walker and Cesar Mendez don't negotiate like that. When they say take it or leave it, they mean it. It's easier and cheaper to kill you and steal the guns."

She wiped her face on her sleeve, forcing a smile. "But it can still work out. Everything can still be okay. We can tell the police what I told you, that I didn't know anything about the guns, that it was all Brett and the others."

"That's why you put two extra bullets in Terry. You didn't care that he jilted your grandma fifty years ago. You wanted to make sure he was dead because he was the last one besides me who could tie you to all of this."

"For God's sake, Jack. I've saved your life twice. You owe me!"

"Not that much. Why would I let you walk away from this?"

She stood, her face grim, her lips peeled back.

"To save Evan and Cara. Back me up, and as soon as the cops say that everything's cool, I'll tell you where to find them and you'll be a hero all over again."

"And if I don't?"

"Then no one ever sees those children again. I'll go to my grave, and their parents will never know what happened to them. You have to choose, Jack. If you want to save those kids, you have to save me first."

Chapter Seventy-five

"I don't think so."

"I'm not bluffing, Jack. I've got nothing left to lose."

I used the cord from a floor lamp and the belts Terry and Brett had been wearing to bind her to a kitchen chair.

"You know what people like you always forget? There's no such thing as a simple plan. There are too many moving parts and too many things that happen that you never thought could or would. Like you paying the utility bills for this house even though it's vacant, in foreclosure, and Nick didn't have the money."

Her eyes widened. "How could you possibly know that?"

I smiled. "See, that's what I mean. It never occurred to you that when you left your office unlocked I'd walk in, look at your computer, and find the connection between Nick Staley and Forgotten Homes LLC. And I'll bet you never thought I would break into your office tonight and steal your mail, but I did. I saw the utility bills addressed to Forgotten Homes and saw that the accounts were current. Nick didn't have the money, but you did and you paid the bills."

"The bank demanded that I keep the power on."

"I believe you," I said, walking out of the kitchen.

She strained against the belts. "Where are you going?"

I gathered my gun and Terry's and the Redhawk. "Upstairs to get Evan and Cara."

She slumped in her chair, defeated. "How did you know?"

"One of the bills was from the cable company. I doubt that the bank made you order Disney movies. At least you let the kids watch

342

TV while they were locked away upstairs. After all, how much fun could they have, especially after you boarded up the windows? Be sure you mention that to the judge before he passes sentence."

There were two bedrooms upstairs, both of them locked. I knocked on the door at the top of the stairs and heard the same hurried footfalls as when I came in the house.

"Evan and Cara, my name is Jack. Your mom sent me to bring you home. Move away from the door."

I waited a moment and kicked the door open. They were huddled together on the bed, wearing pajamas, arms around one another. A lamp on a night-stand next to the bed provided the only light. Stuffed animals and other toys were scattered on the floor along with empty McDonald's bags. A small television sat on a dresser, the screen blank.

"You're safe now, but I want you to sit tight until the police get here."

I left them to go back downstairs. I had to call Adrienne Nardelli, Quincy Carter, Lucy, and Joy. I was buzzing with adrenaline, and, for the moment, I wasn't shaking. I made it to the top of the stairs when I heard a familiar voice.

"Hello, Jack," Braylon Jennings said. "Walk down slow and easy and keep your hands above your shoulders."

He was standing in the front hall next to Cesar Mendez, who was aiming a shotgun at me, one of his men from earlier in the evening backing them up. They were too happy to see me, Mendez taking my guns when I reached the bottom stair, emptying them and dropping them on the floor.

Jennings said to Mendez. "Go see what's upstairs."

Mendez cocked his head at the other man. "Alvaro," he said, passing Jennings's order down the line.

"I told you to go," Jennings said to Mendez, "not Alvaro."

Mendez screwed his face tighter than the grip on his shotgun, swallowed, and trotted up the stairs. It was Jennings's way of reminding Mendez of the pecking order and telling me how wrong I'd been about Jennings.

He was on the Nuestra cartel's payroll, sent by the home office to find the guns Mendez had promised. He needed Brett Staley to do that, which was why he had made certain Quincy Carter let Brett leave the hospital Sunday night and why he pushed so hard to get Roni released from jail when Brett went off the grid.

I wondered how he found me until my cell phone rang. I'd turned it back on a couple of hours ago, long enough for him to have picked up the signal and tracked me down. It was Joy.

"Give me the phone," Jennings said.

I threw the phone across the floor, skipping it like a stone on a pond into the room with the duffel bags. Jennings motioned to Alvaro, who retrieved the phone as he launched a roundhouse punch to my gut, folding me in half and forcing me to my knees.

I clenched my jaw, seeing stars, sucking hard to find my breath as he grabbed me by the hair and pressed the barrel of his gun against my temple, the click of the hammer being pulled back echoing in my ear.

"You're a piece of work, Jennings. How much is Nuestra paying you?"

"A helluva lot more than my pension, and that's all you need to know."

"Too many people know that Roni and I are here. You won't be able to cover your tracks."

"You'd be surprised what a remodeling fire will do."

"Look at this," Mendez said from the top of the stairs, the shotgun resting on his shoulder, aimed behind him and at the ceiling.

Evan and Cara were standing in front of him, quivering, crying silently, Mendez grinning like a wolf that had found his dinner. I knew there would be no negotiations, no keeping them talking while I thought of something clever to say. The kids were an impossible complication. Mendez and Jennings couldn't let them go any more than they could let Roni or me go. They'd kill us, take the guns, and burn the house down before I could give them a reason not to.

Mendez was tall, looming over the kids, an irresistible target out of my reach until Jennings loosened his grip and lowered his gun and spoke what I hoped would be his last words.

"What the fuck?"

I grabbed his gun with both hands, flipping the barrel up, aiming at his chin, forcing my finger inside the trigger guard and blowing a hole through the top of his head. I yanked his gun free and shoved his body toward Alvaro, who fired wildly, hitting Jennings and coming after me.

I spun toward the stairs and put two rounds in the center of Mendez's chest as he racked the slide on the shotgun. Mendez pitched forward, knocking Evan and Cara to the side, tumbling down the stairs and firing the shotgun. I flattened myself on the floor, the blast catching Alvaro in the face.

Bolting up the stairs, I swept Evan and Cara into my arms, the three of us sitting on the floor. They were crying, and I was shaking, their slender arms locked around my chest, squeezing me in a hug that did what no other hug had ever done: It made the shaking stop.

Chapter Seventy-six

Each of us serves different kinds of sentences, some imposed by law, some self-imposed, and some that are part of the inexplicable nature of life. Like everything else, we choose as often as we are chosen.

Roni Chase was sentenced to twenty-five years to life for kidnapping Evan and Cara Martin. All charges relating to the stolen guns and construction materials were dropped in exchange for her cooperation into the government's ongoing investigation of the cross-border gun and drug trade. Her lawyer argued for leniency, citing her mother's physical condition, her grandmother's financial problems, and the fact that she'd saved my life on two occasions as mitigating circumstances, but the judge didn't buy it.

Her lawyer asked me to testify on Roni's behalf at her sentencing, threatening to subpoena me when I declined. She backed down when I assured her that I would do everything in my power from the witness stand to assure that Roni went away for a long, long time.

Lilly Chase did testify, fingering a cameo suspended from a gold chain around her neck as she spoke. She drew a line from her mother, Vivian Chase, to her granddaughter, Roni, shaking her head, saying Roni wasn't responsible for the blood that ran in her veins, acknowledging on cross-examination that even if that was an explanation, it wasn't an excuse.

Jimmy Martin finally spoke, explaining the impossible situation Roni put him in, any chance for leniency lost when it turned out he owned a Dodge Ram and the paint found at the scene of Eldon

Fowler's accident matched the paint on it. Kate wrote a letter to the court on his behalf, saying that she forgave him and did not consider him a threat to her safety, drawing on a well of forgiveness that was deeper than mine. It wasn't enough to save him from a life sentence.

Peggy Martin moved away, taking Evan and Cara, saying that she and her children needed a fresh start. Lucy and I went to see them the day they left. She had been sober long enough to realize how good it felt and how hard it would be to stay that way. The kids were quiet and avoided eye contact with us, Peggy saying that they'd been seeing a therapist who'd referred her to a colleague in Seattle, where she had found a job.

"Debt paid?" Lucy asked me as we drove away.

"In full."

Joy's cancer made her oncologist a prophet when she died six months later. We spent her last weeks at Kansas City Hospice House, holding hands, whispering remembered stories, laughing when our versions didn't match.

Memory, I discovered, is reconstructive, not reproductive, a collage of half-remembered names and faces. We can't reproduce or remember exactly what happened. We bind bits of facts with pieces of our hearts, making the past easier, sweeter, and less painful. And so it was with letting her go, our last moments merging with our first.

Like Peggy Martin, I needed a fresh start. I had lost my children, believing that I could somehow reclaim them by saving others, alchemy for the guilty. I laid down that burden at last when I buried Joy, her words canceling all debts. *You did your best. Now let us go.* Though my body still shakes, my soul is steady.

I sold the house and everything in it. Lucy and Simon adopted Roxy and Ruby and promised me the use of their guest room until they turned it into a nursery.

I packed a bag and bought a ticket, running into Jeremiah Quinn at the airport.

"Coming or going?" he asked me.

"Going."

"Where to?"

"San Diego."

"Kate?" he asked, and I nodded. "One way or round trip?"

"We'll see. Kansas City is a good town. Keep an eye on things while I'm away."

Thanks

Thanks for adding *No Way Out* to your digital library. The ebook revolution has opened new doors. Thanks for walking through one of mine.

Find out more about Joel Goldman at http://www.joelgoldman.com

Follow his blog at http://www.joelgoldman.blogspot.com

Sign up for his newsletter at http://www.joelgoldman.com/newsletter.php

Follow him on Twitter at http://twitter.com/#!/JoelGoldman1

Follow him on Facebook at http://www.facebook.com/joel.goldman

ACKNOWLEDGMENTS

Thanks to Nancy Leazer, superintendent of the Kansas City Municipal Jail, aka the Farm, for giving me a tour and explaining how she and her staff made a difficult job seem so easy.

Thanks also to Anne Rosenthal for telling me that the moon is pink. Though she insists that it isn't what she said, it is what I heard and nothing could make the point better than that. And, thanks to Joe Rosenthal for taking me to gun shows and answering my questions about guns.

I never do anything worthwhile without the love and support of my wife, Hildy, and this book is no exception.

My agent, Meredith Bernstein, and my editor, Audrey LaFehr, as always, were generous with their praise and honest with their criticism, making this a better book.

JOEL GOLDMAN

Shakedown

If you like the knockout suspense of Michael Connelly and the gritty "who done its" by Linda Fairstein, you'll love Joel Goldman's *Shakedown*!

"Goldman tells a story at a breakneck pace…"
—Kansas City Star

"A killer identified via a fleeting facial expression and behavioral cues turns a middle-agend FBI agent dealing with a disruptive disability into an unexpected hero in Goldman's latest terrific thriller."
—Publisher's Weekly

When FBI Agent Jack Davis investigates a mass murder, a leak of crucial information and his imploding personal life throw him into the ultimate danger zone – where truth lies at the heart of betrayal.

Need a thrill pill? Take *Shakedown* and stay up all night!

"*Shakedown* is a really fine novel. Joel Goldman has got it locked and loaded and full of the blood of character and the gritty details that make up the truth. Page for page, I loved it."
—Michael Connelly, NYT Bestselling Author

"*Shakedown* is a chillingly realistic crime novel – it's fast-paced, smartly plotted, and a gripping read to the very last page. Joel Goldman explores – with an insider's eye – a dark tale of murder and betrayal."
—Linda Fairstein, NYT Bestselling Author

James Patterson fan's - take off on a rocket-fueled suspense ride with *Shakedown*, the first book in the Jack Davis Thriller series by Joel Goldman.

Motion To Kill

Lee Child and Michael Connelly recommend *Motion To Kill!* If you like the action, suspense and excitement in their books, you'll love *Motion To Kill!*

"The story line never skips a beat. Fans will set in motion a plea for Mr. Goldman to return with more Mason (Lou not Perry) legal thrillers."
—Harriett Klausner

"Lou Mason is still the sexy, brilliant but flawed counselor who is thrown into chaos and finds order. The plot leads you to the edge like the thrilling Yungas cliff road in Bolivia."
—Elizabeth Wenig

When two of his partners are killed, corruption, sex and murder fill trial lawyer Lou Mason's docket as he tracks the killer. Will Lou be the next victim? Found out in *Motion To Kill*, the action-packed, can't-put-it-down first book in the Lou Mason thriller series!

"Joel Goldman is the real deal!"
—John Lescroart, Bestselling author of the Dismas Hardy thriller series.

"A real page-turner with plenty of action and many surprising twists and turns along the way driven by the wise-cracking protagonist and a great supporting cast."
—David A. Berman

"The plot races forward."
—Amarillo Globe-News

JOEL GOLDMAN

The Last Witness

If you love the twists, turns and suspense of John Grisham, you'll love *The Last Witness*!

"Fast, furious and thoroughly enjoyable, *The Last Witness* is classic and classy noir for our time, filled with great characters and sharp, stylish writing. "
—Jeffery Deaver, author of The Vanished Man and The Stone Monkey

"*The Last Witness* is an old fashioned, '40s, tough guy detective story set in modern times. There's a lot of action, loads of suspects, and plenty of snappy dialogue. It's a fun read from beginning to end."
—Phillip Margolin, author of The Associate and Wild Justice

Lou Mason is back and this time it's personal when his surrogate father, Homicide Detective Harry Ryman, arrests his best friend, Wilson "Blues" Bluestone, Jr., for murder. Mason unearths secrets someone will do anything to keep as he closes in on a desperate killer, setting himself up as the next target. Goldman goes Grisham one better!

"Joel Goldman has written another fast-paced legal thriller. Find a comfortable chair and plan to stay up late."
—Sheldon Siegel, Author of The Special Circumstances and Criminal Inten

"*The Last Witness* is a legal thriller written the way criminal law should be practiced: from the gut…one of the premier crime novels of the year."
—Jeremiah Healy, author of Turnabout and Spiral

Move over John Grisham! Joel Goldman is in the courthouse!

About The Author

Joel Goldman is an Edgar and Shamus nominated author who was a trial lawyer for twenty-eight years. He wrote his first thriller after one of his partners complained about another partner and he decided to write a mystery, kill the son-of-a-bitch off in the first chapter and spend the rest of the book figuring out who did it. No longer practicing law, he offices at Starbucks and lives in Kansas City with his wife and two dogs.